# AFTERLIFE

Also by Claudia Gray

*Evernight*

*Stargazer*

*Hourglass*

CLAUDIA GRAY

HarperCollins *Children's Books*

www.claudiagray.com

First published in hardback in the USA by HarperCollins Inc. in 2011
Published in paperback in the UK by HarperCollins Children's Books in 2011
HarperCollins Children's Books is a division of HarperCollins Publishers Ltd,
77-85 Fulham Palace Road, Hammersmith, London W6 8JB

The HarperCollins website is
www.harpercollins.co.uk

ISBN: 978-0-00-742566-2
Afterlife
Copyright © 2011 by Amy Vincent

Printed and bound in England by Clays Ltd.

Typography by Andrea Vandergrift
1

# AFTERLIFE

# Chapter One

"SUNRISE IS COMING," BALTHAZAR SAID.

Those were the first words anyone had spoken aloud in hours. Although I didn't want to hear anything Balthazar had to say—about this or anything else—I knew he was right. Vampires could always feel the approaching dawn deep in their bones.

Could Lucas feel it, too?

We sat in the projection room of an abandoned theater, where the poster-covered walls still bore marks from last night's battle. Vic, the only human in the room, dozed on Ranulf's shoulder, his sandy hair mussed from sleep; Ranulf sat quietly, bloodstained ax across his lap as though he expected more danger at any second. His long, thin face and bowl haircut had never made him look more like a medieval saint. Balthazar stood in the far corner of the room, keeping his distance out of respect for my grief. Yet his height and his broad shoulders meant he took up more than his share of room.

I cradled Lucas's head in my lap. Had I been alive, or a

vampire, so many hours without moving would have made me stiff. As a ghost, though, freed of the demands of a physical body, I'd been able to hold him through the whole long night of his death. I brushed back my long red hair, trying not to notice that the ends had trailed in Lucas's blood.

Charity had murdered him in front of my eyes, taking advantage of Lucas's desire to protect me rather than himself. It was her latest and most horrible attempt to hurt me, driven by her hatred for anybody who mattered to Balthazar, her brother and sire. She'd violated a vampire taboo by biting someone another vampire had bitten first—who had, in effect, been prepared for the transformation from living to undead. Lucas was supposedly mine to turn, or no one's. But Charity hadn't cared about any taboos in a long time. She didn't care about anyone or anything except her twisted relationship with Balthazar.

Wherever she was now, she was no doubt reveling in the fact that she'd broken my heart, and that she'd thrust Lucas into the very last place he would ever want to be.

*I'd rather be dead*, Lucas had always said. When I was alive and so much more innocent, I had dreamed of him becoming a vampire with me. But he had been raised by the hunters of Black Cross, who loathed the undead and pursued them with the passion of a cult. Turning into a vampire had always been his ultimate nightmare.

Now that nightmare had come true.

"How long?" I said.

"Minutes." Balthazar took one step forward, saw the

expression on my face, and came no closer. "Vic should go."

"What's happening?" Vic's voice was scratchy with sleep. He pushed himself upright, and his expression shifted from confusion to horror as he looked at Lucas's body, bloody and pale on the floor. "Oh. I—for a sec, I thought I'd just had a nightmare or something. But this—it's real."

Balthazar shook his head. "I'm sorry, Vic, but you need to leave."

I realized what Balthazar meant. My parents, who had always wanted me to follow in their footsteps, had told me about the first hours of the transition. When Lucas rose as a vampire, he would want fresh blood—want it desperately, as much as he could get. In the first frenzy of awakening, his hunger could push every other thought out of his mind.

He'd be hungry enough to kill.

Vic didn't know any of that. "Come on, Balthazar. I've gone this far with you guys. I don't want to leave Lucas now."

"Balthazar is correct," Ranulf said. "It is safer that you leave."

"What do you mean, safer?"

"Vic, go," I said. I hated to push him away, but if he didn't understand what was going on here, he needed a dose of harsh reality. "If you want to survive, go."

Vic's face paled.

More gently, Balthazar added, "This is no place for the living. This belongs to the dead."

Vic ran his hands through his shaggy hair, nodded once at Ranulf and walked out of the projection room. Probably he would head home, where he'd try to do something useful—clean house, maybe, or make food nobody else could eat. Human concerns seemed very distant at that moment.

Now that Vic had left, I could finally voice the thought that had been haunting me for hours. "Should we—" My throat choked up, and I had to swallow hard. "Should we let this happen?"

"You mean that you believe we should destroy Lucas." From anybody else, this would have sounded too harsh to bear; from Ranulf, it was simple, calm fact. "That we should prevent him from rising as a vampire, and accept this as his final death."

"I don't want to do that. I can't begin to tell you how much I don't want that," I answered. Every word I spoke felt like blood being squeezed from my heart. "But I know it's what Lucas would want." Didn't loving someone mean putting their wishes first, even with something as terrible as this?

Balthazar shook his head. "Don't do it."

"You sound very sure." I tried to say it calmly. Still, I was so angry at Balthazar that I could hardly look at him; he'd brought Lucas into the battle against Charity, even though he knew Lucas was numb with grief and unable to fight at his best. It felt like Lucas's death was as much his fault as Charity's. "Are you just telling me what I want to hear?"

Balthazar frowned. "When have I ever done that? Bianca, listen to me. If you'd asked me the day before I became a vampire whether I'd want to rise as undead, I would have said no."

"You would still say no, if you had the chance. If you could go back. Wouldn't you?" I demanded.

That caught him off guard. "We aren't only talking about me. Think about your parents. About Patrice, and Ranulf, the other vampires you know. Would they really be better off rotting in their graves?"

Some vampires were okay, weren't they? That was true of most of the ones I'd ever known. My parents had known centuries of happiness and love together. Lucas and I could have that, maybe. I knew he hated the idea of being a vampire—but only two short years ago, he'd hated all vampires with blind, unthinking prejudice. He'd come so far so quickly; surely he could come to accept himself in time.

It was worth a chance. It had to be. Everything in my heart told me that Lucas deserved another chance, and that we deserved another hope of being together.

I traced a finger across Lucas's face: his forehead, his cheekbone, and the outline of his lips. The heaviness and paleness of his body reminded me of a carving on a tombstone—fixed, unliving, unchanging.

"It's close," Balthazar said. He came closer. "It's time."

Ranulf nodded. "I sense it as well. You should step away, Bianca."

"I'm not letting go of him."

"Just be ready to move, then. If you have to." Balthazar shifted his weight from one foot to the next, steadying his stance like a fighter preparing for battle.

*It's going to be okay, Lucas,* I thought, willing him to hear me past the divide between this world and the next. Wasn't he about to cross that divide to return to me? So maybe we were close enough for him to listen. *We're dead, but we can still be together. Nothing matters more than that. We're stronger than death. Now nothing else ever has to come between us. You and I never have to be apart again.*

I wanted him to believe that. I wanted to believe it, too.

Lucas's hand twitched.

I gasped—a reflex of the body I'd created, more a memory of what shock did to a living being than anything else.

"Be ready," Balthazar said. He was talking to Ranulf, not to me.

Shakily, I laid one hand upon Lucas's chest. I realized only then that I was waiting for a heartbeat. His heart would never beat again.

One of Lucas's feet shifted slightly, and his head turned a couple inches to the side. "Lucas?" I whispered. He needed to understand that he wasn't alone, before he realized anything else. "Can you hear me? It's Bianca. I'm waiting for you."

He didn't move.

"I love you so much." I wanted so badly to cry, but my ghostly body created no tears. "Please come back to me. Please."

The fingers of his right hand straightened, muscles tensing, then curled back in toward his palm.

"Lucas, can you—"

"No!" Lucas shoved himself away from the floor, from me, stumbling to all fours. His eyes were wild, too dazed to truly see. *"No!"*

✢ 6 ✢

His back slammed against the wall. He stared at the three of us, his eyes displaying no recognition, no sanity. His hands pressed against the wall, fingers curved like claws, and I thought he might try to dig through it. Maybe it was a vampire instinct for digging your way out of a grave.

"Lucas, it's okay." I held my hands out, doing my best to remain completely solid and opaque. It was better to look as familiar as possible. "We're here with you."

"He doesn't know you yet," Balthazar said. "He's looking at us, but he can't see."

Ranulf added, "He wants only blood."

At the word *blood*, Lucas's head tilted, like a predator catching the scent of prey. I realized that was the only word he'd recognized.

The man I loved had been reduced to an animal—to a monster, I realized, the sick, empty, murderous shell that Lucas had once believed every vampire to be.

Lucas's eyes narrowed. He bared his teeth, and with a shock I saw, for the first time, his vampire fangs. They altered his face so much that I hardly knew him, and that more than anything else tore at me. His posture shifted into a crouch, and I realized he was about to attack—any of us, all of us. Anything that moved. Me.

Balthazar moved first. He leaped—pounced—toward Lucas, colliding with him so forcefully that the wall behind them crunched and plaster dust fell from the ceiling. Lucas threw him off, but then Ranulf was on him in an attempt to push him into a corner.

"What are you doing?" I cried. "Stop hurting him!"

Balthazar shook his head as he rose from the floor. "This is the only thing he understands right now, Bianca. Dominance."

Lucas pushed Ranulf backward, so hard that he thudded against me, and I stumbled into the old projector. Sharp metal jabbed into my shoulder. I felt pain, real pain, the kind I'd experienced back when I had a real body instead of this ghostly simulation. When I put my hand to my shoulder, I felt a luke-warm wetness beneath my fingers and pulled them away to see blood—silvery and strange. I hadn't even realized that I still had blood now. The liquid gleamed like mercury, almost iridescent in the dim light.

The three-way fight in front of me was growing more violent—Balthazar's foot to Lucas's gut, Lucas's fist to Ranulf's jaw—but Balthazar saw that I was injured and shouted, "Bianca, stay back! You're bleeding!"

What was that supposed to mean? Surely vampires didn't drink wraiths' blood, so there was no danger of my driving Lucas further into a killing frenzy. At that moment, I wasn't sure he could become more frenzied than he already was. Younger and weaker he might be, but desperation goaded him on, made him fierce. It was possible he might defeat Ranulf and Balthazar both. I couldn't bear to see that, but I didn't think I could stand the alternative either. My fear sharpened—and became anger.

*Enough of this.*

I pushed myself toward them, blood on my fingertips, and flung out my hand as I cried, "Stop!"

Droplets of silvery blood spattered through the air as all three of the guys shrank back.

At my side, Balthazar whispered, "Don't get into this."

Ignoring him, I stepped directly in front of Lucas. He had backed against the wall, glancing around wildly as though he could think of nothing but escape—or, perhaps, in search of living prey. Death had sharpened his features, making him both more beautiful and infinitely frightening. The only features that remained the same were his eyes.

So I focused only on his eyes. "Lucas, it's me. It's Bianca."

He said nothing, just stared at me, utterly motionless. I realized he wasn't breathing—most vampires did just as force of habit, but it seemed that death had claimed him entirely. No way was I going to let that happen.

"Lucas," I repeated. "I know you can hear me. The guy I love is still in there. Come back to me." Once again, I longed for the release of tears. "Death couldn't keep me from you. And it can't keep you from me, not if you don't let it."

Lucas didn't speak, but some of the tension left his body, relaxing his hands and his shoulders. He still looked edgy, almost crazed, but some semblance of control had returned to him.

What could I do? Was there anything I could say that would get through to him? Something he would remember . . .

When Lucas had first learned that I was born to two vampires, he had to overcome his revulsion of the undead in order to hold true to his love for me. If he could remember what it had meant for him to accept me for what I was, maybe he could begin to face what he, too, had become.

Haltingly, I spoke his words as they came back to me: "Even though you're a vampire—it doesn't matter to me. It doesn't change how I feel about you."

Lucas blinked, and for the first time since he had risen from the dead, his eyes seemed to fully focus. I realized that his fangs had retracted, leaving only the unearthly pallor and beauty of the vampire. In every other way, he looked human. He looked like himself.

He whispered, "Bianca?"

"It's me. Oh, Lucas, it's me."

Lucas clutched me to him in an impossibly tight embrace, and I wrapped my arms around his shoulders. I felt hot tears against my shoulder; I wished I could cry, too. Our legs gave out at the same time, and we sank to the floor together.

I glanced over my shoulder to tell Balthazar and Ranulf to leave us, but they were already halfway out the door.

Once we were alone, I ran my hands through Lucas's hair, stroked his back, and kissed his cheek. "You made it back," I said. "We're together. We'll be okay."

"I never thought I'd see you again. I thought you were dead."

"I am. We both are."

"Then how—how is this real?"

"I've become a wraith. Only, wraiths like me who were born to it, born to two vampires—we have powers the others don't. I can have a body if I want, at least for a while. If I'd realized before . . . if I could have told you . . . this would never have had to happen."

"Don't say it." His voice was strangled.

We rested our foreheads against each other, and the contact should have been comforting, but we were both so cold.

"My body feels heavy. Wrong. Dead." Lucas's hands tightened on my shoulders. "And yet there's this hunger making me wild. Driving me insane. You're back in my arms—I'd lost you forever, and here you are—but the only thing I can think about, the only thing I want—" He couldn't finish; he didn't have to. I knew all he wanted was blood.

"It will get better." My parents had always told me so, and weren't most of the vampires of Evernight proof of that?

Lucas didn't seem to believe me, but he said, dutifully, "Gotta hang on."

"Right."

For a few moments, we simply held each other. The faded film-star faces on the tattered movie posters around us seemed to be watching us, an audience of dark, soulless eyes. When I leaned against Lucas's shoulder, I tried to breathe in the familiar scent of his skin, but that was gone. Either his scent had been lost when he died, or I no longer had a sense of smell like I had before, or both. So many things had been taken from us.

*But not each other,* I reminded myself. *We have to remember that.*

First I had to get him out of the place where he had been murdered. We needed to go someplace better, more familiar. Vic's house, I decided. We'd hidden out there for the past month or so this summer, while Vic's family vacationed in Italy. Our little makeshift apartment in the wine cellar wouldn't be that much more comforting—it was where I had died just the day before—but maybe we could remain there until we figured out what to do.

"Come on." I took one of his hands in mine. The coral bracelet he'd given me for my last birthday jangled at my wrist. "They're waiting for us outside."

"Who's waiting for us?" Lucas couldn't seem to focus; it was like he was listening to a cell phone at the same time he was trying to listen to me. Not in a rude way; he just couldn't help it, which was worse.

"Balthazar—and Vic and Ranulf, too. They came back from Italy after you e-mailed them. Remember?"

Lucas nodded. His hand tightened around mine, so hard it nearly hurt. Lucas didn't seem to have any way to judge his new strength—and this despite the fact that he already had enhanced power from having been bitten. He worked his jaw, as if practicing biting down, over and over.

If he needed me to be the steady one, I would be. Of course I was better at being dead, I decided; I'd had a whole day's practice. It had taken me a few hours to get the hang of being noncorporeal. So no wonder it would take him a while to deal with becoming a vampire.

We left the projection room and walked out through the abandoned theater. The scene in the lobby wasn't pretty: Beheaded vampires lay crumpled on the floor, and I tried not to look at any of the abandoned heads. Vampires didn't bleed much after death—no heartbeat to pump out the blood—but I noticed Lucas looking hungrily at the few droplets on the floor.

"I know you're hungry," I said, trying to comfort him.

"You don't know. You can't know. There's nothing like this." Lucas's grimace revealed his fangs. Just the sight of blood had brought them out again. When I had been alive, part vampire, I had experienced the desperate yearning for blood, but I suspected Lucas was right: The craving he felt now had intensified beyond anything I'd ever known.

We walked outside to see Balthazar, alone, leaning on his car in the otherwise empty parking lot. His shadow stretched out, long and broad, in the beam of the nearby streetlamp. Balthazar spoke to me first. "Vic was hanging around out front. The only way Ranulf could get him to leave was to go along."

"Okay," I said as we reached him. "Let's just get out of here. I never want to see this place again."

Balthazar didn't move; he and Lucas just stared at each other. For years, they'd loathed one another; only in the aftermath of my death had they been able to work together. Now, though, what I saw between them was total understanding.

"I'm sorry." Lucas's voice was rough. "Some of the stuff I said to you—about choices, being a vampire, and everything like that—Jesus. I get it now."

"I wish you didn't. I wish you'd never had to understand." Balthazar closed his eyes for a second, maybe remembering his own transformation centuries ago. "Come on. We'll get you something to drink."

With a pang, I realized that Lucas and Balthazar understood each other now on a level that I would never fully grasp. For some reason, it felt like a loss. Or maybe in that moment, with Lucas seemingly so far from me in spirit, everything felt like a loss.

Balthazar drove us back toward the nicer neighborhood in Philadelphia where Vic lived. Lucas and I sat together in the backseat, his hand gripping mine tightly, his gaze focused in the distance beyond the windshield. Sometimes he frowned and closed his eyes like a person in the throes of a migraine; his feet moved restlessly against the floorboards, as though he were pushing back, or attempting to push through. He didn't want to be here, to be contained—everything around him now was just one more thing between him and the blood he needed. I knew better than to try to get him to talk. After he'd had something to drink, then he would be okay. He had to be.

Balthazar broke the wretched silence by turning on the radio, classic jazz, the kind of thing my dad used to listen to around the house. As Billie Holiday crooned about foolish things, I wondered what my parents would say now, and whether there was any advice they could have given us. We'd parted badly before I ran off with Lucas at the beginning of the summer; at the moment, I missed them so much it hurt. What would they think of everything that had happened in the past couple of days?

I glanced at Lucas—the pale, cool stillness of his flesh, the way that death had brightened his eyes and carved out his cheekbones—and thought bleakly, *Well, they always wanted me to end up with a nice vampire boy.*

The car turned onto the road where Vic lived, an upscale area with broad yards separating the palatial homes. As every house had a four-car garage, we rarely saw other cars out on the street, but there were three right in front of Vic's house. Not the usual kinds of Mercedes or Jaguars that drove around here either—these were beat-up trucks and station wagons. Something about this began to feel familiar.

Then I realized nearly a dozen people were standing in the street and in Vic's yard. When I glimpsed a stake in one man's hands, I realized at least that some of them were armed.

"Is this Charity's tribe?" Balthazar said. "Is she still after Lucas?"

I remembered the e-mails Lucas had sent out just before my death, when he'd been so desperate that he'd asked anyone and everyone for help, even people we had every reason to expect to turn against us. His messages had been answered.

"It's not Charity," I whispered. "It's Black Cross."

# Chapter Two

"BLACK CROSS," BALTHAZAR REPEATED. IF I HADN'T been there when Black Cross captured Balthazar—and tortured him—I might have thought he was being very calm about the fact that a band of vampire hunters had showed up. Instead, I could see the hints of fear and anger submerged in his gaze. His fists tightened around the steering wheel. "We should get out of here."

"We can't just leave Vic and Ranulf!" I said.

Then Lucas leaned forward and whispered, "Mom?"

I saw her, too: Kate, a Black Cross cell leader and Lucas's mother. Her honey gold hair, so like her son's, shone beneath the streetlamp's light; shadows etched the firm muscles of her arms and the stake she wore at her belt. When Black Cross had learned of my true nature and cast us out of their cell, they'd kept her away. I'd always believed this was because of Kate's fierce love for her son, which was often hidden beneath her discipline and duty but was undeniable. Was it strong enough to sustain them now?

"It's okay," I said to Balthazar. "She brought some friends and came here to help Lucas, not to hunt. See?" Pointing, I showed him where another Black Cross hunter was at the front door, apparently asking Vic a lot of questions while Vic did a bad job of looking casual.

"These 'friends' are some of the hunters who captured me and discovered you, Bianca," Balthazar said. "They might have come here to help, but once they see us, all bets are off."

"I need to talk to her," Lucas said. "If you guys want to go, go."

I wasn't afraid for myself; these hunters knew little about the wraiths and would be unable to hurt me. That didn't mean I wasn't afraid. "Do you think Kate can protect you from them? And Balthazar?"

"She'll hold off if I tell her to," Lucas insisted.

"And what about you?" Balthazar said. His hands only clutched the steering wheel harder. "Who's going to hold you off?"

Lucas glared at him. "I won't attack my own mother."

"You think that now. Wait until you get out there and smell fresh blood. You'll be able to feel her pulse, almost—like a magnet, drawing you in." Balthazar knew too well what he was talking about; his first act after being turned into a vampire had been to murder his own sister. Also, the hunters had begun paying attention to our car, moving closer. Balthazar continued, "If we're going, we need to go now."

"We're not going." Lucas's jaw was set, his stare resolute. "I can handle it. I've got to. And—come on, it's my mom."

As he slid out of the backseat, Balthazar glanced at me in the rearview mirror, like I was suddenly going to take his side versus Lucas's and run away. If Lucas trusted himself, then I would trust Lucas. I simply stepped out behind him. Balthazar could get out of the car to back us up or not; I didn't care.

"Lucas?" Kate said. She jogged toward him, a smile lighting her face for the brief moment before she saw me. In the distance, I could see the hunters walking toward us and away from Vic's house, and Vic slumping against his doorjamb in relief.

"Mom." Lucas remained still, as if frozen to the spot. His features tightened, and I could tell that he was staring at her throat. What Balthazar had said was true. He could feel her pulse—sense her blood.

Kate's eyes narrowed as she came closer to us. "Thought you were supposed to be sick," she said. Distrust and contempt laced her every word. "So sick you couldn't move."

"I was," I said. "But—not now." I couldn't exactly claim to have gotten better.

"No more reason for Lucas to stick around, then." Kate held out her hand to her son. "You can come back. It's okay. The people who would hold it against you—we don't need them. All you have to do is realize you made a mistake."

Lucas didn't take her hand. "I didn't make a mistake." His voice was thin, his words forced. His eyes glittered brightly in the dim light, and I could sense the waves of killing madness washing over him. Yet he stood his ground. "I love Bianca. I made my choice. But . . . I'm glad you came."

Movement in the farther distance caught my attention. My eyes widened when I recognized two of the hunters in this small group, standing at the far side of Vic's lawn—a heavyset, dark-skinned woman with her hair in thick braids, and another with golden skin and hair sheared crazily short against her scalp: Dana and Raquel. Dana had been Lucas's best friend since they were little kids, and when my true nature had been revealed, she was the one who had helped us escape. Raquel had been my best friend and junior-year roommate at Evernight Academy, and the victim of a terrible wraith haunting ever since childhood. She had run away with Lucas and me, joining us when we'd become part of Black Cross.

Raquel was also the one who had turned me in to Black Cross when she'd realized I was the child of vampires.

They loved each other. Would Raquel have come around to Dana's way of thinking and stand with us now? Or would Dana side with Raquel instead of the old friend who had abandoned her?

I turned away from them, focusing entirely on Lucas. Kate stood only a couple of feet away from him. Although she radiated disapproval, I could tell that it was only me she loathed; for her son, she had an uncertain smile. "Lucas, think about this," she said. "We're not only your cell. We're your family. Because family's not just about blood—it's about what you share, what you believe."

Lucas winced when she said *blood*, but Kate didn't seem to

notice. She was too angry at me, and too worried about him.

"Bianca can't have told you what she was at first," Kate said. "She lied to you."

Although Lucas and I had gotten past the fact that we'd kept so many secrets from each other at the start, the memory of our old mistakes stung.

Kate continued, "Are you going to forget your duty, forget everything else you learned, and throw away your whole life chasing after some girl who lied to you? I think you're smarter than that."

He *had* thrown his life away, literally dying in an attempt to avenge me. The reminder of what he'd lost to be by my side scalded me with shame. Lucas didn't notice—he shook with the need to restrain himself. His need for blood had become so overpowering that I could tell he might break.

"I need to talk to you." Lucas's voice sounded ragged with strain. "Please, Mom, can the two of us just . . . talk for a while? I have a lot to tell you. A lot of stuff I need to make sense of."

Concern made Kate stop trying to convert him and start listening. "Lucas, are you okay? You look pale, and you've obviously been in a fight—"

"I'm—" His throat choked off the word *fine*. "We have to talk. That's it. I need you to come through for me on this." His eyes met hers. "I really need you to do that."

Kate's expression softened. The mother had won out over the fighter. "Okay."

She took another step toward him and held out her arms.

Lucas paused only a moment before embracing her tightly. I saw him grimace as he took in the scent of her blood—but he didn't break.

*He's done it,* I thought with delight. *Lucas can control the blood hunger.*

Then Kate's arms tensed, and her eyes went wide. I realized that, for the first time, she saw that the blood staining his T-shirt was his own—and she saw the wound at his neck. The wound obviously caused by a vampire's bite.

If I had noticed how cold Lucas felt to the touch, then his mother could, too.

Kate jerked away from him, leaving Lucas to stumble back in confusion. Her hand went to her stake. "What did Bianca do to you?"

Lucas took a step toward her, eyes pleading. "It wasn't Bianca. Mom, just listen."

"Ask the others to leave," I said. Maybe Kate had a chance to accept her son as whatever he had become, but I didn't want to take my chances on the rest of the Black Cross hunters. "Let Lucas explain."

"You've been killed." Kate's voice was almost a sob. "You're a vampire."

There was a ripple of gasps and whispered curses from the other hunters. Dana hid her face against Raquel's arm for a moment. I glanced behind us at Balthazar, who remained behind the wheel with the car's motor idling.

Lucas kept his eyes locked with his mother's. "Yes. I am.

It's not like they told us, Mom; I'm different but I'm still me. At least, I think I'm still me. This is . . . weird and scary, and I need to find out if there's any way for me to be the person I was before. Please help me do that."

Kate straightened. She never looked away from him, her gaze as cool and hard as iron. "You're the shell of what my son used to be. I loved him more than a monster like you can ever know—"

"Mom, no," Lucas whispered.

She acted like she hadn't heard. "And you can taunt me with his voice and his face only as long as I let you." Though her voice trembled, Kate pulled out her stake, her grip sure. "All I can do for Lucas now is give him a decent burial. And that means ending you."

"Lucas!" I grabbed his arm to pull him toward the car, but he twisted away from me, as if unable to believe that his mother could do this to him. Then she swung at him so fast that he stumbled as he dodged the blow.

Most of the other hunters began running toward us. Ranulf burst from Vic's doorway, ax in hand, courageously jumping into the fray despite the likelihood that he'd be staked and beheaded. None of that scared me as much as what was happening to Lucas.

*Wham!* Kate's fist hit his jaw, and his expression went blank.

*Wham!* Lucas blocked one of her blows, and he narrowed his eyes, baring his teeth in rage.

*Wham!* This time he hit her. His fangs extended. I knew then that the threat had pushed him over the edge. The blood madness gripped Lucas now. He was fighting to kill.

I pulled at the clasp of my coral bracelet, the one Lucas had given me for my birthday—and my tether to corporeal existence. When it fell onto Vic's lawn, I felt myself become lighter, insubstantial.

One of the hunters came at me, swinging a stake. I simply turned to vapor, so that his hand passed right through me—a weird sensation, sort of like a stomach cramp. The hunter screamed, which would have been hilarious any other time.

Zooming above the fray, I tried to take in the scene. Ranulf single-handedly held off the three hunters closest to Vic's house. Vic had run out onto the lawn, not to fight but apparently to yell at Raquel, which at least was keeping her out of the battle. Dana, too—she had remained by Raquel's side, maybe to defend her, maybe because she couldn't attack her best friend even if he'd become a vampire. Lucas and his mother stood in the heart of it, locked in combat. He answered every punch she landed and clawed at her every chance he got, while throwing off the two hunters trying to come to her aid. If he got the upper hand, I knew he would kill Kate. And if he did that, if he drank his own mother's blood, there was no way Lucas would ever be able to forgive himself.

At first it looked like Balthazar was just going to sit in the car and watch, which infuriated me. Then the motor revved, and with the screech of burning rubber, Balthazar drove the car straight onto Vic's lawn, making the hunters scatter. He didn't hit anybody, but not for lack of trying.

I wanted to protect the people I could. Quickly I pulled myself together into a physical form on the ground, right by Raquel, Dana, and Vic. Though I remained half transparent, they were able to see me.

"What the hell?" Dana yelled, throwing her arms around Raquel like I was going to hurt her.

"Get out of here," I said. "Dana, take Raquel and try to get the others to follow you. Please!"

"Do it." Vic folded his arms. "You don't know what kind of badass ghost mojo she's capable of. Trust me, I've seen her in action. You don't want to be around."

"Ghost?" Raquel whispered. Her face went pale. "Bianca— you're *dead*?"

"We're leaving." Dana dragged Raquel toward one of the trucks. Raquel's eyes met mine for one tortured moment before she turned to follow.

"Um, Bianca?" Vic tried to tap my shoulder, but his hand went through. "Whoa. Okay, some of that badass ghost mojo wouldn't be a bad idea right now."

A couple of hunters ran toward us, but Balthazar tackled them, taking them both down with his outstretched arms. Ranulf held his own, but I wasn't sure how much longer he could go. And two hunters already lay dazed on the ground near Lucas, who battled his mother in blind rage.

I did have ghostly powers that were useful in combat, but I'd only ever tried them on vampires. Would that kill a human? I wasn't ready to do that, even if the humans in question seemed very ready to kill me.

"We don't need powers," I said quickly. "We need the police."

"Police?"

"Vic, call 911! Tell them there's a—like, a home invasion or an attempted robbery in progress, something!" Black Cross tried to steer clear of the law, because they wanted to stay off their radar. "When they hear the sirens, they'll go."

Vic took off for the house and his cell phone. I ran toward Lucas, not sure what I was going to do but desperate to keep him from either being killed or killing his mother.

Lucas's wild-eyed gaze told me he was beyond reasoning with. So I cried, "Kate, don't! You don't want to do this!"

"Let me give my son some peace!" She never stopped circling her son; one of her eyes was already blackening from his fist. Lucas would never have done that to her, never, if anything of his spirit was in control.

I slipped between them—not like she could do anything to me, what with me being dead and everything. "You can't kill him. You know you don't want to."

Her gaze went right through me, focusing only on the cloudy figure of her son behind my transparent form. "I can and I will."

My desperation peaked. I looked at Kate, pleading with every part of my soul for her to stop and try to see that her son was still with her—to see him through my eyes—until it felt almost like my desperation had become a blade that could cut through her—

Then this bizarre tidal pull seized me, dragging me toward

Kate in the blink of an eye. Before I could ask myself what was happening, I felt myself being drawn into her, absorbed *by* her. Everything went dark for an instant, and then when I could see again, I knew I was looking through Kate's eyes. I could feel her body all around me, like a suit of armor, but one with warmth, breath, and a heartbeat.

Kate's hand dropped the stake as her feet stumbled backward. The only thing I could think was, *I'm possessing someone. I've possessed Kate. How did I do that?* The sheer power of my desperation had acted almost like a battering ram, opening a portal into her very self. Could all wraiths do this? I had no idea. All that mattered was my ability to stop this fight.

Lucas charged at me, and I dodged him, but clumsily, because controlling Kate's body was weird and unfamiliar, sort of like my first driving lesson. I shouted, "Everyone, let's go!" Talking in Kate's voice sounded odd, but I kept giving orders. "We're getting out of here now!"

Then I felt an even stranger sensation—Kate's spirit, struggling against me, trying to push me out. Could she do it? I decided to let her, if it was possible.

Instantly, I felt myself scattered and invisible, floating upward in a dreamlike haze. My reverie was broken when I heard Kate say, voice shaking with fear, "We have to leave."

The hunters ran for their trucks and vans, responding either to her first order or her last. Lucas sprang after her, but Balthazar shoved him aside and took him down, keeping him back.

As their tail lights vanished down the road, Vic jogged out of his house, both hands in his sandy hair, like he was trying to hold his head together. "What, I just called the cops for nothing?"

"First be glad that Black Cross is gone," Ranulf pointed out, brushing himself off and calm as ever.

"Well, the police are coming. So maybe get the car out of the yard." Vic looked at the deep tire tracks in the grass and groaned. "There are not even words for how grounded I'm going to be. They're gonna have to invent words for it. New words."

I coalesced amid the guys. "Ranulf's right, though. This could have been a lot worse."

Lucas turned toward Vic. His eyes remained flat and blind, his fangs still extended. With horror I realized that Lucas hadn't yet drunk blood—and the killing rage from the fight held him in its grasp.

He lunged at Vic. Ranulf managed to knock Vic out of the way, but Lucas tore at him with his whole strength, willing to shred Ranulf if that got him closer to the human, to the source of fresh blood.

Vic's jaw dropped. "Oh, my God," he said, standing in place out of shock instead of running for his life. "This isn't happening."

"Vic, run!" Balthazar said, pulling Lucas off Ranulf. Vic took a couple of shuffling steps, then finally accepted what was going on and ran like crazy toward his front door. Lucas elbowed Balthazar sharply, but Balthazar was able, with difficulty, to maintain his grip. He said to Ranulf, "Get him into the wine cellar. Keep him there until we can get him some blood. After I move the car, I'll come help you."

"Lucas?" I pleaded. "Lucas, can you hear me?"

It was like I didn't exist. Lucas only wanted blood, and he

didn't care if he had to kill Vic to get it.

Ranulf dragged Lucas backward, struggling with him the whole way. All I could do was open the wine cellar door for them. In the distance, sirens blared, coming closer.

"Let me go!" Lucas raged, clawing Ranulf viciously in the side. Ranulf grimaced but held on. "Let me go!"

"You have to calm down," I said. "Please, Lucas, get ahold of yourself."

"He cannot—hear you—" Ranulf managed to say as he wrestled Lucas toward a corner. "I remember the madness."

Lucas roared, a terrifyingly animal sound. Every muscle of his body was flexed in his desperate need to escape, to kill and drink blood. Ranulf could hold him off, because of his great age and power, but after that battle, Ranulf's strength had to be taxed to the limit. Seeing Lucas like this, reduced to an insane shell of himself, here in the little makeshift apartment where we had loved each other so much, nearly destroyed me.

The sirens got louder. Lucas roared again and smashed Ranulf backward against the wall with such force that the wine bottles rattled and Ranulf lost his grip. He leaped toward the door, and I started after him—but Balthazar came through.

*Thank God*, I thought. *Balthazar can stop him, I know he can!*

But then I cried out in horror as Balthazar brandished a stake and swung it, hard, so that it slammed deep into Lucas's chest.

# Chapter Three

LUCAS COLLAPSED UPON THE FLOOR, A STAKE jutting out from his heart.

I fell to my knees by his side. "Balthazar, no! What are you doing?" Just as I grasped the stake to pull it out, Balthazar roughly towed me up to my feet, away from Lucas. I went vapory again, slipping out of his arms easily. "You can't stop me from taking care of him."

"Think," Balthazar said. "We need him to remain quiet while the police are here, and make sure he doesn't go after Vic. I can't come up with any other way to make that happen. Can you?"

"There has to be some way better than staking him," I insisted.

"He is essentially unharmed," Ranulf said, shaking off the impact of Lucas's last blows. "The stake through the heart only paralyzes; it does not kill. When the stake is removed, Lucas will be as he was, except for a scar."

"I know—but—" The sight of him lying at my feet, crumpled and dead as he had been just a few hours ago, was too raw for me to bear.

Balthazar stepped closer. In the relative darkness of the wine cellar, his shadowy form seemed more imposing than usual, which made the contrast with his quiet voice especially striking. "Lucas staked me once to save me. I'm returning the favor."

"You probably enjoyed it." I turned away from him then, but already I'd realized we couldn't unstake Lucas yet. As he was, he was uncontrollable.

"Until we have fresh blood for him to drink, leaving him unconscious is a kindness," Balthazar said. Just when I might have softened toward him, he had to add, "When you calm down enough to act like an adult, you'll see that."

"Please do not force me to listen to romantic bickering," Ranulf said.

Ranulf's request was simple enough, but it was an uncomfortable reminder of everything that had happened between Balthazar and me—how much more he had wanted, and what I had been unable to give. Although I didn't think jealousy drove Balthazar's actions, I wondered if it allowed him to gain some satisfaction by staking Lucas.

Balthazar had insisted on going after Charity the day after my death, and he had brought Lucas along, knowing that Lucas was too grief-stricken to truly fight. Lucas, near suicidal, had plunged in unprepared. The aftermath of Balthazar's mistake would be on Lucas forever. That outweighed everything that had happened between us before, good or bad.

*This is what you get for hanging out with the wrong kind of dead people,* a sardonic voice said.

That would be Maxie, the house ghost. The others couldn't hear her. She'd been connected to Vic throughout his childhood but had never appeared to him or any other living creature— except me. Anticipating my transformation into a wraith, she'd begun appearing to me back when I was a student at Evernight Academy; now that I'd died, she wanted me to abandon the mortal world and join her in other, more mystical realms. The whole idea terrified me, and I'd never been less in the mood to talk to her about it.

An awkward silence filled the room. A dead body on the floor made casual conversation pretty much impossible. Balthazar studied the wine racks for a few minutes, in what I thought was just a distraction, until he pulled a bottle out. "Argentinean Malbec. Nice."

"You're going to sit here and *drink wine*?" I protested.

"We've got to sit here and do something." Balthazar looked around for a corkscrew, failed to find one, and then simply smashed the neck of the bottle against the tiny sink. Spatters of red fell onto the floor. "It's not a particularly expensive bottle. We can replace it."

"That's not the problem," I said.

"What is the problem, Bianca?" He, too, had become frustrated. "Are you freaking out because I look underage? My face might be nineteen, but I'm legal plus four hundred years or so."

He knew that wasn't what I meant either. Before I could snap at him, Ranulf groaned. "Still there is bickering."

"Okay," I said. "Okay. Truce." I was too tired for any of this.

Although Balthazar looked like he might keep it up, he finally let it go. From his pocket he withdrew my bracelet. "Picked this up off the lawn," he said.

"Thanks," I said flatly. But I hastened to clasp it around my wrist again. Since my death a couple of days ago, I'd learned that only a handful of things I'd bonded to strongly in life had the ability to empower me to be fully corporeal again—this coral bracelet, and a jet brooch in Lucas's pocket. Both of them were made out of material that had once been alive; it was something we had in common. As the bracelet enhanced my power, I felt gravity settle around me, and I no longer had to work at retaining a regular form.

Balthazar sighed heavily, grabbed two glasses from the rack beside the sink, and poured for himself and Ranulf. After a moment, he said, "Can you drink wine anymore? Drink anything?"

"I don't know," I said. "I don't seem to need food or water." The mere thought of chewing was faintly disgusting to me now, I realized—one more difference between me and the living world.

*There are better things than eating and drinking,* Maxie said. Increasingly her presence could be felt, a sort of cool spot right next to me, but Balthazar and Ranulf remained oblivious. *Aren't you curious about what they are?*

I ignored her. I had eyes only for Lucas, so pale and broken upon the floor. A thin circle of bloodstains ringed the stake, no more: evidence that his heart had stopped beating forever. The strong features that had always captivated me—his firm jaw, his high cheekbones—were more sculpted now, his handsomeness as compelling as it was unnatural.

The makeshift apartment in the wine cellar was where we had lived for the final weeks of our lives, virtually the only time we'd ever had to just be together without rules to keep us apart. We'd tried to make spaghetti on the hot plate, watched old movies on the DVD player, and slept together in the bed. Sometimes our situation had seemed so desperate, but I realized now that it was the greatest joy we'd ever shared. Maybe the greatest we ever would share.

*We're together,* I reminded myself. *You have to believe that as long as that's true, we can make it.* That belief had never been more important, but it had never felt so fragile.

I heard car doors slamming; Vic had apparently managed to get rid of the police. Ranulf and Balthazar lifted glasses to each other, or to Vic. Within a few seconds, there was a rapping on the door, and Balthazar opened it to let Vic in.

"Those guys did *not* want to believe my home invasion story," he said. Vic remained on the doorstop instead of coming in. "Apparently my neighbors called them even before I did and said it was a wild party, though how that looked like a party, I don't know. They made me take a Breathalyzer—oh, man." Vic saw Lucas on the floor. "What did you guys do?"

"The staking will not harm him," Ranulf explained. "When

it is removed, Lucas will revive. Do you require some wine?"

Vic shook his head. He just stood there in his T-shirt and jeans, awkward and miserable, staring down at Lucas. "He won't . . . he can't . . ."

"He won't attack you," Balthazar said. "For the time being, Lucas can't move. And we won't unstake him until we can get him fed."

Vic crammed his hands in his pockets, and although he had to know Balthazar was telling the truth, he couldn't bring himself to walk any closer.

I realized that, no matter how upsetting this was for me, it had to be a hundred times worse for Vic. He was the only human in the room, and despite growing up in a haunted house and attending Evernight Academy, Vic's experience of the supernatural was fairly benign—or it had been, before tonight, when one of his best friends had tried to kill him.

Balthazar took a pen and a scrap of paper from his pocket and began jotting something down. "Vic, if you can stay awake a while longer, you should head to this address," he said. "It's a butcher's in town. They open within the hour. These guys have a side business in blood. You show up with cash, and they don't ask any questions about why you need it."

"Don't think I could sleep right now," Vic said. "I'm not one hundred percent sure I'm ever sleeping again." Though he was trying to joke, his voice broke on the last words.

I went to him in the doorway and embraced him tightly. "Thank you," I whispered. "You've done so much for us, and we've done nothing for you."

"Don't say that." Vic's hands patted my back. "You're my friends. Nothing else to it."

How could we begin to repay Vic everything we owed him? Not just money—though we owed him that, too—but his loyalty and his courage? I didn't know if I had it in me. The rest of us had powers, but Vic might have been the strongest one.

When we pulled apart, Vic gave me an uneven smile. "All my best friends are dead people. Someday I've got to figure out how that happened." Despite everything, I laughed a little.

"Come, Vic," Ranulf said, clapping him on the shoulder. "I, too, would like to purchase a few pints. And perhaps we can repair some of the damage to the grasses in front of your home later today."

Vic shook his head as they started out the door. "Doubtful. Unless you spent all your time in ye olden Viking days doing landscaping."

The door shut behind them, leaving me and Balthazar basically alone. It was hard to know what to say; the silence between us was terrible. "The blood—that's going to snap Lucas out of it," I said. "Right?"

"That's not how being a vampire works. You should know that."

"Can you please stop lecturing me?"

"You're one to talk."

This situation was only going to get worse. Balthazar and I definitely needed some space between us for a while. I unfastened my bracelet and again released my tie to the physical world. "Watch Lucas," I said as I began to fade out.

"He's not going anywhere." Balthazar sat down and took a deep swallow of his wine.

The cellar became dimmer in my vision, until it faded into a blue-gray fog. As the mists closed around me, I concentrated on my memories of Maxie's face and the first place we'd talked after my death, the attic of Vic's home. As I imagined it—the old Persian carpet, the dressmaker's dummy, the bric-a-brac lying around—the place took shape around me. So did Maxie. She stood there in the long, billowy nightgown she'd died in back during the 1920s, just as I wore the white camisole and cloud-printed pajama pants I'd had on at the end.

"Sorry about your boyfriend," she said, and for pretty much the first time since we'd begun speaking, she truly did sound sorry. Maxie's usual hard demeanor was softer now. "It's lousy that you had to lose him like that."

"I haven't lost him. We'll find a way."

Maxie cocked an eyebrow, her saucy sense of humor already returning. "I already told you. Vampires and wraiths? Not a good mix. A really, really bad mix. We're poison to them, and they're no friends to us."

"I love Lucas. Our deaths don't change that."

"Death changes everything. Haven't you learned that much by now?"

"It didn't change you haranguing me nonstop," I snapped.

Maxie ducked her head, her dark blond hair tumbling

around her face. If she'd had blood flow, I thought, she might have blushed. "Sorry. You've had a rough couple of days. I don't mean to— I'm just trying to tell you how things are."

A rough couple of days. I'd died, found out I was a ghost, seen Lucas get cut down and turned into a vampire, and fought off a Black Cross attack. Yeah, that counted as a rough couple of days.

"You used to play with Vic in this room, when he was a little kid." I glanced at the place he'd shown me, where he used to sit and read his storybooks to her. "You didn't separate yourself from the world after you died."

"But I did. For the better part of a century, I just . . . I was stuck between here and there, and I didn't quite know what was going on. Sometimes I'd stab into people's dreams and turn them to nightmares, just to do it. Just to prove that I could affect the world around me."

I'd heard of wraiths doing worse things, maybe for similar reasons.

Maxie sat on the windowsill, her long white nightgown seeming to glow as the moonlight filtered through the billowing sleeves. "As you can probably imagine, people usually didn't stay in this house long. It was like a game for me, seeing how fast I could scare them out. But then the Woodsons took the place, and Vic was so tiny, just a couple of years old. When I showed myself to him, he wasn't scared. That was the first time in so long that I remembered what it was like to—to be accepted. To care about someone."

"So you understand," I said. "You see why I can't give up on the world."

"Vic's human. He's alive. He anchors me to life and lets me experience it through him, just a bit. I don't think Lucas can do that for you, not anymore."

"He does. He can. I know it." But I didn't know any such thing. There was so much about being a wraith that I didn't understand yet.

"You need to talk to Christopher," she said encouragingly. "He'll make you understand."

I remembered Christopher. He had appeared to me, a mysterious and foreboding figure, at Evernight; he had attacked me there with intent to kill, so that my transformation into a wraith would be guaranteed. Yet when he had appeared to me and Lucas this summer, he had rescued us from Charity.

Was he benevolent or evil? Did the actions of wraiths even fit into any kind of morality I understood? The only thing I knew for sure was that Christopher had power and influence among the wraiths. Now that I had become one, our paths were certain to cross again.

Thinking about this made me nervous. I managed to ask, "He's sort of the . . . wraith in charge, right?"

"Nobody's 'in charge.' But plenty of us listen to Christopher. He has a lot of power, a lot of wisdom."

"How did he get so powerful? Is it because he's especially old?" That was how it worked for vampires. "Or is he, well, like me?" I'd already figured out that my status—as a child born of two vampires, and therefore able to die a natural death and yet become a ghost—gave me abilities most ghosts could never claim.

"Neither," Maxie said. "He wasn't born to be a wraith, like you were. Christopher learned everything on his own. He has this amazing inner strength. You're going to like him, Bianca. Why don't you come with me now?"

I couldn't do it. Christopher might have amazing strength he'd used to save me—but he had also attacked me. The world of the wraiths remained foreign and frightening; I had no idea how my powers related to the cold, revenge-driven creatures I'd encountered at Evernight Academy. Maybe it was crazy to still be frightened of ghosts after I'd become one myself, but the thought of joining them forever scared me deeply. More than that: going into that world felt like giving up on life.

"I can't," I whispered. Maxie's face fell, but she didn't argue.

I pulled away from the room, away from her, and vanished again into the bluish fog that was my mind's way of making sense of pure nothingness. Lucas filled my thoughts, and I willed myself back to his side.

When I reappeared in the wine cellar, I immediately got the sense that more time had passed for Balthazar than it had for me; he'd finished his glass of wine and was across the room, lying on our bed.

Lucas lay exactly as he had fallen. The sight of him as a corpse hit me anew, and it took my whole strength not to fade out again so I wouldn't have to bear the loss for a while. He deserved better than that. No matter how difficult it was to endure, I would remain by his side.

Balthazar realized I was there with a start, but he said nothing.

I didn't want to argue with him anymore; I was too sad for that, too tired. Instead I asked, "Isn't there anything we can do for him?"

"No." Balthazar sat up. His curly hair was mussed, and I realized he'd been asleep. No doubt he was exhausted; it hadn't exactly been an awesome couple of days for him, either. "The urge to kill—it's powerful, Bianca. It can be overwhelming. The vampires you've known have nearly all been the ones who mastered that urge, but they're a minority."

"You mean, most of them end up like—like Charity."

He closed his eyes briefly at the mention of his younger sister's name. "No. Charity and her kind are special cases. Individuals with the strength to keep going, but who have lost touch with what it meant to be human. They're the most dangerous. And, fortunately, the most rare."

"Then what happens to the others?"

Balthazar rubbed his temple. If vampires could get headaches, I'd think he had one. "They self-destruct," he said quietly. "They get taken out by Black Cross, or by humans who've seen just enough horror movies to get the idea. Or they end themselves. Set a fire and walk into it. They'd rather burn than endure the killing rage any longer."

I wanted to say that there was no way Lucas would ever

do that, but I couldn't. No, Black Cross wouldn't be able to take him down easily. But hating his vampire nature as he did, already burdened with the fact that he'd tried to kill both his mother and one of his best friends—it was entirely possible that Lucas could end his existence. He'd see it as the right thing to do, the only way to keep people safe.

"The hunger is stronger for some of us than it is for others," Balthazar continued. "As badly as I crave blood sometimes . . . it's nothing compared to what some other vampires endure. The ones who self-destruct are always the ones with the greatest hunger. It makes them crazy, turns their minds inside out."

Our eyes met, as if he was asking me whether he had to go on. But I knew I needed him to say what came next.

Balthazar, understanding, said, "It looks like Lucas is one of the hungry ones."

"Isn't there anything we can do for him?" I said. "Any way to make this easier?"

Slowly Balthazar rose from the bed and walked toward me, his expression uncertain. "I don't think we can make it easier, exactly, but there's a place where we can keep him away from most humans, and from Black Cross, too. Where Lucas might be able to learn how to handle what he's become."

I brightened until I realized what Balthazar meant. Or did I? Surely he couldn't be thinking about *that*. "Where?"

Balthazar confirmed my worst suspicions by saying, "We have to take Lucas back to Evernight."

# Chapter Four

"TAKE LUCAS TO EVERNIGHT?" I REPEATED. "HAVE you gone insane? Balthazar, think about it! Lucas was Black Cross. He spied on Evernight for them. Mrs. Bethany hates him—everybody there hates him. They'll kill him on sight."

"They won't. They can't," Balthazar insisted. "Any vampire can come to Evernight at any time and ask for sanctuary. No matter who it is or what they've done, Mrs. Bethany has to take them in."

"But that's Mrs. Bethany's rule, isn't it? She can break it any time she wants."

Balthazar's mouth twisted, the closest he could come to a smile on a day as dark as this one. "Mrs. Bethany doesn't break rules. You should know that. Remember, she let Charity in."

True, and Mrs. Bethany and Charity hated each other fervently. I wasn't convinced, though. Lucas had been a vampire hunter; surely that was worse than being any kind of vampire, no matter how dangerous.

Some of my reluctance was more selfish. Going back to Evernight Academy would mean returning to my parents. On one hand, I wanted to see them again so badly it hurt; on the other, I knew that they'd always feared and rejected wraiths. If they rejected me—as Kate had Lucas—I didn't think I could bear it.

I heard footsteps on the concrete steps outside and went to the door to let in Vic and Ranulf, who had a large sack full of what I suspected were pints of cow's blood. Vic did come in this time, but he didn't move more than a couple steps past the door. When he caught me looking, Vic handed over the bag, then fished out a single bottle of Mountain Dew. "I figure I should probably hang in the backyard for a while," he said, his eyes focused nervously on the floor where Lucas lay. "Until you guys chill Lucas out."

"Good idea." I took the shopping bag to the folding table. "Thanks again, Vic."

"Just give me another day or so before we get attacked again. That's thanks enough."

Balthazar and Ranulf each took a pint from the sack, each one in a little plastic container like the kind they use to serve soup to go at a deli. They both opened them up and started drinking, while Lucas still lay on the floor. At first I thought they were being selfish, but I soon realized what they were doing: regaining their strength. If Lucas awoke as savage as he'd been when Balthazar staked him, they'd need it.

I took a couple of pints and put them in the microwave.

Blood always tasted better at human body temperature. When they were ready, I glanced over at my friends. Ranulf was finishing, tipping up his cup to get the last drops; Balthazar's lips were tinted dark red. Drinking blood had been so delicious. I realized that I missed it, maybe more than anything else about being alive.

The guys were prepared. I knelt at Lucas's side, putting the pints within reach. Slowly I wrapped my hand around the protruding handle of the stake. Splinters jabbed into my palm, and I imagined the pain Lucas must have felt in the seconds before he passed out.

"On the count of three," I said. "One . . . two—"

I tugged the stake out. It made a wet, disgusting sound. Lucas writhed on the floor, and his eyes opened wide. He inhaled, deliberately sniffing the air. I knew he'd caught the scent of blood.

"Drink," I whispered. "Drink."

Lucas's hand shot out to clutch one of the containers. In an instant he was gulping down the blood, thick swallows that made his Adam's apple bob in his extended throat. Within seconds, he emptied the first container, dropped it on the floor, and lunged for the second one. That one he drained even faster. I watched him, fascinated.

When that one was done, Lucas looked around wildly, and Ranulf threw him another container from the bag. Though I hadn't warmed that one, he drank it just as quickly. As it fell to clatter on the floor, he didn't go after one more—but he ran his tongue around his mouth, catching stray drops, then lifted his bloodstained fingers to his mouth to suck every last bit of it.

"Is that better?" I asked.

"Bianca." Lucas turned to me, body remaining tense, but his expression no longer looked like that of an animal—it was his own. "That wasn't some hallucination. You're really here."

"Really here. How do you feel?"

Instead of answering, Lucas pulled me roughly into his arms. The embrace was too hard, but it was human emotion, and for that I was grateful. His hands combed through my hair, which must have felt more or less real to him. I was very present in that moment.

I repeated, "How do you feel?"

"Better." His words came haltingly. "Before, all I could think about was—no, I couldn't think. I was just this hungry . . . thing."

"You're okay now."

"As long as you're with me." His voice was tight, and I realized that he remained troubled. The blood hunger wasn't his only problem. He shifted away from me, hanging on tightly to my hand, to look up at Balthazar and Ranulf. "I didn't dream you two either."

"Welcome to death," Ranulf said cheerily. "It is not so bad once you get what is called the 'hang of it.' "

"Thanks, buddy." Lucas simply nodded at Balthazar; apparently he remembered the conversation they'd had. But then he froze, and his face twisted like he was about to be sick. I wondered if he'd drunk the blood too fast until he whispered, "Mom. Vic. I went after— I wanted—"

"Everybody's fine. You didn't hurt anyone." I closed my fingers around his.

"I could have. I wanted to." There was something in Lucas's eyes that made me wonder if, instead of saying *wanted*, he'd nearly said *want*. "Mom's never going to speak to me again."

Balthazar folded his arms. "Do you really want to talk to her again, after the way she turned on you?"

"It doesn't work like that," I said. As bitterly as my parents and I had parted, I wanted to see them again every single day. When my eyes met Lucas's, I could see he felt the same way. He understood Kate's revulsion and distrust of his new nature; he shared them.

Ranulf stepped forward, helpful as ever. "Vic bears you no ill will. He is outside drinking the Dew of the Mountain and will be glad to see you yourself again."

Lucas shook his head. "He can't want to hang out with me after I went for his throat."

"I believe that he is somewhat . . . overwhelmed by the day's events, but he will not abandon you," Ranulf said.

"None of us will." I wanted to embrace him again, but Lucas remained distant, focused inward. When I glanced at Balthazar, he shook his head slightly, a warning for me not to push. The control Lucas had gained was temporary, and we all knew it.

"Can you guys give us a few minutes?" Lucas said, running one hand through his dark gold hair, which was even more mussed than Balthazar's. "I'm glad to see you and everything, but Bianca and I have to talk."

"Sure." Balthazar nudged Ranulf. "Come on, we'll help Vic with the home repair."

After the door closed behind them, Lucas and I looked at each other, and the sadness of it struck me so hard it almost hurt. I found myself remembering a time a few years ago, when I'd first learned he was Black Cross. Once he'd escaped from Evernight, we had faced one another through a pane of stained glass, unable to believe there was any way we could ever be together again. I could picture it so perfectly, each shade of the glass, as though it still hung between us.

"What was it like for you?" I asked. "Being dead?"

"I don't remember anything about it." Lucas leaned his head back against the leg of our folding table, giving in to the exhaustion that followed rising from the grave. We remained on the floor, unable to summon the will to move. "Just now, when Balthazar staked me—that sounds so weird to say—whatever. Well, after that, I dreamed. Thought I saw Charity chasing after us." He half laughed, a bitter sound, and looked up at the ceiling. "The last thing I needed was her in my nightmares."

I shivered. Charity looked innocent, with her youthful face and bedraggled, waiflike appearance; she was anything but. I figured I would have nightmares about her forever, too, if I could still dream. I wasn't sure about that yet.

"What was it like for you?" he asked, focusing on me again. "Did you become a ghost right away, or was there some time between? It'd be nice to think you got a sneak preview of heaven."

"No sneak previews." I folded my arms atop my knees and rested my chin there. "I think I turned into a ghost pretty much instantly, but it took me awhile to realize what had happened. At first I just drifted in and out."

"Do you think there's an afterlife for vampires? Do they— do *we* all go to hell, if there's a hell?"

"Don't say that!"

"Holy water burns me. I'll never be able to set foot on consecrated ground again," Lucas said. "God's made it pretty clear where he stands, don't you think?"

I cupped his face with my hands. "I know you hate this, but there are ways to go on, to enjoy the years to come. Think about it: We're immortal now. We lost each other once, but at least we never have to again."

Lucas pulled away, breaking contact between us. Slowly he pushed himself to his feet. He walked a few steps farther into our makeshift apartment in the wine cellar, studying it as though he were seeing it for the first time: the hot plate, the air mattress on a bed frame, the cardboard drawers that held our things. There were times in the past few weeks when I'd thought this was the most perfect, romantic place on earth. Now it seemed shabby and small, its beauty our last shared illusion.

He said, "Bianca, I don't know if I can do this."

"You can."

"You're saying that because you want to believe it. Not because you do."

"You're giving up without even trying."

Lucas turned to me, his eyes anguished. "I'm going to try. Jesus, Bianca, do you think I wouldn't try for you? As much as I hate this—this hunger inside me, this cold, disgusting, *dead* feeling—if it means being with you, I'll try."

"You'll make it. You'll learn how to handle the hunger. I promise."

"How is that supposed to happen?" He gestured at the empty blood containers on the floor. "That's, what, three pints of blood? It's as much as I can do right this second not to tackle that bag and drink the rest immediately. Already when I think about Vic outside—it's not about Vic anymore, it's about the fact that he's alive and he's got blood I could drink. In another few minutes—"

"We have more blood. Drink as much as you need. We can get more." But that was a purely temporary solution, and we both knew it.

He needed hope, and only one suggestion gave us any hope. I laid aside my own objections and fears about my parents; Balthazar's plan was the best we had.

"Classes start in two weeks," I said. "At Evernight. You're going to go back there."

Lucas stared at me for a second, then thumped his head against one of the wine racks so that the bottles rattled. "Great. I'm already hearing things. Halfway to crazy."

"You're not hearing things. You're enrolling in Evernight Academy again as a student, a vampire student this time, and they'll take care of you."

"Take care of me? Bianca, the last time I visited, I rode with the guys who burned the place down."

I remembered what Balthazar had said and clung to it. "You're a vampire now. If you ask for sanctuary, Mrs. Bethany has to give it to you. They might not be friendly, exactly, but they'll give you a place to stay, and plenty of blood to drink, and advice about how to deal with the hunger. For weeks or months, however long you need."

"Or years," Lucas said. "Balthazar's kept coming back for years."

Balthazar had attended Evernight Academy for different reasons, ones more focused on the school's true mission: helping young-looking vampires pass for human by keeping them up-to-date with the modern world. I wasn't about to point that out to Lucas, though. The last thing he needed to hear was how well all the other vampires could manage.

Lucas added, "Besides, it doesn't matter how much they hate me. We're not going to Evernight Academy because it's dangerous for you."

"For me?" I had hardly had a moment to consider this, but Lucas was right. We knew from the events at school last year that Mrs. Bethany was no longer merely the headmistress at Evernight; she was also using the school as a means of finding— and perhaps capturing—ghosts like me. *Why* she was doing this remained a mystery, but there was no doubt that she loathed the wraiths. Whatever she was up to couldn't be good for us.

Seeing realization dawn on my face, Lucas nodded. His

expression had become truly grim. "I've already screwed things up so badly that you died," he said. "No way am I ever going back to the one place where that situation could get even worse."

What else could we do, though? I forced myself to be brave. "We'll figure it out."

"Don't ask me to go there without you. I couldn't take it." Lucas said it simply, like it was obvious; if he was parted from me, the thin tether of will that kept him going would snap.

"You're going to Evernight Academy, and I'm going with you."

"Bianca, no. It's too dangerous."

"Lucas, yes." He always wanted to protect me against every risk, but it was time for a reality check. "Is it more dangerous than my being a vampire in a Black Cross cell? I made it through that, and I'll make it through this. Besides, there are wraiths who managed to be at Evernight without being destroyed by Mrs. Bethany. Maxie's one of them. It can be done. At least I know to be careful."

Lucas didn't look convinced. "We could do something else. Lock me up someplace until I—"

"Until you stop wanting blood?" I kept my voice low, to soften the impact of my next words. "That's not going to happen. And I'm not turning you into a prisoner in some basement somewhere. I'm telling you, we can do this. We can because we have to."

"I don't like it."

"I don't either, but I'll be all right. You'll have a structure there, a blood supply, other vampires who can help teach you how to handle this. Ranulf and Balthazar will go with you," I promised. "And Vic's going back, too, remember?"

His dark green eyes widened, and I knew that Vic wasn't a source of comfort for him; he wasn't a friend. He was prey.

Hurriedly, I added, "You'll be able to be around Vic while others are there to help you. Eventually it's going to seem easy."

Lucas stared down at the floor, and I hated myself for being so glib, so casual. Maybe he would learn to bear it, but it would never be easy. It didn't help either of us for me to pretend that it could.

I remembered what Balthazar had said, about vampires walking into a fire rather than going on. Lucas knew better than most how to destroy a vampire's body.

"Okay. It won't be easy," I said. "It never has been. And that's never kept us apart."

He held out his arms, and I ran into them. Already his embrace had cooled, but it was still Lucas, still us.

Into my hair, Lucas whispered, "Will I only see you in my dreams?"

"As long as you have my brooch, I can get to you."

He frowned, then pulled the brooch from his back pocket. The Whitby jet flower, ornately carved, had been a gift from him to me when we were first dating. He'd taken it with him when he went into the fight, to die; that was the only thing that had allowed me to reach him. "Why the brooch?"

"Things that wraiths bonded to strongly in life, meaningful things—like this brooch, or my bracelet, or the gargoyle outside the window of my old room—well, we can use them to travel. They're like stops on a subway line; I can travel to them, just sort of appear wherever they are. The coral bracelet and the jet brooch are especially powerful, because they're made out of materials that were once living creatures." I closed his hand around the brooch. "So as long as you keep this with you, I'll always be able to find you. See, you'll still have a way to make sure I'm safe."

"Evernight," he said. "Okay." I could tell I hadn't convinced him as much as worn him down. He remained more frightened for me than for himself. But we truly had no other place to turn.

We hugged again, more tightly this time. How badly I wanted to believe that Lucas had found a reason to hope. Even as we embraced, though, I could tell he was looking over my shoulder, staring at the blood.

# Chapter Five

"REST," I SAID AS WE STEPPED INTO ONE OF THE hotel rooms in downtown Philadelphia that Balthazar had paid for. It was ridiculously luxurious, with white cotton quilts on high platform beds—too clean for undead creatures smeared with dried blood. "We both need to rest."

"Can you sleep?" Lucas asked. He'd eaten again on the way over, several pints, and now had the half-dazed look that I recognized as a result of overfeeding—like Mom and Dad on Thanksgiving. We'd had to give him as much as he could take; it was the only way to ensure he could get through the hotel lobby without snapping. Soon he'd crash.

"I'm not sure ghosts need to sleep. Sometimes I need to sort of . . . fade out, I guess. But it's not quite the same thing."

"Where do you go? When you fade out."

I shrugged. There was so much I still didn't know about my new wraith nature. "Someplace I can get back from. That's the only thing that matters."

He nodded wearily. Through the thin hotel walls, I could hear Balthazar roughly throwing down his gear in the next room. We'd decided to spend the last days before the new semester in the hotel because Vic's parents were due to return from Italy. He was going to be in enough trouble about the torn-up front lawn without his mom and dad discovering an infestation of vampires in the basement.

Besides, we needed to give Vic some more space. He and Lucas hadn't come face-to-face since the attack, by their mutual agreement. It was obvious that Vic was trying hard to come to terms, but it was just as obviously going to take a while.

"Why do vampires need sleep? Doesn't make much sense." Lucas kicked off his boots and slid out of his jeans. Now that he wore only his boxers and a T-shirt, I could see that his whole body had taken on the sculpted beauty of the vampire. The tee outlined every broad muscle of his chest.

Although I had lost my mortal body, I could still feel desire.

I turned off one of the side lamps nearer the window and pulled shut the heavy drapes that would keep out the morning sun. Lucas had fed recently enough that sunlight wouldn't hurt him, but he'd probably hate the glare. "My mom used to say that she thought it was more of a habit than anything else, like the body keeps on doing what it knows it should do. See how you've started breathing again? You won't stop, even when you're sound asleep."

"Though I'll never need air again." Lucas said it as a joke, but it fell flat. I could tell he'd just realized that he'd never feel the relief of a good, deep breath, or a heartfelt sigh.

He collapsed into bed, sinking back gratefully into the feather-plump pillows. Probably he could have fallen asleep within seconds, but I had different ideas.

Maybe Lucas's ravenous blood hunger could be channeled into other things. Other needs. Where being ravenous wouldn't be a problem—quite the opposite, actually.

Carefully, I tried shimmying out of the cloud-patterned pajama bottoms. They weren't so much actual clothes as they were the memory of clothes, so I wasn't sure whether or not they'd come off.

They would. The pajamas crumpled to the floor and just sort of vanished. I hoped they'd come back—but later. Ideally, I wouldn't want them for a while.

Lucas raised an eyebrow.

As I slipped into the bed beside him, he smiled a little—the first sign of real pleasure I'd seen from him since his resurrection. "Does this still work?" he murmured. "You and me?"

"Let's find out."

He pulled me down into his arms; we were cold against each other now, but it was natural to him and to me, to what we had become. Delicate lines of frost laced the sheets around us as our lips met gently. For the first moment, Lucas was so unsure—of his reactions, of mine—that I felt unbearably tender toward him. Like all I wanted to do was wrap myself around him like a blanket and shelter him from everything we'd been through.

His mouth opened beneath mine as he tangled his fingers in my hair. The only thing I wore now was the coral bracelet that would keep me solid, make this possible.

*We made it,* I thought. Every complication we faced seemed to have faded away. *We're back where we began. Death couldn't take this away from us.*

Our kisses intensified and deepened. Lucas's hands were still his hands, strong and familiar. He touched me the same way. I felt pleasure differently now—softer, more diffuse and yet all-encompassing—but it was no less for having changed. And as I grew surer, passion building between us, it seemed as though my joy in him flowed through us both.

He rolled me onto my back, but then his expression changed. I saw his fangs, understood, and smiled. I felt the urge to bite, too—not as strongly, now that I no longer needed blood, but sex and fangs would always go together for me.

"It's okay," I whispered against his throat, between kisses. "You can be hungry for this. You can have this."

"Yes," he said roughly. His green eyes bored into me, a desperate plea.

"Do you need to drink?" I arched against him and let my head fall back, exposing my throat. Lucas breathed in, a hard gasp. "Drink from me."

With a growl, he sank his teeth into my flesh. I felt again the real pain of having a body, and that alone was its own kind of pleasure. My hands gripped him tightly around the back, surrendering to his hunger —

—until he shoved himself away from me, shouting out in pain.

"Lucas?" I sat upright, clutching the sheet to me. "Lucas, what's wrong?"

"It burns!"

As he stumbled from the bed, clutching at his throat, he choked and then spat. Silver wraith blood shimmered on the floor briefly before it faded. I smelled smoke and snapped on the bedside light; on the carpet I could see a couple of faint singe marks. Then I realized the sheets were scorched too—coffee-colored drops from where my blood had fallen. I put my hand to the wound at my throat, but it was already closing. The skin knitted beneath my fingertips, a ticklish sensation.

For a few seconds, we just stared at each other. The only thing I could think of to say was, "Now we know why vampires don't drink wraiths' blood."

"Yeah." Lucas winced when he spoke, and his voice was hoarse. I realized that his lips, tongue, and throat remained scorched. As a vampire, he'd heal quickly, but not instantly. Every place we touched was just a source of pain for him now.

Maybe he saw the pity in my eyes, because he turned his head. "We should sleep." He yanked back the covers on the other hotel bed.

"Lucas—it doesn't always have to involve blood drinking. You remember that."

"I know." He lay down in the other bed, heavily, as though he could no longer support his body. "We'll—we'll figure it out."

Though I wanted to argue, I knew this wasn't the time. I simply shut off the light again and slid back beneath the covers, cold and lonely in the big bed. After a couple of seconds, it felt pointless to remain solid, so I took off my bracelet and dissolved into the blue, misty void by myself.

So much for thinking death couldn't take anything from us.

"Last chance to change your mind," I said a few days later, as Lucas bundled up his few possessions early on the morning of the first day of school. For a moment I regretted the joke; it would be disastrous if Lucas did change his mind, because we didn't have a Plan B.

But Lucas attempted to roll with it. "Always meant to get a diploma someday. I guess after death counts as someday, huh?" He tried to smile for me, but it didn't go far. "Does it feel weird? Not going?"

That was the first time I realized I'd died as an eleventh-grade dropout. "Yeah, kinda."

These days hadn't been easy for us. We had to keep over-feeding Lucas blood, and he mostly refused to leave the room. I'd memorized the hotel maids' schedule, so we could make sure Lucas avoided them. Lucas still thought Evernight was too much of a risk for me, and I wasn't sure I disagreed. But what other options did we have?

The dawn light brightened the edges of the hotel window shade as Lucas shrugged on the uniform sweater—Balthazar had ordered supplies for them both online. He'd gotten a little taller and a lot more muscular since he'd been an Evernight student, so the sweater was a bit tight, but in a good way. "You look great," I said. "Reminds me of when we met."

"When I tried to save you from the vampires." Lucas paused, then stepped closer to me and put his hand on my cheek. "You know the only reason I'm doing this is so I can come back to you. Be decent enough for you, know how to act. You get that, right?"

"I do."

"And you're going to be careful, right? You won't take any chances at Evernight?"

"I'll be very careful." I took his hand in mine and kissed his palm. Then I removed my coral and silver bracelet, going half-transparent as it dropped into Lucas's fingers. "Take this with you. I'll get it there."

"You don't want it with you? Just in case? You can't afford to lose this thing, and your brooch is already in my bag."

"It's not like I can take it myself," I pointed out. "When I go incorporeal to travel, nothing physical can travel with me. Besides, it couldn't be anywhere safer than with you." I folded his hand around the bracelet.

He leaned forward, as though to kiss me. Now that I was incorporeal—a soft shadow of blue mist in the vague shape of my body—our lips couldn't touch. But a little of Lucas passed through me, a faint cool tickle that made me shiver, just where our kiss would have been.

Just as I began to smile, though, there was a rap on the door: Balthazar. Time to go.

\* \* \*

After they'd begun the long drive from Philadelphia, I prepared for my own journey. Maxie had told me that wraiths remained bonded to certain places and things that had been meaningful to us during our lifetimes. We could always travel to them, no matter how far away we might be. I wasn't sure what every single one of those places was yet, though I had ideas: the old maple tree in Arrowwood where I'd liked to play as a child, the theater where Lucas and I had gone on our first date, and perhaps the wine cellar where we'd lived our final weeks. Those were just theories, though.

The only place I knew I could travel was the first place I'd gone, by accident: Evernight Academy, specifically the gargoyle that had perched outside my bedroom.

I drifted into foggy darkness, and at first the sensation was deliciously like sleep, so tempting. But my mind remained focused on the gargoyle. I'd spent so much time looking at his gap-fanged grin that I could picture him perfectly: stony claws, hunched back, pointy wings. Briefly I imagined the way the stone had felt beneath my hands, cold and hard—

Then I could feel it.

The world clarified around me. I perched atop the gargoyle, which would've been massively uncomfortable if I'd been alive but was fine now that I could float when I wanted. Curlicues of frost streaked across the windows, heralding the presence of a wraith.

Would my parents see it? They had the first time I'd accidentally come here. Instead of realizing it was me, though, they'd freaked out, believing the frost came from yet another of the ghosts that had invaded Evernight.

*Not invaded,* I reminded myself. *Drawn here, because of the students. Brought here specifically by Mrs. Bethany.* I had to remain on my guard.

I heard nothing from the apartment. Probably my parents were downstairs, helping Mrs. Bethany welcome the students. Looking downward, I could see that the first few people had already begun to arrive. Mostly humans at this point, too noisy and too happy—but every once in a while silent, dark-clad figures would sweep through the crowd as though they belonged here more than anyone else. They *did* belong here more; they were the vampires.

Quickly I shimmered along the side of the building, invisible except for the trails of frost I left behind. At first I just wanted to get a better view, but then I realized: Something felt odd about the school.

Well, big surprise. Evernight Academy was pretty much made of odd. This was different, though, something I had never sensed before—as if, in places, the school was pushing back at me, trying to keep me out. Probably it was something only the wraiths could feel. In those places, I felt as though I was being watched right through the walls. Curious, I whisked along the side of the building, leaving trails of frost on the windows in my wake. Although there were places I could get into the school, there were places that I couldn't. And one place—the area at the very top of the south tower, right above my parents' apartment—felt shut off to me completely, in a way that gave me cold shivers.

*So don't go there,* I told myself. *It's not like you've ever had a single reason to go up there before. As long as you can get in anywhere in the building, you can get to Lucas. Nothing else matters.*

However, the knowledge of that strange forbidding energy made me uneasy. I darted downward again, the better to get away from it, and to watch the arrivals, which was what I needed to be paying attention to anyway.

As I focused again on the group, I saw my first familiar face and felt a warm glow of happiness that could've been a smile. *Patrice!*

Patrice Deveraux, my roommate during my first year at Evernight, stepped out of a lean gray Lexus. Her tailored version of the school uniform made her look sophisticated and trim, even in a kilt and sweater, and her hair now bounced with its natural curl, a thick dark halo that suited her. She'd skipped last year to have fun in Scandinavia with her new guy, but one or the other of them must have broken it off—probably Patrice, who seemed to think of men primarily as fashion accessories.

Despite her obsessions with appearances and luxury, Patrice had a fundamental grit that made me like her. Sort of to my surprise, she'd tried to reach out to me during the summer after I'd run away, proving that she wasn't as thoughtless as she could sometimes seem. It made me happy to remember that not every vampire at Evernight Academy was sinister and forbidding. Besides, this was the first time I'd seen her since

I'd died. I wished I could have said hello, but of course that was impossible.

Just before Patrice stepped inside, she paused at the door and looked upward, directly at where I was hovering. Could she see me? I realized quickly that she couldn't, but the coincidence was striking. Patrice hesitated a second longer before readjusting her sunglasses and going inside.

A few more familiar faces began to appear, both vampire and human, mostly people I hadn't known too well but had shared classes with and spoken to from time to time. A couple of teachers, too—both Mr. Yee and Professor Iwerebon mingled among the newcomers, saying hello to parents. I looked for my mother and father, half in dread, half in hope, but they didn't make an appearance. Among the human students, I didn't see any old friends but recognized a few faces—like Clementine Nichols, whose ticket to Evernight had been her family's haunted car, and Skye Tierney, Raquel's sophomore-year lab partner. Raquel had said Skye was "good people, basically." Coming from Raquel, who hated most people on principle until they gave her a reason to feel otherwise, that was high praise.

And yet I never tried to have a real conversation with her, or with a lot of these people. *How could I never ask Clementine what it was like to have a haunted car?* I should've reached out to people more often. I'd never been incredibly outgoing, but death made me feel lonelier, somehow.

The Woodsons' car finally showed up, and Vic and Ranulf both emerged. Each of them wore the regulation uniform, but

Vic had on a Phillies cap, as usual—and to my delight, Ranulf wore one as well.

"How very striking." Mrs. Bethany swept out of the school, as if she could sense deviations from protocol at a distance. "Mr. Woodson, your sartorial influence on Mr. White is both profound and unfortunate."

"We'll take them off before class," Vic promised, edging around her. "Absolutely."

"See that you do."

Mrs. Bethany watched them go, her sharp eyes following them like a hawk follows prey. She looked darkly beautiful with her thick hair piled atop her head and her long fingernails painted crimson. But the only thing I could think about was the last time I'd seen her—during the raid she'd led on Black Cross's New York headquarters. She'd killed Lucas's stepfather in front of my eyes without hesitating. The headmistress of Evernight enforced her idea of the law, absolutely, whether seeking revenge for a Black Cross attack or regulating the school dress code. I wondered if those things were any different for her, or whether it was all just a matter of rules.

That was what Balthazar seemed to think. I wasn't sure, though. Lucas and I had met because, two years before, Mrs. Bethany had suddenly changed the rules of Evernight Academy in order to allow human students to enroll—without informing those humans that they would be surrounded by vampires, of course. Each of those many human students had connections, one way or another, to ghosts. She'd been hunting the wraiths—creatures like me—for reasons we had yet to learn. Mrs. Bethany was complicated in ways I couldn't pretend to fathom.

But I had to hope she would play by the rules today, at least, because I recognized the car that Balthazar had rented coming up the long gravel drive.

When Balthazar stepped out, several of the students— vampire and human—smiled at him; he'd always been effortlessly popular, trusted by everyone. But when Lucas got out of the passenger seat, the vampires' smiles vanished, replaced by expressions of pure loathing.

The ones who had been here two years ago knew that Lucas had been Black Cross—that he had first come to Evernight to spy on them, and that he had been raised to kill vampires on sight. All of them would have heard how narrowly he had escaped Mrs. Bethany when he'd been discovered. The fact that Lucas had been changed into a vampire, something they had to sense instantly, didn't diminish their hatred in the slightest.

The only vampire who didn't gape in shock and fury was Mrs. Bethany. She stepped forward smoothly, her long black skirt swirling around her, to face Lucas. Her expression was unreadable as she stared into his eyes.

Could he bring himself to do it? His face betrayed his confusion and doubt, and who could blame him? To ask for the vampires' protection—to declare himself one of them at last— was a kind of second death for him. The death of who he had been, his whole life.

But he didn't have much other choice.

Lucas took a deep breath. "I call upon the sanctuary of Evernight."

Chaos followed. Several of the vampire students tried to protest, either to Balthazar, who refused to be baited, or Mrs. Bethany, who ignored them as she stood entirely still amid the din. The human students, of course, had no idea what was going on or why this new guy was so despised by a lot of the student body; understandably, they were suspicious of him already.

Lucas stood his ground, though I could see how he longed to lash back, and how his dark green eyes sometimes followed one of the human students a little too long. Mrs. Bethany studied him, her eyes searching, until she gestured for him to follow her and walked toward the edge of the campus—toward the carriage house where she lived.

As Balthazar watched them go, a space widening around him as he was shunned by the other vampire students, I willed myself to his side and whispered, "How do you think she's taking it?"

He jumped, then hissed, "You scared me."

"From now on, take it for granted that I'm around."

"Even when I'm in the shower?"

"You wish."

After a glance from side to side, making certain that nobody realized he was talking to "himself," he murmured, "I think if she were going to turn him away, she would've done it immediately.

But she never would, Bianca. Trust me."

Despite everything he'd done for Lucas since his turning, I wasn't ready to totally trust Balthazar again yet. He was the guy who'd led Lucas to his death—the person who had gotten Lucas into this situation to start with. Wasn't he?

I couldn't take the uncertainty between us another second. Instead I darted after Mrs. Bethany and Lucas, eager to hear what I could.

Mrs. Bethany lived in a carriage house at the edge of the school grounds, a place I knew well. But I forgot one very basic thing about it until I swept down toward the roof, ready to sink inside—and felt myself shoved back violently. *Of course,* I realized. *The roof.*

Metals and minerals found in the human body, such as copper and iron, repelled wraiths strongly. This was why Mrs. Bethany had chosen a copper roof: to keep us out. The impact reminded me of the "blocked" areas of Evernight, except that in this case, the entire place was shut off to me.

Well, if I couldn't follow Lucas inside, I could try the same thing I'd done back when I was a student—eavesdrop.

I curled into a soft cloud at the edge of one window, where the branches of the nearest elm almost scraped the glass and would disguise me in their shadows. This gave me a view of Mrs. Bethany's desk—so neat and tidy that everything was at right angles, with only a framed nineteenth-century gentleman's silhouette as decoration. As I watched, she strode into the room, as much in command as ever. Lucas followed her, shoulders tense and gaze wary, the look he wore when he expected a fight.

"There is one question we must address before any other, Mr. Ross," Mrs. Bethany said as she took a seat behind her desk. "Where is Bianca Olivier?"

Startled, I jumped, and the leaves around me rustled. She glanced my way for only a second; no doubt she thought I was merely the wind.

Lucas sat heavily in the chair opposite her, gripping the arm-rests hard. "Bianca's dead."

Mrs. Bethany said nothing. Her dark eyes remained fixed on him in a silent demand for the whole truth.

He continued, "About six weeks ago, her health just . . . failed. She didn't want food. Didn't want blood. I tried taking her to the doctor, but she'd started to, well, to change, so they didn't know what to make of her anymore."

"It must have been clear to you what needed to be done."

Slowly, Lucas nodded. "Bianca needed to turn into a vam-pire to stay alive. I asked her to kill me. I would've let her turn me into a vampire, to save herself. But she wouldn't do it." His voice broke on the last word, and he turned his head away from Mrs. Bethany.

My resurrection as a ghost might have lessened Lucas's grief, but I realized in that moment that the wounds he'd suffered when I watched me die would scar him forever.

"You could not have prevented it," Mrs. Bethany said. She didn't sound sympathetic, exactly, but her voice was slightly softer. "If Miss Olivier didn't transform you into a vampire, who did?"

"That would be Charity." Lucas's jaw tightened. A shudder

of pure hate passed through me. "We had a run-in right after Bianca died, back in Philadelphia. I don't know why she did it."

"With Charity More, reason rarely enters into the equation." That was as close to a joke as I'd ever heard from Mrs. Bethany.

"I didn't know what to do at first. It's— I guess you know how it is, when you change. Balthazar was around, trying to deal with his sister, and he helped me out. I tried to talk to my mother, but she—she's Black Cross."

Mrs. Bethany straightened, her eyes flashing. "You mean that she attacked you."

"Yeah."

"Your own mother." To my astonishment, I realized Mrs. Bethany was feeling righteous outrage—on Lucas's behalf. "Indecent. Shocking. Hateful. The sort of behavior I would have expected from most members of Black Cross, to be sure, but one would think that at least a mother's love would prove more powerful than their anti-vampire dogma."

"Guess not," he muttered.

Mrs. Bethany rose to her feet, walked around the desk to Lucas's side, and put her hand on his shoulder. If his wide eyes were any indication, he was as surprised as I was. "It is unfortunate that you had to learn the error of your ways in such a painful fashion. But you should know that my sympathies are entirely with those who have suffered persecution by Black Cross. Your past as a living man, and the mistakes you made then, have now been wiped away. The sanctuary of Evernight Academy is yours.

We will protect you. We will teach you. You need not be alone any longer."

For one half second, I actually liked Mrs. Bethany.

Lucas wasn't won over quite so easily. "Thanks. I mean that. But it's not going to be so simple. Those guys are about ready to stake me already."

"They'll obey the rules." Mrs. Bethany's smile held a hint of chill. "Leave that to me."

"The human students—" His voice sounded strangled. "I've never killed."

"The urge is strong." She spoke as though this were only to be expected. "In your case, perhaps, stronger than most—I see the signs. But here you will have many guardians over your conduct; I daresay you are in less danger of harming a human here than you would be in the outside world. In time, you will discover how to be a part of the vampire world. You will become one of us."

Lucas shut his eyes for a moment, and I wondered if it was in relief or despair.

# Chapter Six

LUCAS WALKED TO THE WROUGHT-IRON GAZEBO, staring after Mrs. Bethany as she went inside to give the annual welcoming speech to the student body. Finally sure that nobody else was watching, I dared to materialize at his side.

"Hey," he said. He half turned to see me and managed to smile for my sake. "Right back where we first kissed."

"The more things change." As the breeze ruffled his dark gold hair and the ivy leaves around us, I could imagine that we'd gone back to the beginning. The sunlight seemed to pass through me, warming me throughout. Despite the wind, my own red hair hung long and motionless, untouched, unreal. "Why aren't you in there?"

"Mrs. Bethany gave me an exemption this go-round. Said she'd try to find a way to explain to the vampire students and teachers to leave me the hell alone without tipping off the humans. Me walking into a pack of vampires before she gives the hands-off speech—no way am I doing that unarmed."

"She handled it better than I would've thought," I said. "I guess Mrs. Bethany takes the sanctuary thing here seriously."

Lucas shrugged. "She claims she's got my back, but all the same, I'm glad Ranulf sneaked our weapons up here in his trunk."

"Why not yours?"

"If Mrs. Bethany doesn't search mine, she's a fool. And that lady's no fool."

I studied his face, reading the emotions he was trying to hide. "You're not frightened of the vampires. You never have been. It's being around the human students that gets to you."

He grimaced. "I can't look at Vic without thinking— Bianca, I would've killed him. Vic. One of the best friends I've ever had. I'd have slaughtered him just to eat."

"Is that why you won't be alone with him?" When he shot me a look, I added, "Yeah, I noticed."

"No, you didn't," Lucas said quietly. "It's not just me. It's Vic, too. He finds ways to avoid being alone with me." I could hear the pain in his voice.

I put my arms around him; maybe it wasn't a real embrace, but I could feel him next to me and knew he'd take some comfort from it. "He'll trust you again. It's just going to take some time."

"How long will it be before I trust myself?"

There was no answer to that. I said the only thing I could: "I love you."

"And I love you. That's why I'm going to make this work. I have to."

\* \* \*

Just like Lucas was learning to be a vampire for my sake, I was learning to be a ghost for his. This meant I had to get the hang of this haunting thing.

I had the basics down: going invisible, appearing in my mist form and, when I had my bracelet or my brooch, becoming solid and lifelike once more. Moving from place to place required some concentration, but it could be done.

Haunting Evernight Academy, though—that was going to be a lot tougher. I'd need to figure out where I could travel in the hallways and where I couldn't. Leaving trails of frost around wherever I went would tip off the other students and teachers about a ghost, and while I wasn't sure they could do anything about it but scream, I didn't intend to find out.

It was scary, to think about the myriad ways this could go wrong. But holding back meant leaving Lucas alone, and that was something I couldn't do.

As he walked into the school, I followed. The heavy wooden doors were simple enough to slip through, maybe because they, like me, had once been alive. Once again, I entered the Evernight Academy great hall. Dozens of students milled around, each wearing the uniform sweater with the school crest: a shield emblazoned with two ravens on either side of a sword. To my surprise, a wave of nostalgia swept through me. Maybe I hadn't often been happy at Evernight—but sometimes I had. This was where I'd fallen in love and made so many good friends. This was where I'd *lived*.

My happiness lasted only a moment, though, as I focused once more on Lucas. Nobody attacked him, or said anything to him, which had to count as a positive sign; apparently Mrs. Bethany's speech had done the trick. But if nobody planned on killing Lucas, nobody planned on forgiving and forgetting either. Every vampire student stared at him with undisguised loathing. Lucas didn't slow down—he wasn't a guy to crumple because of a little glaring—but that didn't mean he liked it.

*We encouraged him to come here because we wanted him to feel comfortable being a vampire,* I thought. *How can that happen if everybody else rejects him?*

Every time he walked past a human student, his whole body went tense; I could see it in the set of his shoulders and the lines of his face. But he determinedly didn't look directly at them, and his steps never slowed. His resolve was as strong as his hunger, at least for now.

Lucas kept going, heading toward the north tower where the guys roomed. I stayed with him. A few flakes of ice crystallized on the windowsill nearest me, and hurriedly I floated higher, closer to the ceiling. Until I learned how to avoid creating frost, it might be better for me to stay up high, where at least nobody was likely to see it.

The crowd began murmuring, as though there were some commotion. I glanced back and saw that the students were parting—that someone was shoving them aside to get closer to Lucas. Apparently Mrs. Bethany hadn't managed to calm everybody down.

I folded myself tightly in a corner. Lucas cocked his head, hearing the danger before he saw it, and turned to face his would-be attacker. Probably it was some younger vampire guy, only at Evernight for a few laughs, ready to turn into a killer again the first time he felt like it—like Erich, that jerk who'd stalked Raquel during our first year here. Lucas would be able to handle somebody like that easily, I knew.

But when the attacker appeared, it was somebody Lucas couldn't handle. Somebody I couldn't handle.

It was my mother.

Mom stood in front of him, fists at her sides, eyes wild. "Is it true? Tell me." Her voice shook. "I want you to look me in the face and tell me it's true."

Lucas looked like he'd been punched in the gut. As he opened his mouth to answer, though, Balthazar pushed his way to their side and grabbed Mom's arm. "Not here," he said quietly.

Mom didn't even turn her head, like she couldn't see or hear Balthazar, but after a moment she nodded and stalked toward one of the staircases. It was like she was daring Lucas not to follow her, but he did. Balthazar started to come, too, but Mom shot him a look that froze him in place on the stairs.

She led him into a small office on the second floor. I went along, although I desperately didn't want to hear what I knew had to come next.

As soon as he'd shut the door behind them, Mom said again, "Tell me it's true, Lucas."

"It's true," Lucas said. He looked deader than he had the night after he'd been killed. "Bianca died."

My mother stumbled backward, like she'd been spun so hard she was dizzy. Her face crumpled into tears. "She was supposed to live forever," she whispered. "Bianca was going to be our little girl forever."

"Mrs. Olivier, I'm so sorry."

"Sorry? Sorry? You convince our daughter to leave her home and her parents and forsake the immortality that's rightfully hers—her birthright—and she dies, she's gone forever, and the only thing you can say is sorry?"

"That's all I can say!" Lucas shouted. "There aren't words for this! I would've died for her. I tried to. I failed. I hate myself for it, and if I could take it back I would, but . . . but . . ." His voice choked on a sob. He steeled himself and managed to say, "If you want to kill me, I won't stop you. I won't even blame you."

My mother shook her head. Tears streaked her face, and a few caramel-colored strands of hair stuck to her flushed cheeks. "If you hate yourself as much as you say—if you loved her a tenth as much as we loved her—then you deserve immortality. You deserve to live forever, so you can suffer forever."

Lucas was crying, too, but he never turned his head away, steeling himself to keep meeting my mother's eyes. It was more than I could do.

This wasn't Lucas's fault. It was mine.

For one second I considered appearing in the room. If Mom saw that something of me lived on, maybe she wouldn't hurt so badly. But at that moment, I was too ashamed of having hurt her to show my face.

"This isn't over," Mom said. She pushed blindly past Lucas into the hallway. He slumped into the nearest chair. I wanted to take form and comfort him, but I had the feeling that seeing me as a ghost wouldn't be that comforting for Lucas right now.

And there was something else I had to do.

I followed my mother along the corridors. She wiped at her cheeks but otherwise didn't try to disguise the fact that she'd been sobbing. Several of the students, both vampire and human, gave her curious glances, but she didn't seem to care.

We went up the winding stone stairs of the south tower, all the way to my family's apartment. My father lay on the sofa, his arms wrapped around himself and his eyes dull. He didn't look at my mother as she walked in. Dad had put on one of his old records—one I recognized, one with Henry Mancini songs that I had liked a lot when I was a child. Audrey Hepburn was singing "Moon River."

"It's true," Mom said in a small voice.

"I know. I think—I think I knew a long time ago. Just didn't want to . . ." Dad shut his eyes tightly, like he was closing out Mom and memory and the whole rest of the world.

My mother stretched on the sofa beside him, taking him into her arms. As she bowed her cheek against his dark red hair, his shoulders began to shake with heavy sobs.

I couldn't take it anymore. No matter how ashamed I felt, no matter how hard it would be, it couldn't be worse than hearing them suffer. It was time for me to appear to them, to reveal what had happened.

But as I gathered myself together to take form, even as I struggled to find the right words to say first, my mother choked out, "May God damn the wraiths."

I froze.

"It's their fault," she continued. "What happened to her is their fault."

Dad cuddled her closer. "I know, sweetheart. I know."

"I hate them. I hate them all. As long as I'm on this earth, I'll never stop hating them…" Her voice ebbed into sobs again.

They hated the wraiths, for having had a hold on me, for haunting Evernight, for merely existing. If I appeared, they wouldn't think of me as their little girl anymore. I would just be a monster. The way Lucas had been nothing but a monster to Kate.

I'd never known how much I needed their love for me until I'd lost it.

So I didn't appear to them. How could I? I would only have made it worse for them and for me, as impossible as it seemed that anything, ever, could be worse than that moment. Compared to this, dying had been easy. But I remained there for a long time, watching them weep. I deserved to see it.

They cried themselves to sleep, but I couldn't bring myself to leave. For a while I drifted through my old room. Apparently most of my family's stuff had made it through the fire, because many of my things remained there. Klimt's *The Kiss* still hung on one wall, shining, ideal lovers that, in my mind, symbolized Lucas and me.

*We'll get back to that place,* I thought. *We'll find a way.*

I flowed through the window, not bothering about the frost, until I sat beside my old friend the gargoyle again. His stone wings were the same color as the gray autumn nightfall.

"Remember that time we talked here?"

Startled, I turned to see Maxie sitting next to me—actually a few inches off the windowsill, but once you were a ghost, gravity didn't matter so much. She was smiling like this was the greatest day ever.

"Maxie, what are you doing here?"

"Uh, saying hello? Like the last time we met here. You figured out how to fog up the glass so I could write on it. That was when I decided maybe you weren't terminally stupid."

I'd fogged the glass with my breath—a trick I'd never be able to perform again. "Don't take this personally, but honestly, I can't do the banter thing right now."

"Stop sulking, living dead girl."

"Maxie. No." I couldn't feel good about being a wraith, about being dead, after seeing what my death had done to my parents.

"You're not alone, you know." Maxie tried to make it sound casual, but I knew she was reaching out as best she could. After decades of being isolated from the living world, except for visits from Vic, she wasn't very good at the social-interaction thing.

"You don't have to be afraid of us."

But I was. Going to "talk to Christopher" sounded the same as accepting my death, and at that moment, I couldn't. "Not tonight, okay?"

She hesitated, clearly disappointed, but then she vanished.

After a second, I realized that Maxie was right about one thing: It was time for me to quit brooding and go to Lucas. By now, perhaps, he'd be ready to see me again, ghost or not.

The easiest way down proved to be sort of melting along the tower wall, feeling the stones ripple past me. As soon as I reached the new roof, I could feel that it was far more resistant to ghosts than before, but I could go in through the front door or most of the windows. I darted in and out, finding my way, memorizing paths in case I needed to use them later.

Occasionally I felt a small ripple of energy behind me, or in an opposite corner, and figured Maxie was trailing along after me. But then I realized that it wasn't her.

It—they—were other ghosts.

*Christopher?* I thought, with a shiver of fear. He was the only other wraith I'd encountered at Evernight. But his was a powerful, unmistakable presence, one I didn't detect here. And there were several of them: two, three, five, ten, maybe more. They were just slivers of fog, zephyrs of sensation, probably invisible to anyone who wasn't a ghost, too. It reminded me of when I'd been a vampire, the way I'd started to be able to just sense when another vampire was nearby, whether or not I ever saw them. I wasn't exactly seeing these ghosts—more the trails they left behind—but I knew they were there.

Mrs. Bethany's plan to draw them here through the human students had obviously worked.

*We always wanted to know why she was hunting the wraiths,* I thought. *I guess soon we'll find out.*

I rose through the north tower, searching as I went. Mostly I saw a lot of vampire guys hanging out in their rooms, chugging blood, and bragging about how much sex they'd had during summer vacation, and a few other rooms with human guys who were hanging out, eating potato chips, and bragging—less credibly—about the sex they'd had during summer vacation. If I'd had a body, I would've rolled my eyes.

Then I reached a room where the two inhabitants sat on opposite sides of a chess board, and I smiled.

"That pawn is now a queen, baby," Vic said. "Booya."

"Your soul is as devious as your stratagems." Ranulf frowned as he considered what to do next.

I unfolded, willing myself into a visible form. Both Vic and Ranulf jumped, but then they each smiled. "Hey, ghostly lady." Vic rose from his chair, like an old-fashioned gentleman. "How's it going?"

"Not so hot," I admitted. "How are you guys?"

"We compete now for the desirable bunk farther from the windows, which will be less drafty in winter," Ranulf said. "Later, Vic's iPad will be used to watch a film of the winner's choosing. Much is at stake."

"In other words, it's all good." Vic paused. "At least, in this room. On the sixth floor, you're gonna find two guys who are having a suckier time of it."

"So Mrs. Bethany let them room together?" Balthazar had said he would suggest it, and given the attitudes of the other vampires toward Lucas, it made sense for Mrs. Bethany to agree. But I felt better knowing for sure. "Well, that's something, anyway."

Vic was uncharacteristically quiet for a couple seconds. He avoided my eyes, instead studying the kitschy old Elvis Presley movie poster that he'd tacked onto his wall. Then he said, "I should've volunteered. To room with Lucas, I mean. He needs his friends with him—I know that—but I just—"

"No, Vic, it's okay. Lucas should be with Balthazar, because he's going to have a lot of questions that only a more experienced vampire could handle." There were other reasons Vic didn't need to room with Lucas right now, but reminding him of them wouldn't do anybody any good.

"That's not what I meant. I want Lucas to know I believe in him. You know?"

"I know. But . . . give it time. Don't rush it."

Vic nodded and said nothing else. The moment was threatening to become awkward when Ranulf triumphantly slid his queen across several squares. "I believe the superior bunk will be mine."

"Oh, *man*." Vic made a face, and I had to smile despite myself. Waving good-bye, I dematerialized again and went farther up, to the sixth floor. After searching through a few rooms,

I found Lucas and Balthazar. They were already asleep.

No wonder they'd already gone to bed—this day had to have been exhausting and traumatic for both of them. I didn't think they'd unpacked. Lucas's half of the room was as spartan as ever, and Balthazar appeared to have stopped moving in as soon as he laid a pack of cigarettes and a lighter on the window-sill. Balthazar, almost too broad and tall to fit in his bunk, was curled in facing the wall. Ever the fighter, Lucas slept on his back, large, scarred hands above the covers, the better to grab a weapon within moments if necessary. The only time he'd ever deviated from that was when he held me throughout the night.

Although I knew they needed to crash, I felt bad that I hadn't been able to see Lucas again, even if only to wish him sweet dreams.

Then I remembered something Maxie had taught me before Lucas's death, and smiled. Maybe I could tell him good night after all.

I concentrated on Lucas's sleeping form, hoping that he was dreaming. If I remembered right, it was a little like diving into a pool—thrusting downward, inward, every bit of me in one taut line—

Instantly, I was within Lucas's dream.

The surroundings were familiar—this was the records room at the top of the north tower. A few filmy cobwebs clouded the corners of the room, and sepia gold pages were scattered about here and there. Mrs. Bethany used this only to store records of no use to her any longer, report cards from 1853 and similar stuff.

However, a lot had happened here in recent years. This was where Lucas had fought—and killed—Erich, a vampire who had stalked Raquel. This was where Balthazar and I had sought clues to Mrs. Bethany's ultimate plan. And here Lucas and I had reunited after he'd learned that I was the child of vampires. He had accepted me no matter what, just as I had accepted him.

*Good thing, too,* I thought. *Given how many things we've changed into since.*

Lucas stood at the window, staring out at the night sky. His hair was slightly longer, as it had been when we first met. I smiled, realizing as I did so that I had a body now, or whatever passed for one in the world of dreams. That meant I could take Lucas in my arms, and we could share everything that our waking hours denied us. Here, in sleep, we could be alone and safe.

As I came closer to him, I noticed that he had a stake in one hand—strange, I thought. Then the door behind us opened.

"Knock, knock." To my astonishment, Erich walked through the door. "Raquel? Thanks for the invitation. Knew you couldn't wait to see me." His greedy expression shifted into annoyance as he glimpsed Lucas at the window; I couldn't tell whether he saw me or not. "What the hell are you doing here?"

"Waiting to see whether I can forge Raquel's handwriting well enough to get you up here," Lucas said. He walked right past me without a glance. Apparently I didn't play a role in this dream. "Looks like that's a yes."

"You played some stupid joke to get me alone? What are you, some kind of fag?"

"It would be your lucky day if I were." Lucas circled Erich, his entire body tensed and ready. The second that he stood between Erich and the door, he let Erich see the stake. "But it's not your lucky day."

"Black Cross," Erich spat.

"Vampire," Lucas said, with a hatred so deep it seemed to reverberate within his bones.

They lunged at each other, predator and hunter. I cried out as they tumbled to the floor, Erich's hands closing around Lucas's throat.

*This isn't real,* I told myself, but that wasn't exactly true. No doubt this was Lucas's memory of his final fight with Erich. I'd never doubted that Lucas had done what he had to do, but I'd never realized how dangerous it had been for him. How frightened he must have been, for the nightmares to keep coming back.

As Lucas and Erich grappled, Raquel's tawny leather bracelet fell to the floor. It must have been in Erich's pocket. Lucas shoved Erich away, hard, and gasped, "Taking trophies? Marking your prey?"

"Raquel's going to be mine," Erich said. His fangs were out, misshaping his smile. "I'd have had her weeks ago if your stupid girlfriend hadn't gotten in the way."

"Then I'm doing this just in time." Lucas kicked one of the rickety towers of old boxes, sending it toppling down onto Erich. But Erich, like any monster in a dream, suddenly seemed to be standing somewhere else and attacked Lucas from another direction altogether.

"Did you know your girlfriend's one of us, too?" Erich taunted, as he got his hands around Lucas's throat. "Or are you stupid enough not to notice you're screwing a vampire?"

"Leave Bianca—out of this!" Lucas choked, pushing Erich away.

Erich just grinned. "I'm not leaving her out of it. Everything I do to you up here? She's going to get double. Before I'm done, you'll be dead, and she'll be worse than dead. So much worse."

That made Lucas lose it; his fighting focus shook as he gave in to anger. "I will never let you hurt her." He stabbed at Erich, a wild punch; Erich dodged it with the unearthly speed of the nightmare.

*It's a dream,* I reminded myself forcefully. *You can appear to Lucas in his dreams. Just break into this and change it. Take this dream back for the two of you.*

"Lucas?" I called, daring to step closer to the fight. It wasn't as though Erich could hurt me. "Lucas, it's Bianca. Look at me. Just look at me!"

"I think he's busy," Charity said.

I turned to see her perched on another tower of boxes, wearing a cobwebby gray dress, her hair in a rat's nest of tangles. She might have been one of the gargoyles—the most monstrous one. Charity grinned at me, eyes glinting in the night like a cat's.

Of course Lucas dreamed about her, too. She'd killed him. But how many monsters would I have to banish from Lucas's dreams just to win a few hours for us?

"Lucas!" I shouted. I threw myself toward the fray, sliding

between Lucas and Erich. "Look at me!"

"Bianca?" Lucas looked horrified. "What are you doing here?"

Erich's hands seized me from behind, strong as steel. "Hey, Lucas—want to watch your girlfriend suffer?"

"No!" Lucas grabbed me, pulling me back. The struggle felt totally real.

"Lucas, he can't kill me," I said as I tried to twist out of Erich's grip. His fingers felt like claws digging into my flesh; it was difficult to remind myself that this wasn't real. "He can't hurt you either. It's a dream. Don't you remember?"

He couldn't hear me. Panic had gripped him—his fear for my life far greater than it had ever been for his. "Bianca, hang on!"

Lucas kept trying to swing at Erich with his stake, but Erich dragged me that way and this, using my body to block them. "You're going to be the one to kill her, hunter," Erich sneered. "You'll cremate her to stop the pain. You know those old stories they told you in Black Cross? About the worst torture you can work on a vampire? Soak the stake in holy water, stab them deep so the holy water sinks into their blood—and then they're paralyzed forever. Can't wake up, can't move. They just lie there feeling like they're burning alive for all eternity."

"I never did that," Lucas panted. "Not even to scum like you. You, I'm just gonna kill."

"I'm going to try it." Erich spoke into the side of my face; I could feel his cool undead breath against my neck. "I'm going to do it to Bianca. She'll be like Sleeping Beauty, but you'll know she's not sleeping. You'll know she's burning forever. Nobody else will be able to hear her screaming, but I bet you will."

"You won't get the chance," Lucas swore, but I could see his fear mounting. When he risked his own life, he could stay calm; when it came to me, he lost it.

Finally I lunged forward, pulling myself free of Erich's grasp. Sharp lines of pain lashed my shoulder—*Erich's finger-nails,* I thought—but I didn't care as I fell to the floor. Lucas flung himself at Erich, sending them both toppling down. The battle was furious now, blood from open cuts spattering onto the stone wall.

My silver, shining blood oozed between my fingertips. It glistened on the floor, mingling with Lucas's red blood in a way that seemed beautiful, almost mesmerizing.

*Snap out of it!* I told myself. I was in shock.

"Oh, this is fun," Charity laughed from her place atop the boxes. She clapped her hands like a little girl who's just seen her birthday cake. "Save her, Lucas! Save her while you still can! Or . . . maybe you can't?"

Lucas's face took on an expression I recognized, though I'd only seen it once before. I could never have forgotten it—the look of pure torment he'd worn at my bedside the night I died.

At that moment I realized that I couldn't break him out of this memory. I couldn't do anything in this dream except make it more frightening for Lucas. That meant I had to leave.

I closed myself away from sight. Away from him. When I

could see again, I stood in his dark dorm room, at the foot of his bed. Lucas twisted beneath his sheets, then slumped, drifting from the nightmare to deeper, dreamless sleep.

*At least it's over,* I told myself. Yet even in my ethereal form, I could feel physical pain; that had never happened before. Confused, I glanced at my burning, aching shoulder.

The lines of Erich's scratches still showed upon my skin, and each one glimmered with droplets of silver blood.

# Chapter Seven

I LEFT THE DORM ROOM, GOING THROUGH THE door and down the hallway as though I were mortal. More time must have passed than I'd realized, because nearly everyone was quiet, asleep or at least settled in for the night. Although I badly wanted to revisit Vic and Ranulf, in the feeble hope that they could cheer me up, I wouldn't wake them for my own selfish reasons.

Without them, I realized, there was literally nobody else in the world I could talk to, or even watch, without it causing pain.

*How did we screw up so badly?* I thought as I descended the long, winding stone stairs. Around me I could hear the crackling of ice. I was leaving evidence, but at this point I didn't much care. *The only thing we ever wanted was to be together, and to live honestly without all the lies. How did so many people get hurt?*

For the first time, I realized how easy it would be to follow Maxie's advice and let go of the mortal world completely. Effortless, mindless drifting within blue mist seemed really good to me right now. It would have been a relief to be free from sorrow and guilt, from responsibility for the people I'd left behind.

Was that true for the ghosts trapped at Evernight Academy now? Maybe *trapped* wasn't the right word. This could be a sanctuary for them, too—a place where they didn't have to remain in their old haunts and habitations, taunted by the lives they'd lost.

But Mrs. Bethany had attacked Maxie once, and was no friend to the wraiths. There was no way she'd built this place as a refuge for them.

Tentatively, I stretched my consciousness, seeking the other wraiths who lived here. *Can you hear me?*

No response—but I could sense a shift in the air, like knowing that someone was watching.

Then the visions began to flood my mind.

They were like vivid daydreams, almost hallucinations, except that I knew they didn't come from within my own mind. The wraiths were forcing me to see them: Vampires, each of them at their most monstrous, as though students went around Evernight unwashed, bloody, and fanged. They were attacking human students in the hallways, in the classrooms, one brutal assault after another.

"None of that is real," I said, hoping they could hear. "They mostly leave the human students alone, and when somebody screws up, Mrs. Bethany's all over them. The humans you followed here—they're safe."

The wraiths must not have believed me. Every image intensified, coming closer, and now they had sound (screaming) and smell (blood). Disgusted, I tried to turn away, but how can you turn away from something in your own head?

One of the vampires in the visions suddenly went blue and turned into ice. I watched, fascinated and horrified, as deep cracks appeared in his hardening flesh, fragmenting his cheeks, his lips, his whole head. He fell, a crash of bloody slush, and I knew that was what the wraiths hoped to do to the vampires.

What they wanted me to help them do.

"I'm not helping you attack anyone!"

And like that, I was alone. Nothing vanished or went away, but I simply knew that I wasn't being paid attention to any longer.

What were the ghosts going to do? If I'd been terrified of them before, it was so much worse now. I'd learned some new powers, but nothing that could defend me or my loved ones against an attack like that. Could the wraiths hurt Lucas? Balthazar? My parents? If they tried anything, would I be able to help?

*No,* I thought, depression sinking deeper into me. *There's nothing I can do for any of them. I'm useless.*

*I'm dead.*

I drifted through the great hall on the ground floor, which looked larger when it was empty of students. Although it was always a majestic space, it became more beautiful and austere when it stretched out vast and silent. The moonlight streamed through the many stained-glass windows, which stretched from floor to ceiling, but it was brightest through the one window of plain glass. The original stained glass had been destroyed by a member of Black Cross—Lucas's long-ago predecessor here—making his escape. Lucas had damaged it himself once, maybe living up to the family tradition. I'd always wondered why Mrs. Bethany didn't have it repaired so that it would look like the others.

Now, at last, I understood. She'd left it this way so she would always remember. So she would never be careless again.

This building was scarred. Lucas was scarred. And I, too, felt like I would never heal. I was trapped forever with my regrets and cut off from the living world. Lucas suffered the same way. The main difference was that he could end it for himself and probably would, if he weren't sticking around for my sake.

At that moment, I felt like all I'd ever done was hurt everybody who'd tried to love me. I felt worthless. I wanted to give up.

I saw that I was close to the school library. There probably wasn't anything accurate in there about the wraiths, but maybe there was. I decided to search and see. At that point, one question loomed in my mind, larger than any other: whether wraiths had any way to—well, to die. Again. For good.

Not that I wanted to do anything drastic right that moment, but I had to know if there was an out, ever. And maybe I was starting to want to take it.

The library would've cheered me up, most days. I loved the heavy oaken tables, the high walls stacked with books to the ceiling, the musty smell of old pages and the heavy brass fixtures that had gone dark with age and wear. It reminded me of hanging out with Raquel, or flirting with Lucas, or studying with Balthazar. Of everything happy, simple, and alive.

I didn't belong there anymore.

Resolutely I traveled farther into the library, wondering where ghost-related books might be kept —

—and felt the wall start to pull me in.

It was sickening, overwhelming, like that terrible sensation when you're looking over a high ledge and for one second feel like you want to jump, only this time the pull was taking me over whether I wanted it or not. The east wall of the library had some strange magnetism that tied in to the core of me. A thick vibration muffled every sound and nearly deafened me, and a kind of static blurred my vision.

I tried to make myself more substantial, so maybe I could push myself backward, but I couldn't become entirely solid. A strange black gap—not in the world but in my senses—was opening in front of me, towing me forward.

From within that gap, I could hear terrible cries. I realized they were the screams of other ghosts trapped by whatever force held me. Were they the same ones who had taunted me before? Others? No way to know. At any rate, they couldn't rescue themselves, much less me.

"Is anybody there?" I shouted. "Somebody, help! Can anybody hear me?"

No answers.

*Well, you wanted to die,* said that vicious little voice in my head. I wondered if I was wrong to even fight this. Maybe I needed to let it happen.

Then I realized that if I did that, I'd never see Lucas again, or any of the other people I loved.

"Lucas!" I screamed. My mind filled with the image of the nightmarish scene where I'd left him, and I envisioned myself in the records room. It solidified around me, taking shape. Lucas and Erich were again locked in battle—a dream fight so much longer than the real one could have been—sweaty and bloody. The nightmare had begun again, apparently a night-long torment for him. Charity had vanished, like any other whim within dreams, but otherwise everything was just as terrible. This time, though, I had to break through. Once again, with every bit of my might, I called, "Lucas!"

He turned his head from Erich, startled. Lucas's expression was so confused that I thought he couldn't see me, but at least he could hear.

"Lucas, this is a dream, only a dream. I'm in the library and something's got me—you have to find me!"

The scene faded as quickly as it had arrived. Had I reached him, or was that only my own wishful thinking? Already the dark gap had swallowed almost everything I could see, everything I could feel. Of my hearing, all that was left was the wailing of the other wraiths.

I wanted to call for Maxie or Christopher, but I didn't know if they would hear me, or whether Maxie would respond if I pleaded for help. And what if I dragged them in, too?

A shudder passed through me, and I could feel the vapory

outlines of my limbs beginning to dissipate. *Oh, no, no, no, this is it, this is the end—*

"Bianca!"

"Lucas!" I tried to look for him, but I could gain only the dimmest sense of him in the room. He was an outline, a radiation of energy and fear and love, nothing else. "It's got me."

"Give me your hand!" By that he meant, form a hand, give him something to hold on to; I understood that. I just wasn't sure I could do it anymore, or that it would do any good. No simple physical force could pull me back from the vortex.

But I wanted to hold Lucas's hand at least one more time, even if I couldn't do anything else. So with every ounce of my strength and concentration, I thought about the place where my hand should be, and carved out the image of the wrist, the palm, and the fingers. A soft blue form appeared, fragile as a wisp of smoke. It was nothing like it should have been; maybe this was what wraiths looked like just before they vanished forever.

Then Lucas wrapped something around my wrist.

*The bracelet!* I saw the coral and silver in the same second that I felt a jolt of inner power. Within an instant, my body became solid, and I fell hard to the floor. The answering pain was wonderful. It meant I was real, and that I had escaped. Something about turning solid negated the power of whatever it was that had grabbed me.

Lucas dropped to his knees and gathered me in his arms. In horror, I saw the manifestation of the vortex that had nearly swallowed me—a swirl of fog and darkness that had opened up within the library wall. As we watched, though, it shrank and quieted, smoothing out into uneven plaster once more.

"What the hell was that?" Lucas said, clutching me against his chest. "Are you okay?"

"I think so." My voice shook, and I felt a little like I'd throw up, if I still had a stomach. But the disorientation diminished each moment. "Mrs. Bethany's not just hunting the wraiths. She's . . . trapping them."

"Is that what that was?" His eyes narrowed. "Stand back."

Scooting backward, I put as much distance as I could between me and the wall as Lucas went to the wall, ran his hand against it, and then, with all his vampire strength, punched through. Fine motes of plaster dust puffed out as shards of the wall fell to the floor.

"They'll know somebody was here," I said.

"Let 'em know. We need to figure this out." Lucas reached into the wall and pulled out a small metal box—curiously shaped, with odd curves and angles: a little like a seashell made of silver and obsidian. The lid was open, revealing an interior of mother-of-pearl. At first I thought it was no more than a lovely antique jewelry box, but then—as I focused on the mother-of-pearl, on the living substance within, I felt its pull on me anew. With the bracelet strengthening me and keeping me solid, I was in no danger, but the sensation was still terrifying.

"Lucas, close it! Put it back!" I cried. He did so at once, looking back at me in alarm. But as soon as the box was shut, I felt at ease again.

As Lucas ran to my side, I said, "That's a trap. A trap for wraiths. Mrs. Bethany put one here. She could—she's got to have them all over the school. She's hunting us and trapping us." *Why?* I thought. *What can she want with us? Is it only hate, or something more?*

He frowned as he cuddled me close. "Jesus. Don't ever come back in here."

"Not without the bracelet," I said, with a glance down at it. "That was good thinking."

"Figured whatever was after you, you had a better chance if you could hit back."

I brushed my hand against his cheek. "You heard me. In your dream."

"Yeah." Lucas raked his fingers through my hair. "How did you know about that nightmare? Were you trying to visit me, before?"

"I tried, but I couldn't break through. I couldn't make you see me."

His lips brushed against my forehead as he spoke. "We'll work on it. We can get better at it."

"Okay." I realized that this was the first moment Lucas had truly seemed like himself since he'd risen from the dead. Saving me had given him back a sense of purpose—a reason to be here.

And I realized that he was my reason to be here, too.

Lucas studied me in the dim moonlight, once again focused and sure. "We're going to find all these traps. Figure out a way to keep you clear of them. Nothing's going to happen to you,

Bianca. Not again. There's no way I'm letting that happen."

"And I'm going to take care of you." I remembered how frightened I had been for everyone I loved, even while the trap had been sucking me in. Yes, I was dead now, but my heart remained alive. For Lucas's sake, and the sake of the people I cared about—for the love that endured after death—I had to find a place in this world. If that meant I was never wholly part of the living or undead worlds, well, I'd always been in-between. In the shadows. I knew how to do it, and maybe I could get better at it.

Maybe it wasn't the afterlife preached from pulpits or envisioned by painters who liked harps, wings, and fluffy clouds. But looking out for the people I loved seemed like a pretty good way to spend eternity. As Lucas held me tightly, I knew he felt the same way.

*We still have something at stake,* I realized. *Something to fight for.*

# Chapter Eight

LUCAS AND I STAYED UP MOST OF THE REST OF that night, curled in each other's arms out on the lawn. Death had made us immune to autumn's winds or the chill of the soft earth beneath us. So we spooned together beneath one of the large oak trees, half covered by the first fallen leaves as the wind blew them over us for a blanket. The leaves were the colors of our hair—deep red and dark gold. We were part of the fall. And, for the first time in far too long, we were truly part of each other.

"You haven't said we should leave Evernight," I whispered.

"Don't think I haven't thought it." Lucas nuzzled the side of my face. "I hate knowing how dangerous this place is for you. But . . . I have to trust you to make your own call about the risks. That's the deal we made, and I'll stick to it."

With my head still dizzy from the trap in the library, and the scratches on my shoulder sore, I wondered whether I needed to reassess the risks at Evernight Academy. But until Lucas was steadier, I knew, remaining here was our best option. "I'm just fine." I kissed him, soft and deep. "Nothing worse can happen to me. In fact—it's like I finally see that so many good things can still happen to me. That there's a lot I can do here, for you and for everybody else."

Lucas half smiled. "Not a ghost, but an angel."

"There's a lot you can do here as a vampire. Think about how many students my mother and father helped, or how often Balthazar was able to bail us out. Being dead . . . it's not the worst thing that can happen."

He was quiet for a while after that, considering. "It's just—this hunger."

"I know."

"If I ever snap, and if I hurt someone . . . kill someone—"

"You won't." I wanted badly to believe that, and to help him believe it, too. "You're strong, Lucas. As a kid, you made it through Black Cross training that would've crushed some adults. You went undercover when you were nineteen years old and you pulled it off. I mean, you fooled Mrs. Bethany, and you might just be the only person who's ever done that for long."

At that, he actually laughed; it was a rueful laugh rather than a happy one, but I'd take what I could get. It just felt so good, being here with him without the weight of the world crushing us down.

I kept counting off points. "You think for yourself, which is a lot rarer than it ought to be. You can admit when you're wrong, which is even rarer than that. You're loyal, and you're courageous, and you make friendships that last forever. That's all part of you. The best part of you."

Very serious now, Lucas shook his head. "You're wrong."

"Listen to me—"

"You listen." He snuggled more tightly against me. "*You're* the best part of me. Always."

I closed my eyes and rested my head against his arm, finally at peace—at least for one night.

The next day, Evernight Academy continued along in its usual whirl of activity—in its own way, I thought, more alive than most of its student body. People jumbled together in the hallways, the vampires sleek and sophisticated, the rest wondering vaguely why they couldn't fit in. Traveling down the hallways was scarier now, because I never knew where the next trap might lie. But I took it slow and proceeded carefully. So far, so good.

I was searching for Lucas, intending to follow him into class. I wouldn't distract him; he was honestly trying to do the course work, as a way of killing time if nothing else. After our reunion last night, it felt like enough just to be at his side, and I suspected he would feel the same way.

But then I saw someone who looked lonelier than Lucas had—my mother.

Mom's clothing was much the same as it had always been: simple skirt, practical shoes, and a soft sweater. Her caramel-colored hair was pulled back in the ponytail she'd worn as long as I could remember. But the spring had left her step, and there was no light in her eyes as she trudged down the hallway toward her twentieth-century history class.

When I drifted through the door of her classroom, she was writing on the blackboard. I read the words along with the students: THE LOST GENERATION. I saw a few familiar faces in the room, most particularly Balthazar; he'd lived through this, and remained more hooked-in than most vampires, but I realized he had probably enrolled in this class in particular in order to stay close to my mom.

*Oh, sure,* I mused. Now *you're thoughtful. Why weren't you thinking ahead when Lucas needed it the most?* Balthazar had brought Lucas into the fight with Charity knowing that Lucas wasn't himself—something I still hadn't gotten past. But for my mother, if not myself, I couldn't help feeling some gratitude toward him—and toward Patrice, who sat a few rows ahead and was probably enrolled for the same reason, though she would never admit it.

"The Lost Generation. That's what they called the people who came of age during the First World War—or, as they called it then, the Great War. Anybody know why that was?" Mom asked tiredly.

She was directing her question at the human students, of course, or at least the vampires who had been turned after that era. It was an unwritten rule at Evernight Academy that relying on historical knowledge you'd lived through was too much like cheating.

Skye Tierney, who sat in the front row, raised her hand. "Because the Second World War hadn't happened yet."

"Correct." Mom's gaze remained a couple inches above the class, not quite engaged with them. Dark circles ringed her eyes. It looked like she hadn't slept well in weeks. "Because they couldn't believe humanity could ever be that stupid twice."

A couple of the vampires smirked, obviously thinking that was a slam on human beings, instead of what it was—Mom being fatalistic. Balthazar shut his eyes briefly as if trying to shield himself from their stupidity.

My mother clutched her chalk in her hands, fine yellowish powder coating her fingertips. Her gaze was distant, her voice softer than it should've been for addressing a roomful of students. "World War I shattered people's beliefs in every aspect of their society. People could no longer worship an all-protecting God after so many of their sons and brothers died in the trenches. Soldiers who had suffered from mustard gas, machine-gun fire, and starvation could no longer trust the governments and generals who had sent them to the front with promises of a war that would last only a few months. Women who had picked up the slack of war work in factories and managed at home alone for years could never be 'sheltered' again." Pens scratched on notebooks; keyboards of laptops clicked. Everybody thought this was going to be on the exam. I could tell this was just Mom getting lost in sad memories.

She continued, "Some of those women had lost everyone they'd loved. Every promise they'd ever made to their children to keep them safe . . . those promises were broken. After that, you could never—they could never believe again."

*Oh, Mom.* I wanted to put my arms around her so badly. Did I want to hold her and tell her it would be okay, or was I childish enough to want her to reassure me?

A few of the vampires—the older ones, who had been through that time, too—looked as sad as my mother did; Balthazar suddenly seemed acutely interested in his shoes. I realized I'd never asked what he did in that war, if anything. Whatever had happened to him then might darken his memories, or maybe he simply understood Mom's mind-set better than anyone else and felt bad for her.

*Reaching out to other people,* I reminded myself. *Taking care of them, even if I happen to be mad at them right now. That's what I'm here for.*

I went to his side. His fingers weren't holding his pencil very tightly—having witnessed these events, he apparently didn't see the need to take notes. So I took control of the pencil and wrote, within his grip, *Do you think she's okay?*

Balthazar sat upright very quickly, but he got over being startled fast enough. His grip tightened as he took the pencil back from me. *No, I don't.*

He let the pencil slightly loosen again so that I could reply. *What about my father? Do you think he's able to help her?*

*He asked me to leave his class. The reminder would be too painful, he said. So that sounds like a no. Bianca, why don't you appear to them? I hate lying to them that you're completely gone, forever.*

*Mom and Dad hate the wraiths. They did everything they could to stop me from turning into one and wouldn't say one word to me about my becoming anything but a vampire.* The next words were hard, but I forced myself to finish: *I'm afraid they'd reject and hate me, too.*

*They're your parents. They wouldn't do that. They'd accept you.*

*Like Lucas's mother accepted him?*

He didn't have a response for that.

In her seat in front of Balthazar, Patrice started shivering; apparently the presence of a ghost always created a chill in the air. She glanced over her shoulder once, obviously curious about the cause of the draft. I moved toward the door, unable to take much more of this, but I looked long and hard at Mom before I left the room. Every time I saw her now felt like it might be the last time.

I wanted to appear to her and to Dad so badly. I imagined appearing before them, wearing the white camisole and cloud-patterned pajama pants I'd died in, and slipping on the bracelet so that I could become solid. If I did that, there would be nothing I'd want more in the world than to run into their arms and feel them hug me again.

And then I imagined them turning away. If they did that—I would never get over it.

The other students had started talking about the upcoming school trip into the nearby town of Riverton days ago, but I hadn't paid much attention, because I doubted any of my friends would take part. The trips were a recent innovation—a treat for the human students. Vampires tended to skip it entirely, because getting to Riverton involved crossing running water, which for them always induced chills, nausea, and sometimes a kind of shock. Also, anything the humans enjoyed was automatically extremely uncool to the vampires. The only human I spent any time with anymore was Vic, who would probably stick around school to hang with Ranulf.

However, my plans were about to change.

After Mom's class, as students crowded into the hallways, I sought Lucas. I felt like he needed me, and after seeing my mother's anguish, I needed him, too. But as I came along his right side, Mrs. Bethany stepped smoothly to his left. "Mr. Ross."

"Mrs. Bethany," he said, casting one quick glance in my direction; he'd sensed that I was there and obviously felt protective. Although we both knew that I was invisible, something about that woman made it seem as though she could detect me anyway.

But she seemed to be thinking about something else entirely. "You have not yet put your name on the list of students joining our first off-campus trip. I seem to recall that you were fond of such outings."

"Back when I could cross a river without wanting to throw up, yeah."

"Such discomfort is momentary," Mrs. Bethany said. "It can be overcome."

Lucas shrugged. "I don't see the point."

"I will share a secret with you, Mr. Ross. The secret of how

I learned to bear being dead."

What would ever make Mrs. Bethany reveal something so personal? Lucas's face looked just as shocked as I felt. "Um, okay." Then he shook off his surprise. "Actually, that's something I'd like to hear."

"Right now, I suspect, you are attempting to forget what you loved about being alive." Mrs. Bethany's skirts rustled as she made her way through the crowd, people parting to leave a wide berth around her and Lucas. "To distance yourself from those joys, believing yourself separated from them forever. But that is a mistake."

Lucas walked more slowly, obviously trying to take that in. "But it's not like I can . . . I don't know, go get a good hamburger or go swimming in the ocean—"

"No. Some things are closed to us. But surely you can enjoy the entertainments Riverton has to offer."

We'd gone to the classic movie house on our first date. He'd bought me my brooch in the vintage clothing shop. It would be fun to visit some of those places again, together. So what if I had to hide? Call it another take on a "blind" date.

Maybe Lucas picked up on what I was feeling, because he slowly nodded. "That's true. I could still go."

Mrs. Bethany smiled in satisfaction. "Remember your life," she said. "Don't let go of it, any more than you must." Then she straightened, entirely formal once again. "I shall put your name on the Riverton list."

"Thanks."

As we wandered out onto the grounds, I whispered, "I'm so glad you said yes."

"That was kind of weird, wasn't it?" He was clearly thinking about Mrs. Bethany. "Her opening up like that."

It *was* kind of weird. More than weird. I knew I should be grateful to her—she appeared to be looking out for Lucas, in her own way—but she scared me too much for that. I didn't want to talk about her any longer, or even think about her. Better to concentrate on better times ahead. "If it gets us back to the movies, then it's okay by me."

Lucas laughed, and I basked in the pleasure of being just another girl, looking forward to her weekend date.

I could've just ridden the bus into Riverton that weekend, hovering above Lucas, but we agreed that I might end up frosting the windows. Instead, he took the brooch with him so I could zoom to his side once he got there. Lucas took along a spare coat and a set of sweatpants in his backpack; that way, if we were the only Evernight students in the movie house, as usual, I could become solid and we could hang out like before. Maybe make out like before. I was definitely hoping for that one.

My impatience only grew in the half-hour after the bus left. It felt like eternity to wait, hanging out on the roof beside one of the gargoyles and letting the soft rain pass right through me. I knew there was no point in going to Lucas before he would for sure be in Riverton, but I was so anxious to get there. Especially to that movie house, the very first place we'd ever gone on a date.

It was so precious to me that I could envision every bit of golden scrollwork on the walls, the red velvet curtains, the posters—

Wait. Was it possible that I'd loved it enough to bond with it? That it was one of the places I could instantly travel to, and "haunt," after my death?

*Worth a try,* I decided. I faded out slightly, letting go of the material world around me at the school, and envisioned the movie theater in as much detail as my mind could hold. Everything about it, the woodwork, the frame of the theater itself, I willed to take shape around me.

And I was there.

*Yes!* I would've done a fist pump of victory if I'd been solid. The theater hadn't changed in the slightest. There was the old-fashioned popcorn machine, a little brass cage with a red-and-white striped sign. And here was the swirly patterned carpet, so thick and soft I longed to have feet that I could sink into it. Tonight's show, to judge by the spotlighted poster, would be "To Catch a Thief." Cary Grant, total glamour, total romance. Could this be any better?

Well, yes, I realized. It looked like this was going to be a crowded show, so Lucas and I wouldn't have much chance to be alone. The movie wouldn't start for another half-hour, and already several people had taken their seats—though they kept looking restlessly toward the doorway where I had materialized, looking through me, for someone else—

And then it hit me. I recognized some of them—including, down in the front row, Kate.

*Black Cross.* I felt terror wash through me, so hard that I thought I'd turn to ice. *They realized where Lucas went after being turned into a vampire, and they remembered about the Riverton trips from when he was spying for them before. And this isn't a handful of people like she brought to Philadelphia—this is a full Black Cross hunting party.*

*They've staked this place out. They're lying in wait to kill him.*

I rushed out of the lobby; I knew I must have frosted one of the glass doors, but I didn't care. Black Cross wasn't looking for me. If I didn't warn Lucas in time, they'd pounce on him as soon as he entered the theater. Even his strength and fighting skill wouldn't save him against a dozen vampire hunters.

As I made my way down the street toward the town square, though, I realized that the party in the theater wasn't the only one. There, sitting in a booth at the diner, ignoring a plate of fries in front of her, was Eliza Pang, the leader of Black Cross's New York cell. And, worst of all, lurking in one alleyway near the square were Raquel and Dana.

The Riverton bus pulled in, and students began to pour out. I only had eyes for Lucas and so paid no attention to the others, who were laughing and talking, walking past me with no idea I was there.

Lucas was one of the last ones off the bus. He looked badly shaken, almost weak. The running water must have affected him strongly. "You okay, buddy?" said the driver.

"Okay. I'm going to get a coffee real quick. That will help," Lucas said. What he meant was that he could sit down in the coffeehouse without anybody bothering him for a second. He thought I would come to him in the theater and didn't want me to see him looking so weak.

*It doesn't matter, just get someplace private, so I can warn you!* I didn't see any Black Cross hunters in the coffeehouse, but that didn't mean there weren't a couple I didn't recognize. Quickly I darted after him, hoping to whisper in his ear before he could go inside anywhere.

And then I just—stopped. Went blind. Lost everything.

Within an instant, I'd become unable to move forward, back, up or down—anywhere. *A trap!* I thought in panic, thinking of that creepy box back at Evernight, but this was different. Instead of a steady, inexorable pull, I was simply held firmly in place. It was like the difference between sinking in quicksand and merely being stuck in an elevator. Well, an elevator with the lights out.

Had Black Cross done this? Were they after both of us? What was going on? All I knew was that this imprisonment, whatever it was, kept me from warning Lucas that he was in terrible danger.

Then I saw a single shining circle open up before me, shimmering just like a pool in the moonlight. Carefully I peered out—and saw my captor staring down at me in shock.

"Bianca?"

"*Patrice?*"

# Chapter Nine

"BIANCA?" PATRICE LOOKED AS ASTONISHED AS I felt. Her face seemed to fill the whole sky, or ceiling, or whatever else I saw above me in this black, formless place. "You're— You've become a wraith?"

"Patrice, I don't have time to discuss this right now!"

"We have lots of time, seeing how we're both dead," Patrice snapped, her expression clouding over. The old animosity between vampires and wraiths seemed to be at work. "Eternity, in fact. Start with how you died."

"Black Cross is here in Riverton, and if you don't let me out *this second*, they're going to kill Lucas and any other vampire they find, probably including you!"

The strange tar-pit drag on my movements released me so quickly that I felt like I went flying. Light seemed to explode all around—but it was only the streetlamps of downtown Riverton, in contrast to the darkness that had enclosed me. As I made sense of the world again, I realized that I was just in front of

Patrice, who in turn stood in an alleyway just off the main strip. She held in her hand a small makeup mirror, which was crusted with frost. I must have been visible, but only just—as I reached out one hand, I saw only the faintest gray outline of fingers and palm. Nobody would see me if they didn't know to look.

Patrice knew. She blinked once, then shook off her astonishment. "Where are they?" she said. "Tell me quickly."

"The theater. The diner. I don't know where else. Lucas is headed toward the coffee shop; we have to get to him before they do."

She took off across the street, running as hard as if it were her existence on the line instead of Lucas's. I followed her, but slowly. Being trapped had taken something out of me—I needed time to get my strength back, time Lucas didn't have.

Patrice got to the coffee shop while I was still two dozen feet away. She didn't so much open the door as burst through it, violently enough that most of the customers looked up to see what the commotion was. One of those was Lucas, who had been sitting in one of the green velvet armchairs with his head in his hands. As he stared at Patrice, she held out her hand to him, clearly urging him to leave.

That was the moment my view was blocked by the hunters.

Kate. Eliza. Milos. Ten or fifteen more that I didn't know, but each of them with the brawn of Black Cross troops. Somebody had given the word that Lucas was in town, and told them his location. Patrice and I had been too late.

*Oh, no,* I thought. *Please, no.*

"Weapons," Kate said. The word fell as heavy and unyielding as iron. She'd come here to kill her son, and the weight of it deadened her eyes. As the hunters shouldered their crossbows, Lucas rose and walked toward Patrice, ready to go—and saw his mother. He saw the attack about to happen, and there was nothing he could do about it.

That meant it was up to me.

I stretched myself thin, into one long horizontal line, and imagined myself like the sharp edge of a sword—then plunged forward.

"Fire!" Kate cried, just as I swept through the hunters. It must have hit them like a slimmer, swifter stroke of ice, because they all shouted and most of them fired blindly, their arrow-stakes slamming into the pavement or nearby walls. But at least one got through, because the coffee-shop window shattered in a spray of glass. People inside started screaming, and I could see passersby on the street begin to freak out.

*Lucas!* I couldn't see him. Though I desperately wanted to find out whether he was okay, I knew I had to end this before anybody else got hurt. My strength remained shaky, but I had to do whatever I could.

Already the hunters were regathering. Although a few of them had doubled over in pain from my blow, they were straightening up, readying themselves for another assault. My first thought was to possess Kate again and order them to stop. Could I do that? If desperation was the key, as I'd suspected before, then yes, I could do it. But as I rushed toward her, I felt something pushing me back, until I came to a halt.

*What the*—? Then I saw, shining on her fingers, half a dozen copper rings. Copper, like any other mineral found in the human body, repelled wraiths. Black Cross only knew a little about wraiths, so far as I'd been able to find out, but apparently Kate had discovered enough to protect herself from possession. I could strike at her, but I could never again take over her body.

I'd just have to take them out one by one, then.

I plunged toward the hunter closest to me. To punch him with that fist of ice, I would have to take form, and I knew that was probably a bad idea; not only would it give me away to tons more Evernight students, but it also would give Black Cross somewhere to aim. They'd probably looked up ways to harm or demolish wraiths since our last encounter.

Instead, I whirled around him, a breeze becoming a gale, willing myself to be colder and colder. As my speed increased, I could see icicles beginning to form at the ends of his hair and beard. His skin went bluish, and he cried out in pain.

*Enough.* I let him go, hearing him fall in an apparent stupor, and rushed toward another hunter. Dimly I could sense the rest of the fight around me: Patrice had taken on Kate, matching her blow for blow with a ferocity I'd never realized she possessed. Lucas was in the thick of things, too; he roared with rage as he tackled Milos to the ground. My emotions were torn between being glad Lucas was okay, and terrified that this would be it— the time he would take a human life, the sin for which he could never forgive himself.

But right now, the best thing I could do to help Lucas was keep fighting. I forced myself to become a whirlwind yet again, whipping colder and colder. Within moments of my wrapping myself around the next hunter, she, too, fell prey to frostbite, or hypothermia, or whatever it was I was doing to them. So I went after another, but as I began, I heard Lucas shout out in pain.

I couldn't focus. In terror, I looked behind me to see Lucas—fangs extended, face monstrous—on the ground as Milos raised a stake. Blood flowed from a cut on Lucas's forehead. They were too far away; I couldn't get to them in time—

Then Raquel appeared, running from a nearby side street, and slammed something into the side of Milos's head.

Milos fell to his knees, stunned. As I watched in disbelief, Raquel cried out, "Lucas, get out of here! Now!"

"What the hell are you doing?" Kate shouted. But Dana had arrived, too, holding a crossbow aimed directly at Kate.

"This ends," Dana said. She was shaking so hard that her voice trembled. "This ends now."

From the distance, I heard sirens begin to wail; somebody in Riverton had called the police.

Lucas stumbled to his feet, obviously somewhat dazed from the blow to his head—and deep in the urge to fight, and to kill. I went swiftly to his side, unable to be anything more than a cool breeze against his cheek, but maybe that would at least remind him of who he was.

Behind me, I heard Kate's voice trembling with rage. "You two will regret this."

"I've got plenty of regrets," Raquel said. She hadn't budged from her place between the hunters and Lucas. "What's one more?"

"Damn you." Quick as a blink, Kate dodged left and shouldered her crossbow. Dana slammed into her side, sending the arrow flying askew—thank God, it wouldn't hit Raquel or Lucas—but then I realized it was headed straight toward one of the Evernight students gaping at the fight, a human girl who would never be able to dodge in time.

Although the next moment lasted no more than a fraction of a second, it seemed to unfold before me in slow motion. The arrow, slicing lethally through the air. Lucas, leaping with his vampire strength and speed, directly at the girl in danger. Their bodies colliding, her shining dark hair trailing behind her, both of them falling to the ground—just a couple of inches short of the arrow, which thwacked into the side of the building, burying itself inches deep in the wood.

The sirens came closer, and the crowds were growing—dozens of witnesses, now, something Black Cross hated. Kate must have given some signal, because I heard the hunters take off, running or stumbling as best they could.

Dana called, "Lucas!"

From where he was sprawled on the sidewalk with the rescued girl, he looked up at her. His whole body shook, and he didn't smile. I knew that, while Lucas might have overcome his blood hunger to protect another, he was still too close to snapping.

"Don't approach him right now," Patrice said. She'd seen

the signs that Lucas was close to breaking. "Both of you have weapons. The police will think you were part of the group attacking us."

"We resigned last night, when Kate said we were gonna go after Lucas," Dana said. "Not that we exactly mentioned it to her or anything."

Raquel said, "What was that—ice cyclone thing?"

"That was me," I answered, still invisible. Everyone jumped. "Dana, Raquel, you guys have to listen to Patrice. You'll get arrested if you stick around."

"And no Black Cross to post bail this time." Dana sighed. "Raquel, baby, time to run."

Dana took off, but Raquel hesitated a moment, searching the air in vain for a glimpse of me. "Bianca . . ."

"I get it," I said. "I understand." Which wasn't totally true— I didn't know what, exactly, had brought Raquel around from the fear that had led her to betray me. But I knew that *something* had, and that she and Dana had risked their lives and left Black Cross in order to protect Lucas. As far as I was concerned, that mattered more than anything else.

Raquel ran after Dana, disappearing around a corner just as the police car pulled up. I realized that Patrice had stepped away from me and turned to see that she had put herself smoothly between Lucas and the human girl he'd saved—Skye Tierney, I recognized her now—so that Lucas couldn't look at her. Her quick thinking might have saved him from snapping. Or, more accurately, saved Skye's life.

As the cops got out of the car, Patrice whispered, quietly enough so that only Lucas and I could hear, "Leave the explanations to me."

Within a couple minutes of the police officers' arrival, I understood why Patrice had wanted to take charge of this. A century and a half's experience of providing supposedly rational explanations for supernatural events was paying off. With expertise, Patrice played the part of a terrified young girl, sure she had seen gang members from the city, and they'd said something about an initiation, and it was just like those e-mails you got sometimes where you heard that gang members were going to kill some innocent person at random, wasn't it?

The cops might not have believed that, but they believed that her fear was genuine and, more important, that neither she nor any of her friends had anything to do with starting the fight. The other witnesses' testimony, including Skye's, would back that up. By the time they got to Lucas, the only questions they asked were about his head and whether he needed to see a doctor.

He was able to answer their questions calmly enough. Although I knew he was struggling, Lucas had won out over the blood hunger awakened by the fight, at least for now.

Once the police left, I was eager to talk to him, to see how he was—but so was someone else. Skye stepped to his side, glowing with excitement and relief. "I just had to tell you, that was amazing," she said. "You saved my life. For real. I can't thank you enough."

"Just glad you're okay," Lucas said, and despite the turmoil I knew he had to be in, he smiled a little for her. That made Skye beam at him, and I realized with a start just how pretty she was: sleek dark hair, pale blue eyes with thick lashes, perfect skin, thin but not emaciated looking—

All at once, I wasn't entirely thrilled about the fact that Lucas had saved her. Not that I wanted Skye dead, but she was a gorgeous girl who was probably about to have a huge crush on my guy. And that was not good.

"Do you really think they were gang members?" She looked doubtful. "They looked kind of old for that."

"Guess you never get too old to be stupid." Lucas couldn't quite meet her eyes.

Skye put one hand on Lucas's forearm. I was this close to hating her when she said, "I'm kind of shaken up. . . . I want to go call my boyfriend back home—but before I take off, thanks again. Seriously."

Just like that, I suddenly liked Skye a whole lot more. When Lucas waved good-bye to her, I murmured in his ear, "It's okay. We got through it. You didn't break. Lucas, see how strong you are?"

"I need to be alone." Lucas stalked away from me, and I wanted to follow but didn't. His mother had just tried once again to kill him; no wonder he couldn't take any pleasure in his small victory over himself.

As I sadly watched him go, I caught sight of someone else— Patrice, who now sat alone on a small bench. She appeared to be studying the hem of her floral-patterned skirt for any rips or tears. Typically, she'd gotten through that entire fight, giving as good as she got, without messing up her hair.

I went to her side and said, "Thanks for all of that."

"Bianca." Patrice lifted her head, with that faraway look people got when they talked to me while I was invisible. "You're a wraith now?"

"Yeah."

She settled herself onto the bench, clearly getting comfortable. "Tell me the whole story. Start back when you and Lucas broke up, which I now assume was not exactly the truth."

Patrice had never been someone I confided in much, but after the way she'd come through for us, I knew that I could trust her. So I told her the whole story, as concisely as I could, from the beginnings of my clandestine relationship with Lucas to our deaths to the current situation at Evernight Academy. She listened—not as sympathetically as some people might have, talking about how terrible it was and how bad they felt for us— but she didn't judge. After all the guilt and recrimination going around, that alone was a relief.

Once I'd finished, I realized I had a few questions of my own. "Why did you trap me? How did you trap me?"

"I'd felt something following me around. Or following Lucas around, I see now, but I knew I sensed it. Something ghostly. I wasn't positive, but I decided to take action if I felt it again. You're chilly sometimes, you know that?"

"How come you aren't scared of me? Most vampires are."

Patrice's full lips quirked into a smile. "Most vampires are pretty stupid about wraiths—I heard about the panic last year. What a lot of silliness. But in New Orleans, where I started out? Back then, there was a woman named Marie Leveau who knew everything about vampires, ghosts, spirits, you name it. I went to her when I was newly turned." She gazed into the distance as though she were trying to look into the past. "There was a man who'd died . . . someone I wanted to see again . . . well. Bringing someone back against his will turns out to be a bad idea."

"I can imagine." Adjusting to being a wraith had been hard enough for me. For someone who had been peacefully dead, it was probably a lot worse. "Did you trap him in a mirror?"

"And in the end, I broke the mirror to let him go." From her purse she pulled out the compact she'd used to trap me. The frost had melted, and when she opened it, I saw the reflecting pane remained intact. "Since then, I've figured out how to release ghosts without breaking any mirrors. It's such a pain, replacing them."

That was Patrice for you—worrying about her cosmetics case while she was messing with the line between the living and the dead.

"Where do ghosts go when you use the mirror to trap them?"

"I was hoping you could tell me," she said. "Into the mirror, as far as I know."

To me it felt more like no place, some area between existence and nonexistence, but mysteries like this were beginning to feel almost routine now that I'd become a wraith. Besides, earthly concerns felt more pressing at the moment.

I began, "You know, Lucas could use a few more friends at Evernight Academy. And it would be nice to have somebody else to talk to." Particularly, I thought, another girl. Lucas, Balthazar, Ranulf, and Vic were each terrific in their own ways, but hanging out with only them did get a little sweat socky after a while.

"I don't tend to make friends with Black Cross hunters, unlike some people," she sniffed. But I could see her regal features softening slightly. "Though I guess Lucas isn't with them anymore. So backing him up is basically the same as giving Black Cross the finger."

Not much of an avowal of eternal friendship, but I would take it.

"And I guess I did miss you," Patrice added. "I'd been thinking about you earlier tonight, actually."

"Really?" That made me feel nice, being missed.

"You always did have wonderful taste in vintage jewelry, and I wanted to hit the shop here to find something to wear with this outfit. Worth a ride over the river, don't you think?"

Patrice would stop at nothing to have the perfect look, but I no longer found that annoying—instead it was funny, and kind of great, and, well, just her. "Okay, I'll go with you. They won't see me. I may be dead, but I can still shop."

She perked up. "Ooooh, we need T-shirts saying that."

I shopped with Patrice, urging her toward an antique charm bracelet, but while it was nice to reconnect, on another level I was basically killing time. When we were in the clothing store, I couldn't help remembering how Lucas and I had come here on one of our early dates. He'd been so happy, trying on awesome long coats and crazy hats, so carefree. So *alive*.

It wasn't that I loved him any less for being dead—how could I?—but I knew that his life was something that I had loved about Lucas, and it was gone.

When the students began to gather in the square to catch the bus back to school, Lucas didn't appear with the rest. Nobody except Skye seemed to notice. As everyone started boarding, she went to the chaperone and said, "We're one person short. He might be hurt."

"Ross? He's not hurt." The driver—a vampire—shrugged it off. "He told me earlier that he had another ride back to school tonight. You'll see him tomorrow."

Skye didn't look very happy about Lucas being left behind, and I could understand why. At any normal school, that would've been a cause for concern; even at Evernight, if it had been a human student who had gotten lost, there would have been search parties and considerable worry. But vampire students were allowed more independence and were assumed to be able to take care of themselves.

I hoped that was true.

"Go find him," Patrice whispered before she stepped onto the bus. "See you later."

Swiftly I moved away from the square, toward the woods that lay between the town and Evernight. Once the houses were few and far between, and the night breeze stirred around me, I had the solitude I needed to concentrate.

I imagined my jet brooch, the one he had bought for me here in Riverton. The black stone, the shape of the flower, the stone filling in the life that had once pulsed at the core of the wood.

Everything around me swirled like so much smoke, changing colors, taking shape. To my surprise, I wasn't with Lucas; the brooch had been in the pocket of his jacket, which now lay discarded in a heap on the forest floor. As I peered down at it, I saw that it was stained with blood. His from the fight, I assumed—but then I saw that other things were lying around it. A dead raccoon. A dead bird of some kind. A dead fox. Their bodies hadn't just been drained; they'd been torn apart. The pile was the aftermath of a killing frenzy, taken out on small animals instead of human beings.

In the near distance, I could hear a *thud, thud, thud*—blows against wood, like with a mallet or maybe an ax. Taking hold of the brooch and becoming solid, I walked toward the sound until I saw Lucas, stripped down to his undershirt. He stood facing a tree, punching it the way a boxer would a bag.

I came closer. Lucas was oblivious to me, maybe to anything. He hit the tree so hard that bark flew with each punch; on either side of the trunk were stripped-down places of splintered wood, glistening with his blood. Horrified, I realized that he'd beaten through the skin of his own hands, and a sliver of bone jutted through one finger. The pain he felt with each blow had to be tremendous, and yet he kept going, relentless.

"Lucas!" I ran to his side and grabbed at one of his arms. "Don't do this to yourself!"

He stopped, but he didn't look at me. Sweat slicked his skin, making his T-shirt stick to him and his face shine in the moonlight. Lucas kept staring at that tree like he hated it. "I wanted to kill her."

"She's your mother," I said. "She's betrayed you, as badly as anybody could ever . . . it's okay to be mad."

"Not just her. I wanted to kill Dana and Raquel, while they were trying to save me. I wanted to kill Skye the whole time I was rescuing her. And now I look back on it, and I'm not proud, and I don't feel strong. I'm just so mad at myself for not killing them and drinking their blood when I had the chance, and I hate myself for it, and I— Damn it. Damn it."

Lucas punched the tree again, so fiercely that I knew he wasn't imagining hurting anyone but himself.

"Please don't do this." I took both his arms in my hands and brought his broken hand to my face. It was a twisted mess of bone and sinew and blood, like he'd been in a car wreck. "It hurts to see it."

"I keep trying to break my hand worse and worse, so it won't heal," he said. "But it *is* healing. I can feel the bones coming back together even while I break new ones. It goes back to the way it was before. I can't tear myself down. I can't escape from this. There's no way out."

He was right. I couldn't argue with him. So instead I flung

my arms around his neck and held him tightly.

After a moment, Lucas embraced me back. He shuddered, as though the madness was leaving him.

Only for now, I knew. But if that was the only help I could give, then I would give it. I closed my eyes and hoped that love truly could win over death.

# Chapter Ten

AFTER THAT NIGHT IN RIVERTON, LUCAS BECAME quieter. Harder. Although he continued to reach out to me, and to try to find fun stuff for us to do, it was increasingly obvious to me—and, no doubt, to him—that he was in a desperate struggle for his own sanity, and I could only help him so much.

And every time he would build himself up, get to where he might have a good day or two in a row, something else would happen to tear him down.

A couple of days later, I sneaked into his calculus class, one I generally avoided, because I'd taken that the year before and once was definitely enough. As usual, Lucas sat near the back of the room, but this time, there was no invisible barrier around him. A couple of guys—vampire guys, lean and pale—were on either side of him, and they were paying more attention to Lucas than to the equation on the board.

As I dipped down closer, I heard Lucas mutter, "Shut it, okay, Samuel?"

The skinnier of the vampires, a new student apparently called Samuel, answered, "Can't shut it *out*. You know it as well as I do. You smell it, too."

The other vampire, silently giggling in an incredibly creepy way, pointed with his middle finger toward a girl sitting two rows ahead of them, one with blond hair in a pixie cut.

"Breathe that in," Samuel whispered. "Nothing better than a girl on the rag."

I'd never realized full vampires could smell when girls had their periods. Retroactive mortification from every month of my two years at Evernight hit me at once, and if I'd had a body, I would have blushed hot pink.

Lucas looked mortified, too, but that was clearly not the main problem. Samuel and his loathsome friend weren't trying to embarrass him; they were trying to make him hungry.

Samuel leaned farther out in the aisle, his desk at the point of tipping over, his mouth right next to Lucas's ear. "You just got turned this summer, huh, hunter? Bet you've never even had a kill. Never had fresh human blood. But you want it, don't you?"

Lucas's hands gripped the edge of his desk. His still-scarred knuckles were white. He kept staring down at the notes he'd made, but it was obvious he wasn't seeing any of it.

"This place is like a freakin' all-you-can-eat buffet these days," Samuel said. "So many humans. So many girls. Don't you want a drink, Lucas? Or did Black Cross make you too self-righteous to feed yourself?" He spat out the words Black Cross like they tasted bad in his mouth.

"Shut the hell up."

Samuel's voice lowered further, but he kept talking. "You're gonna starve. You're just gonna get hungrier and hungrier until it claws out the center of you. A pretty girl like that, maybe—she'll send you right over the edge. Someday you'll snap, hunter. Someday you'll kill."

Lucas shut his eyes tightly.

*Enough,* I decided. I flattened myself at the floor, cold and strong, and swept beneath Samuel's desk—toppling it, and him, over.

He crashed down, books and paper going everywhere, and everybody started laughing. Professor Raju crossed her arms. "Mr. Younger, you'll never learn to balance equations if you can't balance yourself." Lame teacher humor, but people snickered anyway; Samuel looked furious but sullenly righted himself. I knew he wouldn't make fun of anybody else for at least a day or two.

Lucas didn't join in the laughter. The hunger had taken him over, and I realized it was taking every bit of his focus and will to keep from attacking the girl two rows ahead.

When class was dismissed, Lucas got up so quickly that his desk scraped across the floor. Samuel and his creepy friend laughed, and Samuel said, "What's the big hurry, Lucas? Gotta change a Tampax?"

A couple other vampires laughed, but Skye, who had been in the front row, whirled around. "Don't you guys ever leave him alone?"

"What do you care if we don't like this jerk?"

"I'm looking at the biggest jerk in the room, and it's not Lucas."

While Samuel and Skye had it out, Lucas grabbed his stuff and rushed out of the room. I followed him, and only my ability to travel above the crowds of students allowed me to keep up. Lucas shoved and pushed, going faster and faster, ignoring every annoyed look he received. He was focused on only one thing: getting out.

Lucas flung the great hall's huge wooden doors open with both hands. Gold and tan leaves on the lawn crunched beneath his feet, and I could tell he was preparing to run. He'd vanish into the woods again, kill as many creatures as he could, beat himself into a pulp. *Not again*, I thought in despair. *Please, not again!*

At that moment, Balthazar appeared, like he'd materialized in front of Lucas. He must have called on his vampire speed to reach him. "Bad day?" he said.

"Get out of my way," Lucas growled.

"No." Balthazar grabbed Lucas's arm and towed him back into the building. "You're coming with me."

"What are you doing?" I whispered furiously into Balthazar's ear.

"Stopping him from tearing himself up."

Which was what I'd wanted, too, but this would only make a bad situation worse. "He needs out of there. Away from the humans. Can't you see that?"

Balthazar smiled grimly as we went through the hallways.

It looked weird—him basically dragging Lucas along like that, Lucas almost out of it—but Balthazar didn't seem to mind making it worse by talking to me out loud. "I know you don't trust me anymore, but you're just going to have to deal."

Their destination turned out to be the fencing room. No lessons at this hour: It was deserted, the gear neatly stowed away. A few mats remained on the floor, but otherwise everything looked bare. "Okay," I said after the door shut behind us, as I allowed myself to take visible form. "We're out of the crowd. Is that enough?"

"It's enough," Lucas said. He looked like he wanted to double over. "Just leave me alone, okay? I can— Just leave me alone."

"No can do," Balthazar said, right before he punched Lucas in the face.

I gasped. Lucas staggered back a step, one hand to his jaw. His eyes darkened, and I could see his self-control straining, stretching, right at the point of failure.

"You need to get it out," Balthazar said. He pulled off his sweater so that he stood there in a T-shirt. "So let's get it out."

"I'm not fighting." Lucas's voice shook.

Balthazar grinned. "Then I guess I'll just have to beat the crap out of you."

He swung at Lucas again, but Lucas's fighting instincts took over. He blocked the blow and shoved Balthazar halfway across the room. In an instant, Balthazar returned, smashing his fist into Lucas's gut. Lucas hit him back harder, snapping Balthazar's head back.

"Guys, stop this!" I shouted, but Balthazar didn't listen, and Lucas couldn't hear. They were two vampires—two monsters—struggling for dominance, and nothing else in the world mattered.

Fists. Blood. Sweat. They tore at each other like animals. Freaked out, I tried to think of how best to stop this and decided, *Right, time to ice the room.* But even as I began, I realized what was happening.

The crazed look had left Lucas's eyes. Instead, his gaze was sharp, directed, like he was on a Black Cross mission again. Every punch was focused; every move was tactical. Fighting like this, against an opponent just as strong as he was, had given him an outlet for the desperate energy building inside him.

What Balthazar was getting out of this, I had no idea, but even when Lucas kicked him in the jaw, sending him sprawling across the floor, he had a lunatic grin on his face.

Balthazar laughed from his place on the ground, holding two fingers to his mouth and pulling them back to see the blood. "Only some Black Cross redneck would stoop to kicking a guy in the mouth."

"Only some half-rotten corpse would let me." Lucas sort of blinked, like he couldn't believe he'd made a joke. Like that, apparently, the fight was over.

Everything was quiet for a few seconds, until I said, "Lucas, are you all right now?"

"Yeah." He thought that over, his attention drifting from me to Balthazar. "Yeah. Thanks, man."

Balthazar said, "If you get wound up like that again, and you need an outlet, just find me. We can spar. Fence. Whatever it takes to get it out. It helps; you'll see."

Lucas didn't look like he entirely believed that, but he nodded. He held out a hand to help Balthazar from the floor. When Balthazar's eyes met mine, he smiled, maddeningly smug. "What, you're not going to thank me, too? Or would that mean admitting I was right about something?"

"You enjoyed it," I retorted.

Balthazar shrugged, unable to deny it. He grabbed his sweater from the floor. "I'm going to shower before class. See you guys later."

Once we were alone, Lucas said, "Bianca, I'm sorry."

"What for?"

"Breaking down like that, in front of you."

"You *didn't* break down," I insisted. "You were able to control it."

"Balthazar was able to control it," Lucas corrected me.

He had a point, but I knew we needed to focus on the positive. "You're feeling better now. I can tell." He looked better; in fact, with sweat glistening on his skin, his hair mussed and his uniform askew, he looked pretty amazingly hot.

*If only we could touch each other without him feeling the urge to bite,* I thought longingly. *I know better ways for him to burn off that energy.*

"I feel . . . good." Lucas stood a little straighter. "Calmer than I have in a long time. It's like all this white noise in my head finally went quiet and I can actually *think*."

I joked, "Maybe this would be a good time for you to work on your psych paper."

"Actually, you know what?" Lucas stepped back and straightened his sweater. "This is as good a time as any to break into Mrs. Bethany's carriage house."

"Wait. What?"

"Mrs. Bethany's hiding traps for wraiths around the school, right? We can't protect you until we know more about where she's putting them, and why." He grinned, and for a moment he looked like his old self, when we first met—handsome, aggressive, and quite possibly up to no good. "Feel like a little breaking and entering?"

"We should wait until she's off the school grounds sometime. Or at least in class. I don't think she's teaching this period. It's dangerous," I said, as Lucas kept going down the stairs.

"It's always going to be dangerous. At least right now, I can focus on what I'm doing. That's got to help our chances."

I wasn't wholly convinced, but Lucas did have a point—and besides, he seemed dead set on doing it now. "I'll be your lookout. If she comes out there, I'll throw pebbles against the window, something like that."

"Sounds good." Lucas grinned, and in that moment, it felt like we were on some great adventure together, like it had been back when we first sneaked around to see each other. Apparently burglary could be very romantic under the right circumstances.

Nobody else seemed to be around on the school grounds; Lucas was currently cutting class. (Plenty of the vampire students did this—they were here less to learn the subjects than to learn how to fit in, which the teachers tacitly recognized—but when they skipped class, they usually did it for something more fun than lounging around outside.) At his nod, I darted forward to circle Mrs. Bethany's carriage house. I peered through each window, slightly frosting a couple of the panes. She wasn't inside. "The coast is clear."

"Okay. Keep an eye out."

Lucas went to one of the side windows. I watched as he worked at one of the small metal frames around a pane, wiggling it back and forth until the top strip slid free into his hand. The other three strips of metal around the windowpane came out easily then, as did the rectangle of glass. Apparently Mrs. Bethany hadn't replaced the windows recently. Lucas put everything out of the way, then reached through the open pane to turn the lock, quickly setting aside the small row of potted African violets kept there. Then he put his hands on the sill and neatly flipped over and through, into Mrs. Bethany's house.

That was a lot faster and neater than I'd been able to do it. I consoled myself a little by thinking that he had his full vampire powers to work with. Maybe I'd tease him later about having more natural criminal instincts.

Through the window, I could see Lucas walking through the house toward her desk, where any materials about her hunt for the wraiths would most likely be kept. I shifted around the edges of the walls, eager to keep an eye on him, as well as a look-out for Mrs. Bethany. But as I did so, I felt it again. The pull.

*A trap!* Before I could panic, I realized that it wasn't the same as in the library—or, while it was the same kind of trap, there was a barrier between us that could keep me from fall-ing in—the wraithproof roof or walls, perhaps. Apparently she put the traps together in her home before installing them within Evernight Academy.

Though it didn't capture me, the trap's power was over-whelming. I could feel that strange pull all through me, and I was suddenly slow, sluggish, and inattentive. It was like running a high fever, when nothing quite made sense, and movement was possible but seemed to take too much effort.

As I came close to losing the ability to focus, I saw Lucas brush his hand against something sitting on her desk—another seashell-shaped box, just like the one he'd found in the library. Maybe it was the same one; he'd reported that the library wall had been immediately fixed, no questions asked. Quickly he shut the box, and the dizzying pull of the trap vanished. How-ever, I still felt terrible; just being near an active trap was enough to seriously drain me.

For a moment, I was tempted to fade out—to rest, just for a little while—but I realized it might be a long time before I woke again. I gathered together my will and tugged myself free of it, returning to the here and now of Lucas's search—

Just in time to see Mrs. Bethany walking to the door of the carriage house.

I threw myself against Mrs. Bethany's window so hard it rattled. Lucas looked up from her desk, instantly alert, but too late. Mrs. Bethany walked into the carriage house and entered her study before Lucas could do more than stand.

She paused in the doorway. For a moment, they simply stared at each other across the room. Horror chilled me so deeply that it was like I'd become pure frost. Lucas looked seasick.

*She's going to attack him, or at least throw him out of Evernight Academy. I shouldn't have asked him to do this. I shouldn't have let him do this.*

I was just about to fly to the school in an attempt to get help when Mrs. Bethany said, evenly, "Mr. Ross, it would be more efficient if you simply asked me whatever it is you need to know."

He didn't relax, didn't move. His eyes remained locked on hers, ready to defend or to attack. "Doubt you'd tell me."

"Doubt." Mrs. Bethany laid aside her things and sat in one of the wooden chairs on the far side of the wall. Another, empty chair sat next to her, a wordless invitation to Lucas. "Black Cross teaches its hunters to doubt everything new to them, and to believe only their own decrees about duty. Or sacrifice. Or who is and is not a monster."

Lucas's jaw tightened, and I knew he was remembering Kate's attack.

"They asked so much of you, and what do you have in return? Nothing except a few bad habits, such as your penchant for breaking and entering."

Quietly Lucas said, "Don't make me leave school." The

words seemed to choke him. He hated to beg.

"The sanctuary of Evernight protects you," Mrs. Bethany said. Her voice sounded so weird; I couldn't place the difference at first, until I realized that she actually sounded—warm. "I don't intend to punish you for behaving in the only way you've ever known. Black Cross has encouraged you to be underhanded. There is a better way to conduct matters. Here, I hope, you can learn it."

Yeah, Evernight Academy was the home of honesty, what with lying to the human students about most of their new friends being vampires. As I scoffed, though, I could see Lucas's expression changing, becoming less wary. Mrs. Bethany was saying exactly what he wanted to hear.

More unbelievably, I thought she actually meant it.

"Now," she said. "Tell me what you were looking for."

"More information about the wraiths."

*Lucas, don't!* I couldn't believe he was going to spill our secrets to her that easily.

Instead he said, "I heard they were after Bianca last year. I don't understand why she died. If they had something to do with it, I want to know. And I want revenge."

Mrs. Bethany straightened, obviously pleased to have found a kindred spirit. Lucas had convinced her that he wanted the same thing she wanted: to hunt the wraiths. That was probably the single best way to get her to open up. I should've had more faith in him.

She gestured to the chair next to her, and Lucas took a seat.

"To the best of my knowledge, the wraiths believed themselves to have some kind of claim over Miss Olivier," Mrs. Bethany said. "Are you aware of the circumstances surrounding Bianca's birth?"

"You mean, the part where two vampires can't make little baby vampires without some wraith assistance? Yeah, she told me."

"Rather like a fairy tale," Mrs. Bethany said. Lucas shot her a puzzled look. "I suppose your warrior mother didn't spend much time telling you stories out of Grimm. Suffice it to say that the magical godmother at the christening usually hides a curse among her gifts. And so it was with the wraiths. They drank of Celia's blood, and gave Celia and Adrian a chance to create life, for a little while."

Lucas considered that. His dark green eyes focused upon the window; although I knew he couldn't actually see me, he knew exactly where I was. "So her mom and dad always knew this was going to happen."

"To be precise, her parents thought that she would fulfill her dominant vampire heritage by taking a life and completing the transformation. They knew the only other alternative was for her to die."

"Being just a regular girl—"

"Was always impossible," Mrs. Bethany said coolly. "Bianca was given life, but only so much."

I sank down to the ground, mist taking form into a shadow of my body. Had anybody walked by at that moment, they probably could have seen me, but I didn't care. I needed to feel something solid to rest on. It wasn't that what Mrs. Bethany had said hurt; to the contrary, it felt weirdly and yet undeniably *right*. My astonishment at my own reaction seemed to knock something out of me.

Mrs. Bethany's voice gentled. "It's hard for you to hear, isn't it? But in time, I think, knowing this will lessen your pain. You could not have saved her, Mr. Ross. You endangered her no more than her parents did—though they will never accept that."

"I don't think I can either."

"You still see death as the worst thing that can possibly happen. It isn't."

"I know there's something worse than being dead," Lucas said, each word grinding out. "Because we're there."

"You miss being alive." I expected her to say that he was foolish to do so; nobody seemed to get more pleasure out of being a vampire than she did. But Mrs. Bethany added, very quietly, "So do I."

Lucas said, "Never gets any better, huh?"

"I didn't say that."

Astonishment overcame my melancholy. I became transparent again so that I could peek once more through her window; Mrs. Bethany sat with her hand on Lucas's shoulder, her thick, grooved nails dark crimson against his black sweater. He didn't shy away from the touch.

*Is she . . .* hitting *on him?* I rejected the idea instantly; it wasn't that kind of gesture. There was no denying that a bond had been formed, however—and that in some ways, right now,

Mrs. Bethany could understand what was going on with Lucas better than I could.

Wordlessly, she patted his shoulder. Lucas obeyed the unspoken suggestion by rising to his feet. Mrs. Bethany walked him out of the carriage house—completely unconcerned about his having broken into it—and the entire way back to Evernight itself. They didn't part until they were both inside the great hall; a few people studying during their free period glanced at the scene, registering to their surprise that Lucas had apparently gotten teacher's pet status. I wondered if that would make the other vampires back off, or target him even more.

"English class calls," she said. "Dare I hope that you've done the reading?"

Lucas said, "I read *Catcher in the Rye* on my own a couple years ago, actually."

"Of course. You would be primarily self-taught. What did you think?"

"That Holden Caulfield is a self-pitying loser who needs more to do with his time."

Mrs. Bethany smiled slightly. "Although I would phrase things more delicately, our analyses are similar in substance. Which means I will call on you. Be ready." She checked the old-fashioned gold wristwatch she wore. "You have several minutes yet if you wished to shower," she said, in a tone of voice indicating that he should definitely consider it.

She went on her way, and Lucas immediately started jogging upstairs to do what she'd said. He was smiling—really smiling, like it came from his heart. I felt almost jealous, more like a tag-along than his constant companion, until he whispered, "Can you believe that?"

"You *did* get kind of sweaty sparring with Balthazar."

"No, I mean, can you believe she let me off?"

"Nope. Then again, you are pretty charming."

"Charm's not my strong suit."

"I disagree." Carefully, I said, "You know not to trust her, right?"

Lucas remained silent as he walked out onto the floor of the guys' dorm where he lived. Finally, when we reached his room, he said, "She cut me slack, and she didn't have to."

"She hates Black Cross a lot, and I get that she feels sorry for you because of what happened with them, but . . . the traps, Lucas. She's out to get ghosts like me. One of those traps nearly killed me."

"Maybe she's just scared of what she doesn't understand," he protested as he stripped off his sweater and shirt, dumping them on the floor atop the wet towels no doubt left over from Balthazar's shower. Guys never seemed to realize that doing laundry was an option. "Bianca, you're still frightened of the wraiths, and you are one. So it's not an unreasonable reaction."

I had trouble imagining Mrs. Bethany being scared of much of anything. But Lucas wasn't totally wrong about her either; she'd come through for him when none of his friends could, not even me.

Just the same, I couldn't have any real faith in her. Not

yet. "You won't tell her about me, will you? That I've become a wraith, and that I'm here with you?"

Lucas got a weird look on his face. "Are you kidding? Of course not."

Relief washed through me. "So you don't trust her."

"I don't know if I trust her or not. But when it comes to you, I'm not taking any more risks than we have to. Your secrets are my secrets, Bianca. Never doubt that."

I brushed against his cheek, a soft breeze, and he closed his eyes and smiled.

He was so strong right now. So happy. I suggested, "You know, I realize we can't actually . . . be together . . ."

Lucas opened his eyes, his smile dimming.

Before he could apologize, I said, "But I *could* watch you shower."

He laughed out loud.

The next ten minutes were awesome, in terms of the view. However, the whole time, I couldn't totally concentrate—not even with gorgeous, wet, naked Lucas to focus on. One thought had lodged itself in my mind, and I couldn't shake it.

I kept thinking, *It's like everyone else in the world can help him a little bit—but not me. Never me.*

# Chapter Eleven

WATCHING LUCAS SHOWER DID THINGS TO MY brain.

I let him go to class, but seeing him again, with his muscled chest and legs, and water streaming through his dark gold hair and over his full lips—remembering everything we'd had together during the short weeks we'd shared in Philadelphia—awakened my hunger to be with him again. Desire was different for me now that I didn't have a living body, but that didn't mean I wanted Lucas any less.

And I wanted that closeness between us again. I knew that I helped tether Lucas to the world as much as he helped me; surely we didn't have to be celibate forever, did we? We could find a way. As long as I had my bracelet on, I didn't see why it would even have to be difficult.

Lucas hadn't made any moves in that direction since our first terrible attempt. Given how traumatizing that whole time had been, I'd respected the fact that he needed some distance;

I knew he loved me just as much. Maybe I'd taken it too far, though. Maybe I was the one who needed to make the first move.

As darkness fell, I slipped down the side of the guys' tower and into Vic and Ranulf's room. They were sharing a companionably silent dinner, Ranulf sipping blood from an Eagles mug, Vic wolfing down a Hot Pocket. When I appeared in their room, Vic grinned and waved. "Yo, Bianca! It's good you dropped by. We were just gonna watch Jackie Chan movies. The old ones, where he's badass, not the American stuff where he's funny."

"His ass remains bad in all incarnations," Ranulf interjected. "In the laudatory sense of the word *bad* and a rather nebulous sense of the word *ass*."

"Ever and always badass," Vic agreed. "Just more badass in the *Drunken Master* days. You want to join us, Bianca? See for yourself?"

"Actually," I began, "I was hoping you guys might ask Balthazar to join you. For a couple of hours or so."

Vic nodded sagely. "A little necktie-on-the-doorknob time is called for, I see." When Ranulf frowned, he added, "Bianca and Lucas want to be alone."

"I see at once the symbolism of the doorknob and the necktie," Ranulf said.

"Wait—no," Vic said. "That is *not* what that means. At least, I don't think so—"

This conversation was about to derail. "Could you maybe go ahead and ask him? It would mean a lot."

Vic grinned. "Consider it done."

About ten minutes later, when I went up to Lucas's room, I found him alone; Vic and Ranulf had already collected Balthazar. Lucas sat amid a pile of schoolbooks, like he was cramming for all his exams at once. "Wow," I said as I took shape. "Did you get hit with a homework tsunami or something?"

"Studying helps," Lucas said quietly. "When I study, I can focus on something outside my head for a little while."

The books and papers and laptop in front of him looked different now; at once I was reminded of him in his Black Cross cell, surrounded by his hunter's weapons. His newfound drive for his schoolwork was one more way for him to defend himself—this time, against the demons within.

I hoped I had another way. "Do you think you could take a little time away?"

Lucas looked up at me, his green eyes so warm and liquid that I felt myself melt. "For you? Always."

"We're alone." I brushed my hand through his hair; he shut his eyes, clearly relishing the touch. "You've got my jewelry, so I could be solid for a while. Maybe we could . . . give being together another try?"

He remained silent for a long moment. His hand closed around mine, and I felt again the sparkly sensation of connecting when I wasn't 100 percent solid—deliciously cool, sending ripples of pleasure through me. I bent to kiss Lucas, but just before our lips met, he said, "We shouldn't."

"Lucas—why not?" I didn't feel rejected; his longing and love for me radiated from him. So I didn't understand what kept us apart. "I know last time was bad, but we realize what's going on now. What we can and can't do." As far as I was concerned, the stuff we could do was a whole lot more interesting than what we couldn't.

"The need for sex and the need for blood—they're so tightly linked, Bianca. They always have been, for us."

"But they aren't the same thing." I kissed his forehead, his cheek, the side of his mouth. He breathed in sharply, and I knew he wanted this as badly as I did—more, perhaps. "You know now that drinking my blood would hurt you. Maybe destroy you. So that means you won't lose control and bite me."

Lucas gripped my hands tightly and met my eyes. "I know that drinking your blood could destroy me," he said. "And that's why I'm afraid I'll bite you."

Silence fell over us, as heavy and horrible as the new knowledge I had to bear. I'd known that Lucas was struggling, but I hadn't realized that his desire for self-destruction remained so immediate and strong.

My face must have looked crushed, because Lucas said, "Oh, God, Bianca, I'm sorry. I'm so sorry."

"You told me the truth," I managed to say. "That's the main thing."

Lucas embraced me as tightly as he could in my semisolid state. "I daydream about being with you all the time," he whispered into my hair. "All the time. If I couldn't remember being with you, I don't know how I would go on. But sometimes I think—if I could end it, just end it, while I was with you, it's as close as anything like me could ever get to heaven—"

"Lucas, no."

"I would never do that to you," he said. "Never. But . . . Bianca, we can't."

I nodded, accepting the barrier between us. It wasn't forever; just until Lucas managed to control his blood hunger and the terrible self-loathing Black Cross had programmed into him. But how long until that day came?

Would it ever come?

As though he could hear my doubts, Lucas said, "Someday."

"Someday," I said, a promise to him and to myself.

Later that night, still dazed with disappointment and worry for Lucas, I drifted down into the main area of the school— deserted, this late at night. Even the vampires were asleep.

*How many vampires don't make the transition?* I thought. *How many give in to suicidal impulses or blood hunger, or both?* I suspected the number was far larger than my parents had ever let on. Once again I felt a fierce surge of longing for them. Not only did I miss Mom and Dad just as themselves, but if we could talk—really talk, without all the lies between us—maybe I could learn how to help Lucas bear his burdens.

Perhaps it was the intensity of my concentration as I wondered about this, the way it dragged me so deeply into my own mind rather than the here and now—or maybe it was some trick of where I was at that moment, because Evernight's traps and guards and passageways created a kind of spiritual architecture within the stone. Whatever it was, in that moment, I suddenly became sharply aware that I was not alone.

I could sense the wraiths.

They were more distinct at that moment than they had ever been. Instead of simply knowing that they were there, I could now tell roughly how many there were—dozens, at least. They seemed to stand out in my awareness, each of them distinct but part of a whole, like stars in the sky, maybe, different points of brightness that formed constellations all around me. It was like suddenly seeing the night sky for the very first time, as though I'd been blind to it my whole life and then been dazzled all at once.

Except that constellations were beautiful, peaceful—and what I sensed around me now was desperation and madness. Instead of being dazzled, I felt the cold grip of fear.

Some lingered alone, crammed into tiny slivers between stones or at the edge of windowpanes. It was as though they were beating their heads against a wall, cramping and hurting themselves just to remind themselves they continued to exist.

The trapped ones were the worst, because I couldn't feel anything from them but pure terror. They'd become nothing but long wordless screams.

And then there were a few others, clustered tightly together, who, when I sensed them, sensed me in return.

Once again, the visions began.

I saw an image of Mrs. Bethany in my mind—not a product of my own imagination, but something projected into my head like a movie on a screen. Something was tearing her apart, literally, graphically, bone and sinew and blood and guts, more disgusting than anything I'd ever seen. My throat tightened, and I gagged, but the image filled my whole mind now, and I couldn't push it away.

The Plotters—that was what I called them—repeated, *Help us.*

Or what? Would they attack the people I loved like this? Or would they come after me? What could a ghost do to another ghost? I had no idea, but terrible possibilities unfolded in my mind, becoming part of the gruesome destruction of Mrs. Bethany.

Her mouth was open, her jaw unhinging, but the desperate scream in my mind was my own—

Then a shaft of light seemed to penetrate my dream. Mrs. Bethany vanished, and the "constellations" disappeared as though it were dawn.

When I could see again, I realized that Maxie was standing with me in the great hall. Her white nightgown floated slightly on some unseen breeze, so that she seemed to be part of the fog outside.

"You saved me," I said.

"I pushed them back. That's as much as I can do." She cocked an eyebrow, like it was weird that *she* had to save *me* from anything. "You're the girl with the superpowers, if you'd just realize it already."

What else could a ghost do to another ghost? That sharp new

fear controlled me as powerfully as the Plotters had a moment before. I stabilized myself as best I could, becoming more solid. "Are those Christopher's . . . henchmen? Or henchghosts? Or whatever?"

"Christopher doesn't have anything to do with them," Maxie said. "They'd be better off if he did. They're too tied to the human world to come to terms with the fact that they're wraiths."

"They hate Evernight," I said. "They hate Mrs. Bethany. Why don't they just leave?"

Maxie folded her arms. "You keep thinking all of us can do the things you can do. We can't. Most wraiths can't move around the way you can, or even the way I can. They followed their human anchors here because of the strength of that bond; every instinct they have tells them not to abandon it. And because they're so screwed up now, they can't think past instinct. They can't think, period. They're just emotions, going in every direction."

"What's wrong with them?"

"This is how we end, if we're not careful."

Cautiously, I said, "You mean, we end up . . . crazy?"

"Unhinged. Unstable. It comes from being in the human world but not of it." She gave me a pointed look that suggested I was headed in that direction.

"You've spent time with Vic since he was a child," I said. Vic was her biggest vulnerability; I wasn't above using that.

She smiled softly when I said his name. "You can watch

them. You can even—you can love." Her voice broke on the last word. "But you can't live. The damage comes from pretending that you can."

"I'm not pretending," I insisted.

"Aren't you?"

"Bianca, if you would just come talk to Christopher—"

Fear swept through me again, and I shook my head. "Don't."

Maxie's usual sarcastic demeanor had faded into genuine pleading. "Bianca, you're important to the wraiths. Don't you see that? The stuff you can do that the rest of us can't—it's not just so much smoke and fog. It means something. You mean something." My curiosity began to get the better of my fear, but just when I wanted to ask her more, she grew desperate, almost scarily so, and said, "We *need* you."

"You're not the only ones who need me." I swept out of the great hall, afraid she was going to chase me. But she let me go.

"You're sure you want to learn how to do this?" Patrice folded her arms, studying me as severely as Mrs. Bethany had during midterms.

The real answer was that no, I wasn't sure. This was, in its way, as scary as training with Black Cross had been—it never felt good, learning how to attack creatures like myself.

The only way to make myself free was to give myself power. And that meant learning how to strike back against the wraiths, if necessary.

"Let's begin," I said.

Patrice pulled out her compact. "To catch a wraith," she said, "you first have to detect that a wraith is there."

"Done and done." When Patrice glared at me for interrupting, I said, "I've kind of got an edge there, okay?"

"I see your point. Now, watch." She opened the mirror slowly, with exaggerated movements, like a preschool teacher. I would have laughed if the situation had been any less serious and the setting had been any less spooky. Outside, heavy cold rain had been falling steadily the whole day, draining the sky of any color besides gray. Although Patrice had turned on both of the lamps in her dorm room, they weren't able to counteract the gloom outside. One of the lights danced on the open mirror, sending a little spot of brightness darting around the stones surrounding us. "You need to open the mirror after you've sensed the presence of the wraith, but before you've actually confronted it. This isn't like Mrs. Bethany's traps—a wraith can resist a mirror, if she knows the attack is coming."

My amusement got the better of the moment. When I started grinning, Patrice cocked her head in confusion. I said, "I'm sorry. It's just so weird hearing you talk about attacking people."

"Excuse me?"

"You know, aren't you worried about breaking a nail or something?"

Patrice looked annoyed, until she realized I was only teasing. She raised one eyebrow. "Did you see me worrying about that while I kicked some Black Cross butt?"

"Absolutely not," I said.

"Mind you, I'm a bit out of practice. I've done all the killing I ever intend to do. Drinking blood can give you skanky breath. If you ask me, Evernight Academy should add a hygiene class, because some people here? They haven't gotten that critical message."

I wasn't interested in gossiping about who had blood-induced halitosis. "You've . . . done a lot of killing?"

"Not so much," Patrice said easily. "Just a few slave owners and redneck sheriffs, back in the day. Before the Emancipation Proclamation, if you were black in this country, there was always someone trying to take your freedom away. Literally, I mean; figuratively, it never stops. After I became a vampire, I didn't have to put up with that anymore."

Pretty much every vampire I'd ever known had killed sometimes—except my parents, though maybe they just hadn't shared with me. Even the best of them, like Patrice and Balthazar, had drunk from, and murdered, humans. Balthazar's kills had mostly taken place during wartime, and I couldn't blame Patrice for striking back at anyone who wanted to enslave her. But just the same, they'd drunk human blood. Balthazar had even murdered his own sister, with consequences that continued to haunt us.

Did that mean there was really no choice for Lucas? That sooner or later, he would inevitably snap? Knowing him as I did, I was sure he'd never be able to forgive himself. No wonder he was desperate to find a way beyond the bloodlust. Mrs. Bethany might be able to offer him the thing he wanted most in the world.

"Can we get back to the lesson here?" Patrice tapped one perfect, lilac-tinted nail against the mirror. "Okay. It helps if you have some sense of a draft, or a breeze, some idea of which way the wraith is traveling. If they're visible, easy. If not, you have to pay close attention to things like the chill in the air, any signs of frost, so on and so forth. And you want to angle the mirror perpendicular to that direction."

"You just hold it out there like a catcher's mitt, and the wraith flies right into it?"

"If only." Patrice hesitated. "Essentially, you have to think of your own death."

Caught short, I said, "Why?"

"Not just think about. Be one with. It's like you have to reach inside yourself and sort of . . . resonate on a dead frequency, I guess. Find the way that you're like the wraiths. That's what pulls them into the mirror—they're coming close to you, because of that resonance, and then that weird mirror mojo does its own thing."

She didn't have to explain "weird mirror mojo" to me. One of the unsolvable puzzles of being a vampire was why mirrors stopped showing reflections when a vampire had been too long without blood; the phenomenon didn't make any sense, and yet it was true. The simple physical property of reflection had a power to it none of us understood, but all of us respected.

Patrice continued, "It should work better for you than for vampires, as I guess you can resonate with other wraiths pretty easily. But this trick wouldn't be much use to a human."

"Okay. Sounds simple enough."

"Sounds simple," she scoffed. "It takes a few tries to learn, or at least it did for me."

Our eyes met, and her mask of indifference fell. I must have looked terrified.

"They frighten me," I said. "I am one, but—I don't know."

"You're strong, Bianca." Patrice spoke in a whisper. I'd never seen her this serious before, or this sincere. "Stronger than I ever would've thought, for somebody so young. If anybody can face them down, it's you."

"I don't know if I'm scared they'll hurt me, or . . ."

"Or what?"

"Or if they'll take me away from here, from Lucas and the rest of you. Keep me from ever coming back."

Patrice shook her head. The lamp behind her made her curls seem to glow. "Not you. I know you'll always find your way home."

I wished I could be as certain.

Seeing my reluctance, Patrice sat up and smoothed her tailored uniform back into perfect order. "What we need to do is give you more of a home to come back to."

"Where are we going?" Lucas asked as I led him up the winding stairs of the guys' tower. "Is this more fun than astronomy?"

"You always acted like you were interested in my astronomy!"

"I was. Just more interested in you."

"It's a secret," I said, ruffling his hair as a cool breeze. "You'll see when we get there."

Samuel Younger came down the stairs as we went up, and I could sense Lucas tensing as they came close to each other. Samuel said, "Talking to yourself, freak?"

"Sometimes that's what you've gotta do for some intelligent conversation," Lucas answered. Samuel flipped him off but kept going down the stairs.

Once we were truly alone again, I said, "We've *got* to watch that."

"We do okay. Besides, it's crazy what people won't notice."

By this time Lucas and I were almost to the top of the tower—the old records room. "Anyway, Patrice and I were thinking that it's not good for any of us to be alone so much."

"I'm never alone as long as I've got you."

As Lucas said this, he opened the door to reveal the group gathered within: Patrice, who was smoothing a scarf on one of the dusty trunks before sitting on it; Vic and Ranulf, who seemed to have brought his movie posters and an inflatable chair; and Balthazar, who was blowing smoke from his cigarette out the window. Somebody's iPod and speaker dock had been parked in the corner, turned up about as loud as it could be without attracting attention.

While Lucas gaped at this, I whispered, "We'll always have each other—but we can have this, too."

"Hey, guys!" Vic was the first to spot us. "We thought we'd

try to cheer this place up. Nothing like some vintage Elvis movie posters to add a touch of class."

"I could make some other suggestions," Patrice said, in a tone of voice that suggested "a touch of class" was not what had happened here. But she was smiling.

"Is this safe?" Lucas said.

Balthazar stubbed out his cigarette on the stone windowsill. "I don't see why not. We might get caught, but they'll probably think we're just hanging out up here."

"And we *are* going to do some hanging out," I said, "but seriously, we need a place Mrs. Bethany doesn't know about. A place to . . . strategize. Figure out what she's up to. Find a way to communicate better with the wraiths. All of that. I can't just keep muttering to you guys between classes."

"There's no reason for anybody to realize Bianca's up here with us," Patrice agreed. "And if someone overheard a lot of us talking, they wouldn't think anything of it. She's right. If we keep meeting up with her one on one, it sounds like we've started talking to ourselves, and *that* makes people wonder. Besides, Bianca can leave something here to help anchor her. It would be good for her to be hooked in to a place, as well as to people."

Vic's initial cheer had faded somewhat, and he and Lucas studied each other warily. Lucas said, "I'm not sure about—about this."

About being around Vic, he meant. About being around any human for long.

Vic blurted out, "I'm daubed."

"What?" Lucas looked confused; I couldn't blame him.

"I mean, I got my parents to send me some holy water, which took, like, some serious explaining, and now I think they believe I want to become a priest, which, come on, *hardly*, but they sent it. I keep it in a cologne bottle on my desk. And now I'm daubed." Vic yanked open the neck of his shirt; his hula-girl painted tie swung slightly. "Holy water, daubed all over my neck. So even if you did lose it and bite me, which I'm hoping you're not going to do, it would burn. Like biting into a—a . . . jalapeño pepper. Me equals jalapeño pepper. So you'd back off immediately." He glanced around at the rest of us. "Right?"

"Um, maybe?" That was as much as Patrice could come up with; the rest of us had nothing.

Lucas obviously was as nonplussed as we were, but slowly, he nodded. "You know, weirdly, that helps. I don't think we should be alone up here, but—yeah. Okay."

Vic relaxed a little. There was still distance between them, but less. Maybe Lucas could get the hang of being around a human if it was one he couldn't easily bite; maybe their friendship could start to heal. "Come on, man. I haven't kicked your ass at chess in more than a year. Time for you to learn some humility."

Ranulf said, "He now challenges you because he can no longer defeat me." Vic mock-shoved him away from the chessboard.

Lucas handed me my bracelet, and I slipped it on, taking form again. For the first time in what felt like forever, I could just spend time with my friends like anybody else. It was as close to normal as I could possibly get. "This is going to work. You'll see."

"Yeah," Lucas said. But I knew he remained uneasy about Vic and the rest of it.

*Give it time,* I told myself, and him, too.

As dusk came earlier and the leaves began to cover the ground more thickly than the branches of trees, Lucas gave me back my bracelet for good. He kept my brooch, so I could reach him at any time. But, at Patrice's suggestion, I hid a small box beneath a loose stone in the wall, and I stored the bracelet there. That way I could reach it anytime I wanted to turn solid.

"If anything happened to me or my stuff, I wouldn't want you to be stuck," Lucas said as he placed it into my hand.

"Nothing's going to happen," I insisted, but I knew he was right. I just couldn't have guessed how quickly events would prove it.

Later that night, Lucas and I decided it was time for me to try entering his dreams again. "This time I'll know you're coming," he said, obviously trying hard to psych himself up for it. "That's going to help me break out of the pattern of the nightmare."

His one assumption—the way he matter-of-factly said *nightmare*—told me that all his dreams were nightmares, now.

"It's going to be okay," I said. Although I felt sure it was true, it felt a little like a lie. I hadn't mentioned the mysterious scratches I'd received during his dream about the fight with

Erich. They had stopped hurting very quickly and had completely vanished after only a few days. Besides, they were only scratches. How much could something like that injure me?

Lucas, I decided, was already too worried about me. If I got some kind of mystical bruise or scratch while visiting his dreams, it wouldn't mean much afterward—but if he was concerned about it before we began, it could infect his mind and maybe his dreams. He needed an escape from that anxiety, not another reason for it. I knew it was best to remain silent.

After hours, I drifted downward into Lucas's and Balthazar's room, where they were clearly in the last stages of getting ready for bed. I didn't announce myself—I knew Lucas would sense my presence—but wished I had when Balthazar promptly stripped off his uniform.

His whole uniform.

"Uh, Balthazar?" Lucas said.

"Yeah?" Balthazar threw his boxers in the laundry hamper. I was trying hard not to look, but what sliver of a view I'd gotten was exactly the kind of thing that made me want to look more.

"You get that we're not exactly alone, right?"

Balthazar froze for a second, then quickly grabbed a pillow and held it in front of himself. "When I said that about following me into the shower, I was joking, Bianca!"

I traced a shaky word in lines of frost across their window: *Sorry!*

Lucas scowled. "When were you two joking about her showering with you?"

Balthazar, trying to get his bathrobe on without dropping the pillow, scowled right back. "I'm going to the communal bathrooms for privacy. Which is pathetic, but that's what we're stuck with." He grabbed his pajamas and hurried out.

Into Lucas's ear, I whispered, "I wasn't talking about showering with Balthazar."

"I know," he said, flopping back onto the bed. "I trust you. I just like giving him hell sometimes. It's fun."

"Ready?"

He nodded, taking a deep breath, as if already trying to calm himself toward sleep. "Yeah. Let's try it."

Within half an hour, Lucas was sound asleep, and Balthazar was apparently taking the world's longest shower. I waited for the rapid movements of Lucas's eyelids and thick lashes before gathering myself together and taking the long, deep dive into what I hoped would be the world of his dreams.

That world took substance around me. However, my triumph faded as I realized where we were: in the shabby, abandoned movie theater where Lucas had been killed. He stood several steps ahead of me in the lobby. One hand clutched a stake, and the other covered his nose and mouth. I didn't understand why until I smelled smoke and realized that was the reason for the haze around us.

From the movie screen came a warm flickering that I knew wasn't a movie—it was a fire.

*Yeah, it's another nightmare,* I realized. *Now to see if I can wake him up.*

Before I could speak, Lucas said, "Charity."

"Hello, baby." Charity emerged from the shadows. She didn't say *baby* like it meant honey or sweetheart, more like she was talking about an actual infant. The firelight danced in her pale curls. Her long, lacy dress was clean for once—only in dreams. "How is my dear baby tonight?"

"Let me go," he said. His voice broke on the words.

"Couldn't if I wanted to." She smiled triumphantly. "And I don't want to."

"Lucas," I said. "It's okay. Don't look at her. She's just a dream. Look at me."

But he didn't look at me. I stepped between him and Charity, hoping to break the dream spell that kept him from fully recognizing me, but it did no good. He only looked through me, as if I weren't even there.

"Are you searching for Bianca?" Charity's concern would have sounded genuine to anyone who didn't actually know her. "She might be trapped in the fire. You must save her!"

Lucas ran from her, straight toward the flames. As I whirled to go after him, Charity said, "He's mine now, Bianca. You'll never have him again."

How was it possible for Charity to see me when Lucas hadn't been aware of my presence, when she was only part of his nightmare?

Her eyes locked with mine. Her smile changed character until it was less defiant, more conspiratorial. Almost as if we were in on a joke together. How could that happen in Lucas's dream?

It couldn't.

I realized she wasn't part of his nightmare. She was the cause. This wasn't a dream of Charity; this was the real thing. Here. In Lucas's mind.

She must have seen the realization on my face, because her grin widened, showing her fangs. "I told you. Lucas is mine."

# Chapter Twelve

"HOW ARE YOU DOING THIS?" I SHOUTED OVER the crackling of the fire. "How are you in Lucas's head?"

"I created Lucas." Charity twirled her finger through one of her pale blond curls as though she were flirting. Having died at fourteen, she looked too young to be so evil, baby softness in her cheeks. "I sired him. That means his mind and all the rest of him belong to me now, and forever."

Nobody had ever mentioned this to me before. It would never have applied in my case; as the child of two vampires, I would never have required a "sire" to turn me. Although I'd always known the relationship carried with it a powerful bond, I'd never realized it extended so far.

"Don't make him dream about this." I hated to beg her, but I didn't know what else to do. "He has enough to deal with."

Charity cocked her head to one side as she came closer to me, creepy and threatening even in the realm of imagination. "I didn't create this nightmare. Lucas did. Or was it you? You're the one he keeps trying to save."

From deep within the burning theater, I heard my own scream.

"Over and over, they threaten you," Charity said. "Over and over, they kill you. Some vampires dream about their murders; others about their remorse. But not Lucas. The phantoms of his mind, the thousands of nightmares he endures, they're all about one thing—losing you time and again."

And in waking, Lucas didn't have the comfort of knowing that it was only a dream. I really had died. Being with him as a ghost couldn't entirely heal that wound. By making him experience that moment over and over, Charity kept Lucas on the verge of losing it and turning into a killer.

"They're his dreams," she whispered into my ear. "I just make them worse. I make the fire burn hotter and the blood flow faster, so he can be even more afraid for you. Instead of drinking his blood, now I drink his pain."

"I hate you."

"His pain, and yours."

I ran from her into the theater. It would've been faster to just think myself to Lucas's side, but quickly I remembered that, in dream worlds, I didn't have ghostly powers. The old human limitations held me fast.

As I ran, I heard Lucas calling, "Hang on, Bianca! I'm coming!"

The scene in the theater horrified me. The movie screen itself was on fire, falling away from the wall in blackening strips that writhed and curled in the heat. Plastic cornices on the walls were melting into bubbling streaks. And in the seats, which had been empty on that night, were dead bodies, lying crumpled and bloody. Every one of their throats had been torn out.

*They're the victims of vampires,* I realized. *The ones Lucas has seen. The ones he's scared he'll create.* Some of the corpses were on fire, too.

Disgusted and nauseated, I stumbled away from the corpses and fell backward. As I hit the ground, I felt the sharp lash of fire across my calf. With a gasp I pushed myself up again to see a red, blistering weal just under my knee; a piece of still-smoldering wood on the ground must have burned me.

The danger was becoming more real. I had to get us out of here. "Lucas!" I shouted.

Once again, I heard my own voice—yet not mine—calling his name as well.

Pushing my way through the smoke, eyes itching and throat raw, I finally caught a glimpse of Lucas. He was at the very front of the theater, where part of the ceiling had collapsed into a jumble of metal and timbers. Beneath the timbers, face creased in pain, lay . . . me. Or Lucas's dream version of me, anyway. My long red hair was splayed out on the floor, mirroring the blood pooling around my abdomen. The dream me was even more badly burned and blistered than I was. It was hard even to look at her.

"Lucas, no! I'm over here!" I came closer, willing him to hear me.

And he did, turning to see me. But his expression remained desperate, and he said only, "It's okay, Bianca. I'm going to get you out."

Still he hadn't broken through the powerful spell of the dream, but now I understood why Lucas believed in his illusions so desperately: Charity made sure that he would. Determined to get through to him, I started forward, but a cold hand closed fast around my wrist.

"He has to learn that he can't save you," Charity said. Her blond curls were the color of the firelight. "And you have to learn that you can't save him, because he's *mine*."

A searing jolt of power arced through me, like electrocution times a thousand. I screamed harder than I'd known I could scream—and the pain stopped.

I opened my eyes to see that I was once again hovering in Lucas's and Balthazar's dorm room. Charity had flung me out of the dream.

"What the—" Balthazar pushed himself upright just as Lucas's eyes opened wide. I must have screamed in this world as well as in the dream.

Lucas saw me and blinked hard. "Bianca?"

"I'm here!" I flung myself into his arms and hugged him tightly, willing myself to be as solid as possible. "I'm okay!"

"In the dream, you were— That didn't happen to you, did it? You didn't have to go through that?"

"No," I said, thinking only of the broken, burned version of me he had glimpsed. But as my leg brushed against the side of his bed, I winced, and Lucas looked down in concern. Silvery blood oozed through the pajama bottoms, revealing the long line of the burn against my calf.

"Bianca!" Lucas slid off the bed to look more closely. He peeled the pajamas upward, which stung—but made him wince harder. Of course; my wraith's blood was burning him. He just didn't care. Wisps of smoke drifted up from his singed fingers as he examined the wound. "This really happened. Things that happen in my dreams have the power to hurt you."

"It'll heal. It's not anything major. Once I've faded out once, the worst will be over." Although I tried to sound reassuring, my voice shook despite myself. The burn hurt worse than I'd thought I could hurt, after death.

Balthazar, rubbing his head sleepily, wandered over to our side of the room. His eyes widened as he saw my burn. "How did that happen?"

I turned to him, fear instantly transmuted into anger. "Why didn't you tell us about a vampire's sire?"

"What are you talking about?" Taken aback by my shift in mood, Balthazar didn't seem to know how to answer. "You both know what a sire is, right? I don't see how you could *not* know."

"I mean, the part about the sire coming into your dreams." I rose from Lucas's bed and stepped closer to Balthazar, close enough to make him straighten up. My leg ached, but I ignored it. "Why didn't you tell us that?"

Balthazar's face fell, and he sagged backward as he realized what I was saying. "Damn it," he swore. "Charity."

Lucas went pale. "Wait—in my dreams—Charity's *real*?"

"Did you assume your sainted little sister wouldn't do that?" I demanded. "Or was it just more fun to let us figure it out for ourselves?"

Balthazar's mood shifted so fast it startled me. He got right in my face, his expression twisted in anger darker than I'd ever seen from him before. "First, nothing about this is fun. Not for you, not for Lucas, and not for me."

"Then why didn't you—"

"Shut. Up." Balthazar said. Lucas rose from his knees at that, maybe ready to get into the argument and defend me, but Balthazar never glanced toward him. Our eyes remained locked. "Second, I didn't warn you guys because it doesn't happen often. The sire has to really want to mess with somebody like that, and besides, doing that—it weakens a vampire for days. Maybe weeks. That's why nobody does it. If she's taking over Lucas's dreams every night, Charity would have to be . . . beyond obsessed."

"In other words, Charity," I retorted.

Lucas wasn't part of the argument, but what we were saying had its own effect on him. "Charity's really in my head," he murmured. "She's the one making me so crazy."

Balthazar grimaced. "Yeah, she is. It's sick and twisted—and yes, I understand by now that Charity's sick. Even when I miss her, even when I think I can fix her—" His voice broke, but he kept going. "I always know she's broken."

"Balthazar—" I said, more softly, trying to give him an out.

"God, you cannot be quiet and let anyone else talk, can you?" He got closer to me—closer than he'd been at any moment other than the times we'd kissed. "Third, and last, I want you to get one thing straight. Whatever mistakes I made after you died, I'm not the one who turned Lucas. Charity did. And I didn't force you to let Lucas rise from the dead. So stop blaming me for it."

With that, Balthazar turned, grabbed his bathrobe and cigarettes, and went for the door. I wanted to protest but knew it would just drive him over the edge. But Lucas said, "Hey, Balthazar."

He paused with his hand on the knob. "What?"

"You shouldn't have yelled." Lucas winced and then said, "But you're not wrong."

Balthazar simply stalked out, slamming the door behind him. Down the hall, I could hear a couple of people muttering about the noise.

Lucas, hearing it, too, said, "Hope nobody recognized your name when he was shouting."

"I can't believe you took his side."

"I'm on your side. No matter what." Lucas put his hands on my shoulders, which were solid enough to bear the touch. "But you've been giving him attitude at the slightest excuse ever since—ever since we died, I guess. That is never going to stop sounding weird."

"He shouldn't have taken you along that night!"

"I shouldn't have gone with him. But it was my choice, my call. Besides—" Lucas clearly didn't like admitting this, but he went ahead. "Losing you hit him almost as hard as it did me. If I wasn't responsible for my actions that day, neither was he."

I drifted slightly farther from Lucas, allowing myself to float to the windowsill, where I could tuck my knees against my chest. Hugging myself like a child, I realized, a kind of comfort I hadn't outgrown. At the moment, I felt like there were way too many things I should've outgrown, but hadn't.

"I know how badly you want someone to blame," Lucas said. "Someone who's here, now, so you can give him hell. But Balthazar's our friend, Bianca. He's done a lot for us."

Slowly I nodded. "I feel stupid."

"You're not stupid." After a moment he said, "You thought about destroying me before I rose as a vampire. Balthazar talked you out of it."

"Yeah. But I let him talk me out of it." The heaviness of that unspoken question was too much to bear, now; I had to know. "Did I do the wrong thing? Lucas, I love you so much. I couldn't let you go. But I realize . . . I realize it's what you probably wanted."

"It's done. I know you made your choices out of love. That's enough," Lucas said. Although I still felt horrible—both for even having considered destroying him, and for not carrying through—I knew he forgave me. I wished it truly could be enough.

"I wish I could cry."

He caressed my hand, as though he could massage away my sadness. "How's your leg?"

"Not great." I flexed it and winced. "If I fade out, it will help, though."

"We're never doing this again," Lucas said. His face was stark. "If Charity's able to hurt you in my dreams, then you can't come into them."

I remembered the first dream we had shared, back when Lucas had still been alive. We'd held each other in a bookstore where we'd hung out, while the night sky miraculously stretched out overhead. It had been so beautiful and romantic; at the time, I had thought it was the only consolation we would have for my being dead. Now that, too, was lost.

My face must have fallen, because Lucas kissed my forehead, my cheek, and then my mouth, the lightest and most tender of touches. "It's okay." He didn't look as depressed as I felt. Given the burdens on him, I would've thought the realization that Charity was torturing him in his dreams would be all it took to send him over the edge. Instead, he seemed steadier. "I mean, think about it. Balthazar's heard of this, the invading of the dreams. Apparently lots of vampires have. That means they might know some way to handle it. A block or—or something like that."

"Maybe." That was encouraging. I brightened despite myself. "It's possible."

"Even if Balthazar doesn't know how to push Charity back, Mrs. Bethany probably does. Gotta be something, right?"

"Right," I said absently. Suddenly Charity didn't seem like the only problem we had to deal with.

Lucas wanted to trust Mrs. Bethany. He wanted to share his deepest fears with her, and to turn to her for help. She might be able to save him when I couldn't. And in that moment, I couldn't blame him for not caring about the traps she'd laid.

It seemed to me as though everyone and everything— Charity, Mrs. Bethany, and his own blood hunger—was fighting me for Lucas's soul.

The next morning, I returned to the fencing room. Although the class had ended for the day, the room wasn't empty. Balthazar stood in his fencing whites, mask pushed atop his head as he wiped sweat from his brow. After the others in the class had finished, he'd stayed behind to practice his technique—to fight invisible opponents that existed only in his mind.

I remembered that he often did that when he was stressed out; last night had been as rough for him as for me.

Slowly I took shape in the far corner of the room, giving him plenty of time to leave if he didn't want to talk. He stayed. Within a few seconds we were face-to-face again, though the whole broad expanse of the wooden floor lay between us.

"Hey," I began. Lame, but maybe it was better to keep it simple at first.

"Hello." Balthazar tested the weight of his blade in one hand, then the other, like the saber was new to him instead of an old friend. "Here to practice?"

"I never was any good at fencing."

"You learned a lot. Don't knock yourself."

He could be kind to me, even now. "I'm sorry," I said. "I shouldn't have yelled at you last night. I shouldn't have yelled at you about what happened to Lucas, not ever."

Balthazar took a halfhearted stab at a nearby dummy. The steel curved into a thin arc under pressure. "I shouldn't have gone off on you like that. You were injured, and clearly you were upset."

"You didn't say anything that didn't need to be said."

"But I could've picked a better way to say it." He slipped the mask off his head and tucked it under one arm as he walked closer to me. The fencing whites had always been a good look for Balthazar, and I remembered for a moment what it had felt like to be so close to him.

I could never regret choosing Lucas, but that didn't mean I wasn't aware of what I'd lost when I chose.

As though he could read my thoughts, Balthazar smiled. "Friends again?"

"Yes, please." I wanted to hug him, but that was probably a bad idea.

"Actually, most of the time, when you're not upset, you're very good about listening."

Just as I was about to simply say thanks—and be relieved, since his words last night about me not shutting up had stung— I realized he might be giving me an opening. "Do I need to listen now?"

"Charity." The name fell between us like a stone. "You were right when you said I was in denial about her. You've always been right about that. And on some level, I've always known."

Already I could feel anger pricking its way back into my consciousness, but this time I forced myself to remember that it was Charity I was angry at, not Balthazar. "She's your sister." The words came out calm and steady, for which I was grateful. "You love her. How could you help it?"

"That's no excuse for letting her run wild. Letting her hurt people. Or not making myself think about what she might be doing to Lucas, and to you."

"He didn't tell you about it, though." Lucas shared his feelings so openly with me that I'd had to stop and realize that he wasn't as free with everyone else; even with the greater trust and liking between them now, Lucas would never have thought to talk to Balthazar about his bad dreams. "And you said Charity's weakening herself to do this. I wouldn't have expected that either."

"I've heard him tossing and turning in his sleep for a month now, and I never put it together. That was criminally stupid, and worth yelling at me about."

"I'm done yelling at you, okay? Forever." Guilt slumped his shoulders and darkened his eyes, so I stepped closer and gently laid a hand on his arm. "You said yourself, invading people's dreams like that—it's rare."

Balthazar nodded. "I've never done it. Never had it done to me. Charity must be sleeping almost all the time, because it would be exhausting for her. On the other hand, since she's asleep, that means she gets to be there every single time Lucas dreams. Damn it."

Only one thing mattered. "Is there a way to protect Lucas against it? Against her?"

"Not that I know of. But let me think about it." He studied my face for a few moments. "Some of what you and Lucas said last night, and that burn on your leg—it sounded like Charity goes after you in the dreams, too."

I nodded. "But she can't manipulate me as much as she does Lucas. I guess that's because it's his dream, and I'm just visiting."

"Be careful, Bianca." Balthazar's voice was unexpectedly firm. "It's Lucas's dream, and that probably does mean Charity has more influence over his mind. But when you're in the dreams—that's all of you, not just your subconscious. That's how you got burned last night. I don't know how much worse you could get injured, but you shouldn't find out."

"We're not going to try it again," I admitted.

Some of the sadness I felt must have showed, because Balthazar became gentler again. "How does your leg feel?"

"Not great, but not terrible." I pointed to show him I could move it. Whenever I became solid or nearly so, I could still sense the tight, prickly line against my calf, but the pain wasn't as bad any longer. Other, pettier fears crept into my heart, and I blurted, "Do you think Mrs. Bethany knows how to get Charity out of his dreams?"

"I doubt it." He cocked his head. "Why did that make you look . . . relieved?"

"It's weird to feel like she can help him more than I can," I admitted.

"That's what we came to Evernight Academy for, though, right? To call on the experience of everyone here, give Lucas a safe place to adjust? Mrs. Bethany is a large part of what keeps this school safe."

"I don't trust her."

"I don't exactly trust her either. But I trust her dedication to this school and the vampires who come here."

"As long as she's hunting the wraiths, she's our enemy."

Balthazar paused. "We don't know that. There's too much we don't know."

"Well, at least we agree there."

He smiled, and despite my other uncertainties, it felt so good to know our friendship was mended.

After Balthazar left to get ready for his afternoon classes, I went incorporeal and drifted through the school, deep in thought. For a while I watched my dad teaching physics, scribbling out formulas on the board with so much energy that anybody who didn't know him well would miss the sadness in his eyes.

When I couldn't take that anymore, I escaped to Mr. Yee's modern technology class, where he was explaining to a group of older, out-of-touch vampires how to operate a washing machine. As he lectured about the spin cycle, I curled in a vacant corner and mulled over everything we'd learned—and everything we hadn't.

We needed to know how to keep Charity out of Lucas's dreams, and whether I as a wraith could be hurt there, or per-haps help Lucas through it.

We needed to know how many traps were in Evernight Academy, and their locations, so I could stay safe.

Most important, we needed to know what Mrs. Bethany's plans were, not only for the sake of the wraiths, but also to be sure whether or not she could be trusted.

None of the vampires I knew and trusted had that information or could get it. That meant that if I wanted those answers—I was going to have to confront my fears.

I would have to go to the wraiths.

Determined, I straightened from my corner—to see half the class staring at me.

*Oh, crap, am I visible?* I realized that I wasn't, but that in my deep concentration on my new plan, I'd allowed a deep lacing of frost to cover the wall and the windows. To anybody in the know, that was as good as a huge blinking neon sign that said WRAITH FOUND HERE.

"Mr. Yee!" someone yelped.

"Everyone remain calm," Mr. Yee said, though his normally unshakable mood was slipping into a full-on freakout. "We'll summon Mrs. Bethany right away."

*Get out of here!* I started thinking of the different places I felt connected to, all the "subway stations" that I was capable of traveling to in an instant. Something far away would be ideal right around now—and just as fast, I realized there was a way to get out of here and pursue my latest idea.

*Philadelphia. Vic's house, where Lucas and I lived together. The attic room—*

Instantly, Evernight Academy disappeared around me, swirling around like so much fog. The vapor took new shape quickly and outlined the attic of Vic's home, with its comfortable clutter.

And Vic's mom, who was holding a couple bags of old clothes and staring right at me.

"Jerry!" she screamed, dropping the bags and scurrying for the stairs. "It's the ghost again! We have to call those people on cable TV!"

As the attic door shut, a voice behind me said, "Great, thanks. Now I'm going to have camera crews running around up here, and a bunch of nerds pretending they know how I died."

"Hi, Maxie," I said, turning to smile at her. She didn't look thrilled to see me, at least not until I said what I'd come for. "I'm ready to meet Christopher."

Her entire face lit up. "You're really doing it," Maxie said. "You're joining the wraiths."

# Chapter Thirteen

"EVERYTHING WILL BE DIFFERENT, NOW THAT you're one of us." Maxie was aglow—literally—in a golden haze of joy. "Wait and see."

"I've been one of you ever since I died."

"Not for real. Not while you were hanging out with the vampires. This is going to be so much better."

I didn't tell Maxie that I had no intention of abandoning Lucas or anybody else. It felt uncomfortably like lying, and I was beyond tired of lies. But I wasn't ready to fully trust the wraiths just yet.

"So," I began. "How do we do this? Finding Christopher, I mean." I glanced around. "I don't guess he hangs out in this attic with you."

"Of course not," she scoffed. "Like Christopher spends any time on the mortal plane." Then she paused. "I take that back, actually. He comes here every once in a while."

"To the attic?"

"To the mortal plane, dumbass. But he comes here only when he has a purpose. Like trying to help a lost wraith find his way. Stuff like that. Christopher doesn't haunt."

"Like you, you mean?"

I intended that to be a jab at Maxie, to point out that she hadn't surrendered the mortal world entirely either. But she nodded, solemn and sweet. "If I know you're coming with us, then I can let this place go at last. Even—even Vic." She gazed down at the spot on the carpet where Vic had once sat to summon her. "That's going to be hard, but I can do it."

"Why *me*? You and I know each other, I guess, but we're hardly best friends—"

"I'll let Christopher explain." Maxie practically sparkled with anticipation. "Ready?"

I couldn't answer that question without knowing what I was supposed to be ready for. "Maybe?"

"Fade out with me. Come on."

For some reason, it was difficult for me to fade out this time, where it never had been before. Maybe it was a little like trying to fall asleep when it's important to get some rest, so of course you lie awake for hours. But as Maxie turned into a pure glow, I managed to follow her lead. Slowly the world around us turned into nothing but blue-gray mist, a mysterious haze that had no up, no down, no center, and no boundaries. Maxie's glow twinkled slightly amid the swirling mists, then was gone.

*Okay, Bianca.* Her voice wasn't something I heard so much

anymore—just something I perceived without really knowing how. *You have to let go.*

*Let go of what?*

*Everything.*

*You mean, Lucas and my friends—*

*No, I mean, EVERYTHING. Of yourself. Just pull it all tight within yourself and then . . . let go.*

What was that supposed to mean? Without much optimism, I tried doing what Maxie said. As I tried it, though, I started to get some sense of it—and then I let go.

It was terrifying. Like discovering you had the ability to make your heart stop beating, or to make gravity stop working. To turn every law of the universe upside down. There wasn't any blue-gray mist now; there was only total nothingness, both alien and yet weirdly familiar, like something so vast that I'd simply never been able to see it before, though it had always been around me. I floated free within my mind—or something's mind—not entirely myself any longer.

*Will I ever be able to get back?* At that moment, it seemed like there could be no returning from something like this. Was this what lay on the other side of the traps? *Lucas, I'm sorry, I didn't realize what this would mean.*

Then I heard another voice, deeper and masculine: "Be here."

Instantly, I was myself again. I stood on ground, saw light, had a body. As I blinked, this new place took shape around me, and at first the only thing I could do was stare.

How can I describe it? I stood in the heart of a city, amid an enormous bustling crowd, that was simultaneously the most terrifying and the most beautiful place I'd ever seen. A brilliantly painted Greek temple stood in front of us, next to a squat, sturdy stone turret and, beyond that, a small grove of plum trees with thick clouds of clover beneath the branches. Beyond them were skyscrapers, houses, tents, hills, a castle, a chalet—every kind of structure and landscape imaginable, some glorious, others in ruins. Next to the cobblestone road Maxie and I stood upon wound a small, silt brown river, rushing so rapidly over rocks that I felt sure, if I fell in, I would be swept away by the current. Around us thronged people in all kinds of dress, from jeans to Victorian finery to Bedouin robes to togas. They could see me—a few glanced my way—but nobody approached. My old timidity in crowds had returned a hundredfold, so I was grateful.

As I looked down at myself, I realized I wasn't in the pajamas I'd died in any longer. "It's my green sweater!" I said. "I could never find it after we moved to Evernight. It was my favorite—and hey, these jeans—I loved them, too, but . . . didn't I outgrow them?"

"Pretty much everything you've ever lost can come back to you here," Maxie said, preening in a thick furry coat. Her hair was sleekly bobbed now, and she wore shiny silver shoes with buckles—the height of flapper fashion. This is what she'd looked like when she was alive, I realized, when she'd been at her happiest. "I'll warn you now—that includes some of the bad stuff along with the good stuff. You just never know."

Now that I'd wrapped my mind around something as mundane as our clothes, I began to comprehend the broader implications of what we were seeing. "Maxie, are we . . . no, this can't be heaven." I felt sure heaven wouldn't be quite so dirty, and despite the beauty of many of the buildings around us, this place was filthy. Magnificent and yet vaguely disgusting—actually, it reminded me a lot of my first impression of New York City.

"You have not yet reached paradise," said the masculine voice. "This is a place of refuge, I think, but I would never claim to understand it. It's best to accept where we are on its own terms."

I turned to see him—dressed in his nineteenth-century finery, with his long, thick brown hair. He was an adult, but not quite middle-aged yet—or, at least, he hadn't been when he died. His solid, firm-jawed face was like those I'd seen in old-fashioned paintings of great soldiers or admirals, going into battle beneath improbably beautiful skies: broad shoulders, slim waist, firm gaze, and piercing eyes.

Maxie grinned as she snuggled into her coat. "Christopher, I brought Bianca here with me. Bianca, this is Christopher."

"We've met," I said, though that was inadequate to describe the strange ways in which our paths had crossed. When he had first begun appearing to me during my junior year at Evernight, he'd threatened me so fearsomely that I'd been terrified of him; he'd also prevented Charity's tribe from murdering me and Lucas last summer. I started at the beginning: "I'm pretty sure you two tried to kill me once."

Christopher didn't deny it; he didn't even seem fazed. "You had only so much life to live. Sooner or later, you would have become either a vampire or a wraith. We came to you at Evernight when you were drinking blood—becoming closer to your vampire self."

"You guys wanted me for yourselves," I said.

"And for your sake as well," Christopher replied. "Becoming a vampire would have been less a sacrifice for you than for most, but so much less than you have the potential to become."

"Besides, vampires are gross," Maxie said. I glared at her, but she just shrugged. "No offense, but come on. They're *dead bodies*. Walking around. Eww."

"I assure you, that did not enter into my decision." Christopher looked slightly pained at Maxie's rudeness. "Bianca, as a vampire, you would have been merely one among many. As a wraith, you have powers beyond almost any other of our kind, and abilities you have only begun to grasp."

"That's why you saved me and Lucas from Charity this summer. Just to stop me from being turned into a vampire. It's never been . . . personal, for you. Killing me or saving me."

He looked amused. "How could it be personal when we have only just met?" Apparently he could see how angry that made me, because he quickly added, "When you have been dead as long as I, your perspective is altered. But no less true."

Great, I had centuries of undeath waiting for me before this was going to make sense. I decided there was no point in freaking out about it, though. I'd become a wraith, and I had to deal with that reality. Christopher was the only person who could help me through it.

Not the wraith leader, Maxie had said—apparently there was no such thing. But Christopher was the most powerful among the wraiths, for reasons I hadn't yet learned. He not only had significant power of his own, but he also seemed to suggest that I had greater powers still waiting to manifest. Discovering my own abilities, coming into my own as a wraith, meant accepting Christopher. I decided it was a small price to pay. "Okay. Let bygones be bygones, or whatever. I just want to understand."

"Will you walk with me?"

"Sure."

Taking the hint, Maxie waved good-bye to us, hurrying off to something that looked sort of like an old-fashioned soda shop. One of her shiny-buckled shoes caught on the cobblestone path, making her stumble—even here, it appeared, you could fall—but she caught herself. That left Christopher and I alone in this mysterious place. "If we're not in heaven," I asked, "how did we get . . . here?"

"Those of us who have achieved clarity after death, who no longer need to haunt the mortal realms, bring that which we loved here with us." Christopher's wavy brown hair ruffled in a soft breeze that smelled like the seashore—simultaneously fresh and foul. On a hill in the distance ahead of us, I saw an Egyptian riding along the road in a chariot, just ahead of an old pickup truck that spewed exhaust from the tailpipe. "Not the people we loved, alas. Each individual's soul is their possession alone. But the places that mattered to us, keepsakes of the best and worst of our lives—all of that finds us here, where everything lost can be found once again."

*The land of lost things*, I thought. It seemed to be as good a name for it as anything else. "If ghosts can come here, why do they bother hanging around and haunting people? This beats lurking in somebody's attic."

"Not every wraith can come here." His dark eyes could be unsettlingly intense, more so now that he was in his human form. "Most of us are created by murder. And only the foulest of murders, none committed in the heat of passion—but premeditated, selfish killings that arise from betrayal."

Christopher's voice grew rough, and I wondered what had happened to him, and to Maxie. To the many ghosts bustling around us on the road.

Composed again, he continued. "That kind of death is not easily overcome. Most of us awaken as wraith alone, unable to believe that we have passed away, that we have been so betrayed, or that heaven is delayed for us, perhaps forever. Sometimes we see those we thought loved us glorying in our demise. Is it any wonder that so many become—twisted? Sick inside?"

"I guess not." The thought of it turned my stomach. "Did that happen to you? Somebody you loved—"

"Friends," he said quietly. "Men I thought faithful comrades had plotted against me. Of those I held dearest to me, only my beloved wife was true. And the worst fate awaited her."

That sounded seriously bad. I wondered if the friends had

killed her, too, or left her alone and broke to starve—back in those days, a woman on her own might not have been able to get a job, or maybe inherit money, though I wasn't sure about that. Or maybe one of the killers had insinuated himself into her life and married her, without her ever knowing that he was responsible for Christopher's death. Any of those options seemed too terrible to contemplate, and I definitely wasn't going to pry further. I changed the subject, asking, "So, you're telling me that most wraiths get stuck. They can't get over their own murders, and it drives them crazy."

"Essentially. If our murderers are caught, it provides some sense of justice. That helps many of us let go and ascend." Christopher looked up above us longingly—still, after all this time, waiting for heaven. "But many are not caught, and for others, justice is not enough to heal the wounds. Those remain on earth forever, growing sicker and stranger, and sometimes dangerous. For many of them, there is no chance that they could ever be restored enough to come here. They become as evil as the forces that destroyed them."

"I've heard of wraiths like that," I said. "But the rest of you—everyone here—why aren't they in heaven? Or whatever it is that follows this?"

"They remain anchored to the mortal world."

"Anchored." I'd been hearing that a lot lately. "What does that mean?"

Christopher led me around a fountain, ornate and elaborate, perhaps something from the Renaissance; instead of burbling merrily, the water inside was motionless and dank, overgrown with algae that slicked the stone. "An anchor is someone or something that ties you to the earth. The best anchors keep you sane and strong. They can be sources of deep, lasting love." He glanced back at the soda shop where we'd left Maxie; I could just make her form out as she sat at the counter, drinking something out of a tall frosted glass. "Maxine was on the verge of leaving the mortal world behind entirely when the small boy in her house discovered her and began reading her stories."

"Vic."

"Yes. Her love for him has tethered her to the earth once more—much to her chagrin, I suspect." For the first time, I heard a glint of humor in Christopher's voice. "Although she will not admit this, she could let go of him at any time, and trust that his life will be happy and full. But she has already lingered eighty years after death; another decade, or several, will make little difference."

"The best anchors, you said. There are other ones—bad ones?"

"Sometimes it is not love that binds us to our anchors, but obsession. Sickness. When that happens, the wraith becomes more twisted over time." As Christopher spoke, I remembered the wraith that had haunted and tormented Raquel. No doubt this was an example of what he was talking about. "The danger of this is so great that even wraiths better anchored, such as Maxine and myself, consider any ties to the mortal world fundamentally unfortunate. Even we hope to move on someday, as hard as it will be to let our loved ones go."

I started to ask him whether I was anchored, but I already knew that I was. Lucas, my parents, Balthazar, Vic, Ranulf, Patrice, Raquel—they kept me down-to-earth, so to speak. Even if I could let go of them, I didn't want to. One thought occurred to me and made me frown. "Who is the ancient Egyptian guy hanging on to?"

Christopher smiled. "He helped to design the pyramids and remains rather proud of them. I believe he likes to return to Giza in the mornings and watch the sun rise there."

In the distant sky, darker clouds swirled, illuminated briefly by a flash that might have been lightning. "Okay, you guys really wanted me here," I said. "What is it that makes me so powerful or special or whatever? Besides being able to form a body, I mean. Though that is pretty awesome."

He faced me, serious once more. "You already know that you can travel within all our realms, and you can do so more easily than any of us—even me."

"Maxie can do it."

"At times, but not easily, save for when she is in your presence," Christopher said. "You are able to sense other wraiths, something very few of us can do. Sometimes we are invisible to one another, particularly for those who remain lost and frightened in the mortal world. Once we have established communication with each other, it is easier, but it is never easy."

I realized what he was getting at. "You want me to help you find those people. To make them let go of the sickness inside before they get permanently screwed up."

"While they have a chance to come here and find restoration."

"You want me to help find every ghost in the *whole world*?"

He shook his head. "Most can find their way here eventually. But those who cannot—for their sakes, and the sakes of those they come to torment on earth—you have the power to reach them. To guide them. To help them find their way here. You can travel between worlds, Bianca. You are a bridge between the worlds of the living and the dead."

Those distant clouds weren't so distant anymore; the entire sky seemed to me to be darkening, although sunlight shone down on everyone else. The cool, damp breeze that rushed through my hair didn't touch anybody else on the road. I realized that the skies above were, for each person here, a reflection of their spirit; as I grew more afraid and unsure, the storm came.

Christopher didn't answer. "This work is important. It will demand much of you. But the good you could do is beyond measure."

I agreed with him. It sounded worthwhile—more than worthwhile. Important. The kind of thing I'd wanted to spend my afterlife doing. But the idea of letting go of the people I loved held me back. "Why don't you do it? You're so super-powerful and everything, according to Maxie."

"I was not born to the wraiths. I have not your natural power. My talents are meaner, and self-taught over time."

"Why don't you train everyone else here to do the same?"

"They are not as powerfully anchored to the mortal realm as I have been," he said. His gaze was distant. "My connection has lasted longer than most, more intimately than most."

Lightning flashed, and I felt rain begin to patter onto my hair and jeans, despite the fact that nobody else was getting wet. "I can't. I'm sorry—I see that what you want me to be is a good thing—that it's important—but I can't."

Christopher didn't look as discouraged by my refusal as I would've thought. "You have time to consider the matter," he said. He was right, of course; we literally had eternity to go over this. As I edged away from him, already eager to leave, Christopher hurriedly added, "You need not be entirely separate from those you care for, even here. Your powers would allow you to hear them."

"Really?" Not that this was that big a selling point for me—I mean, I wanted to remain with the people I loved, not just able to reach them. But knowing that those bonds survived here was encouraging, somehow.

Apparently encouraged himself, Christopher nodded. "Reach into the depths of your own spirit until you find, within, someone that you love."

What was that supposed to mean, reach into my own spirit? Then I remembered what I'd thought about the skies overhead. They were a reflection of my innermost self; I should concentrate on the darkening storm.

I closed my eyes but could still see the brilliance of the lightning through my eyelids. Cold raindrops spattered on my face, but I held out my arms, accepting the storm as part of myself.

And then my eyes flew open wide as I heard my name—as a scream.

*Someone's in trouble,* I realized. My first thought was Lucas, but I realized that the voice in the thunder sounded familiar.

It sounded like my father.

# Chapter Fourteen

"DAD," I WHISPERED. I COULD HEAR HIM—THOUGH "hear" wasn't quite the right word. It was more a matter of sensing him, feeling his fear and anguish through the sound of the thunder and the chill of the wind whipping around me.

"Will you go to him?" Christopher didn't seem to approve or disapprove; he just watched, like he was taking my measure.

Could I face my father again? Face the risk that he would reject me forever, or turn against me?

Then the thunder rumbled one more time, and I felt the fear in my father's heart more strongly than the fear in my own. Something terrible was happening, something much more important than the answers I needed. If Christopher turned against me now—if he tried to trap me in this place—I had to find Dad if I could.

"Yes," I said. "I'm going."

Christopher wasn't angry; that was the first moment I felt that perhaps I could trust him. "Then I shall hope for your return."

"I'll come back," I promised Christopher. "I want to know more."

"And I want to tell you."

"How do I reach my father?"

"When the person you love wishes for you so desperately," Christopher said, "you will find it impossible to be anywhere else."

His face looked sorrowful as he said it, so much so that I wondered who had wished for him. But I couldn't worry about Christopher for very long, not with Dad in danger or despair or whatever it was that clouded the skies above. I couldn't worry about myself, either. My fears had been only a kind of selfishness; I saw that now. This land of lost things gave everything, whether seen or unseen, a brilliant clarity.

I closed my eyes and thought of my father. For the first time in months—since I'd died—I didn't just think of the *idea* of him. I let myself remember so fully that it filled my heart. Tucking me into bed when I was a baby. Slow-dancing with Mom while Dinah Washington played on his old hi-fi. Making small talk with our neighbors in Arrowwood in an effort to fit in. Taking me to the beach because I loved it, though he hated sunlight. Griping about having to get up early in the morning, with his hair sticking out all over the place. Acting out his resurrection from the dead with one of my old Ken dolls, to an audience of one very interested little girl and some highly surprised Barbies. Everything that made him *Dad*.

When I opened my eyes, he was there.

Or rather, I was back with him, at Evernight. Night had fallen—no telling how long it had been since I'd left. It had felt like minutes but could have been hours or days. My father stood in the center of the school library—

*The library!* I thought, terrified, remembering the trap that had been here. But Lucas had taken it away, and perhaps it hadn't been replaced. I felt fine. My father, on the other hand, seemed to be bracing himself against high winds. No, not "seemed to"—a gale-force wind had whipped up inside the room itself, each gust ice cold. I realized he was trapped; ice had formed between the bookshelves, creating a ten-foot-high frozen maze with my father in the center and no way out. A blue-gray shimmering form could just be made out in the far corner, someone skinny to the point of boniness, very old, almost bald. It could've been male or female. It was certainly a wraith.

"It tries," the thing wheezed, in a voice that sounded like cracking ice. I recognized it: one of the Plotters. "It tries, but it's too stupid to know what it's doing wrong."

Dad said, "You'll be pulled in. You can't hold out forever." But he didn't sound like he believed it. His eyes didn't look angry or scared, just sad—the way they had when I'd seen him on the couch when I first returned to Evernight. The way Lucas had looked when he went into his fatal battle with Charity. I realized why Dad had been thinking about me, calling to me; my father believed he was about to die his final death.

He'd been trying to lure this ghost into a trap, I realized—I could see one of the coppery seashell boxes at his feet, cracked in two and now apparently powerless. Why was Dad helping Mrs. Bethany?

The wheeze turned into a cackle. "Freeze it cold. Break it in two. No more head, no more noise."

Dad's face didn't change, because he probably didn't know what the wraith was talking about. But I knew. I'd used the power myself—the ability to reach inside a vampire and turn its body to ice. I'd seen how powerfully it could hurt vampires, and I didn't doubt it could kill them.

The wraith swooped down, the malevolent spirit from my worst nightmares, the embodiment of everything that still terrified me about ghosts. I didn't know what to do; I didn't know if I had any power over other wraiths. Could it destroy me as well as my father? What could I do?

Instantly, I thought of my coral bracelet and the records room, and my spirit rematerialized there. Vic, who was sitting on a beanbag and reading a comic book, half snorted, half choked on a mouthful of soda when I appeared. "Whoa! Bianca, you gotta warn a guy."

I'd hoped for Lucas or Balthazar, but I'd take whatever help I could get; even a simple interruption might make the wraith leave. "My dad's in trouble—get to the library! Quick!"

Just as fast, I thought of the gargoyle outside my old window—and I was there, hovering outside my old room. It was worth scaring the crap out of my mother if that got her down to the library to help Dad, but she wasn't there. Frustrated, I zipped down along the stones, seeking a familiar face; luckily, Patrice was there, alone, putting the finishing touches on her manicure. I realized she was the one I'd needed all along. I frosted the window so fast it shook, and she opened it to thrust her head outside. "Bianca?"

"The library! Bring your mirror, now!"

*I have to get back to Dad.* But the tether I'd traveled along before had snapped; that kind of connection didn't seem to work here in the mortal world. I'd have to take the long way. The only way to avoid leaving ice in my wake was to calm down and slow down, but this was no time for that.

I zoomed through Patrice's room and down the hallways, ignoring the frost and the eerie blue lights that rippled around me, even when the other students began to scream. Skye, emerging from the shower, nearly dropped her towel, and I could see the wet strands of her hair freezing into icy points. *Sorry,* I thought absently. I couldn't worry about anyone right now besides my father.

My journey to the library probably took no more than a couple of minutes, but it seemed like eternity. When I went through the doors, a quick swipe of wood through my whole body, I could see flickering blue light reflecting on and within what was now an enormous cage of ice. Somewhere in the middle of that crackling, sparkling prison was my dad. I pushed through the ice to the center.

There, to my horror, I saw Dad—swaying on his feet, leaning back at an impossible angle, pushing desperately against the fist of ice that was buried within his chest.

The wraith cackled. "Stupid it. Stupid it."

"Get away from him!" I screamed. Not knowing what else to do, I threw myself into it from the side, as hard as I could. It simply went filmy and let me topple through. But I at least provided a distraction; the wraith pulled its icy hand from my father and turned toward me.

It was the ugliest thing I'd ever seen. At first I'd thought it was only old, but old people didn't look like this. The "flesh" that it manifested didn't seem to fit any longer—its lower eyelids sagged so far that I could see the full eye socket, and its lips drooped over its jaws, down by its chin. I backed away until I touched the ice; I could've gone through it, but that would have meant abandoning Dad.

I heard a soft voice say, disbelieving, *"Bianca?"*

*Dad!* But I couldn't look at him right now; this wraith needed to stay focused on me and not him.

The wraith's round, eerie eyes lit up—literally, as though they were gas flames. I had no idea we could do that and seriously did not want to start. "A baby," it said.

"I might be new to this, but I promise you, I can—" What could I do? "I can out-haunt you any day if you don't leave him alone."

"You can take us there," it said, shuffling forward with an eagerness that was slightly childlike, and therefore more disturbing.

Was this what Christopher had meant? That I was supposed to help creepy things like this?

Then I felt bad. If I hadn't been able to create a body, and interact once more with the people who loved me, maybe I would have turned creepy, too. If it could go to that land of lost things, maybe it would stop being so scary and start to look like itself again. If I'd thought working with dead people was going to be pretty all the time—especially given some of the dead people I'd already known—then that was stupid of me.

"I'll take you," I promised. I didn't exactly know how to do that yet, but already I understood that if I couldn't pick it up quickly, Christopher could help me. "Just let this man go, okay? We can go there right now."

The wraith hesitated. Maybe it couldn't believe its good luck.

But then its flaming eyes narrowed, slits of unearthly fire blue. "It doesn't get to run away," it hissed. "Not after what it did."

"I don't care what he was doing. It doesn't matter! You can leave this place now. Isn't that more important?"

It didn't answer me. The wraith had to think, I realized—it was divided between hope and hate, unable to choose one over the other.

Softly, I added, "Where we're going . . . it can be beautiful. It's better than haunting a school, anyway. You have to see it. Come on." I forced myself to offer my hand to the wraith, though its fingers were clawlike and bony.

For another moment, the wraith hesitated. I dared to glance over at my father and wished instantly that I hadn't; tears were running down his cheeks as he looked up at me, and I thought maybe he was crying because I had turned into something so horrible—something just like this creature that had tried to hurt him.

Then the wraith suddenly shrieked in rage. "It doesn't! It doesn't get to run away."

Hate had won.

It dove for my father, and I tried to get between them. I couldn't stop the wraith, exactly, but it was like we somehow tangled up in each other—neither of us solid, neither of us distinct. Like peanut butter in a sandwich: a gooey, sticky mess. The wraith's spirit curled around my own, sicker and sadder than I'd realized, and I shuddered in revulsion.

"Get away from me!" I pushed the wraith away, and it worked. The ghost sprang above us, a coiled blue streak of electricity just beneath the ceiling. I had a sudden image of it coming down as a thunderbolt. Who would it strike first? My dad or me? And what would happen when it did?

Then the wraith screamed, a pitiful sound, and dissolved into bluish smoke that swirled down toward the library door. Within a second the light had gone out, and there was silence.

I realized what must have happened. "Patrice?" I called.

"It's in my new compact!" she called from beyond the ice. "Which just happens to be Laura Mercier. This thing had better not break it."

Then I heard the sound of Vic's amazed laughter. "That was incredibly cool."

"I try," she said.

The ice walls surrounded my father and me. Although I guessed they'd melt eventually, I didn't like the idea of leaving him in there alone to be found in the morning. "Can you guys break us out?"

"Yeah, hang on!" Vic sounded excited about the whole process. "I'm gonna use the emergency fire ax. Try out some of Ranulf's moves."

As I heard them going into the hallway for the fire ax, I knew that there was no other way to avoid it. Bracing myself, I turned to once again face my father.

"Bianca," he said again. His cheeks were wet from tears. "It's . . . really you?"

"Yeah." My voice sounded so small. "Dad, I'm sorry."

*"Sorry?"* Dad grabbed me and hugged me so hard that my semisolid body almost gave way, but I held on. "My baby girl. You don't have to be sorry for anything. You're *here*. You're here."

And I knew that he didn't care that I was a wraith, or that I'd been so stupid and wrong about so many things, or that we'd fought the last time we talked. My dad still loved me.

If I could have cried, I would have. As it was, the joy that spread through me turned into light and warmth, a soft glow like a candle—and I could feel it soothing my father's pain. "I missed you," I whispered. "I missed you and Mom so much."

"Why didn't you come to us?"

"I was scared you wouldn't want me anymore. Now that I'm a wraith."

"You're my daughter. That never changes." Dad's face was creased with pain. "We hated them so much . . . were so afraid of them. Of course you were scared. We were so—obstinate and shortsighted about this. We should have talked to you."

"If I'd known . . ." I didn't know what I would've done, if I had known. Would I have turned into a vampire? Chosen my present path? I couldn't tell, and it didn't matter. We were here now. "I'm sorry I ran away like that. I know I scared you."

My dad's expression suggested that I hadn't known the half of it, but he never stopped embracing me. "It's that boy. He was always a bad influence on you—"

"Dad, no. I made the decision to go on my own. Lucas helped take care of me, but it was my choice. If you're angry about it—and I don't blame you—you have to understand that it was my fault. Only mine."

Dad stroked my hair, but said nothing. I knew he didn't believe me.

"Lucas needs your help," I whispered. "He's having trouble with the transition. He hates what he is and can't get over it. You could help him."

"That's too much to ask."

"That's what I'm asking." But after what I'd put my father through in the past few months, maybe I didn't have the right to demand a whole lot, at least not now. "When you're ready. Think about it."

The library doors squeaked, and I heard Vic yell, "Fire brigade's here!"

My dad and I took hands as Vic and Patrice started chopping their way through the ice. They were laughing—apparently it was wet, messy work—which let me whisper to him privately, "Can we go see Mom?"

I thought he'd be so thrilled, but instead he hesitated. "We should wait. Not long—I need to think about how best to handle it."

My heart sank. "You think Mom wouldn't be able to accept this. She hates the wraiths. Is she going to hate me?"

"Your mother loves you forever," Dad said fiercely. "Just like me. But her experiences with the wraiths have been worse than most. After the Great Fire of London, and the mass destruction of the ghosts there, the few wraiths that remained were—*insane* doesn't even come close. Celia lingered for days with her injuries, and would've died if I hadn't—well. While she was trapped between life and death, she had some terrifying experiences. You'll never know how hard it was for her to agree to the brief encounter with the wraith that created you. This stuff frightens her pretty badly to this day."

"Mom would be . . . scared of me?"

"We'll get her through it," he promised. Already Dad looked better than I'd seen him since before I died. Younger, if that was possible. There was a light in his eyes, and no shadow behind his smile. "I don't want to leave her mourning for much longer. It would be— I'm not going to do that to her. I just want to think about how best we can break it to her."

"Okay." That sounded fair. As badly as I wanted to see Mom

again, to double the happiness I felt at this moment, I trusted Dad's judgment. He'd loved my mother for about four hundred years now; he knew her better than anyone else ever could. "Wait—you said the Great Fire of London. It destroyed all the ghosts?"

He seized my arms. "Bianca, don't you know? If a wraith is trapped within a structure, and that structure burns, the wraith is destroyed. You have to be careful. Fire could hurt you."

Dad might have been lecturing my three-year-old self about why it was a bad idea to touch the stove while it was on. "Don't worry. I don't intend to let myself get trapped."

The ice wall closest to us shattered, and Dad and I jumped back. Standing on the other side, sprinkled with flakes of ice, were Vic and Patrice. Vic, who held the ax, looked like he'd never had more fun in his life; Patrice gingerly brushed dripping curls of hair away from her eyes. "How's it going, Mr. Olivier?" Vic said cheerfully.

Patrice held out her expensive compact, which was completely caked with ice. "Any ideas what I should do with this thing? I'm not putting it back in my makeup bag."

Dad stared at them, then at me, like he was just putting something together. "Wait—your friends, they all . . . know about you? Spend time with you?"

"Yeah. It took me a little while to figure out how to make it work, but we got it."

"Lucas . . . Balthazar . . ." Dad's forehead furrowed.

"Yes, they've always known," I said. "And don't get mad at

them for not telling you. That was my decision, too."

"Oh, man, awkward." Vic tucked the ax behind his back, like that was the reason things might be difficult. "Should we go?"

"I'm *not* taking this with me," Patrice said, holding the ice-coated compact out from her with two fingers, like it smelled bad.

"Give it to me." Dad saw her hesitate and sighed. "We'll return the mirror later."

Patrice looked doubtful, but she handed over the compact. "Well, that's done. Glad to help. See you later, okay?"

"Okay," I said. Vic just nodded at us and sheepishly followed Patrice out. As they went, I saw her staring down disapprovingly at her nails; apparently, in her rush to help me, she'd wrecked her new manicure. For Patrice, that was a sign of real dedication.

My father and I were alone again. Wordlessly, we stepped out of the winding blocks of ice into a snug corner of the library, where a small sofa sat between two of the tallest bookshelves. It was a good place to sit and talk, though at the moment we weren't talking. There was so much to say that I couldn't think of where to begin; I started with the place where tonight's confrontation had begun. "What were you doing with that box?"

"Trying to catch a wraith." His eyes tracked over to the far wall of the library—the place where the trap had been set. Dad's hands closed around mine, like he was unwilling to let me go even for a second. "It had settled in here without—"

"Without being caught. Because the trap was broken." I realized for the first time that my father might already have the answers I'd been searching for. "Dad, what's going on? Why is Mrs. Bethany setting these traps for the wraiths?"

"To stop them, of course. They're not all like you. Most of them are like that thing we just captured."

"No, most of them are more like me—ourselves, mostly, the people that we were before. You just don't see those. They don't haunt places the same way."

He opened his mouth as if to argue, before realizing that I really did know more about this. "If we'd understood that . . ."

Although Dad had trailed off, I could follow his train of thought. "You would have told me about my turning into a wraith, wouldn't you? But because you thought it meant being some scary, horrible thing—something that could never be your daughter again."

"I couldn't stand to say the words. And we thought it would scare you." Dad looked very tired. "We just tried to make vampirism as attractive as possible. There didn't seem to be any reason for you to question it, or turn away."

*Not until I fell in love with a human,* I thought. That was the real source of their anger toward Lucas, I realized; it didn't have much to do with anything Lucas had done or not done. He had given me an alternative—made me question everything I'd taken for granted. I wondered if Dad realized it, too.

I turned back to the subject. "Anyway, most ghosts aren't as crazy as that one."

"Most of the ones here seem to be," he pointed out. "Remember the autumn ball last year?"

Like I'd forget nearly being crushed by massive spears of falling ice. "If they're so dangerous, why is Mrs. Bethany bringing them here in the first place?"

"Bringing them here? Bianca, what do you mean?"

Quickly I explained the secret common element that every human student at Evernight shared—each of them came from a haunted home and was connected to a ghost or ghosts. Some of those ghosts had followed them here. "That's why she let humans in to begin with. To bring the ghosts."

"You don't think it might have something to do with the fact that human students help the vampire students acclimate to the present day? There's no better preparation for fitting in with humanity than actually spending time with human beings." He squeezed my hands tightly, like he thought I was being a little silly, but didn't mind.

But I shook my head. "Maybe that helps. But seriously, Dad, every single one of the humans? There aren't that many wraiths. Not even close. There's no way that's a coincidence."

"So she has some purpose behind trapping ghosts. Some purpose we don't know. I'll try to find out." My father's expression changed then, turning sharp and distant, like he was mad at someone not in the room.

"Dad?"

"It's just— Nothing." He turned his attention back to me and hugged me tightly. My glow of happiness lit up the entire library and turned it to gold. "It doesn't matter. Nothing matters except having you back."

We stayed with each other for a while after that, but we'd already said the most important things. Soon he would tell Mom; until then, the two of us agreed to meet up after his classes so we could at least spend a few minutes a day together checking in, finding out how to navigate being father and daughter now that so much had changed. It was a place to start, and I felt like all we needed was that beginning.

When, after midnight, my father finally went up to his rooms, I felt exhausted—like I needed to "fade out" for a while, the closest I could get to sleeping. But I knew I had more important things to do. Though I had now met Christopher, and had changed my mind about being scared of all ghosts, I'd just gotten a big wake-up call about how dangerous they could be to the people I loved. I'd struck back against a wraith once now; it was time to discover what else I could do, without Patrice by my side.

Whatever else Black Cross had done to me, they'd made me a fighter. It was past time for me to act like one.

Of course, to test myself in a fight, I needed a wraith to fight with. But for a few days now, I'd had a candidate in mind—one ghost that I knew absolutely, positively used his powers in the most evil way. That sounded like a good place to start.

"That's awesome," Lucas said as he sat on the stone steps with me the next afternoon. "I mean it, Bianca. It's great that your father knows, and it's going to be good between you and your parents."

His eyes were shadowed as he said it. I knew that had nothing to do with his feeling about my reconciliation with Dad; it was the memory of Kate's brutal attacks that shadowed him now. The cruelty of her rejection struck me harder now that I, too, had faced my father—I knew the fear and vulnerability of that moment. Lucas had shown even more courage and faith than I had; his trust in her had been immediate and total. His reward had been betrayal. I couldn't imagine how much that must have hurt.

"Your mom might come around," I said softly. "Given time."

Lucas smiled grimly as he shook his head. "I'm nothing but a monster to her now. Never will be anything else."

I touched his face. "You're not a monster."

"Yes, I am. Got the fangs to prove it."

"Then you're not *only* a monster. You're also a good man." I smiled, scattering a soft glow around us in the stairwell. Hopefully that had helped him, but I thought it would be a good idea to change the subject, too. "So, what do you think of my plan?"

"I hate it."

"You think it's a bad idea?"

"No," he admitted. "It's a good idea. You've got to go up against a wraith sometime, and I can't think of a better candidate than that creep. But it's dangerous. I hate the fact that I can't protect you."

"I can protect myself."

An unwilling smile spread across Lucas's face. "I know that.

I trust you. And I've seen what you can do when you set your mind to it. But I always wanted to be the one looking out for you, you know? I've gotta learn to let you fight your own battles—at least the ones I can't fight for you."

Understanding, I said, "You just don't have to like it."

"Exactly . . ." His voice trailed off as we heard footsteps on the stairs above us. Quickly I vanished, turning into a fine cloud of mist that could easily hide in a corner. Lucas stood up, adjusting his uniform sweater, and said to the unseen person, "Hey!"

His voice was a little too loud, an attempt at forced cheer, and it must have scared somebody who thought she was alone. I heard a feminine cry of surprise, and then a thudding on the stairs. Lucas ran up, taking two steps at a time, as I followed behind.

There, uniform kilt practically around her waist and books scattered around, lay Skye. She scrambled into a sitting position when she saw Lucas, tucking her kilt back into place as her cheeks flushed with embarrassment. "You scared me! I thought I was alone," she said. "And these stairs—they're slippery—"

"You don't have to apologize for falling down," Lucas said. "I startled you, and yeah, the steps suck. You okay, Skye?"

"Mostly just humiliated."

"No need to be freaked out because of me. So you're okay." He bent over, maybe to help her up or to pick up some of her books—and froze.

I saw it only a moment later. Skye had skinned her knee when she fell. Crisscrossing the pale skin of her knee were stripes of blood, beading up thicker by the moment.

Lucas's eyes narrowed, and I could see his entire body tense as he breathed in the scent.

Skye saw it too and winced. "So, not just a bruise. Don't guess you happen to have any Band-Aids on you?"

"No," Lucas said slowly. His gaze—his whole being—was focused entirely on the blood. As his jaw worked, I realized his fangs were threatening to emerge.

*Lucas, no. Lucas, snap out of it.* Did I dare to materialize? It would scare the hell out of Skye, but if Lucas was about to bite her . . . but he wouldn't. He couldn't.

"Of course you don't have a Band-Aid. Guys don't carry purses," Skye said as if she were scolding herself. She bent the leg, bringing the knee closer to her face—and his. "Maybe I've got a tissue in my backpack, but I think I left my first-aid stuff in the stables. Let me check."

As she unzipped her backpack, her shining brown hair fell across her face and obscured her view of Lucas. I could feel temptation radiating from him like heat. He wanted blood— her blood—this second. He wanted it worse than anything else, enough to forget that I was watching, maybe enough to forget everything but his vampire hunger.

I made up my mind to appear and was gathering myself together to do it, when I heard someone else walk onto the floor above. The *click-clack* of footsteps made Skye look up, though Lucas never took his eyes off the bleeding wound.

"Miss Tierney." Mrs. Bethany's rich voice echoed slightly in the stairwell. I saw her appear first as a shadow in the darkness, as if she were made out of nothing but night. "I see you've had an accident. And Mr. Ross is helping you."

Skye smiled unevenly. "Yeah, tripped and fell."

As they spoke, Lucas finally pulled himself together with a start. He didn't seem to remember where he'd been or how he'd gotten here. Hurriedly he held out his arm to help Skye to her feet.

Mrs. Bethany held out a lacy white handkerchief. "Bandage it as best you can until you can get the first-aid kit."

"It's so pretty," Skye protested, her fingers brushing over the delicate lace. "I don't want to bleed on it."

"If you rinse the linen in cold water as soon as possible, there will be little chance of any stain," Mrs. Bethany said. "And a ruined handkerchief would be infinitely preferable to a student bleeding profusely in the hallways."

Obviously Mrs. Bethany knew better than to tempt the undead half of the student body.

Skye thanked Mrs. Bethany and Lucas as Lucas returned her books to her backpack and handed it over. Just as she was leaving, she cast a curious glance at Lucas, maybe realizing that he'd hardly spoken a word since he'd seen her skinned knee. But she said nothing about it as she went limping back up toward her dorm room.

When Mrs. Bethany and Lucas were again alone, except for me, she gave him a hard stare. "You found that difficult, didn't you?"

Lucas just nodded. He couldn't meet her eyes. I knew that shame had to be consuming him from the inside out. He hated himself for craving blood, and being tempted to attack a human—especially a human who had always been kind to him—would be unbearable.

"Take heart, Mr. Ross." Mrs. Bethany put that familiar hand on his shoulder again. "There is a way beyond your present difficulty."

"What, is there a way to stop vampires from wanting blood?" he scoffed.

"Yes."

He stared at her in blank surprise, at least so far as I could tell; I was too astonished to notice anything but my own shock.

Wanting blood—that was what made a vampire a vampire. Besides, Evernight Academy was almost wholly made up of vampires who didn't attack humans; wouldn't they teach this kind of thing instead of driver's ed?

At Lucas's stunned response, Mrs. Bethany smiled thinly. Her fingers tightened on his shoulder. "A way to silence the bloodlust forever," she murmured. "It's real. And it's going to be mine."

Lucas was utterly still, staring up at her raptly. "Teach me," he said.

"When you're ready." She turned to go, but said, as she began to walk upstairs with her long skirts in her hands, "I think that will be very soon."

When we were alone again, he whispered, "Is it real?

Bianca, can she be telling the truth?"

"I don't know."

The rest of the day passed in a weird sort of blur for me. My anxiety about Mrs. Bethany's increasing hold on Lucas kept me from focusing properly on anything, including the task at hand. But as night fell and Lucas and my friends went to bed, I forced myself to get it together.

If I failed tonight, I would never have the courage to stand up to the wraiths again. And that meant I might never be able to control my own destiny.

I concentrated on an object that had been meaningful to me during my life—a potential "subway stop" I could travel to at any time. This would be tricky, though; this object hadn't belonged to me. It was owned by someone else. Someone who maybe never wanted to see me again—but she was about to.

I filled my mind with the image, willing myself to see it, to be one with it: a braided, tawny leather bracelet.

Evernight Academy vanished. Everything around me went dark. As I looked around, I could see a few points of illumination—strips of lights through Venetian blinds, revealing the garish neon of a cheap hotel's sign and blocky numerals on a digital alarm clock.

To my relief, this was a private room instead of a full Black Cross lair. I'd suspected as much, but all the same, it was better to know for sure. I decided the room needed another light source and turned up my own glow, filling the room with soft blue light that outlined my spectral form. Now I could see the hotel bed, and the two figures who slept there.

One of them shifted beneath the covers, then sat bolt upright. She blinked once, then said, "Bianca?"

I smiled. "Hey, Raquel."

# Chapter Fifteen

RAQUEL STARED AT ME, HER SHORT BLACK HAIR
rumpled and her eyes wide. "Am I dreaming?" she whispered.

"No," I said.

She punched at the other person sleeping in the bed—her
girlfriend, Dana, who sat up slowly, rubbing her eyes. "What is
it, babe?"

I brightened a little more, daring to take firmer shape. "Hey,
Dana."

Dana did a double take that, under other circumstances,
would've been funny.

"Are you here to haunt me?" Raquel asked. She had scooted
backward, against the headboard of the bed, like she wanted to
get away. One of her crazy-quilt montages had been pinned to
the wall, a collection of magazine snippets and found objects
that Raquel liked to turn into art. "I knew it."

"What? No." Then I realized why Raquel looked so scared
and guilty; she thought I remained angry about her having

turned me in to Black Cross.

Which I was, a little bit. I hadn't quite realized that until I saw her again, without any horde of Black Cross fighters to get in the way.

Dana interrupted, "How's Lucas doing? In Riverton, he didn't look good."

"He's having a hard time." That was totally inadequate for what Lucas was going through, but I didn't know what else to say.

Dana slumped, as if crushed. She and Lucas had grown up together—and she also had been indoctrinated by Black Cross, to the point where she would consider vampirism the worst possible fate. Maybe she was the only person who could fully comprehend the depth of Lucas's self-loathing now. Then her eyes fixed on mine, flashing with anger. "How come you didn't behead him?"

As horrible as that was to contemplate, I'd considered it difficult enough to know my answer: "Because I'd been a vampire myself. I knew it wasn't always the worst thing. I thought maybe he could handle it, and maybe he can."

"You were never anything but a vampire," Dana shot back. Raquel watched us argue with wide eyes, as if afraid to remind either of us she was there. "How do you know what's the worst thing? I know for damn sure that if I got changed, I'd want somebody to make sure I never woke up undead. It's the most sacred promise we make to ourselves. Lucas and I promised each other that a thousand times." She was breathing hard, her outrage growing. "If you loved him, you'd have done that for him."

It was a slap in the face, even though I knew Lucas had forgiven me for it. "It's easy to make promises. But if you had been there—if you'd seen Lucas lying there dead, and knew that you could either lose him forever or talk to him again in just a couple of hours—it's not that easy anymore." Once again, I wished it was possible for wraiths to cry; it hurt to carry such a sad memory and have no way to vent my grief. "As difficult as this is for him, he has his friends. He has me. Is that honestly worse than never having anything else, ever again?"

Dana sat in silence for a few seconds. "I don't know," she finally admitted. "But what I say goes, okay, babe?" Her eyes met Raquel's. "If I get changed into a vampire, you make sure I never, ever see the sunrise."

"I promise." Raquel's voice was so quiet, so sure, that her love for Dana filled the room. If Lucas and I had talked more about this—if I had made him that promise—could I have been strong enough to let him go? As strong as Raquel? I wasn't sure.

For a few long moments, Raquel and Dana looked only at each other, and Raquel held Dana's hand tight. But then Dana turned back to me. "Is that what you came to talk about? Lucas?" Her tone softened slightly. "Does he need to speak to me? Because . . . if you need me to sneak into that crazy vampire school for him, I'll do it."

Raquel blurted out, "What are you guys doing back at Evernight Academy? Are you nuts?" Then she shrank back again, still afraid of me.

"It's working out, sort of. Mrs. Bethany wasn't even angry. It's like she hates Black Cross so much that . . . she *enjoys* having taken Lucas from them." I hadn't realized that until now, but I didn't doubt that was part of her reaction. "Anyway, I wouldn't suggest showing up there as a Black Cross hunter. But there's another Riverton trip coming up fairly soon. Unless . . . would Black Cross come after him again, if he leaves campus?"

"Next time Mrs. Bethany's going to have people there waiting for them," Dana said, shaking her head. "Black Cross knows that. If they ever run into Lucas again, they'll turn on him in an instant, but they wouldn't target Riverton after failing there the first time."

"Then that works. Maybe you could come to Riverton again, Dana. Lucas—I think he thinks you wouldn't want to see him."

"That boy never did have any sense." Dana's scowl told me that she loved Lucas as much as ever. "Name the day. We'll get there."

I took in our surroundings for the first time—a cheap but comfortable hotel room, with enough clutter around to show that they'd been here for a while. Saving up money for private accommodations was impossible in Black Cross, where any money was supposed to belong to the group rather than the individual. "So, you guys really did it. You left Black Cross for good."

"Not like we had much choice in the matter after we'd fired at Kate," Raquel said. For the first time, she met my eyes without flinching. "But we'd do it again in a heartbeat." Then she winced, obviously afraid that was a tactless thing to say to a dead person.

Dana sighed. "We started having doubts after what they did

to you two in New York. Then, when they turned on Lucas in Philadelphia—that was the breaking point. We lit out a couple weeks ago. Holed up here, but we'll find a real place sometime. We're making minimum wage and feeling fine."

"We might be eating ramen," Raquel added, "but we're eating."

A weird silence fell in the room. I began, "Raquel, I actually came here to talk to you."

"I'm sorry." Raquel was trembling, but she got out of bed. She wore a beat-up old T-shirt and sweatpants—and of course the leather bracelet, the one I remembered so well it had possessed the power to draw me here. "Bianca, I'm so, so sorry. You'll never know how . . . forget it, how I feel doesn't matter. You were a good friend to me, and I should've protected you, and I didn't. I suck. If you want to haunt me or—or whatever, I know I deserve it."

I hadn't realized how much I needed to hear that. But there were also things I needed to say. "I lied to you. I had my reasons, but still. If I'd told you the truth in the right way, maybe it wouldn't have been so bad."

"That doesn't excuse what I did," Raquel said, her voice shaky. She kept balling her hands into fists, so worked up that it startled me. "You could've been killed. I mean, *killed* killed. You know what I mean. When I realized what they were going to do—if I had known that, I would never have told. Not ever."

"I know. I always knew that, I think. Besides, you guys came through for Lucas when it mattered the most. That's the main thing."

As I smiled unevenly at Raquel, she tried to smile back. The weight of her old betrayal hung between us, but lighter somehow than it had been before. It was going to take more time to heal, but at least now it was all out in the open. We were back on the same side. Everything else, I decided, could heal over time.

"I didn't come here to talk to you about that, actually," I said.

That caught Raquel up short. After glancing at an equally bewildered Dana, she said, "Then why are you here?"

"The wraith who haunted your old house," I said, bracing myself for what was to come. "The one who hurt you."

Raquel's dark eyes searched mine, as if pleading with me not to bring up anything that painful. "What about it?"

"We're going to take care of him—for good."

As it happened, Dana and Raquel were living in a suburb of Boston, not terribly far from where Raquel had grown up. Also, when they'd left, they'd taken one of the Black Cross vans with them.

"Some might call it stealing," Dana said cheerfully as we piled into the old van, which smelled like gunpowder and Fritos. "But seeing as how Black Cross stole it from a dead vampire in the first place, I think of it as repurposing the vehicle. Sounds nicer, don't you think?"

"Looks like you repurposed some weapons, too." I glanced over the armory in the back. "Stakes, holy water, and . . . is that a flamethrower?"

"You never know when one will come in handy," Raquel said, and I had to smile.

Our joking around didn't last for long, though. The closer we got to the house, the tenser Raquel became. She had a shotgun in front; I was the phantom in the backseat. "How is this going to work?" she asked.

"It's pretty simple." I sort of didn't mention I hadn't done this before. No need to add to her nervousness, right? "We just need a mirror. Does one of you guys have a compact? You know, for powder, makeup?"

We were at a stoplight, which was why both Dana and Raquel were able to turn around and stare at me. After a second, Dana said, "Hi, have we met?"

"Okay, no makeup in the car," I said. "But we have to get a mirror."

A quick stop at an all-night drugstore yielded one powder compact. Although I had more substance than not, getting through the packaging was difficult for me, so I let Raquel handle it. She tore at the paper and plastic, hands shaky, making way more of a mess than necessary.

"I haven't talked to them in a long time," she said, prying the compact out. "And now I'm just going to show up at two A.M. and be all, hey, remember that ghost you said doesn't exist?"

"Maybe we don't have to wake them," Dana said. A fine rain began to fall, and she hit the windshield wipers, with their soft *slap-slap* sound. "Is this ghostbusting business loud, Bianca?"

"Um, it can be. But it doesn't have to be." I hoped that was true. "We'll try."

Raquel had always been very clear about the fact that she wasn't wealthy, like most of the living and dead students at Evernight. Her neighborhood wasn't as bad as I'd always imagined it, though. Maybe I was just naive and thought being poor meant living in a slum like one they showed on bad TV shows, with burning cars and gang members everywhere. It was just a quiet neighborhood with small houses that didn't have much in the way of yards. Instead of squalor and violence, everything was just kind of gray and run-down, with some half-hearted, sloppy graffiti on the trash cans.

"We're lucky it's raining," Raquel said. "Everybody would be out on the corners if it weren't."

The house in the middle of the block belonged to Raquel's family. We realized as soon as we got out of the car that no one was home. "Where would they be?" Dana asked, as we peered through the windows at packed-up boxes. "The furniture's in place, so they haven't moved."

"With Frida, maybe?" Raquel squinted. "It looks like they've pulled up part of the kitchen floor. Maybe that water pipe burst again, and they're fixing the damage."

"They're not home," I said. "That's the important thing. We can do this now."

Raquel went very still. "I'm not sure I can."

Dana put an arm around her shoulders. "It's okay. If you want to stay out here, that works, too. Right, Bianca?"

I started to agree with her, then stopped myself. "You can stay out here if you want to," I said. "But I think you should face this thing."

Her white lips pressed together, Raquel shook her head.

"Come on, Raquel! Since when do you run away from a fight?" She wouldn't look at me any longer, but I kept going. "If you don't see this happen, then you'll always be scared of it. Always. But if you see us defeat it, then that's the last way you'll remember it. Beaten. Isn't that what you'd rather see?"

"Back off, okay?" Dana got between us. "Don't push her."

"No," Raquel said. She touched Dana's shoulder, gently edging her aside. "Bianca's right. I'll go in."

As the rain fell softly around us, pattering on the metal awning overhead, Dana jimmied the front-door lock as swiftly as Lucas could've done. *Too bad I wasn't in Black Cross long enough to learn that trick,* I thought.

The door swung open with a creak. Dana tiptoed in, trying not to make a sound; Raquel, face pale, followed. I allowed myself to become mostly vapor, a soft blue mist right behind them.

"Whoa," Raquel said, clearly taken aback. "That's . . . spooky."

"Shhh! We're trying to be quiet here!" Dana held the compact in front of her, like she hoped to use it as a shield. I would need to take the compact from her, but that would come once I could take form again.

"That's okay," I said. "Sooner or later, we want it to know we're here."

I stretched my consciousness throughout the house, discovering that I could sense the layout of the rooms without seeing them, that I knew which one had belonged to Raquel—part of her essence lingered there.

So did something else.

The voice resonated on a frequency that wasn't quite sound, merely vibration, in the ether we shared. *Little girl. Little girl. You've come back to play.*

Raquel started to shake. "It's here," she whispered. "I can tell."

She hadn't heard the voice, I realized, nor had Dana; they were both looking around wildly, as if expecting the wraith to appear from any direction, at any second. And yet Raquel knew the presence of this thing on a deeper level than I could comprehend. I wondered how deep a link had been formed—how deeply this wraith had sunk its claws into her.

*Did you bring playmates for me?*

Suddenly I could see a room, not this one—a different, false reality surrounding me, slightly transparent but enclosing, too, like a cell made of glass. It looked like a small child's bedroom. At first I thought this must have been what Raquel's room looked like when she was a child, but then I corrected myself; she would never have spent so much as one night in a room this pink and frilly, with a canopy bed and dolls stacked in row after row. I'd never seen so many dolls —

And I'd never seen any dolls who were watching me right back. Somehow they were looking at me, their glassy black eyes all too alive. I heard a soft rustling among their fluffy petticoats, and one of the dolls leaned sharply to the side, as if it had fallen. They were alive but not alive, watching but not watching, and just completely creepy. It was enough to scare the crap out of me, and I was a *ghost*.

*This is somebody's idea of a child's room,* I thought. *Their over-the-top imitation of where a little girl would sleep. Created by some guy who's spent way too much time thinking about little girls in bed.*

"Show yourself," I demanded. In the other reality—the actual one—I could see Raquel and Dana both jump. "Stop hiding behind the dolls. Come out."

"The dolls," Raquel whispered. She must have dreamed of them before.

In the dream bedroom, the dolls rustled some more, toppling into piles so that their gold and brown curls tangled together. In the center, I saw him.

If I hadn't been able to feel the depth of Raquel's fear, I might have laughed. This wraith didn't look scary—just fat and kind of bald. Not very tall, either. And yet, as he studied me, tilting his head from side to side, there was something in the vacancy of his stare, and the greediness of his smile, that unsettled me on every level.

*Pretty. Pretty red hair. Have you come to play with me?*

He shuffled out from the cloud of dolls. His body was naked, and disgusting, and my fear turned quickly to revulsion, then to anger.

I said, "I'm not here to play."

Resonate, Patrice had said. I didn't know how to do that, so I just concentrated on him, and thought of my own death. I remembered that strange sinking feeling of my body giving in, giving way. I remembered Lucas's tears as he clutched my hand. It came back to me too vividly to bear—and yet I could feel the wraith being brought closer by the memories. I found my mind shaping words as though they were an incantation:

*By all that divides us from the living, I divide you from this place. By all the darkness that dwells within us, I consign you to darkness. By all the death that gives me power, I take your power from you.*

The wraith began to shriek, an unearthly wail that reverberated throughout the house. Dana grabbed both of her ears, perhaps in pain, and dropped the compact to the floor. Raquel didn't flinch. She grabbed the mirror and tossed it toward me, and I materialized just enough to catch it in my hand.

The moment I did, the force of the magic began drawing the wraith into the mirror. As I angled the mirror, the way Patrice had said, the wraith came apart before my eyes, not in a pretty mist like I was used to, but as though it were a physical thing being dismembered, blood and sinew, shrieks of pain. Yet it turned into so much dust as it flew into the mirror, howling the whole way—

Until there was silence. The dream world had vanished. We stood in the living room, staring at the ice-caked mirror I held high above my head.

"Is that . . . did we get him?" Dana asked breathlessly, her hands still at her ears.

"Oh, my God." Raquel took a shuddering breath. "We caught it."

"And as long as we don't break the mirror, it can never get out again." I'd fought it. I'd won. I knew how to stand up for myself against a wraith now; did that mean I was finally free?

"It's trapped in a mirror?" Raquel blinked. "It's not in the phantom zone or something?"

I shrugged. "Wherever it is, it can't get out again."

Raquel started to laugh, a sound of pure joy, and then she flung her arms around me. With all my strength, I kept myself as solid as I could, because the hug felt way too good to miss.

"You did it," she gasped. "You did it. That horrible thing—"

"It's okay." I patted her back as I realized her laughter was turning into tears. "It can't get you again."

"You did that for me after what I did to you."

"I did it for me, too—"

"Just shut up, okay?" Raquel hugged me tighter, and I took her advice and just held her while she cried. Over her shoulder, I could see Dana smiling at me beatifically, like I was her new favorite person in the whole world.

Once Raquel had settled down again, I handed her off to Dana for more hugging and returned my attention to the mirror. It was thickly iced, yet it seemed to me that I could glimpse something moving in the reflection.

"What are we going to do with that thing?" Raquel said. "Encase it in cement?"

"That's not a bad idea."

Then I felt the pull—almost physical, like I was being dragged.

"Bianca?" Raquel took a step forward. "You're turning invisible."

"Riverton! Don't forget!" I called, before I lost the ability to make sound. "I'll make sure Lucas is there!"

"Bianca!" Raquel shouted again, but in an instant I was gone, somersaulting through the blue misty nothingness. I landed—or so it seemed, anyway. I looked down at soft green grass, then turned my face up to see Maxie standing above me. She wore a strange coat of some dark fur that looked more creepy than luxurious.

"What are you doing?" she demanded. "You're siding with them against us now?"

"That thing had to be stopped."

"That thing? *Thing?*" Maxie looked like she might slap me. "I guess you might as well help Mrs. Bethany set the traps."

A third voice interrupted our argument. "There's a difference between what Bianca has done and Mrs. Bethany's efforts."

We turned to see Christopher. So I was in the land of lost things again—brought here, this time, against my will. Maxie had told me he was powerful, but this was my first evidence of exactly how much stronger Christopher was than the average wraith.

And yet it didn't frighten me, because now I knew I had the power to defend myself. Any power Christopher now had, I might gain for myself in time—probably less time than it had taken him to learn.

The sunlight brightened Christopher's dark brown hair, and his old-fashioned long coat was a deep bottle green. We were at the foot of a building that looked like some sort of pagoda, except that a rattling elevated train straight out of the 1910s was rushing along behind it.

"I got her out of there before she could do anything worse," Maxie said. So it was her, and not Christopher, who had intervened. "You shouldn't have let her go back, anyway."

"Maxine, calm yourself." Christopher put his hands on her shoulders. "It is not my role to allow or disallow Bianca's travels. She is freer than the rest of us. She does not share our limitations. I realize that is hard for you to accept, but you must."

Maxie snapped, "I don't see the difference between what Mrs. Bethany's doing and what Bianca did. She's turned against her fellow wraiths. That doesn't matter?"

I said, "That thing—"

"*Thing* again!"

"It hurt people, Maxie," I continued. "Nobody has the right to do that."

Christopher nodded. "It is one matter to act in defense of others. Another to act from selfish desires—no matter how understandable those desires may be."

He seemed so sad that I hated to ask more. And yet his sadness itself drew my attention more than anything else. It was like whatever Mrs. Bethany was doing wounded him personally, deeply. Did he care so deeply about the wraiths—all the wraiths? No, this was something that affected him, not as the leader of this ghostly world or whatever else he'd become, but as the man he had been.

A laughably bizarre idea occurred to me, and yet I couldn't shake it. Christopher watched me closely, able to see that I was struggling with something. Even his smile was sad.

"You know, now," he said. "Trust your insight. You will see many things here that would be hidden to you elsewhere."

This world's clarity had worked its magic on me again—or had it? Still, I couldn't quite believe. I asked the less direct question, in case I was wrong: "Christopher . . . what anchors you to the world? Or . . . who?"

"My beloved wife, though I have not spoken to her in nearly two hundred years."

Was he saying what I thought he was saying? "Then you're—"

"Christopher Bethany," he said. "Of course, you already know my wife."

# Chapter Sixteen

"MRS. BETHANY IS YOUR WIFE," I REPEATED. Although I'd guessed it myself, I couldn't fully wrap my mind around the information. The leader of the wraiths, married to one of the most powerful, ruthless vampires in existence? "Then why does she hate the wraiths so much?" Surely if she was married to a wraith, she'd have to like them a little. But maybe not. Maybe they'd broken up or something. A divorce would probably be extra-nasty after two hundred years of marriage.

But Christopher shook his head. "I have not spoken to her since my death."

"Why not? Is it because she became a vampire? Did she—was she the one who killed you?" I corrected myself. "No, of course not. You said she was the only person loyal to you."

"This is my history, mine alone," Christopher said, and his voice held a sharpness I hadn't heard since his first frightening manifestations at Evernight. Sensing my tension, though, he visibly calmed himself. "And yet, it concerns you now, and those close to you. It is not wrong for you to ask."

Maxie gaped at him, her earlier outrage at my special treatment forgotten. "Are you going to tell us where you come from?" I got the impression this was a closely guarded secret.

Christopher glared at her. "I shall tell Bianca, as it relates to her existence," he said. "It does not relate to yours."

With a huff, Maxie stomped away, her shiny heels loud on the pavement. She disappeared into a crowd of people who seemed mostly to be dressed in feathers and paint. I turned back to Christopher. "If you don't want to talk about it," I said, "honestly, that's okay. It's your business." I wanted answers, but that wasn't the same as wanting to pry.

"You will soon see how our paths intersected. These events are becoming part of your history as well."

He swept his hand across the sky, turning it instantly black—as though, instead of being outside, we stood in a kind of planetarium. Instead of the flowing, chaotic land of lost things around us, we were entirely alone, in a sort of void. I understood, without being told, that this was beyond most wraiths' power, including my own; this uncanny ability was something Christopher had forged from his long centuries trapped between worlds.

"Wow," I said. "What is this?"

"We are traveling to see the past."

"We're going back in time?" After everything else that had happened, it was weird that this had the power to surprise me. Like something out of a science-fiction movie; Vic would think this was extremely cool.

But Christopher shook his head. "Traveling to *see*," he said. "The past is unreachable by any power, mortal or immortal."

I wasn't sure what the difference was, but there was no time to ask. Taking shape around us was a forest, through which wound a narrow dirt road, striped with tracks from wheels and horses. A carriage came toward us, pulled by two pale gray horses and lit by actual lanterns on each side. It seemed romantic to me, something out of a novel by one of the Brontës.

At least, it seemed that way until figures jumped out of the dark—out of nowhere, it seemed—and sprang upon the carriage. The horses whinnied and snorted as one of the figures grabbed their harness, bringing everything to a halt.

I gasped, but nobody seemed able to hear me—the difference, maybe, between seeing the past and being there. Christopher stood quiet beside me as we saw the highway bandits or whatever they were pull open the doors of the carriage. In the lantern light, I could see their faces, their wicked grins, and their fangs: vampires on the attack. "Well, well. What have we here?" one of them snarled. "Guests for dinner?"

"I shall tell you what you have." Mrs. Bethany—in Regency costume, her hair piled high upon her head—leaned out of the door, completely unfazed by the attack. Was this the moment she was changed?

Then she hoisted a crossbow.

"You have to run," she said.

The vampires scattered, but not fast enough. Mrs. Bethany shot one straight through, the wooden shaft staking it in the heart. In a flash, the carriage driver and liverymen leaped into action, each of them armed, each of them sure and determined as they ran into the forest after the vampires.

"Quickly!" Mrs. Bethany cried, jumping from the carriage so that her skirts fluttered. Already she had reloaded the cross-bow, and despite the darkness, she took aim and brought another vampire down in a single stroke. Her smile was brilliant in the night. "We have them now!"

She laughed out loud as she pulled a broadsword from within her cloak. As she lifted it high, I turned away; I'd seen one vampire being beheaded, and that was enough for a life-time. As I heard the sick wet thud, I winced—and then my eyes opened wide.

"The way they're fighting . . . the way she throws herself into it . . ." I'd seen this before.

"Trained well, don't you think?" Christopher never looked away from Mrs. Bethany.

"If she was hunting vampires, and if she knew just what to do, then she was—she had to be—Mrs. Bethany was in Black Cross?"

I had to look at her again now. The fight was over, the vam-pires dust at her feet. In the moonlight, her smile softened and became warm as she rushed forward toward one of the livery-men—who, I now realized, was a slightly younger Christopher. They embraced each other, her arms tight around his neck, and kissed so passionately that I felt my cheeks flush.

"We were both raised among Black Cross hunters,"

Christopher said as he watched his long-ago happiness with his wife. "When I emigrated to America in the first years of its independence, I connected with the first Boston cell. There we met. Few women hunted in those days, but nobody questioned her. She was the best fighter among us. And the vampires—they always underestimated her until it was too late. There sprang up a legend among them of a huntress both beautiful and deadly, which they disbelieved at their peril. Sometimes it was the last thing they said, even as the stake sank into them. 'It is her.'"

The forest had darkened into indistinct gloom, but now shapes began to form anew. I saw a small house, simple, with one large room that seemed to be both kitchen and parlor. The fireplace was enormous, deep enough to walk into, tall as a person and as long as the house itself. A teakettle hung near the flames as Mrs. Bethany busied herself cutting cake; at the table, Christopher sat with a few men dressed as he was, with long coats and white kerchiefs tied at their throats. They had large metal cups filled with something that looked like beer, and they were laughing loudly.

Was it the clarity of this place that showed me the others weren't as happy as they pretended to be? That their eyes watched Christopher cagily as he took another drink?

"Business associates." Christopher's face was illuminated by the long-ago fire. We seemed to be standing at the very edge of the room, in deep shadow. "Friends, or so I thought. We joined in a shipping venture. Trade between Europe and America, in fine goods—a growing industry in that time, and therefore a likely bet to increase my family's wealth. But I was accustomed only to the company of Black Cross hunters; say what you will of Black Cross, but they do not engage in such gross trickery. I had been brought up to think that all evil was embodied by vampires. I did not look for it in men who called themselves my friends."

"What did they do?" I whispered, though I knew by now the figures before us couldn't hear.

"They did not want to establish a shipping business. They only wanted to steal the family money I gave them as investment." He still sounded slightly bewildered—like after a couple hundred years, Christopher hadn't yet wrapped his mind around the fact of his betrayal. "After some months, I began to press them for returns. Profits. To examine the books. They had countless excuses and nothing to show me. One night I swore I would take them to court. As I walked home that night, they attacked me. I was unarmed, and recovering from a winter illness. My Black Cross training was to no avail. They left me dying in a ditch. The last sound I heard was their laughter as they walked away."

"I'm sorry." Before us remained the happy scene with everyone being friendly. Maybe he preferred this to remembering his death; I wouldn't blame him. I didn't like remembering my death either, and at least I'd been in my bed, with Lucas by my side. "That's awful."

Christopher stared hard at his killers, who were at that moment laughing at one of his jokes. Mrs. Bethany set the slices of cake in front of them; she didn't seem to be in as good spirits as the others. In fact, her expression was wary. She'd picked up on trouble even if her husband hadn't.

Then the room shifted again, with Mrs. Bethany remaining motionless at the center of it, her dress flowing from one color to another and her expression changing from unease to rage. "What do you mean, you cannot act?"

The scene in front of us was now some kind of meeting-house or storeroom. Black Cross, I realized, seeing the weaponry mounted on the walls. A man with his hair tied in a tail sat on a slightly raised platform, obviously in charge. He shook his head. "Mrs. Bethany, as lamentable as your husband's death is, it was not the work of any supernatural agency. Therefore it does not concern Black Cross."

"The magistrate will not listen," Mrs. Bethany said. "He believes it was the work of bandits and says I am a foolish woman, doubting two such 'fine gentlemen.'" She spat those two words, as if she thought they could poison her. "I could kill them myself, but they are gone to the Caribbean. His family's money is lost, because of their deceit. At least give me the funds to travel there, to see justice done."

The Black Cross leader looked at Mrs. Bethany pityingly— the same look, I realized, that Kate had worn when she refused to give back Lucas's coffee can full of cash. "Our funds are used for our struggle, and every penny is needed. You know this as well as I. Your grief has brought you to the point of hysteria."

Mrs. Bethany's proud face never changed, but I saw something I'd never expected to see: her eyes filling with tears. Yet she spoke steadily. "After everything I have done, everything I have given, this is your answer."

"What other answer could there be?"

She stepped back slightly, cocking her head in that familiar gesture of contemplation and contempt. *Like she's seeing him for the first time,* I thought.

Christopher said, "In that instant, her dedication to Black Cross turned to hate. We can always hate that which we loved, and with a fire as great as our love once was."

The room vanished, replaced by the same forest pathway we had seen first. But the scene had changed to winter; the naked tree branches glittered with ice, and the ground was thick with snow. Mrs. Bethany rode alone on horseback, sidesaddle, with a heavy cape of dark furs around her. Her eyes searched her surroundings despite the deepening shadows—it was dusk, the sky a piercing cobalt blue. Then she sat up a little straighter; she'd spotted something.

A vampire stepped from behind one of the larger trees, obviously uneasy. "Whatever trap you set, huntress, it's a dangerous one for you. Your help is too far away."

"I set no trap," Mrs. Bethany said. She dismounted from her horse and walked slowly toward him in the snow. "I bear no weapons."

"Then I suppose you have come to die, huntress."

It was a taunt, but Mrs. Bethany lifted her head. "Yes."

The vampire appeared as shocked as I was. He didn't say anything at first, didn't rush at her or run away.

She held up her hands, gloved in dark green, to show that she had no weapons. A gust of wind ruffled her hair and sent down a shower of snow from the branches above, scattering white on her dark hair and cape. "I was bitten once. Did you know? Do they tell the story?"

"Many claim it," the vampire said. "Many lie."

"One tells the truth," she said. A quick tug at the neck of her cape revealed an old scar upon her throat. "I was rescued, then. But I have always known that I am prepared. If a vampire were to bite me, and kill me, I would rise again, undead."

The vampire took a step closer, disbelieving. "This is a trick."

"No trick."

"You hate our kind. Why would you become one of us?"

"I need to be free of human ties, human cares." Mrs. Bethany's expression faltered, but only for a moment. "I—I need to travel beyond the reach of my mortal means."

That won her a burst of laughter from the vampire. "Mad. You've gone mad."

She said, "Change me and see."

The vampire sprang at her, taking both of them down to the ground in one pounce. Mrs. Bethany didn't resist and didn't scream, not even when her blood spurted onto the white snow, steaming.

"Revenge," Christopher said, "is a powerful motivator."

The next place he showed me was obviously someplace a lot warmer. A palm frond brushed against the window and tropical flowers were piled high in vases. We seemed to be in an island villa, one that might have been very nice before it had been trashed. Furniture was upended, mirrors broken. Two dead bodies lay on the floor, and Mrs. Bethany stood in one corner, taking in the scene with some satisfaction. She wiped blood from her mouth with the back of her hand.

"She got them back," I said. Despite the horror of the murder scene before us, I couldn't help feeling like those guys had it coming.

Christopher nodded. "But at what cost? Her life. Perhaps more important, her mission. Her soul."

"Where were you during all this?" I said. "Why didn't you appear to her? If she'd known you were a ghost, that she could maybe talk to you—"

"I could not yet appear to her." The Caribbean scene with Mrs. Bethany faded, and we were once again in the land of lost things. Were we in the same location? Our surroundings had changed; instead of the city, we stood out in the open, in a desert too stark to be beautiful. Sunlight beat down hotly, and I noticed a scorpion scuttling across the ground. Christopher sat on a low, flat rock; his handsome profile was outlined against the dark stone, and for the first time, I recognized him as the silhouette on Mrs. Bethany's desk. "As you know, learning to use wraith powers takes some time—and far more time for most than it did for you. By the point when I could have appeared to my wife, she had learned to hate the wraiths as the natural enemy of the vampire. She had shown me, through her actions, that her hate was stronger than her love."

I wanted to argue with him, but I remembered how hard it had been for me to appear to my parents. That fear of rejection was powerful. And as Lucas's situation showed, not every person was strong enough to love despite the change.

*Lucas,* I thought. Of course Mrs. Bethany had been sympathetic to Lucas. Of course she reached out to him and understood him. She had been *exactly* where he was. But that didn't make her generous and good. It just made her somebody who hated Black Cross a lot. He needed to realize that, and the sooner the better.

"I have to go," I said. "I'll come back, okay?"

I'd expected Christopher to protest, or throw some ice-storm tantrum to keep me here, but instead he kept gazing at the scorpion as it skittered upon the sand. "Go," he said. "I am weary."

Watching Mrs. Bethany's death—even as a long-distant memory—had been as hard for him as it had been for me to see Lucas die. I put one hand on his shoulder. "Thank you for showing me."

"Go," he said, more quietly, and placed his face in his hands.

I concentrated on a place, on the records room, and traveled through the blue until it materialized around me. Patrice was up there alone, studying her German; she started when I appeared, but only for a second. "Hey, there you are. Lucas was getting worried."

"I'm going to him right away," I promised, going to the loose brick in the wall and retrieving my bracelet from behind it. When I'd put it around my wrist, I took completely solid form and felt an enormous wave of relief. "I just need a second to be . . . less ghostly. If that makes sense."

"Whatever works," Patrice said, not unkindly. "But he's got a test this afternoon, remember? He'll do better if he knows you're around and okay."

"I know it." Though I hated to give up the bracelet so soon, I decided I'd better. "Okay, fine. Come with me?"

"Sure. I have to head down to class anyway."

I trailed behind her as vapor the whole way down the stairs. "Could you keep out of my hair, please?" she muttered. "You're awfully damp sometimes. I'll frizz."

"This isn't easy, you know."

"Neither is fixing my hair."

I wanted to laugh, but just then—as we were re-entering the classroom area—we heard the commotion. People shouting, shoes squeaking against the floor, the thud of a body against the wall—

"A fight," Patrice said.

"Lucas." I knew it without having to be told.

Patrice ran, me above her, until we reached the fracas. Sure enough, Lucas and Samuel were on the floor, grappling with each other, their noses bloody.

"I said," Lucas rasped, "leave her alone."

"You want her for yourself, huh? Is that what you want?" Samuel's sick grin made it clear that he wasn't talking about flirtation. Whatever human Samuel had been picking on—and Lucas had been defending—was all too appetizing as an evening snack. I realized who it must have been when Skye, amid the crowd, threw one of her books at Samuel, but he dodged it easily. "Hit me a little harder, and she's yours, man. Take what you want."

Lucas head-butted the guy, so hard that Samuel flopped back, stunned. Groggily, a hand to his forehead, Lucas said, "Mostly I just want you to shut up."

The laughing crowd around us went very quiet, parting to allow Mrs. Bethany to sweep into the middle of this. She looked so different to me now that I had seen her younger, human, in love, alive. And yet she was still Mrs. Bethany, made of starched lace and long skirts and chilly authority. The fight scene got no more reaction from her than a raised eyebrow. "Mr. Ross. Mr. Younger. I take it you've settled this matter between yourselves?"

"Yeah, it's settled." Lucas got to his feet, somewhat unsteadily, and dabbed at his nose with his sleeve. Samuel continued to glare up at him, like he might tackle him anew whether the headmistress was watching or not.

"Mr. Younger?" Mrs. Bethany repeated. "I hope I won't have to undertake any . . . disciplinary action. I suspect you wouldn't care for my methods."

"Yeah," Samuel said, which wasn't exactly an answer, but he rose and slouched off without another word.

As everyone else went about their business, scattering from Mrs. Bethany like leaves in a strong gale, I wanted to talk to Lucas—but Skye was a little faster, reaching him before I had a chance to say a word. "Thanks for standing up for me."

"No prob."

She had a crooked sort of smile that somehow made her beauty more approachable. How come my funny smile only made me look silly? "You're kind of like a one-man SWAT team, you know. Who would've thought anybody would need so much rescuing in high school?"

Skye was only making a joke, but it obviously struck a chord for Lucas. He took her arm by the elbow and said, "We've gotta talk."

"Our test is starting in five minutes—and don't you need to clean up after the fight?"

"Forget cleaning up. Forget the test. This is important."

I followed them back into the stairwell; Patrice cast a worried glance after us but didn't try to join them. Good thing, too, because she probably would've freaked out. Knowing Lucas as I did, I knew what he was about to say—and I thought it was a good idea.

It was time to tell Skye the truth.

"What's up?" Skye's expression clouded as they stood together in the stairwell, light from the narrow arched window illuminating her dark hair. "Are you finally going to talk about what's wrong with you?"

Lucas grew wary. "What do you mean?"

"You're just so . . . angry," she whispered, her voice gentle. "So angry about everything, all the time. I'm not saying you're wrong to be angry, but Lucas—it's burning you up inside. What is it? Can you tell me?"

If she'd tried to hint or trick it out of him, Lucas would never have spoken. But simple honesty always broke down his barriers. "My girlfriend, Bianca . . . she died last summer. I still love her. I always will."

The truth, if not the whole truth, and it had the power to warm and thrill me all over again. What surprised me was the power that it had over Skye; her pale blue eyes instantly welled with tears. "I lost somebody this summer, too. My older brother."

"Oh, Jesus." Lucas was clearly caught off guard. "Skye, I'm sorry."

She squeezed his hand. "Believe me, I get it. I might hide the anger better than you do, but sometimes I just want to . . ." Skye breathed out in frustration but managed to smile for him as she wiped away one tear. "Was Bianca just—amazing? I bet she was amazing."

Lucas's expression faltered. Talking about me in the past tense reminded him of my death and brought the pain back. "You have no idea."

"If it helps any, I believe—no, I *know*—the dead aren't truly gone." She spoke with the deep assurance that could only have come from growing up in a haunted house. Skye knew about the undead, at least on that level. "They watch us. They're close by. And I think they realize how much we love them, maybe more than they did when they were alive."

As Skye finished saying this, I took the risk of brushing, gently, against Lucas's hand. I saw him straighten, reassured of my presence and safety, and yet more emotional than before. "I believe that, too."

"She'd want you to be happy," Skye said. "Not angry all the time."

"I'm trying." I knew Lucas was speaking to me as much as to Skye.

They just watched each other for a second, struggling for composure. After swallowing hard, Skye managed to say, "So, what did you want to tell me?"

"This school is dangerous, Skye. Everywhere around here is dangerous. You have to watch yourself."

"Yeah, I kinda got that after the time those weird old gang members fired an arrow at me. What kind of gang uses crossbows?"

Lucas took a step closer and looked her straight in the eyes. Through the one crescent-shaped window, afternoon sunlight flooded in, turning his hair pure gold. "No, I mean it. Some of the students here—they're not just students."

She folded her arms. "You mean, they're also enormous dickweeds?"

"I mean, they're vampires."

Skye stared at Lucas. Lucas stared right back at her. I wondered if she would scream, or ask questions, or just run like hell out of the school.

Instead she burst into laughter.

As Lucas pulled back, startled, she gasped, "You almost had me!"

"Skye—"

"It's okay, I get it." Her giggles almost masked her words. "We were getting way too heavy for people who need to think about calculus. Thanks for making me laugh. I needed it."

Lucas struggled for words, then surrendered. "Anytime."

"Come on, let's get to class." Skye headed for the door. Lucas glanced back, and I shimmered slightly in the light, so he'd know I was near. His bashful smile was the best welcome-home I could have had.

Of course I wanted to tell Lucas about Mrs. Bethany, but it could wait. Lucas's dedication to his studies this semester might be mostly a way of distracting himself from pain, but that was a good reason to respect it. I supposed it wouldn't hurt to wait forty-five minutes.

Not everybody could be as disciplined about waiting for the right time to speak, though. As I settled back into the records room upstairs, alone and ready to spend a little more quality time wearing my bracelet, someone else decided to pay me a visit.

"Well, if it isn't the prom queen of the dead," Maxie said. I sat up, startled; she'd materialized across the room, and I'd been so deep in thought I hadn't noticed. She was back in her flowing nightdress, like I was back in my usual pajamas. "Tell me, what's it like to be *so special* that the rules don't apply to you?"

"Awful," I said. "It means even people you thought were your friends don't like you."

Maxie hesitated. She ducked her head, so that her cropped

hair fell into her eyes, slightly blocking her view. "I like you," she said in a small voice.

"Sometimes you don't act like it."

"We have to make choices," she said. For the first time since I'd known her, she sounded more like an adult than a petulant child. "We have to recognize that we're dead."

"I get that. Trust me."

"Vampires are our enemies."

"Maybe that's true most of the time," I admitted, thinking of Mrs. Bethany, "but it's not true for Lucas. Or for Balthazar, or Patrice, or Ranulf. Why do you keep trying to create these black-and-white categories? Why are you looking at what everyone is, instead of who they are?"

"It helps," she whispered. "When you're not alive but not totally dead—it can feel like everything is gray. You want black. You want white."

"I know." And I did.

At that moment, the door opened, and Vic and Ranulf walked in. They had lunch period now. "Wait, wait," Vic was saying. "You got *Cristina Del Valle* to go to the Autumn Ball with you? How did you work that? She's the hottest girl in school."

"I am wise in the ways of comely maidens," Ranulf said. Then they both stopped as they saw me—and, I realized, Maxie, who hadn't made herself invisible in time and now seemed to be too startled to do so, or anything else but gape at them.

Quickly, I said, "Maxie, obviously you already know Vic, but have you met Ranulf?"

"Still more wraiths," Ranulf said. He'd been uneasy about socializing with me at first, after my death, but it only took him a second to get past it now. "Welcome. Will you be here often? If so, please do not frost too many of the seating places. Bianca often leaves them too cold to be of use to others."

"Hey!" I protested, but Ranulf suddenly seemed very interested in the Elvis posters.

Vic just kept staring at Maxie. She'd interacted with him throughout his life, but always invisibly; this had to be the first time he'd ever actually seen her. "Wow," he said. "Uh, wow. Hey there."

"Hello," Maxie whispered. I knew that was the first word she'd ever spoken to him. She'd crossed the line—the one she didn't want me to cross, and I liked it. Was she starting to think for herself? To understand that the lines between vampire, wraith, and human were as blurry as the ones between life and death?

"Do you want to . . . hang out for a while?" Vic looked around the room wildly, obviously trying to figure out what might entertain her. "We could just talk or . . . I've got some music—"

"I should go," Maxie said. But before I could be disappointed, she added, more quietly, "I'll come back sometime."

Vic grinned. "Great. I mean, that's— That would be great."

Maxie vanished, but I could sense her. She was drifting out of the room very slowly, as if more reluctant to leave than she'd let on. As she finally rose through the roof, Vic turned to me and said, "That was unbelievable!"

"Was it great? Finally meeting her?" I grinned up at him. His mouth was partway open, half smile and half amazement.

"I guess . . . I never realized . . . I mean, I knew she was a she and all that, but I never realized my ghost was a *girl*."

Ranulf said, "Vic has not yet learned the arts of interaction with females."

"You gonna teach me your tricks, buddy?" Vic said.

"It is only a small matter of observation over several centuries."

"Great." Vic sighed, throwing down his backpack.

"I'll be right back, okay?" I slipped off my bracelet and dematerialized, drifting up through the roof. As I'd suspected, I found Maxie high in the sky. We could see each other, mostly—misty outlines of ourselves that would be invisible from the ground.

"I talked to Vic!" she said. Her smile was part of the afternoon sunlight. "I talked to him, and he talked back!"

"See how much fun it is, crossing the lines?"

"It's not wrong to move on," she said, more firmly. "You know how much better it is there than here. But—as long as we are partly here—"

"I think our afterlives have to be about the people we love." I started drifting higher, mostly out of curiosity to see how high we could go. "Nothing else makes any sense."

"But I didn't know Vic before. Not when I was alive," Maxie protested.

"If you ask me, it doesn't make any difference when you

start to love somebody. Just that you love them."

Merely saying the word *love* reminded me of Lucas and the news I wanted to share with him so badly that it burned inside me. But I had half an hour to kill. So I pushed myself higher; Maxie followed.

"How high up can we go?" I asked.

"Oh, crazy high. Above the troposphere. You can see the stars during the day, if you want."

"Really?" I could go stargazing right now—anytime, in fact. I wouldn't have a telescope, of course, but nevertheless, that view would be something to see, like a picture from the Hubble. "Let's go, okay?"

Maxie started to laugh, and I knew that this was what she'd wanted all along. Not for me to choose sides—just for her to have a companion in her in-between world. "Okay, sure."

We rose up, farther and farther, until Evernight Academy was only a speck on the ground, then obscured by clouds. The sunlight above was brighter than bright. Blinding.

Then this enormous silver shape appeared in the distance, coming closer, faster than I could imagine. "What in the world is that?"

"Hang on!" Maxie yelled.

*Is that—is it an* airplane?

A commercial jetliner zoomed straight toward us, until I could see the outline of it—the front windows—the pilots inside—and then, *wham,* Maxie and I slamming directly through the center of the plane, front cabin, the long aisle, dozens of passengers, the little drink cart, the tail—and it was gone. We'd gone straight through.

Maxie and I drifted there, dazed, for a long second. She finally said, "Do you think anybody on the plane saw us?

"We were going too fast," I said. "But maybe they hit some turbulence."

She started to laugh, and I did, too.

Although Maxie wanted to keep creating "air pockets" for plane traffic out of Boston, I parted from her when I sensed that Lucas's class was probably over. We promised to go stargazing soon, and while that prospect delighted me, the closer I got to earth, the more pressing my real concerns seemed.

I found Lucas out at the gazebo, waiting for me as usual. His backpack had been tossed on the floor, and he was resting his forearms on his knees, his head drooping. "You look tired," I whispered, becoming a soft mist near him.

"I am tired."

"Up late worrying about me?"

"Up late worrying," he confirmed. "But I know you can take care of yourself, so I also stayed up studying. And listening to music. And surfing the Internet. And doing whatever else I could think of to avoid going to sleep."

I didn't have to ask why. "Charity." Lucas didn't reply, but he swallowed hard, making his Adam's apple bob in his throat. I brushed gently against his cheek, hoping he could feel the cool touch. "Is she getting worse?"

"Worse? No. She started off making my dreams as bad as they could be, and since then—well, you have to give her this, she's consistent. It's horrible every night. Every single night." Lucas stood abruptly. He braced his hands against the cast iron of the gazebo, every muscle in his back so tense I could make them out through his uniform sweater. "Sometimes it's Erich again, threatening to torture you with stakes soaked in holy water. Sometimes other vampires drink your blood, and for some reason it kills you instead of turning you into one of them. Sometimes my mom cuts off your head. Or those drunk guys— remember, our first date? In my dreams, they're not trying to take care of you. They're trying to burn you. All the dreams are about losing you, over and over again."

The ragged pain in his voice made me wish I could risk becoming corporeal, so I could put my arms around him. "Charity only turned you to take you away from me," I said. "It's my fault."

"It's not your fault," Lucas said. I wished I could be as sure as he sounded. "But yeah, Charity likes the idea of me losing you forever. Enough to have it on infinite replay in my head."

"Please, let me come back. If I were in your dreams, I know I could get through to you."

Lucas shook his head. "Absolutely not. Anything she did to you in there could really hurt you. That's not a risk I'm willing to take."

Even if the only alternative was his enduring pain? I hated this, but for now, we had no better choice.

He said, "Bianca, I've been meaning to ask you about this for a while now. What happens after Evernight?"

"What do you mean?"

"I can't stay at this school forever," Lucas said. "I mean, I guess technically I could, but I don't really see me repeating English Lit every other semester for the next several centuries. And you can't want to spend the rest of eternity hiding in corners. Waiting on me."

I hadn't thought that far ahead—hadn't let myself. Now that I understood my own powers, the many places I could go and things I could do, I no longer feared the eternity that lay before me. But it was different for Lucas.

I said, "Vampires usually start out . . . wandering, I guess. Taking advantage of their immortality to explore the world. Once you get a few decades of experience, apparently it's not so hard to start making money. And after you get rich, well, you can pretty much do what you want."

Lucas's face looked pained at the words *a few decades*. He said, "I don't need to get rich. I don't need to do what I want. Because right now, I'm not sure I'd use that power well."

"You have to stop being frightened of yourself. Of what you've become."

"I know what I've become," he said. "That's why I know I need to be afraid."

Fear gripped me as I realized that the next thing he was going to say was something along the lines of "You should be free." He still thought he was a burden to me, when he was anything but. "What you've become is my anchor," I said. "The person who connects me to this world."

He couldn't fully believe me. "Really?"

"Always."

Lucas breathed out heavily. "I only wish I could believe I could give you something worth having."

"You do every day. Every second. Never doubt that."

"Okay," he said, but I knew he wasn't completely convinced.

Time to focus his attention on our real problems. "Listen," I said. "I want to talk to you about Mrs. Bethany."

He half turned, so I could see his face. "Do we have to go over this again?"

"This is new."

As quickly as I could, I told him who Christopher was, and what he had revealed to me about her past. When I said that she'd been Black Cross, Lucas's eyes went wide, but he said nothing. Once I'd finished, I said, "She's not being sympathetic because she suddenly turned nice. She just hates Black Cross as much as you do."

"Why do those have to be two separate things?"

I stared at Lucas, stung. He seemed more frustrated than before.

"Bianca, does being mad at Black Cross mean you lose the power to think rationally forever? Or to care about other people? If so, I'm screwed."

"That's not what I'm saying."

"Isn't it?" Lucas kicked at the iron scrollwork nearest his feet, making the ivy rustle. "Why do you hate her so much?"

"She's a killer." I hadn't realized I could speak so loudly, or so sharply, while hardly more than a vapor. "She murdered Eduardo, remember? And how many other members of your cell?"

"The Black Cross cell that invaded this place to try and kill her? And Eduardo—" His hands gripped so tightly around the gazebo railing that I would've thought it would hurt. Lucas hadn't been very fond of his stepfather, but he worried about his mother being left alone, even now. "That happened when she came to the New York cell to try and rescue you. Or have you forgotten?"

"She wanted revenge for the attack on the school! That's what it was, revenge! And have you forgotten the traps she's laid for the wraiths?"

"You wanted to trap them yourself before you turned into one!" Lucas realized we were starting to shout and took a deep breath, calming himself. I couldn't exactly breathe in this state, but I tried to be more still. The few fights Lucas and I had had were always bruising, and besides, we didn't want anybody to start staring at us. More quietly, he said, "People can do things for more than one reason."

"If it's Mrs. Bethany, it's not a good reason."

"Why do you believe that? Seriously, Bianca, do you have a reason for distrusting her besides the fact that she's a hardass in the classroom?"

That caught me up short. "The people she's killed—"

"I've killed plenty of vampires," Lucas said. "I see now that they were people, too. Do you trust me?"

"Of course. Always." My mind raced. When had I begun to fear Mrs. Bethany? Was it nothing more than a juvenile dislike of a strict teacher? I couldn't believe that, but I couldn't give any better reason than this: "Call it instinct, Lucas. I don't trust her."

"We can't write her off on instinct alone. Not when she's offering me—"

"What is she offering you? Besides vague promises?"

"A place to live," he said. "The right to figure things out. And maybe an end to this hunger."

Lucas looked across the grounds, where a group of students were lounging. Humans. I could tell. Even now, while we were in the heart of a passionate discussion, he could smell their blood and long for his first kill.

"Oh, Lucas." I dared to add a bit more substance to myself, enough to touch his hand. He closed his eyes tightly as I did. "Do you think that could be real?"

He stepped back from the railing, newly energized. His jaw was set as he looked at me—knowing, somehow, as he always did, how to look into my gaze. "I'm about to find out."

"Lucas, wait!" But I was too late. He descended from the gazebo and headed straight for the carriage house.

Lucas was walking right into Mrs. Bethany's lair—and I knew at that moment, if she made him the right promise, I could be in danger of losing him forever.

# Chapter Seventeen

I FOLLOWED LUCAS TO MRS. BETHANY'S CARRIAGE house. Although I could have called out to him again, to try and stop him from doing this, I didn't.

*We need to know,* I told myself. *If she really can help him, then I should let her do it.*

Was I resisting only because I was jealous that Mrs. Bethany could give him something that precious—something I couldn't? How petty. How small. No wonder Lucas felt he could trust her, if I was so weak by comparison.

I would listen, and watch. Maybe I would hear that Lucas could be free from the blood hunger. If so, then I promised myself I'd never say another bad word about Mrs. Bethany again.

As Lucas knocked on the door, I cautiously took my now-familiar place at her windowsill, relieved to sense no traps nearby—then was startled. Someone already sat in front of her desk: Samuel, no doubt being taken to task for the fighting earlier. Probably Lucas wouldn't get a chance to have a serious conversation with Mrs. Bethany about anything. I couldn't decide whether I was happy about that or not.

But when Mrs. Bethany opened the door and saw Lucas, she said, "What excellent timing, Mr. Ross. Please, step inside."

Lucas didn't look any happier to see Samuel than Samuel did to see Lucas. "Is this about our altercation earlier?"

"Not exactly." Mrs. Bethany gestured toward a chair in the corner of the room. "I was just having a conversation with Mr. Younger about his many disciplinary difficulties this year. There is another matter—one I had planned to bring up with you later, Mr. Ross—but upon consideration, this seems as good a time as any."

Mr. Younger, aka Samuel, drew himself up, obviously offended. "Since when does that Black Cross scum have anything to do with running this place?"

"I alone am the authority here." Mrs. Bethany walked toward her desk, long dusty-violet skirt swirling around her. As she laid one hand upon her desk, I noticed again the framed silhouette she'd always kept nearby. Christopher: She still looked at his face every day. Kept him close. That made me wistful, and for a few moments I felt that I might have judged her wrong from the beginning. She continued, "As the authority at this school, I notice that you have been reprimanded by multiple instructors for offenses ranging from talking in class to bullying."

Samuel had always looked like an average thick-headed jerk to me, but his expression hardened, and for the first time I could see the ancient monster within the boy. "This isn't actually a school, or did you forget? I don't need to study algebra. I need to figure out how to pass for human. Everything else here is a waste of my time."

"Harassing the human students seems, to you, a better use of your time?" Mrs. Bethany arched one elegant eyebrow.

"Why are they even here?" Samuel shot back. "If you didn't bring them in to serve as our dessert tray, I don't see the point."

She smiled, just a little, her eyes darting briefly toward Lucas, who looked as confused as I felt. "You don't see many things, Mr. Younger."

"I've had enough of this." Samuel rose as if to go, but Mrs. Bethany's withering glare pinned him in place.

She steepled her hands upon her desk and spoke slowly and carefully. "I asked human students to this school because they were necessary to fulfill a . . . pet project of mine. An interest of Mr. Ross's as well." Mrs. Bethany looked directly at Lucas as she said, "The elimination of the bloodlust of our kind."

Samuel snorted. "So leave me out of it. I don't want to be free from bloodlust. I like bloodlust. Best thing about being what we are."

"You enjoy being a vampire too much, I think," she said. "You've forgotten the alternative."

"So what if I have? As far as I remember, being human kind of sucked. I was weak, I had to eat vegetables, plus don't forget having to go to the bathroom, what, like, multiple times every day? What a waste of time."

Mrs. Bethany cocked her head, taking his measure as she took something from one of the drawers of her desk—a small metal container. A trap. And yet I felt no pull toward it. "We shall see."

"What?" Samuel said. But she wasn't paying any more attention to him.

To Lucas, she said, "Do you know what this is?"

"A trap," Lucas replied. His gaze was fixed on the box. "For a wraith."

I realized that ice flaked the metal container, meaning that a ghost was already trapped inside. That was why it had no power over me; the trap was full.

"Very good, Mr. Ross." She rose to a standing position. "Now, observe."

Mrs. Bethany whispered something in Latin as she opened the box. The wraith within came out—as a bolt of light that struck Samuel squarely in the chest. He collapsed onto the floor, twitching violently; the wraith seemed to be circling him, stuck to him, a writhing vapor going over each limb, covering his face, trying to get away but unable to move.

"What the hell?" Lucas rose to his feet, obviously trying to figure out how to help Samuel, if that was possible. But Mrs. Bethany shook her head no.

Fascinated, I stared as Mrs. Bethany withdrew a long knife with a black blade—obsidian, I realized. Despite the barrier of the house's walls, the obsidian seemed to push me back.

Then she stabbed downward—through the wraith, into Samuel. Silvery blood mingled with red, and both of them screamed.

The wraith suddenly sank within Samuel, clearly being absorbed by him. Samuel twitched one moment more, then sucked in a deep breath. Then another. He pushed himself up on his elbows, staring at the oozing wound in his arm. The blood was pulsing out—

Pulsing—

*He has a pulse,* I realized. *A heartbeat.*

Samuel stared up at Mrs. Bethany, mute with shock. His eyes were wild and vacant. She straightened, throwing back her shoulders and smiling so brilliantly that she looked younger for a moment. Beautiful. Terrible. Lucas took a halting step backward, then sat heavily in the chair, like his only alternative would've been to fall down.

"It works," she whispered.

"I'm—" Samuel kept patting himself down, like that would make sense of it. "Oh, God, I'm human."

Mrs. Bethany began to laugh. "You're *alive.*"

My mind seemed to blank out, like where I should've had thoughts, there was only white light and static. What I'd just seen was impossible—and yet, I'd seen it.

"Make it stop. Make it stop." Samuel clawed at his uniform sweater, like he was trying to rip through his own chest to tear out the beating heart.

Lucas had to open and close his mouth a couple of times before he could say, "What—what did you do?"

"The wraith and the vampire represent two halves of death, Mr. Ross." Her voice was again crisp and professional, but the hot light in her eyes hadn't faded. She stepped closer to Samuel, who was by this point writhing on the floor, his living body apparently excruciating to him. "And yet, we also represent two halves of life. The flesh, and the spirit. Unite them once more, and the result is . . . resurrection."

"I never heard of anything like that," Lucas said. "Black Cross never told us this."

"And yet they are among the very few who have ever known it. It was among Black Cross documents I stole that I discovered this." Mrs. Bethany leaned over Samuel. His distress did nothing to diminish her delight. "Why didn't they share the knowledge? You would think anything that resulted in fewer vampires—but no. Black Cross didn't merely want safety for humans. They also wanted vengeance. And what vengeance could they have had in giving vampires renewed life?"

"Make it stop," Samuel repeated. His voice was reedy now, which made it almost unrecognizable. It was like coming back to life had driven him crazy.

Lucas took a step toward Samuel, but he didn't know how to help any more than I did. He said, "This can't be real."

"Feel his pulse!" Mrs. Bethany grabbed Samuel's wrist; he whimpered but didn't resist her. Then she let go, visibly steadying herself. "Forgive me. I have known the theory for nearly four years, but this is my first successful test."

Then Lucas lifted his head, awareness dawning. "Bianca," he said, and for a moment I thought he was talking to me. But he continued, "Bianca was created when her parents made a deal with a wraith—"

"Another way for the combination of wraith and vampire to

create life," Mrs. Bethany said. "Though there, the result is the creation of a third, independent being. Here, we take the energy of a wraith and unite it with the body of a vampire. Ideally, the wraith's consciousness is erased, leaving the energy to resurrect the vampire as the person he or she once was."

The wraith's consciousness was erased? When you were a wraith, all you were was consciousness. Mrs. Bethany wasn't just trapping the ghosts. She intended to kill them, a sacrifice so that vampires could live again.

And Lucas hadn't yet walked away.

*He's in shock,* I told myself, and I knew it was true; I was in shock myself. But I also knew how profoundly Lucas hated being a vampire. If he had a chance to live again—to be fully human—what might he do to make it happen?

Lucas had focused again on Samuel, who had begun thumping his head against the floor. It should've looked funny, but the disjointed, jerky way he moved was too unsettling for that. "What's wrong with him?"

Mrs. Bethany sighed. "As I feared, using an unstable spirit results in an unstable human. This one I had thought was a superior specimen, far more cogent than most of the wraiths we've managed to ensnare thus far—and yet, obviously, not steady enough."

"Please," Samuel whispered. He'd started to cry, and I realized that in his fists were strands of his own hair; he'd pulled it from his own scalp. I saw that the wraith's insanity had become a part of him now, as much as his blood or his bone. Mrs. Bethany had restored him to life, but she had also wrecked him.

"You just—" Lucas glanced at her. "Did this as an *experiment*."

"I didn't intend to go first myself," Mrs. Bethany said, "and Mr. Younger had serious behavioral problems. I have better uses for my time than hosting detention."

Lucas frowned in a way I recognized as a sign of growing anger. As much as he'd suffered from Samuel, he obviously never would have wished this on him. "Seems like you could've warned the guy."

"I thought there was a reasonable chance he'd be restored to life and health," Mrs. Bethany said. She opened the front door, and Samuel stumbled to his feet and ran for it. His steps were unsteady, and he didn't go toward the school; instead, he streaked toward the woods. Somehow I knew we would never see him again. Mrs. Bethany came right to my window, so close I shrank myself within the branches of the nearest shrub, and watched him go. "Who can say? In a decade or so, he may gain some stability."

"Shouldn't we go after the guy?" Lucas demanded. "And if that's the best you can manage, you shouldn't have tried it on him in the first place."

"Angry, Mr. Ross?" Mrs. Bethany looked more amused than anything else. "Why so? Though I have no reason to doubt your good intentions, I cannot imagine your outrage is solely on Mr. Younger's behalf."

"You just—destroyed him! To test your theory!"

The angrier he got, the warmer Mrs. Bethany's smile became. "You're upset because it didn't work, not in a manner you'd wish to experience. Because you think I don't have the answer I promised you."

"That is *not*—"

"Isn't it?" She put her hands on his shoulders. They were face-to-face now, so close. "We can rise from the dead. I have proved it. We can trap the wraiths. I have proved that, too. Now it is only a matter of finding suitable wraiths—those who are especially strong, especially stable. Connected to the world in a meaningful fashion. If we can only find such wraiths, and trap them, you and I will live again."

Lucas's face was a mask of rage, and yet her final words, *live again*, made him shut his eyes tightly.

Her voice became lower, softer, sweet. "I see how you look at the human students. I know your hunger—it's something we share. I traded my human life to a vampire for the sake of love, and revenge, and two centuries later I remain trapped in the prison of my corpse. It's so heavy, isn't it? Carrying around your own dead body? Knowing yourself to be a monster and hating every urge you feel? But it's almost over, Lucas. We're almost free."

He opened his eyes. They looked deeply at each other for a long second, and I thought, in desperation, *I've lost him. For real, this time.*

"Join me," she said, "and live again."

Lucas flung her hands from his shoulders. "No."

Mrs. Bethany stepped back, one hand to her throat. "Mr. Ross—"

"You threw that guy away like he was nothing," Lucas said. "You trashed him, and it doesn't matter to you one bit. You'll destroy the wraiths like they're nothing, including—including the ones most like living things—and that doesn't matter to you either. I can't do that, not ever, not even to. . . . You know, I don't care what magic you work. Even if you pull it off, even if you give yourself a heartbeat, you'll still be dead inside."

Silence. They stood there, regarding each other as though they were strangers. Mrs. Bethany looked—sad. Crushed. At last she said quietly, "I had hoped you would be a part of this."

"I had hopes," Lucas said. "But I'd never be a part of this." He ran for the door and out onto the grounds.

How could I have doubted him, even for a second? Lucas had stood by me. He had kept my secret. In the face of the ultimate temptation, he had walked away without any doubts. Amid my astonishment and horror, I also knew a deep, powerful joy. I raced after him, a breeze high above the grounds, shaking down red and gold leaves from the trees so that they scattered behind me.

Lucas ran into the forest, and at first I thought he must be going after Samuel, though I couldn't imagine what we could do to help him. Instead, as soon as the trees concealed him from the school—in a small glade that I recognized as the place we'd first met—he collapsed to the ground, on his hands and knees. His breaths came raggedly, and I realized he was on the verge of tears.

I took form slowly, giving him time to tell me to go, if he wanted to be alone. But he fumbled in his pocket, grabbing my brooch, and handed it to me. As soon as I felt the jet, my body became entirely solid, and Lucas clutched me to him with all his strength.

"There's a way out," he gasped. "There's a way out, and I can never take it."

I held him tighter. Why hadn't I realized how much worse this would be for him? He'd been promised a release from an existence he considered worse than any jail—and it was true; every one of Mrs. Bethany's promises was true. It was the doorway out, and he would never walk through it.

Then I considered that. A small, scared feeling quivered inside me, but I didn't let it take me over.

I held Lucas as he buried his face in the curve of my shoulder, his whole body shaking with suppressed emotion. Until I was sure, I couldn't speak.

Finally I said, "We could do it."

Lucas shifted back, enough to see my face. "Do what?"

"The ritual. What Mrs. Bethany did." I steadied myself. "I could bring you back to life."

"No. You'd be giving up whatever life or existence you have left, and then you'd be gone forever."

"You offered to do the same for me," I said. "Remember?"

"And you were brave enough to die in my place." Lucas brushed his thumbs across my cheeks and cradled my face in his hands. "I'm not gonna give you anything less."

I hugged him again, and he sank against me like he was exhausted. Mrs. Bethany would never hold power over him again, I knew, and yet his burden was heavier than ever. It would never get any easier. Neither of us would ever die, or ever live again.

# Chapter Eighteen

LATER THAT NIGHT, UP IN THE RECORDS ROOM, we told the others what we'd seen. So, instead of just Lucas and I being in total shock, each of us sat around mutely for about an hour. Mrs. Bethany's feat—returning a vampire to life—defied every physical and supernatural law any of us had ever known, and yet there was no denying what we'd witnessed.

Balthazar repeated, for about the eighth time, "It's still so . . . unreal to me. That there's a way back to being alive."

"Doesn't tempt me," Patrice sniffed, as though she hadn't spent the first ten minutes after our revelation repeating "Oh, my God," over and over. "I found out the hard way—once someone's dead, in whatever way they happen to be dead, it's best to leave things as they are." She suddenly seemed to be highly interested in her rings, but I knew she was remembering her long-lost love, Amos, whom she had brought back as a ghost. Although Patrice was too private to ever share the full details, it was clear the results had been tragic.

Vic nodded. "Raising the dead brings up serious monkey's paw issues, definitely. What do you think, Ranulf?"

Ranulf, by far the calmest of the vampires in light of this news, shook his head. "I was alive for seventeen years," he said. "I have been a vampire for approximately thirteen hundred years. This is truer to my nature, now."

"I'd do it," Balthazar said. His eyes met mine apologetically. "If it didn't involve killing a sentient being, that is. If it were anything else—I mean, *anything*—I'd go back in a second."

"So we know what she's after now," Lucas said. His eyes had an unearthly focus; he was strategizing, I realized, as a way of distracting himself from pain. "And we know we want to stop her. So we need to find the traps. Clear this place out and make it safe for Bianca, not to mention any other wraiths Mrs. Bethany hasn't already snared."

"Sounds like a plan," Balthazar said. He had taken the only real chair in the room, while Vic and Patrice took the beanbags. Ranulf and Lucas were both sitting on old crates, and I was levitating about halfway to the ceiling. "Do we just want to divide the grounds up into sections, go through them when we can?"

Lucas shook his head. "I want to make one massive sweep. She's probably laying new traps all the time, but if we could get this place cleared out for a little while, it might make it easier to track what she does from here on out."

"When are we supposed to do that?" Patrice said. "Someone's going to notice."

Lucas began, "Late at night, maybe—"

"Hang on," Vic interrupted. "I'm about to be brilliant. What about the Autumn Ball?"

Evernight Academy's biggest dance—the vampire version of the prom—was only a week away. Ranulf had a date, but to the best of my knowledge, nobody else did. As I rolled the idea around in my mind, I liked it more. "Everyone will be out, be busy, and lots of people will go into different rooms to make out or sneak a beer or whatever. That makes it good cover for pretty much anything we would need to do."

"There's no we here," Lucas said. "It's too dangerous for you."

I wanted to argue, but in this particular case, Lucas wasn't being overprotective. Sending a ghost to find ghost traps would be a little like sending a vampire to inspect a stake factory. "Well, then, it gives me something to watch while you guys are busy. It's a perfect distraction—Balthazar, remember how you and I were able to go through the school records last year?"

After the words came out, I wished I could have pulled them back; it was never a great idea to remind Lucas, or Balthazar, that Balthazar and I had been on a date last year.

The silence that followed hung awkwardly in the room, until Vic couldn't take it anymore. "Okay!" he said, too cheerfully. "So we're all going to the Autumn Ball. Ranulf and I have dates—what about you guys?"

"Since when did you get a date?" I asked, joining his effort to brighten the mood of the evening.

Vic looked sheepish. Ranulf said, "Upon questioning, my

date revealed that she has a friend lovely in visage yet unfortunate in matters of romance. We have therefore arranged for Vic to accompany her to the ball."

"You found him someone," I said. "Hey, it works." It occurred to me that Maxie would probably be somewhat jealous about that.

"I'd planned to travel that weekend," Patrice said, "but I suppose if I stayed, I could wear my new Chanel. What do you say, Balthazar? Let's be partners in crime."

Balthazar sighed. "Sure. But one of these years, I hope to go to this party with somebody who actually wants to date me."

"So that just leaves Lucas," Vic said. Then his face fell. "And that gets kinda awkward."

Lucas shrugged. "I'll be the guy who doesn't go. I can just dig around up in the dorms."

"No," I said. Although I hated this, I knew it was true: "The people who go to the party are the ones who have the most freedom that night. Otherwise, the teachers will think that if you're not in your dorm, you've got to be up to something."

"You want me to ask some other girl out on a date?" His disbelief would've been funny, if it weren't such serious business.

"Uh, no. But is there someone you could maybe go with just as a friend?" I hesitated, realizing that Lucas only had one other friend at school—but maybe she would do. "Like Skye?"

"Would she understand it's not a date?" Patrice said.

"Sure," I said. "She'd only be looking for a friend to go with, because she's got a boyfriend back home."

"Actually, not so much," Lucas said. "I heard her telling Clementine earlier today—apparently her boyfriend just dumped her hard. But she said she'd date a guy again 'about six months after hell freezes over,' so I'm guessing she'd only want a friend right now. That's not the real problem, though."

"You wouldn't attack her," I said, trying to be soothing. "You're getting stronger. Besides, you'll meet her downstairs and be in the center of a crowd the whole time. If you did snap, which you won't, somebody would be there to stop you."

Lucas shook his head. "Too risky. Let me go with Patrice, and Balthazar, maybe you could ask Skye."

"I've never so much as spoken to her," Balthazar said. "She probably doesn't know who I am."

Patrice and I shared a look. Balthazar could be obtuse about his own good looks. Maybe he and Skye had never spoken, but there was no way any straight girl or gay guy at Evernight Academy didn't know exactly who he was.

"So ask somebody else," Lucas said.

More firmly, Balthazar said, "I think spending some time with a human would be a good idea for you." He glanced at Vic. "An . . . undaubed human. You can't stay at Evernight much longer, now that things are getting weird with Mrs. Bethany. Eventually you've got to test yourself. Try to strengthen your self-control. And like Bianca said, this is as good an opportunity as any."

"I guess." Lucas gave me an uneasy look. "Bianca, are you sure about this?"

Honestly, I felt a little jealous. Not of anything happening between Lucas and Skye—I had total faith in him. But Skye would get to dress up, go to the ball, and dance with Lucas the whole night long, while I was stuck watching from the ceiling in the spectral version of the pajamas I'd died in. That was a pretty stupid reason to fret, though. "As long as she gets the whole friends thing, yeah. It's fine."

From his place in the beanbag chair, Vic hung his head backward and grinned at Lucas. "Okay, it's slightly losery to have your best friend find you a date," he admitted. "But way less losery than having your girlfriend find you one."

Lucas scowled at him, though I could tell, despite his bleak mood, he thought it was funny. "Shut it."

The preparations for the dance took a fair bit of time; since I wouldn't be able to take part in the search, I did what I could on the prep work. We mapped out the different areas of the school and decided who would slip out to which area, and when.

Lucas seemed possessed by a wild, desperate energy. He strategized more than any of the rest of us, studied longer than before, and made Balthazar practice fencing with him for hours. I thought that he was trying to keep himself in a perpetual state of exhaustion—so that he would be too tired to fully contemplate the fact that there was a way for him to live again, but it was one he could never take advantage of. Even the dancing lessons he took from Patrice were intense and joyless, with Lucas memorizing the steps as though they were Black Cross battle moves.

As important as our plans were, though, I couldn't spend all my time preparing for the Autumn Ball search. At moments, I had trouble so much as thinking about it. Something else, just as important, was on my mind. Finally, Wednesday night, the time came.

I waited in the forest grove with my coral bracelet nearby, eager and yet nervous, until I saw my father coming toward me. Quickly I slipped on my bracelet and ran forward for a hug. He gathered me into his arms, so strong and warm that for a second it was as if I were a little girl again, scared of thunderstorms and trusting my daddy to protect me from the lightning.

"Is she here?" I whispered.

"She's coming." Dad squeezed my hands. "I broke it to her a couple hours ago."

"Is she okay?" Despite my father's reassurance, I couldn't stop worrying that my mother wouldn't be able to accept me as a wraith.

"Yes." There was a strange note in his voice. Uncertainty. Fear pierced me; Dad must have seen it, because he quickly shook his head. "Your mother loves you. She just . . . she can't accept that something so terrible has happened to you. That's what upsets her. But it means the world to her to be able to be with you again."

*Something so terrible.* Those words resonated with me, not in a good way. I wanted to turn them over in my mind and discover why, but there was no time—I could hear my mother's footsteps on the thick carpet of pine needles upon the ground.

I peered past my father, searching for her. As a wraith, my

night vision was no longer as sharp as it had been during my vampire life. So I heard my mother gasp first.

"Mom?" I stepped away from my dad, venturing closer to the edge of the grove, and then I saw her. She stood shock-still, trembling slightly, hands shoved into the pockets of her long coat. "Mom, it's me."

"Oh, my God." Her voice was almost too quiet to hear. "Oh, my God."

She didn't seem to be able to move, so I went to her—not running, as I had toward my father, but going slow, giving her time to take it in. Mom's face didn't move; she just blinked at me, for all the world like a rabbit too scared to run away from the hunter. But when I finally got close to her, she sucked in a deep breath and said, *"Bianca."*

Then her arms were around me, and my dad was hugging both of us, and for a short time there was nothing but warmth and tears and us saying how much we loved each other. It was pretty much totally incoherent, but I didn't care. The only thing that mattered was that I finally had my whole family back again.

"My baby," she said as we broke apart at last. "My poor baby. Are you—trapped here?"

"Not trapped, but no thanks to Mrs. Bethany." Time to bring that up later, I decided. "This is one of the places I can travel, and stay. I've been here for a while now, because Lucas is here"—my mother's eyes narrowed, but I kept going—"and Balthazar, Patrice, Vic, Ranulf, you guys, everyone."

She glanced from me to my father. "You've been here for the last couple of months, and you can just . . . hang out with your

✢ 283 ✢

friends? As though it were normal?"

"It *is* normal," I said. "For me, anyway."

"We can—we can fix up your old room." Mom smiled hesitantly. "You could live up there with us, if you wanted to."

The thought of hanging out in my bedroom, watching winter snow fall on the gargoyle's head, seemed like the loveliest pastime imaginable. "I can already travel there. If you guys make it safe for me, I'll be up there the whole time."

Mom's expression clouded. "Safe. You mean—getting rid of the traps."

"Your mother is frightened," Dad interjected. "She's disturbed by what we've seen here so far."

"Most wraiths aren't like the ones trapped here at Evernight." I knew I needed to set the record straight. "Some of them, yeah, they get creepy. Just like some vampires do. But there are a lot of them who aren't that different from me. They're—they're just people. You don't stop being who you are just because you died."

My mother clearly hadn't been convinced. "Then why are there so many attacking this school?"

"They're attacking this school because they've been drawn here. Trapped here. By Mrs. Bethany," I insisted.

To my surprise, Dad cut in again. "Celia, think about this. Everything Mrs. Bethany's taught us, warned us about at this school—it's more about attack than defense. I think she's known since the beginning."

"Exactly," I said. "She's been planning to capture the ghosts all along—"

Before I could finish, revealing the miracle within Mrs.

Bethany's plotting, my dad continued, "What I mean is, she's always known about Bianca."

Mom's hand clutched at the neck of her coat, gathering the wool together against a new chill. "Adrian, what are you talking about?"

He said, "I mean that Mrs. Bethany is after the wraith, and she always knew that our Bianca had a chance to turn into a wraith someday. Looking back, I suspect that's why we were offered jobs here in the first place."

"Mrs. Bethany is after the wraiths," Mom said. "And you think Mrs. Bethany is specifically after Bianca. That can't be true. Why would she do it?"

Everything fell into place. Mrs. Bethany wanted to live again. She knew that capturing wraiths gave her the power to create life—but only the sacrifice of a powerful, stable wraith would ensure her sanity after the transformation. And I, thanks to my special status as a born wraith, the many relationships that anchored me to this world, and the guidance of other powerful spirits that had found me when they, too, were drawn to Evernight—I would be a perfect example.

I was Mrs. Bethany's best chance at returning to life. Not for one second did I think she would hesitate; if she could resurrect herself by murdering me, she would do it, gladly.

"I know why," I said. They took hands, as if expecting a terrible blow, and I broke it to them as gently as I could.

The rest of our family reunion wasn't as heartwarming as I might've wished. When Mom and Dad weren't sick with anger at Mrs. Bethany, they were angry at themselves for coming to Evernight Academy in the first place. Instead of reminding them that I'd been against this plan from the start—sometimes "I told you so" isn't the best thing to say, even if later events have proved you *totally correct*—I told them what my friends and I were planning. They agreed to serve as chaperones for the Autumn Ball, the better to make sure that the rest of us would be able to leave and return easily. Although they were thrilled that Balthazar and Patrice were playing a role in this, they both went very quiet anytime I mentioned Lucas. Rather than force the issue, I hoped they would wind up talking to him on the night of the ball. By cooperating on a common goal, maybe they could find a way to be civil to each other.

Because of that, I started looking forward to the ball—the dance, the hunt, everything. By the time the night arrived, I was way too excited to just lurk in the great hall until everyone arrived. I decided to enjoy some vicarious glamour by visiting Patrice's room and helping her get ready for the dance.

The envy almost did me in. Her ball gown looked like it cost more than some cars. The ice blue sheath was beaded from straps to hem, and her shoes were embroidered in fine crystals. "Why couldn't I appear in a dress like that?" I said wistfully, helping to hold back the rest of her hair as she worked on the last few fine braids. "It's sort of a wraith-y color. Way more angelic than these stupid pajamas."

"They're cute pajamas, and thank goodness." Patrice squinted at the mirror. Like most vampire girls at the school, she'd cut back on her blood to look thinner and hungrier at the dance; however, that meant she no longer reflected in a mirror very well. "If you'd died in one of those old T-shirts you used to sleep in sophomore year? I shudder to think."

"Even if these were the cutest pajamas in the world, an evening gown would have to be better."

"True," Patrice said. Her smile was luminous. There was nothing she liked more than dressing up.

Or was that maybe not the only reason she was glowing?

"So, you and Balthazar," I began. "Just friends?"

She snorted, the least ladylike thing I'd ever heard her do. "I told you before, remember? Not my type."

"Yeah, I remember." Poor Balthazar was going to have to wait a little longer for romance. At least Patrice was having fun getting dressed up.

No wonder, given that her clothing was this expensive and beautiful. Her drop earrings glittered with diamonds, as did the fine bracelet she wore. She'd coiled her thin braids into an elegant twist.

Once she was getting done, I said, "I'm going to head on, okay? I'll try to say hello during the dance?"

"Are you headed down already?" Patrice wore only her lacy underthings as she curled her eyelashes; the ice blue dress waited on a hanger upon the closet door. "What for?"

"Um, I might actually be going to watch Lucas pick up Skye."

Patrice shot me a sidelong look. "You know nothing's going on there, right?"

"I know. But she gets to go to the party with my boyfriend, and I don't. So if I go right now, after seeing how amazing you look, I'll feel as though she's totally average by comparison. It helps, you know?"

She laughed, pleased as ever by flattery. "Sure, go ahead."

I drifted down to the base of the stairwell, where most girls would come down to find their escorts for the evening. Ranulf and Vic had just met up with their dates; the glamorous Cristina snuggled on Ranulf's arm happily enough, but Vic and his date regarded each other suspiciously.

No sooner had they walked out of the common area than Lucas walked in. He'd managed to rent or borrow an evening suit. I knew him well enough to know he hadn't paid much attention to the process, but somehow the suit fit him perfectly, outlining his shoulders, his waist, and his hips. His dark gold hair was combed back, something he rarely did. The style made his hair seem darker, giving him a slightly older look. I'd never actually seen Lucas dressed up before; this might have been the first formal occasion he'd ever attended in his life. But his rugged good looks turned out to work just as well in midnight black as they did in jeans and flannel. He could've been in a Cary Grant movie. No—he could've been Cary Grant himself.

*I can't wait to see him after this and tell him how amazing he looks,* I thought dreamily. *Oh, I wish we'd been able to go to this dance together just once.*

My giggly delight at Lucas's appearance lasted until Skye appeared on the stairwell.

Every guy in the room went quiet. Even the girls had to stare, including me. Skye's dark brown hair, which normally hung straight, had been swept into a soft bun that left little tendrils free to curl around her oval face and exposed her long, slender neck. Her one-shouldered dress had a richly embroidered band just beneath her breasts, from which the chiffon material rippled to the floor. The deep wine color set off her skin and her pale blue eyes.

On the average day, Skye looked like a cute girl. This was not the average day. When she wanted people to notice her, it turned out nobody would be able to look away.

Sick with jealousy, I wanted to dart from the room that instant, rather than see Lucas offer her his arm. If I did that, though, I'd torture myself wondering what he'd said to her, what she'd said back, everything. Though I knew Lucas loved me, I couldn't help feeling insecure when comparing myself to a beautiful girl who had such a gorgeous body—heck, even one who just had a body, period, all of the time.

So I stayed put to see Lucas walk up to her. His smile was appreciative, but something else, too. Uncertain, maybe? "Hey. Wow, Skye. You look amazing."

"Thanks." She seemed to wilt; why would a compliment have made her feel so awful? But then she caught a bit of the chiffon between two of her fingers. "Some dress, huh?"

"You can say that again."

"I bought it to sweep Craig off his feet. Craig, who is now dating a girl named Britnee. With two Es. Somehow the two

Es make it worse." There was no flirtation in her, I realized; her exquisite appearance tonight was like a battle flag—a symbol of her refusal to surrender, though her heart was broken.

"Don't let it spoil your night," Lucas said quickly. "Forget about that jerk, okay?"

Though her shoulders still drooped a bit, Skye nodded, and I relaxed. There wasn't any reason to be jealous of her. Well, except for that awesome dress. "I'm done crying over him. Tonight I just want to hang out with my friends and dance."

"I can oblige." When Lucas offered his arm to her, I found I didn't mind.

The Autumn Ball was always a spectacle—something out of another century, harkening back to the grander events so many of the vampire students remembered from when they were young. Instead of a DJ or a band, a small orchestra played classical music, which turned out to be a lot more danceable than you'd think. Instead of glittery lights or modern decorations, the great hall was illuminated with hundreds of candles, many set in place in front of hammered brass or old-fashioned, smoky mirrors to reflect the light throughout the room. Every guy wore an evening suit or a tux; every girl wore a floor-length dress, and some of them had gloves to match. It was the kind of grand occasion every girl—and more of the guys than would readily admit it—wanted to be a part of at least once.

I'd attended twice with Balthazar, and had loved my dresses, the dancing, and everything else. However, it turned out to be just as much fun to watch, from above, where I darted amid the hanging chandeliers lit by candles. Sometimes I laughed, either watching Lucas carefully navigate Skye through the waltz, almost visibly counting *one-two-three,* or Vic and his date, keeping each other at full arm's length and obviously both plotting an early escape. Other times, I watched in admiration; some of the dancers were clearly expert and eager to show off their many years of experience. Balthazar and Patrice were the most beautiful of all, moving gracefully at the heart of the dance. And, of course, every once in a while, one of them would slip out to continue the hunt. My parents would always nod at them as they went past—Mom pretty in a cream silk dress I hadn't seen before.

Lucas went most often, as much as everyone else put together. Was that because of his crazed drive to do something productive? Because Skye excused herself frequently to goof around with her friends on the outskirts of the dance? Or because he didn't trust himself to be in such close proximity to a human? All of the above, I suspected. Each time he went out, he walked by my parents, and the three of them would get very tense. But they were acknowledging each other now, Mom and Dad getting over their anger, and I hoped it was a positive sign.

Everything was going perfectly, until I felt a chill—and the visions began.

My mind filled with image after image of the humans below, people I'd never known well but now felt an intimacy with that was as powerful as love. Different faces, different emotions, different ages: Every human being down there felt precious to me now. And above this, a darkening veil of terror for those humans' safety, and hatred of the vampires who danced in their midst.

The wraiths. The Plotters, to be exact. Suddenly I could feel them over the entire dance, gathering like storm clouds. Was this how the attack had begun a year ago? "What are you doing?" I whispered, safe that I was far enough above the crowd for the orchestra to drown out my words.

The images changed to violence: vampires being set aflame, being frozen within blocks of ice, being caught in the kinds of traps that Mrs. Bethany set for ghosts. No one plan took form, but I could tell what it meant. These ghosts feared for their anchors' safety, and for their own. And they wanted revenge on the vampires below, for Mrs. Bethany's plan.

*Those people are safe,* I promised. *If you want to move on, you know that I can help you.*

I expected surprise, happiness, maybe a rush to depart. Instead I felt only a deeper wave of fear. Honestly, I wasn't much less frightened myself, and I didn't yet know how—or if—I could perform the wonders Christopher claimed. So how could I make them any promises?

Yet I felt that, if they would follow me, I had to try. If I was able to usher several of the wraiths away from Evernight Academy in one swoop, that would be as effective at stopping Mrs. Bethany as anything else we could do.

But a hard rush of refusal hit me, like a hard-breaking wave on the shore in winter. And then a rising tumult of energy, aimed downward, in points like a hundred arrows—

*What's happening?* I thought. I looked wildly at the crowd; Balthazar and Patrice were off hunting traps, but everyone else I cared for was down there dancing. There was no time even for a warning.

The energy streaked toward the floor like thunderbolts, and I expected a rain of ice or snow. Maybe ghostly apparitions.

I didn't expect every single human in the crowd to instantly collapse, unconscious.

The orchestra's music snarled into something unrecognizable as instruments stopped, one by one, and the vampires began to react. A few of them were obnoxious enough to laugh, but most of them were worried—either about humans they cared for, or because something obviously dangerous was happening. Lucas knelt on the floor, two fingers at Skye's neck to check for a pulse. Ranulf held Cristina in his arms, though she was completely limp, her head flopping backward. Vic lay facedown, his arms and legs splayed awkwardly like an abandoned rag doll.

And then he moved—or, I should say, his body moved. Because I knew from the first moment that whatever was rising wasn't Vic.

I realized: I wasn't the only wraith with the power to possess humans.

The other humans began coming to as well, but their eyes were clouded—a milky greenish color all over, with no pupil or iris. Yet none of them were blind. Their movements were slow and awkward, as though they had not moved in a very long time. Lucas drew back as Skye, or something that looked like Skye, stared malevolently at him from her place on the floor.

Vic squared his shoulders as he pulled himself fully upright. If I hadn't already sensed that Maxie wasn't among the attackers, I would have known that she wasn't the one possessing him just from the expression on his face. It was so unlike Vic, so strange for him, that it took me a while to recognize the emotion I saw—cruelty.

He shouted, "Mrs. Bethany!"

It wasn't Vic's voice. It was a hoarse rasp that made me instantly think of someone whose throat had been cut. I wished desperately for a mirror to free him—but would the traps work if a wraith was possessing a human being? Remembering how securely armored I had felt when I'd possessed Kate, I suspected not.

Mrs. Bethany stepped forward. She didn't look scared. Just mildly interested. Her long, starched dress of lace was stark white.

"Free our kind," Vic said. The crazy raspy voice seemed to make the entire room shiver. "Free us. Or we shall strike, and your kind will perish."

Smoothly she replied, "If you force me to exorcise you from your anchors, they will suffer terribly. Some might die."

The mask of cruelty on Vic's face didn't waver. "You have been warned."

Then, suddenly, as if the marionette strings had been cut, all the humans collapsed again—but this time, only for a second. Within moments, they were up, rubbing their heads if they'd fallen, confused about what had just happened. Nobody seemed to remember exactly, which was probably a mercy for everyone involved.

I tried to take hope. We were collecting most of the traps tonight. Once we figured out how to act safely, we'd be able to free the wraiths ourselves. Given time, I could probably convince many of them to leave this realm with me, if they could no longer remain safe here.

And yet I sensed that something terrible had already been put into motion—something we might not be able to stop.

# Chapter Nineteen

"I CAN'T BELIEVE I WENT ALL EVIL." VIC SAT ON the steps of the gazebo, where we'd gathered after the chaos had died down. Although it wasn't yet midnight, the Autumn Ball was definitely over. "Did I shoot fire out of my eyes or something cool like that?"

"No, you were just scary as hell." Lucas leaned against the gazebo railing. He'd loosened the tie of his evening suit and undone his collar, a view I wished I had time to appreciate more. Skye, like most of the human students and plenty of the vampires, had long since retreated to their rooms for the full-scale freakout that evidently followed a mass possession. "They just wouldn't listen to you, Bianca?"

"They listened, but they were afraid." I sat on the railing next to him, all but solid; nobody outside our group was around to see. "Whatever they're planning, it's coming soon. If we don't free the wraiths quickly, I'm scared they'll start hurting people—humans, vampires, everybody."

Patrice, who hadn't witnessed the possessions and, as such, was thinking more clearly than most of us, began analyzing our position. "We were able to sweep most of the areas we wanted to. A total of forty-seven traps are in the records room. It stands to reason that we didn't find every single one of the traps, but we must have the majority of them by now. So if we're able to do that, it should change the wraiths' minds, right? Or at least give them some reason to hope, and show them that we're on their side."

My mother shifted on her feet, and my dad slipped his arm around her shoulders in a half hug. I knew she found it difficult to think of herself as being on the side of the wraiths, but she hadn't fled; she stood here with us.

"We have to free the trapped wraiths," I said. "And after that, destroy the traps we've got, to stop Mrs. Bethany from using them again."

"It is unlikely that anyone so determined as Mrs. Bethany would allow herself to be stopped by the destruction of a few traps," Ranulf pointed out.

I nodded. "But when we've freed the trapped ones, the wraiths who have traveled to Evernight will stop being so afraid. I can convince some of them to leave then, maybe."

"And maybe it's not a bad idea to start tipping off the human students," Balthazar said, catching on to the idea. "The hauntings didn't scare them off, but possession might."

Lucas added, "And if possession doesn't, vampires certainly will. I'm not above showing my fangs if it will get some human students out of this school for good."

"So we can really shut her down." I began to get excited; for the first time in far too long, it felt like I was getting the upper hand over Mrs. Bethany. "Destroy the traps, empty the school of everybody except the vampires who need to be here."

My father looked wary. "When we destroy the traps, we'll disrupt the deep magic inside. It's going to be an enormous release of energy. Nobody will be able to miss it."

Lucas grimaced. "In other words, Mrs. Bethany's going to know we've messed up her plan. Not later, when we start telling the human students—right away."

From his place within the gazebo, where he sat on one of the long benches, Balthazar said, "And she'll act. Immediately. When we do this, we have to be ready for the repercussions."

"She wouldn't actually kill—" Another vampire, I wanted to say, but I couldn't, not after seeing what she'd done to Samuel Younger. Mrs. Bethany had nurtured this plan as her dearest wish for two centuries, and she wouldn't hesitate to destroy anybody who got in her way. When I looked at my father, he nodded once in confirmation.

"She would," Dad said. "And she's played favorites a lot this year—among the faculty and the students. I suspect other vampires are in on her plan. If we don't want to get staked or worse, we need to get out of here as soon as we've set the wraiths free."

Lucas turned to my parents—the first time I'd seen him directly speak to one of them since that initial altercation with my mother at the top of the school year. "Any chance she's going to be gone for a while anytime soon?"

There was an awkward pause that made me cringe, but then Dad seemed to pull himself together. "No such luck. But we could come up with a distraction, maybe. A crisis to get her off the grounds for a day. She'd hear about it when she got back, but that would buy us some time to cover our tracks."

"She'll know I'm in on it," Lucas said. "After I turned her down flat the other day—she's got to know. But hopefully I can cover for the rest of you."

Mom cleared her throat, like it cost her some effort to speak to Lucas politely. "Mrs. Bethany will suspect us, too, especially if we're involved in getting her off campus. So we should just agree now that it was the three of us. Nobody else."

"Hey, that's not necessary," Balthazar said.

"Spare me the noble routine, okay?" Lucas shot him a look. "Nobody wants that woman on their bad side if they can help it. So don't be stupid."

To my surprise, Balthazar grinned. "You're a good friend, Lucas. Though you'll never admit it."

They shared a smile, and I could see my parents realizing that—against the odds—Lucas and Balthazar had actually gotten fairly tight. For some reason, the fact that I loved and accepted Lucas didn't have as much impact on them as that simple proof of friendship.

Vic made a T sign with his hands. "Time out from the male bonding, okay? There's one thing we haven't talked about—Bianca."

"What about me?" I said.

"You're, like, Superghost, right? So you're exactly who Mrs. Bethany is gunning for." Vic looked from person to person, as if hoping someone would contradict him, but of course nobody could. "Okay, so how do we stop her from figuring out that you're a wraith? And that you're here? Because she's got to be on the lookout."

"You've all been really careful," Mom said. Her eyes briefly met Lucas's, as if thanking him for helping to protect me. It was a small moment, but it made me want to hug her harder than ever. "She has to know that Bianca's changed into a wraith, but maybe—maybe Mrs. Bethany doesn't realize that she's here. If she did know, wouldn't she have tried to capture Bianca before now?"

I had to admit that was a good point. The traps weren't for me specifically; Lucas's room hadn't been targeted.

Mom continued, "I don't like not knowing how much Mrs. Bethany knows, but hopefully it's about to be a moot point. Within a couple of weeks, I suspect the three of us will have left Evernight Academy forever, and . . . you'll come with us, won't you, Bianca?"

"Wherever you guys are." I leaned my head on Lucas's shoulder, with enough weight to make him smile. The glowing strands of my hair fell across his chest. "That's where I'll be."

Afterward, as everybody prepared to go back into the school, I went invisible, becoming no more than a vapor trailing overhead.

Balthazar, I noticed, rose from his seat but didn't walk away with the others, lingering at the gazebo a moment longer. The moonlight outlined his silhouette amid the scrollwork iron and the ivy.

I drifted a little lower and whispered, "Are you okay?"

"Sure," he said, though his voice was odd. I remembered the Autumn Ball two years ago, when we had walked out here together to watch the stars; it was the night I'd told him that I loved Lucas, and I was still learning how deeply that had affected him. Was he recalling that night, too?

Balthazar looked up in my general direction and said, "Lucas is heading up to double-check the traps, make sure they're well hidden. So he won't be going to bed for at least an hour or so."

"Yeah. What about it?"

"I want you to come into my mind when I'm dreaming tonight."

Immediately I knew why he was asking, what he planned to do. "Balthazar . . . I don't know if that's a good idea. We're headed into a fight. You need your strength."

"I'll be all right. It's taken me a long time to face what I have to do—but I see it now. We can't put this off any longer." His expression was unreadable, but his voice was firm. "Trust me."

After spending a couple of months second-guessing him at every turn, for something that hadn't been his fault to begin with, I owed him that, didn't I? "Okay. I'll come."

We went back into the school. The great hall's grandeur was in shreds—the candles were out, the flowers had been knocked on the floor by panicking students, and the orchestra's bandstand had clearly been abandoned in a hurry. Balthazar unfastened his bow tie and cuffs as he went up the stairs; his footsteps echoed on the stone. After what had happened earlier tonight, I was willing to bet that most people remained wide awake and would be for hours, but nobody was risking wandering around alone at midnight.

Balthazar didn't turn on the lights when we entered his dorm room. That was probably so he could have some privacy while he undressed; of course, I looked away regardless. The moonlight was at work again, though, so I could see his shadow against the wall as he slipped off his shirt and unbuckled his belt.

*And he's not Patrice's "type"?* I thought. *I just don't get that.*

When I heard the covers on his bed rustle, I returned to watching him, hovering just above his bed. Balthazar lay on his side, and he appeared to be one of those lucky people who only had to close his eyes before sleep began. Within a few short minutes, I could sense that he was dreaming.

Although I felt awkward about doing it—almost as though I were cheating on Lucas just by sharing this with anybody else—I stretched myself thin and dove downward, into the very center of Balthazar's sleeping mind—

And found myself in the forest, again at nighttime.

At first I thought these were the woods near Evernight, but then I realized that wasn't right. Most of the trees here were taller, and some of them were hugely thick—ancient, perhaps. In the distance, I could hear a few people talking, and some other sound: horses' hooves. As I peered through the inky night,

I realized that the people were riding in an old-fashioned wagon along a dirt road, and the clothes they wore were unfamiliar, with large hats and long cloaks. It reminded me somewhat of the scene I'd glimpsed in Christopher's memories of his life, but I sensed this was longer ago.

"You made it," Balthazar said.

I turned to see him standing next to me, wearing the same kind of clothes; because he was closer, I could see that he wore trousers that only came to his knees, with high boots that flared out slightly at the top. His coat was belted, his cloak trimmed with fur. His hat—well, despite everything, I had to smile. "You look like the star of the Thanksgiving pageant."

"I'll have you know, this was colonial high fashion in the year 1640." Balthazar readjusted his hat so that it sat at a slightly more rakish angle.

More serious now, I said, "Is this what you dream about? Your life?"

"Sometimes." Balthazar pointed toward a distant light—the glow of an oil lamp in the window of a small cottage. "Let's see what we can see."

I walked with him through the woods until we reached the clearing for the cabin. It was more primitive than I would have imagined, though when I thought about it, this made sense; Balthazar had probably helped his father build this house with their hands and whatever few tools they'd possessed. Smoke curled up from a slightly crooked stone chimney, and the single window was covered with some kind of waxy paper, rather than glass. A shaggy dog slept next to the chimney, his back to the warmth. Balthazar smiled and leaned down to pet him. "Hello, Fido."

Fido didn't stir. Maybe he couldn't feel the touch, in dreams.

Then, from inside, I heard a woman's voice, sharp and angry. "Your disobedience tasks us, Charity."

"I'm ever so sorry, Mother." Charity's voice rang out, clear, strong, and not sorry. "But I'm afraid I have to disobey you even more."

I'd known this moment was coming from the time Balthazar had first asked me to come into his dream, but that didn't make it easier to face. To judge by the dread in Balthazar's eyes, he felt the same way.

Balthazar walked to the front door and pulled it open. There I could see Charity, standing in a long, dark dress with a white apron, and a small white cotton bonnet on her head. Her face was younger than I remembered—this was her a couple years before death, when she was only a child. In front of her sat two people who were clearly Charity's and Balthazar's parents, dressed in the same stark fashion as their children, their faces stern and unamused.

Charity grinned, a too-adult expression on a face rounded with baby fat. She tugged her bonnet from her head, exposing her fair curls. "I'm not going to cover my head any longer. In fact, I don't think I'll cover any of my body, if I don't want to."

"The devil has gotten into you, my girl," boomed their father. He looked like an older, heavier version of Balthazar—but harder, somehow. Unpleasant. There was no love in him as he scolded his daughter, only disapproval.

"That's right!" Charity laughed out loud, glorying in disobeying her stern parents. "Do you want to see what the devil can make me do?"

To Balthazar, I whispered, "Was she always like this?"

"I used to think it was just rebellion," he said. "But, yeah. Charity was always looking for trouble, from the beginning."

At that moment, Charity noticed us. Her face instantly shifted from gleeful triumph to confusion. "What are you doing here? What is *she* doing here?"

"Let me at her," I whispered. After what she'd done to Lucas, I felt like I could rip her apart.

"No," Balthazar said, stepping between us. "She can hurt you here. But for me, this is just a dream. She doesn't have any power over me."

*Just like she's attacked Lucas—he's attacking her.*

Balthazar leaped forward, tackling Charity and sending them both sprawling to the ground. Although their parents protested, neither Balthazar nor Charity paid them any heed; they were dream phantoms only. This fight was for real. She backhanded him savagely, but Balthazar managed to twist one of her arms behind her and thrust her toward the fireplace. When her face was only a few inches from the flames, she started to scream. "Stop it! Stop it! Balthazar, you're hurting me!"

"And I hate it." His voice shook. "You know that I do."

"It wasn't enough to kill me!" She twisted violently in his

grasp, trying to claw at him with her free arm, but she couldn't quite reach. The scene, terrible enough as it was, looked even worse when I realized how childish and helpless Charity seemed. "Now you want to torture me?"

"I want to leave you alone. Just like you want to leave me alone. But you have to let Lucas go."

Charity laughed, though her gold curls began to smolder. "He's mine. All mine. You loved her better than me, and she loved him better than you. But she'll never have him the way that I do."

"You're going to let Lucas go," Balthazar repeated. "Or else . . . every single night you go into his dreams to torture him? I'll come into your dreams and do the same thing back to you."

"You don't have the right! Not after what you did to me!"

"If I could go back in time and kill myself rather than turning you, I'd do it." Balthazar was shaking now, either with the effort of holding the struggling Charity close to the fire or from pure emotion. "But I've let guilt control me for too long. You're a menace, Charity. You hunt, and you kill, and I should have stopped you a long time ago."

"By killing me?" Charity's voice had changed; real pain had slipped in. "Again?"

Balthazar didn't answer. "You're going to let Lucas go. You're going to stop invading his dreams forever. If you ever break your word—ever—I promise you, I'll know, and you'll be sorry."

Charity tried again to claw at him, but without the same strength. I could smell burning hair. "It hurts. Balthazar, it's hot."

"You're going to let Lucas go." Balthazar never flinched, but I saw the dampness shining in his eyes. Despite everything, he wanted to protect his little sister—and despite *that,* he was willing to do this, for Lucas and for me.

After a long moment, she whimpered, almost too quietly to hear, "Okay."

"Swear it."

"I swear! Now stop! Just stop!"

Balthazar pulled Charity away from the fire and shoved her toward the far corner. Soot had blackened her apron and her cheeks, where I could see the outlines of tears. "This is for her, isn't it?" She pointed at me, her hand shaking. Her face was so terribly young. "Did you pick another girl to save because you can't save me?"

"I can't save you," he repeated dully. "But I love you, Charity."

She threw the fireplace brush at him and swore at him. That was probably Charity's version of "I love you, too."

As she wept brokenly beside the fireplace, Balthazar rose and walked out, past the now-mute, reactionless forms of his parents. I followed him, saying nothing at first. He paused by the dog for a few more seconds, watching it sleep.

When I dared to speak again, I said, "You didn't have to do that."

"Yeah, I did." Balthazar pulled his fur-trimmed cloak more tightly around himself. "Charity wouldn't have stopped any other way."

"Will she keep her word?"

"Yes. Strangely enough, when she actually makes a promise, she keeps it."

We began walking farther away from the house into the woods. The air smelled so fresh and clean—there would have been no pollution yet, no engines, no smog. "I know that was hard for you," I said. "To violate the bond in that way. To hurt her."

Balthazar winced, but he said, "I did what I had to do. Maybe Lucas can find some peace now."

"Do you think so?"

"Maybe," he said again, and I knew that Balthazar had seen the same desperation in Lucas that I had.

Then he lifted his head, looking toward the distance, and a small smile flickered upon his face. I followed his gaze toward another cottage in the very far distance. "What's that?"

"That's where Jane lived." It was the only time he'd ever openly acknowledged his long-lost love to me. I'd never learned what had gone wrong for them, but I knew that his passion for her had endured the four hundred years from then until now.

Greatly daring, I said, "Do you want to go see her? I could leave."

"She would only be a dream." Balthazar looked down at me sadly. "I'm done with dreams."

We took hands for a moment, the briefest of touches. Then I willed myself up and out, toward waking.

When I appeared again in the dorm room, Balthazar

remained asleep. Now, though, he wasn't dreaming; he just rested. I brushed a hand against his dark curls in gratitude.

The next day, a cold hush had fallen over the school. Winter's first hard frost had silvered the trees and the ground, but after last night, that seemed less like nature taking its course and more as though the wraiths had claimed the entire world for their own. The vampire students, mostly petrified of the wraiths, kept to their rooms; even the human students—usually calmer about these things, given that they came from haunted homes—seemed disquieted by the possessions. A few kids had already dropped out; we might not have to work too hard to get the rest of the humans to leave. As I zipped around the school, free at last to move around without fear, I saw almost no one in the hallways and heard no talking or laughter. *Frozen,* I thought. *Frozen in place.*

Mrs. Bethany remained in her carriage house. Once or twice I saw her silhouetted against her windows. Although I doubted she was scared of the wraiths, or of anything, she had apparently decided to remain in a structure that was completely safe from ghostly invasion.

Had she discovered that her traps were missing yet? If so, she gave no sign. In the meantime, her absence from the school building gave us a brief window to meet without worrying about being observed.

Everyone gathered in my parents' apartments. Vic sprawled on the sofa, a slight fuzz on his cheeks from where he'd failed to shave. Next to him, Ranulf and Patrice drank cups of the coffee my mother had made for us. Lucas took the chair at the farthest end of the room, like he thought my parents might chuck him out at any second, but Mom brought him coffee, too. I stayed near him, and Maxie dared to materialize right at the doorway, where everybody could see her.

"Next weekend will be our best chance," Mom said as she set the coffeepot down. "Mrs. Bethany sometimes takes advantage of Riverton trips to leave the school for a couple of days. We can encourage that."

Vic brightened. "Yeah, and with the rest of the humans in town on the Friday trip, less chance of us getting found out, right? Oh, man, I just called people *humans*."

"Actually, no," Dad said. "The vampire students throw their biggest parties of the year when the humans are gone. Which is hell on the chaperones, but more to the point, makes it hard for us to get something done. But if we wait until the next night, that Saturday—a week from today—Mrs. Bethany won't have returned yet, and we'll have freedom to work."

Lucas and I shared a look. He said, "We were going to talk to some former Black Cross friends of ours in Riverton."

"Black Cross," Mom muttered, in the same tone of voice she used when she swore.

"It's Raquel, Mom," I said. "And Dana, who helped us get away when we were nearly caught last year. They're our friends, plus they're fighters, and they have a little experience in capturing wraiths. We should make them a part of this. They could help, both with the wraiths and with getting you and Dad and Lucas away afterward."

Mom and Dad clearly weren't sure what to think, but they nodded. I turned to Maxie. "Okay, when the wraiths are freed, they're going to . . . freak out."

"You got it," Maxie said. "We're talking about fireworks, like the Fourth of July. Energy and light and frost going in every direction. Bianca will have to guide them where they need to go, whether that's back to their original homes or on to the next realm, whatever. Away from here—that's the main thing. I'll help if I can."

"Awesome," Vic said, and he and Maxie shared a quick look before she ducked her head, which hid her smile.

Patrice nodded. "So, once the traps are emptied, we destroy them. That's not easy, though, given that adds up to, like, a couple hundred pounds of metal."

"A great cataclysmic force will be required," Ranulf said. "I shall handle the explosives."

"Whoa, there, cowboy," Lucas cut in. "We don't have to break them down to atoms. All we have to do is make them useless as traps. Mrs. Bethany can't have an infinite supply of these things."

My father said, "Our bigger issue is the magical element within the traps. I don't know much about that—I don't think any of us here does—but it's not as simple as demolishing scrap metal. I should be able to come up with a chemical solution that will work, but the results will still be . . . How did you put it, Maxie?"

"Fireworks," she replied.

"I do not see how this is different than explosives," Ranulf said.

That won a round of laughter, and then people began talking animatedly about the plan and our chances of success. For some reason, it hit me then how extraordinary it was that these people had come together. The only obvious thing they had in common was that they each knew me, but they weren't here for me—at least not only, or not mostly for me. They were here because they'd learned to look past their old prejudices and fears and see each other for who they were. Maxie's willingness to engage again with the living world, the vampires' acceptance of wraiths and humans as their equals and allies, Lucas taking what was good from his Black Cross training and leaving behind what was bad, Vic's ability to deal with the supernatural world as easily as the natural one—that was what bonded us now.

For a moment, our plan seemed easy. If we'd managed to come together like this, surely we could do anything.

# Chapter Twenty

"HOW DOES A TOWN THE SIZE OF RIVERTON KEEP a classic movie house going?" Lucas said, standing before the red-and-gold blinking lights of the marquee.

"It's a very small town with very good taste," I whispered into his ear.

Behind us, in the town square, the charter bus from Evernight Academy was emptying out the last students who had come along to Riverton—fewer than before, due to fears of "gang violence." There wasn't much to the city—a pizza place, a diner, a couple of vintage shops, and this amazing movie theater. This week, they were showing *An Affair to Remember,* my favorite Cary Grant movie ever. It made me wish we'd actually come here to see the film.

Lucas had his hands stuffed into the pockets of his jeans. In one of those pockets was my jet brooch, but I didn't think he was checking to make sure he had it. He looked more like he was attempting to stay calm.

"You're nervous," I said, keeping my voice low. "Dana was right about Black Cross not coming here again, right?"

"That sounds right. But, yeah, I'm nervous anyway. Can you blame me?"

He still had trouble believing that Dana would accept him as a vampire. Maybe he still doubted that he would be able to keep himself from attacking her. "It's going to be okay. I promise."

Lucas bought a single movie ticket, and I floated invisibly in along with him. He half grinned as we went up the steps to the balcony. "Can't say you're not a cheap date."

"Shut up, or I'll make you buy me dinner after."

"You don't even eat!"

"Doesn't matter."

We took our seats just as the film began, with loopy cursive text for the credits and the lush theme song. Although there were other viewers on the bottom floor, we were alone in the balcony, so I went ahead and materialized; Lucas pressed my jet brooch into my hand, so that the process became effortless for me. I pinned the brooch to my camisole, and Lucas offered me his coat, so it wouldn't be totally obvious that the girl he was sitting next to was wearing pajamas.

I felt weird being away from the school when so much was going on. My parents were keeping tabs on Mrs. Bethany; if she left tonight, they would have to find out how long she'd be gone, and if not, they'd have to come up with a way to get her to go, at least for a day. Meanwhile, everyone else was smuggling the traps to the Great Hall, preparing for tomorrow night's efforts.

Going to a movie—one of my all-time favorites—felt a little like playing hooky.

*Enjoy it,* I told myself. *Everything's about to change.*

As Vic Damone crooned about a love affair, a couple of other people edged their way onto the balcony and sat by us: Raquel next to me, and Dana on the other side, next to Lucas.

"I got popcorn," Raquel said.

The two of us grinned at each other, and for a moment it was like nothing had ever happened—*no,* I corrected myself, *it happened. And we got through it anyway.*

Next to us, Dana and Lucas didn't seem to be able to find words. Lucas leaned back in his seat, as though he were exhausted and couldn't go any further; despite the darkness in the theater, I could see that Dana's eyes were filling with tears.

She took his hand in hers, and I remembered what a shock it had been to me the first time I touched Lucas when he had no warmth, no pulse. He had always been the most alive person I'd ever known. No matter how many powers and abilities he now had as a vampire, there was no forgetting what he'd lost.

"Little brother, what happened to you?" Her voice shook.

"I keep thinking it's a bad dream," Lucas said. "But there's no waking up. Not from this."

"And yet—you're still you," Dana said.

Lucas sighed. "More or less me."

"They never told us that, in Black Cross." Dana wiped at her cheeks with the back of her free hand. "How come they never told us that?"

He turned his face toward the movie screen, where Cary Grant was striding along the deck of an ocean liner. I could tell he didn't care about the movie; he was fighting to remain steady. "Mom always said that, if she got turned, I should forget I'd ever had a mother. I guess she forgot she ever had a son, huh?"

Raquel put her hand to her mouth. That small gesture— compassion for a vampire—told me how much she, too, had changed.

"It's okay," Lucas said, before he corrected himself. "It's not okay. But it's over."

Dana swaddled Lucas in a bear hug, just as the soundtrack swelled. "I've always got your back, Lucas. You know that, right?"

"That's good to hear," I said, "because we need your help."

While Deborah Kerr flirted with Cary onscreen, I explained what we were trying to do. Neither Dana nor Raquel hesitated for a second. "We can get you guys out," Raquel said. "And we'll take you wherever you want to go."

"Black Cross taught me how to fake IDs nobody will ever catch," Dana promised. "We can get you guys clear and free, for whatever you want to do next. What is that, exactly?"

Lucas and I looked at each other. We didn't have an answer.

After the pause had stretched for a few seconds, Dana said, "Y'all can make up your mind about that later. Tell the others to expect us, okay?"

"And tell Balthazar—" Raquel had trouble saying this, but she managed. "Tell him I should've done more, when I saw him last. I should have helped him out, like you guys did."

"He'll be okay," I promised. "But tell him that yourself, okay? Balthazar would probably like to hear it."

Raquel nodded. "We should go. If anybody who was at Evernight last year sees me, there could be questions."

"Thanks," I said.

"You don't have to thank me," she said firmly. We smiled at each other, and it felt so good to know we'd found our way back to being friends.

Once they'd gone, Lucas and I remained in the movie theater, watching the story unfold. Normally that would've been because there was no way I would walk out of a Cary Grant movie. But this time, I felt as though the unanswered questions between us were weighing us down, so we were held in place.

Finally I said, "Where do you want to go after Evernight?"

"I don't know," he said. "Never spent much time out west. Maybe we could try that."

"Or Europe," I suggested. "Balthazar says it's actually easier to cross a large body of water than a river."

Lucas grimaced; the trip over the river on the way into town had shaken him. "If he says so."

On screen, Cary and Deborah promised to meet each other at the top of the Empire State Building if their love held true. I took Lucas's hands in mine. "I know it's scary—going to a new place—"

"I'm not scared of that. I never lived more than a few months in any one place—not once in my whole life. But what are we going to do? We couldn't support ourselves in Philly, and that was when you could work, too."

I hadn't thought about it before, but being a ghost pretty much eliminated my chances of getting a job. "Mom and Dad will help us this time. They've got plenty, and besides, they know how to fit into the world. They'll teach you. We don't have to worry about that."

Lucas didn't like the thought of borrowing yet more money, I could tell, but that obviously wasn't our biggest problem. "Sitting here, between Dana and Raquel—I could hear their heartbeats."

"You'll get past the hunger. I know you will. Look at Baltha-zar, or my parents, or Ranulf."

"It's harder for me, and we both know it. And if I haven't gotten any better at this after a couple months at Evernight, there's not much chance I ever will."

"You're not crazy. You'll never be a killer like Charity."

"If I kill even once—if I ever slip, and God, Bianca, I just know in my heart I'm gonna slip—I'd rather be dead."

"No," I insisted, taking his face in my hands. "Lucas, I'll always be here. I'll never leave you. You have to promise not to leave me behind. You have to be strong."

Lucas's eyes met mine, and I knew he was making me a more solemn promise than he ever had before. "I'll never leave you behind. Never. Whatever happens, we're together."

That should have made me happy, because I knew how deeply Lucas meant it. But instead, I realized what I'd demanded of him. He hated being a vampire, and suffered from such powerful blood hunger that it ground him down, every day, every moment. For him, going on like this was torture; our love for each other could only provide temporary comfort. He'd sworn to endure countless centuries of that existence rather than leave me alone. I could get Lucas to carry on, but he would never be right again. Nothing would ever really be right again. Our last shot at true happiness had died when Charity changed him.

I hugged him tightly, and he returned the embrace. His voice muffled against my shoulder, he said, "I wish she'd never showed me. It's worse, knowing there's a way out I can never take."

Mrs. Bethany had shown him how to live again. She'd wanted to win him to her side, but she'd realized the other side, too—that if he turned her down, he'd be tormented by the possibilities forever.

I tried to tell myself that it would be okay, as long as we were together, but the world wasn't that simple. I knew that now.

On the movie screen, Deborah Kerr was trying to reach the Empire State Building, but I'd seen the movie before. I knew she didn't make it.

That night, I'd planned to enter Lucas's dreams again. With Charity permanently exiled from his mind, it was finally safe for us to be together there. But, weighted with guilt from the night's realizations, I felt as if I couldn't face him yet. I drifted through the hallways, restless. For the first time, I really felt like a ghost.

*I should put a sheet over my head,* I thought. *Start going "Boo!"*

*every time I see someone. I could haunt the girl's dorm, or the great hall—*

And then it hit me. If our plan worked the way we wanted it to, this was the last night I would ever spend at Evernight Academy.

Despite every terrible thing that had happened here, I realized, I loved so much about this place. I couldn't imagine what it would be like never to be here again. This school had become a part of me—literally, now that I was a wraith. I had bonded to the very stones of this place. Even when I left forever, part of Evernight would always be able to draw me back.

So I went to all the places I remembered, hearing words spoken long ago, seeing everyone as we had been then. Raquel, on her first day here, scowling in the back of the great hall while Mrs. Bethany gave the welcoming speech. Balthazar, learning how to take pictures with a cell phone in Modern Technology class. Vic and Ranulf, stargazing with me out on the grounds. Patrice, braiding my hair for my first-ever date. Courtney, gossiping in the stairwell. Mom and Dad, smiling at me as we passed each other in the hallways between classes. And everywhere, Lucas: whispering to me in the library, running to rescue me after the fire last year, kissing me for the first time at the gazebo.

But thinking of Lucas reminded me of the dilemma before him.

*How can I ask him to face immortality, when it's the last thing he ever wanted?*

I decided that I needed to be solid for a while. Often it made me feel steadier about things, and there was just something comforting about being able to hug yourself. So I drifted up to the records room and began to take shape.

By that time of night, everyone else was in bed, so the records room was deserted. The traps had all been moved to the lower levels of the school, hidden in trunks; the room was just our hangout once more. Patrice's German textbooks lay in the center of the beanbag chair, and Vic had left behind one of his hula-girl ties. Smiling slightly, I removed the brick in the wall where we'd hidden my coral bracelet—

And a sick, horrible tidal pull seized me.

*A trap!* I tried to claw at the windowsill, the stones of the wall, anything, but I couldn't solidify my hands. My bracelet had been taken out of its cubbyhole, leaving the greenish copper trap in its place; my jet brooch was with Lucas, sound asleep, far away. I tried thinking of him as my anchor—of any of the other places I could go—but it was too late. The trap was too close, and I'd practically put my hand right into it. As I began slipping toward the shimmering sinkhole, I tried one last time to call out to Lucas—but I could only just manage to think his name before everything went black.

It was like sinking into hot tar. I couldn't materialize, couldn't dematerialize. I had no sense of the world around me, or whether I was anyplace in either the mortal or ghostly worlds. After I'd died, there had been a moment like this—and again when I had first traveled to the land of lost things—but those terrible, depthless voids had lasted for only a second. This stretched on, and on, and on. A suffocation of the soul, made more horrible by fear.

*No wonder they go crazy,* I thought wildly, recalling the many shrieking spirits I'd sensed within Evernight's traps. *It's going to drive me crazy, too, any second, and I've only been in here a few minutes—or has it been longer? Would I even know? Is this eternity? Is this the death beyond death?*

*Make it stop,* Samuel had said. *Make it stop.* The ghost within him—the one that had been trapped like this—had lost the ability to think anything else. I would, too. Already I felt myself boiling down to the desperate instinct to escape, nothing more.

Then, in that formless void, a soft rectangle of light opened. I rushed toward it, not caring what it was or what it meant: It was something, in a world of nothing, and that was reason enough.

Then, in the frame of the rectangle, far bigger than life, I saw Mrs. Bethany.

"Miss Olivier." She smiled as placidly as ever, but there was no mistaking the avid light in her eyes. "At last. I've been waiting for you."

# Chapter Twenty-one

I COULDN'T LASH OUT; I COULDN'T ESCAPE. ALL I could do was stare up at Mrs. Bethany—at this moment, quite literally the only thing in my world.

"I had thought Mr. Ross would be the one to bring you to me," she said. "But he was more devoted to you than I'd imagined. Then I finally found your little trinket in the records room—after weeks of searching—and realized how simple it would be to replace it with a trap and claim you for myself."

She had always known about our visits to the records room. She had always known about me. "How did you know I was here at the school?"

Mrs. Bethany tilted her head, as though she felt sorry for me. "Based on your past behavior, it was natural to assume that where Mr. Ross was, you would be also."

I hated her so much at that moment, I was surprised the trap didn't shatter. My anger was hot enough to melt metal, to break stone. "I'm the reason you gave my parents jobs here in the first place, aren't I? You set us up from the beginning."

"I gave you every chance, you know." She sounded calm. Satisfied. "If I enjoyed victimizing the helpless, I'd hardly have founded a school such as Evernight. Furthermore, I quite liked your parents; they're fine teachers. So I felt bound in honor to explore every other possibility. I changed the admissions policy in order to bring in students attached to other wraiths, in case one of those spirits might work equally well. Whenever you deviated from the path your parents had in mind for you, I urged you back onto that path. This summer, I told you that throwing away your chances for the sake of love wasn't worthwhile. But you would never listen. You ran headlong toward your ultimate destiny. And now I am free to act as I see fit."

"You don't want to be a vampire anymore," I said. "But if you use me for this—you'll be worse than any vampire."

"I will be alive." Mrs. Bethany displayed not a flicker of hesitation. "An old betrayal will at last be set right. I will be able to die as I ought to have—as a human woman. And you will be no less dead than you already are."

A swirl of light, and the world took shape around me. At first I thought myself free, and prepared to vanish or run or do whatever I could—but then I saw where I was.

Mrs. Bethany stood in front of me, trap in hand, in the middle of a room that shimmered in every color—floor, ceiling, walls. I realized that it had the exact same dimensions as the records room, but instead of bare stone and dust, this glittered, deep and translucent. Mother-of-pearl, I realized. And the copper roof on the south tower—the strange sensation I'd often detected from the empty room above my parents' apartment—she'd brought the trap into the other tower, into this place. And now I knew what it was.

"You turned this entire room into a trap," I said. Already I knew I wouldn't be able to get out.

"My theory is that you can provide the power for many of us to revive," Mrs. Bethany said. "You will be returning life to nearly a dozen individuals, Miss Olivier. Perhaps that is some small consolation."

I backed away from her. The mother-of-pearl felt slippery against my feet—but no, that wasn't it. I couldn't be solid or insubstantial; I couldn't float, couldn't run. Everything was in-between, robbing me of the abilities I could use in either state. Although I had a sense of place within this trap, it was still a trap, eating away at my very sense of reality and self. It just took longer. A slower death. No wonder I'd heard the wraiths screaming. . . .

More gently, Mrs. Bethany said, "Think of it like being an organ donor."

I had been able to hear the wraiths screaming, even when they were trapped. . . .

With everything I had, with every ounce of strength, I screamed, both aloud and within my soul, *"Help me!"* In the scream I put the place I stood, Mrs. Bethany in front of me, everything I thought and felt and knew. The effort alone seemed to make me less than I'd been before—as though I had screamed out part of myself.

"The room is soundproofed," Mrs. Bethany said. "No one can hear."

Not with their ears, maybe. But if Maxie or Christopher detected it, or if Lucas could hear me within his dreams—

A rap on the door startled me into hope. But Mrs. Bethany didn't seem surprised. She simply held up the trap and opened it, then set it on the floor. The grayish swimming void unfolded before me again, and I desperately tried to keep from sinking within it. As I flailed about wildly, unable to resist, I heard a murmur of voices—hardly the rescue mission I'd been hoping for.

The trap swung shut. For a couple seconds, I felt a dizzying rush of relief, and I tried to make sense of what I could see. We remained in the mother-of-pearl room, but the door had already been closed again, cutting off my chance at escape. And now Mrs. Bethany and I weren't alone. Half a dozen vampires ringed the room, each of them staring at me as eagerly as Mrs. Bethany had. Most were teachers; a couple were students. None of them were people I knew very well, but I knew one thing—they were ancient and powerful. Mrs. Bethany had chosen her accomplices well.

"I do not know how many of us you can resurrect, Miss Olivier." Mrs. Bethany reached into the pocket of her long skirt and pulled out the blade I remembered from Samuel's transformation. "But for myself, and those who follow, may I express my most profound gratitude?"

"You can go to hell," I said.

"We're vampires," Mrs. Bethany said, and for a moment I

saw an echo of the darkness and self-hatred I'd glimpsed within Lucas these past months. "We're already there."

"You're killing me." I still couldn't believe it, although it had begun.

"If it helps, you are also killing me." Mrs. Bethany smiled, like that was great news. "I do not intend to live long as a human. This extended existence has been more torment than pleasure to me. I want only to die as I ought to have done."

"To die? You're doing all this just to—to die all over again?"

"To die as I ought to have done," she repeated. A deep sadness darkened her eyes. "To go where I should have gone, after death, and be reunited with those I knew in my one rightful life."

*Christopher*, I realized. *She thinks if she dies as a human, she'll be with Christopher again.*

She pushed up the sleeve of her lacy blouse, angled the knife, and sliced open the skin of her wrist. Her vampire's blood began flowing down her hand, and I felt a crazed hunger unlike anything else I'd ever known. I didn't want to drink her blood; I wanted to be one with it. The instinct to rush into her—to become a part of her and lose myself forever—was more powerful than anything I could've imagined.

*Don't! Hold back! Think about Lucas, think about everyone else you love, hold on for them!* But as I thought this and I tried to cling to it with all my strength, I could feel my resolve breaking down with the rest of me. My humanlike form began turning into cloudy vapor. Mrs. Bethany lifted her head, triumphant.

Soon she would be human again, and I would be . . . nothing.

Then the door thudded, making the vampires jump. It thudded again and gave way, splintering wood and mother-of-pearl in a thousand directions as Lucas burst into the room, crossbow in hand.

Either he instantly understood what was happening, or he was going to kill Mrs. Bethany first and ask questions later. Lucas shouldered his crossbow to fire, but Mrs. Bethany lunged for him, pushing the crossbow up so that the arrow smacked the ceiling.

"Let her go," Lucas said as they struggled for the weapon.

"She is no longer yours," Mrs. Bethany said, shoving him back. "She is mine."

The other vampires began to go after him, too, but Lucas hadn't come alone. Balthazar and my mother smashed through what remained of the door; Balthazar had grabbed his fencing foil, and Mom just seized the vampire nearest her and punched him hard.

As I swirled, disoriented and unable to resist, the fight intensified around me. To me, it seemed to be happening in slow motion, dreamlike and yet more terrifying for the clarity of the violence. I caught a glimpse of my father, wielding a broken chair leg as a kind of stake. I saw Balthazar go sliding across the floor, grimacing in pain before staggering to his feet. Lucas reclaiming his crossbow and firing—Mrs. Bethany smoothly dodging the arrow that sank into another vampire, with a plume of blood and the vampire's cry.

Vampire's blood, drawing me in, dragging me further down into nothingness.

Beyond the trap, I heard Maxie's voice. "Bianca! You have to get out of there! Come on!" I could just make out her form as she stood on the very edge of the room, risking her own existence to try and help me. A few other faces appeared behind her—female students who lived in the upper floors of the dorm, no doubt startled by the noise, and Vic, who appeared to be trying desperately to get those students to go someplace safer.

I tried to do what Maxie said, but I was too weak. Too lost.

At that moment in the fray, Mrs. Bethany ran for the door at vampire speed, grabbing the smaller trap as she went. She opened it—just in front of Maxie.

*No!* I thought, but it was too late. There was just time to see the dawning terror on Maxie's face before the vortex swallowed her up, enclosing her within the trap.

"Hey!" Vic yelled. For the first time ever, I heard real fury in his voice. "That's my ghost!"

Mrs. Bethany smashed Vic across the face with the trap, which sent him sprawling to the floor. The human students began screaming and shouting as Mrs. Bethany pushed through them.

"She's getting away," Balthazar shouted.

"I don't give a damn!" Lucas arrow-staked another vampire; the room fell quiet, but he hardly noticed. "We have to get Bianca out of here!"

"She's got *my ghost*!" Vic started running down the stairs, and Balthazar followed him. My parents and Lucas remained.

"Go," I whispered. It was the only thing I had strength to say. Maxie didn't deserve to be destroyed like this.

"The trap—this room—oh, my God, it's killing you," Lucas said. "Bianca, come on. The door's open. You can leave."

So it seemed. And yet even reaching toward the door was impossible.

"Sweetheart, please," Mom pleaded. Dad's eyes filled with tears as he gripped her shoulders. "You can do it."

"Your brooch!" Lucas fumbled in his pocket and held out my jet brooch. For a moment I felt something like hope; if I could become substantial again, even for a second, I could get out the door and maybe recover. But the brooch just dropped through the blue smoke where my hand had been—I no longer had the ability to touch it, and so I could no longer call on its power.

The jet black flower clattered on the stone floor, dark as ink in this shimmering world, and I remembered the long-ago dreams that had led me here. They had warned me that when I reached out for love, storms would come. And in all my dreams, I had never made it to safety. To Lucas.

Lucas shook his head. "This isn't happening." His voice was hoarse. "This can't be happening. Bianca, come on. Come back to me."

"Bianca?" said an unfamiliar voice. A female figure, wearing a bright blue robe, standing in the doorway—

"Skye, what are you doing here?" Lucas said. "It's not safe! Go downstairs!"

Skye didn't budge. She was a lot cooler than most people would be in a situation like this, but then again, she'd grown up in a haunted house. Maybe it came with the territory. "You said Bianca. That's the girl you loved, the one who died—she's a ghost?"

"She's a ghost and she's trapped and we're getting her out of here," Lucas said, never taking his eyes off me. "Now you get out of here, too!"

Instead, Skye took a couple of steps forward and spoke again—this time, to me. "Bianca, come into me. Like the spirits did at the ball."

She wanted me to possess her? Could I do that?

"What are you doing?" My mother tried to push Skye back. "This is dangerous!"

"I know what it is to lose somebody," Skye said. "If anyone could do this for my brother, I'd want them to try. So I'll try. Bianca, it's okay. Come on! Do it!"

I let go of my vapor self and let the swirling energy in the room carry me down toward Skye. Everything vanished—and then suddenly I felt hard stone against my back, and pain. I tried to inhale, but the breath had been knocked out of me—

Breath. Pain. A heartbeat. I opened my eyes—her eyes—and looked up to see my parents and Lucas kneeling above me.

"Bianca?" Lucas said, hesitantly.

"It's me," I said. "It's us."

Because Skye was there with me, totally. This wasn't like possessing Kate; Skye had welcomed me, and because of that, her spirit and mine existed side by side. Although she was frightened—her heartbeat fluttering as fast as a bird's—she didn't flinch.

*Thank you,* I thought to her.

She thought back, *You're welcome. But shouldn't we maybe run?*

"Good plan," I said. Her voice sounded so strange as mine. Lucas and my parents stared at me, and I grabbed on to Lucas's hand. "Let's go. We have to save Maxie if we can."

"We should just get out of here," Mom said as Lucas helped me to my feet. I was startled to be able to look him directly in the eyes; Skye was taller than me. "Sweetheart, I'm sorry about your friend, but we have to think about your safety."

"Maxie didn't think about her safety when she came after me," I said. "Besides, Vic's trying to help her. Are you going to make Vic go up against Mrs. Bethany alone?"

Lucas guided me toward the door. "No way. Come on."

My mom and dad glanced at each other for a second, but they followed us. Now that I was enclosed in Skye's body, as though it were a warm, living suit of armor, the trap room had no more power over me; leaving was as simple as taking the stairs. Of course, those were a little clumsy—I didn't wholly know how to move in Skye's body yet, and both of us were shaky after what had just happened.

As we started going down the stairs, I said, "Was it Maxie who told you where I was?"

"Yeah," Lucas said. He put his hand around my waist, the

better to steady me; he touched me gingerly, which I realized was because he didn't want to upset Skye. "We realized this morning you were missing, because there's no way you wouldn't have been talking to us about the night's plans—"

"I was in that trap a whole day?" It had seemed to last forever, and to end in a split second, at the same time.

Lucas nodded. "Apparently. We've been turning the school upside down looking for you."

"When we stole her traps, Mrs. Bethany must have realized we were on to her," Dad said. "She stopped biding her time. Went on the offensive."

*After this is over,* Skye thought, *will one of you explain what's going on?*

*Sure,* I replied. *As soon as I understand myself.* "What about the traps? Mrs. Bethany's got to be going after them."

"Hopefully she won't have the chance," Mom said as we went farther down the stone stairs. The entire student body seemed to be awake now, and aware that something dangerous was going on; there was murmuring and shouting on every floor. "Patrice and Ranulf should be taking care of that right now. . . ."

Her voice trailed off as the stones of Evernight began to scream.

That was the only word for it, though it didn't sound like any human scream. It was like the building itself had come alive, and hated it. The sound was the grinding of the real versus the unreal, existing in dimensions that had nothing to do with sound but echoed within us regardless. We clapped our hands over our ears, except Lucas, who kept holding on to me but grimaced in pain. "What the hell?" he shouted over the din.

I felt them, then—snaking their way up through the bones of the school, climbing toward freedom. "The wraiths," I said. "They're free."

They were free, and they were angry. Instead of flying straight to the people who anchored them, or letting go of the mortal realm, or wishing themselves back to the places they'd haunted before, they were attacking Evernight Academy and everything within it. Before, I hadn't been able to understand why they wouldn't be reasonable, why they acted purely on instinct. Now that I had spent a day in a trap, I understood; those things stole away your sense of yourself. It wouldn't take long to turn into nothing but fear and rage.

My breath had become foggy now, and frost began to lace its way along the walls, the steps, the ceilings. My father nearly slipped on the ice that was caking underfoot, so fast it stung my feet, nearly entrapping them. The murmuring upstairs turned into shrieks.

"Hurry," I said, feeling strength flow into me with a fresh sense of purpose.

We ran the rest of the way, although it was difficult. The ice now was thicker than in any other wraith attack I'd witnessed—as though the school itself were made of ice. As stones creaked and cracked from the pressure of ice in the crevices, we slipped and stumbled through a stairwell that increasingly looked more like a cavern of snow.

At last we reached the great hall, and even if I hadn't already known this was the place the wraiths would be freed, it would have been obvious that this was the heart of the storm. The entire great hall seemed to be no more than a great maze carved from one block of ice. Shivering at the sides, white with frost, were Patrice and Ranulf. Both of them slumped near the entrance, apparently unable to move.

"Are you guys okay?" I said, hurrying to Patrice's side. Her hand was like ice in mine.

"I'm fine, Skye," Patrice said through chattering teeth. "You need to get out of here."

"We're all getting out of here," Lucas said. He let go of me to pick Patrice up in his arms; she hung stiffly in his embrace, but he was able to get her out the door. Mom and Dad put their arms on either side of Ranulf to help him out.

I ran out of the school onto the grounds. When I looked up at Evernight, I gasped; it now looked as though it had been carved of crystal, its outline blurred and fractal like the edges of snowflakes. Other students had congregated outside, shivering in their nightclothes as they looked up at the bewildering sight. Snow must have fallen that day, because some of them were knee-deep in it.

*It could take hours for help to get here*, I thought. *People could die of exposure in that time. I have to do this now.*

*Do what?* Skye thought, increasingly worried. Given what I'd put her through in just the last couple of minutes, I couldn't blame her.

In the near distance, I saw Balthazar fighting with one of Mrs. Bethany's surviving guards. Their fangs extended as they roared and leaped toward each other.

Skye screamed, momentarily taking her body back just by sheer force of terror. *What are they?*

*Vampires. Remember what Lucas told you? He's a vampire, too. Plus my parents. Plus—you know, a lot of people. We have to go over this later. Right now, I have something to do.*

She repeated, *Do what?*

*Don't worry; I can only do this alone.*

With that, I let Skye go. We both fell to the ground, and it seemed as if the impact of her body against the ground snapped us in two. I rolled over, semisolid, but leaving no impression in the snow; Skye sat up, sputtering, icy flakes spangling her dark hair. Her expression was strange—horrified, maybe as if she didn't remember giving me permission. But she said, "I can feel them."

"Feel what?"

She clutched her hair in her fists, as if she were trying to use pain to block some other sensation. "The ghosts—all of them— it's like they're *in my head*—"

Had my possessing her for so long opened her up to some other realm of perception? We'd have to find out later. "I'm going to take care of them, Skye. I promise."

From his place a few steps away, where he was trying to revive Patrice to full consciousness, Lucas said, "Bianca, what are you doing?"

"I'll be back soon," I swore. "Did you get my brooch?"

He patted his pocket—then went still. "We've got trouble."

Like we hadn't had trouble already? But I followed his gaze to see Mrs. Bethany's carriage house, shutters fastened tight, with only slivers of blue-hot light coming through the slits. They looked like knives cutting open the night. Mrs. Bethany was beginning her spell; soon, she would have destroyed Maxie, and resurrected herself. Maybe a few of her cronies were in there, too. I could just make out the outline of Vic, who was throwing himself against the door again and again, trying to save Maxie.

"Go help them," I said. "I promise, I'll be back soon."

With one last look at Patrice, who finally seemed to be sitting up under her own power, Lucas took off running toward Mrs. Bethany's carriage house.

I let go of my physical self and floated upward, pure energy now. Evernight was below me, less something I could see and more something I could feel as the collection of so many lost, desperate spirits, no longer able to feel anything but fear. Before, when I had never been trapped, I couldn't understand what they felt. I hadn't been able to communicate with them. Now I knew what to do.

Remembering my time in the trap, I created around me the memory of that dark, fathomless void. As strongly as I could, I sent that downward, so that the wraiths would recognize it for what it was. Just as I felt them react in pain and panic, I opened up that brilliant circle of light—the way out.

And past that circle, I envisioned the land of lost things in all its beauty and ugliness and chaos. It seemed to take shape in miniature, like the magical castles at the center of a snow globe: an old Tudor mansion, a mobile home, a brown horse with knobby knees and friendly eyes, a twisty dirt road—not things I had seen there before, but the things these spirits were bringing along with them.

The energy beneath me changed from fear into something like hope.

I took hold of them. Every one of them. I couldn't say how I did it, but the power must have been within me from the beginning. In that instant, I knew each of them, could envision their faces, their personalities, sense fragments of the lives they must have led. They were as familiar to me, in both their virtues and flaws, as my dearest friends, and I felt them recognize me in return. More important, I felt them recognize themselves—the people they had been before darkness and fear had taken them over. Then I lifted us together, soaring upward into that sphere of light.

Then there was laughter, and cheering, and embraces. I stood in a patch of sunlight near what looked like a version of the Taj Mahal, though it was black instead of white, and even more beautiful. A crowd of perhaps a hundred people milled around me, wearing clothes that varied from T-shirts and jeans to one woman in a full, hoop-skirted dress who carried a parasol.

"Thank you," she whispered as she hugged me tightly. "You got us out. You brought us here."

I hugged her back, but I remained vividly aware of how

quickly time could pass here, and how badly I needed to return.

Christopher seemed to appear in the middle of us—no puffs of smoke or bursts of light, but one minute he wasn't there, and the next he was. His smile transformed him into the younger, happier man he had been in his memories of his life. "Bianca. I knew you could do it."

"Yes, and it's awesome and tremendous and all of that, but we have a situation," I said. "Mrs. Bethany's captured Maxie. She's going to destroy her. Is there anything we can do?"

His smile faded. "That poor child. She must be terrified."

"What can we do? Your wife—I know you love her, but we can't let her do this!" Beyond my fear for Maxie, I was also terrified for Lucas, as well as for Balthazar, my parents, Vic—everyone I'd left back at Evernight. She had fighters around her who knew she was their only chance to live again. The battle going on now would be desperate, and for some, fatal.

"No, we cannot." Christopher squared his shoulders. "We shall return to the world below, together."

"Can you get Maxie out of the trap?" I asked, though I felt sure it must be impossible.

"There is one way," he said, surprising me. "Only one way."

He vanished. Apparently explanations would have to wait. I thought of my brooch, the beautiful black flower from my dreams, and tried to fold myself into the heart of it.

I took form—then fell bodily into the snow, Lucas toppling beside me. Blood marred his face, streaking his skin and making his green eyes seem unearthly. He glanced at me only for a moment before raising his crossbow just in time to deflect an ax. One of Mrs. Bethany's loyalists was swinging at him, repeatedly, and from the looks of things, he'd landed a few blows.

My brooch had tumbled out when Lucas fell, apparently; it lay on the ground, stark against the snow. I grabbed it, grateful for the ability to do so, and put it in my pocket. Now embodied, I tried to take in the scene.

A battle raged around me. My vampire friends were locked in combat with other vampires loyal to Mrs. Bethany. Across the grounds, Evernight Academy was melting—or, at least, the ice that had encased it was vanishing. Half-frozen students were already stumbling back inside for shelter and to get away from the fighting. I couldn't find Vic, and nobody seemed to have breached Mrs. Bethany's carriage house.

The roaring of an engine pierced the night, and I turned to see a pair of headlights fast approaching the school. With a rush of relief and hope, I recognized the van. I ran through the snow, crying out, "Raquel! Dana!"

They skidded to a stop. Dana leaped from the vehicle and took in the scene. "I told you guys not to start the party without us."

"They're all vampires," Raquel said, clutching her stake. "Which ones do we go after?"

"If they're attacking a vampire you know, take them out! Tell Dana who's who!" I looked for a weapon for myself and grabbed a small hand ax.

"Raquel!" Vic ran toward the truck. He must have been in

the woods—probably looking for something to use to smash into Mrs. Bethany's house. "Give me something! Anything!"

I left them behind, running through the snow, determined to help Lucas and the others. As I saw how well armed Mrs. Bethany's crew seemed to be, I reached up and pulled off my brooch. My body remained solid.

The closest people to me were my father and the tallest vampire in school, a guy almost as broad as he was high. He was pounding my dad with one hand; the other held a knife certainly big enough for a beheading. Dad had already gone down on one knee, unable to defend himself. I shouted, "Hey!"

The vampire turned. With a lazy grin, he swung the knife toward me—

—as I dropped the brooch and became vapory. The knife went directly through me, and I felt nothing. The ax I'd been carrying kept swinging through the air at the same speed, undeflected, to bury itself in the guy's back.

He fell to the ground, obviously not permanently taken out but dazed and in pain. Quickly I grabbed my brooch again and took Dad's hand. "Come on! We have to get in there!"

"We have to get out of here," Dad protested.

I shook my head. "This fight doesn't end until Mrs. Bethany's stopped, and we won't be out of danger until the fight ends."

Mrs. Bethany's cottage was only a few steps away. But Vic beat me to it, and when I saw what he was carrying, my eyes went wide.

I never thought they'd give him the flamethrower.

Vic pointed the weapon at one wall—and a plume of fire set the place ablaze.

I realized, *Vic doesn't know that fire could kill Maxie forever.*

I ran toward the cottage, unsure what to do or how to help. Then I saw a faint outline of a figure against the snow—Maxie, drifting in a daze away from the flames.

"Maxie!" I shouted. Vic reached her at the same moment I did, and I pressed my brooch into her hand. Although she hardly had any substance, she was able to hang on to it; the magic within the jet solidified her and seemed to give her some strength.

"Are you okay?" Vice smoothed her golden brown hair away from her forehead.

She shook her head no. "Christopher," she managed to say.

"What about him?" I said. "Did he get you out?"

"Yes, but he—" Maxie stared back at the fire consuming the carriage house. "He took my place." Suddenly undone by grief and exhaustion, Maxie slumped against Vic's shoulder; he let the flamethrower drop and held her tightly.

I left them alone and rushed toward the blaze. Though I knew it was dangerous to be so near fire or a trap, I couldn't let Christopher perish if there was any way to save him.

But as I remembered his sad expression as we prepared to come here, I knew immediately that there wasn't. Christopher had done this knowing he would be lost forever. He had sacrificed himself for Maxie.

I peered into the very heart of the flames. There, I could

see Mrs. Bethany, her long hair tumbling down loose around her shoulders. Soot stained her face, and she looked very young. "Christopher!" she cried out. She must have seen him, in the instant that he had taken Maxie's place. "Christopher, I'm here, I'm here!"

Despite the fact that she was on the verge of burning to death, Mrs. Bethany was—smiling. I realized then that Christopher had been wrong; her love for him really had been stronger than her hate. But they'd both found out too late.

Maxie had been freed before Mrs. Bethany could transform herself. Mrs. Bethany had enough time, maybe—to sacrifice Christopher and live again. She had to know that. But she wouldn't do it. "We can get out of here," she gasped, reaching through smoldering woodwork despite the risk to herself. I realized she was trying to retrieve the trap that held him. "We'll be together, I promise you."

I heard Christopher's voice, hardly a whisper amid the crackling of the flames, "My dearest Charlotte."

Then a surge of sparks drove me back, and I gaped as the roof of the carriage house crumbled. Nothing remained but glowing embers, and flame, and smoke. Sure death for any vampire, or any wraith. The Bethanys were gone, forever.

Shaken, I turned to see the battle—or what had been the battle. The vampires fighting my friends had been subdued, either by Dana and Raquel as reinforcements or by surrender when they saw that their leader, and the resurrection magic she alone knew, had perished. I could see my mother helping my father to his feet, Raquel and Patrice herding the enemy vampires farther away from the rest of us, and most of the others gathered around a fallen figure in the snow —

Around Lucas.

# Chapter Twenty-two

I FLASHED MYSELF TO THE SMALL GROUP OF people huddled around Lucas's fallen form. He lay motionless and bloodied on the snow, his chest and forehead sliced deeply by a weapon. Dana cradled his head in her hands, and Balthazar ran one finger along the edge of the chest wound and winced. Vic and Maxie, still holding on to each other, stood nearby, while Ranulf clutched his ax to his chest as if he were a child with a security blanket. Lucas appeared to be totally unconscious.

"What's going on?" I knelt beside Lucas. "He's wounded?"

"Badly," Balthazar said. But in his voice I heard real dread.

I said, "As awful as it is, as much as I know he's hurting . . . he'll be okay." Nobody spoke. "Won't he?"

Balthazar turned to me, expressionless. "The other vampire had laced his weapon with holy water. It's a dangerous tactic for us, but—"

I held up a hand; I couldn't bear to hear what came next, and besides, I already knew. Black Cross training had covered the technique, and it had been whispered by Erich in Lucas's own dream—claiming that stakes soaked in holy water could paralyze and torture a vampire forever.

That it was like burning them alive, just from the inside out.

They'd never claimed to know for sure. Maybe it wasn't so. But Lucas wasn't moving. He was trapped deep in that terrible, unending fire.

I took his hand in mine; it was colder than usual, deeply chilled by the snow around us. His fingers were heavy, unresisting. "Lucas?" I whispered, but I knew he couldn't hear.

The only release from his torment would be to behead him. To lose him forever. In the hours after Charity's attack, I'd been faced with the decision of whether or not to kill Lucas; now I had to face it again. But I couldn't. I just couldn't.

I squeezed his hand tighter. Dana, who had begun to sob, reached up with one hand to wipe her cheeks. Lucas's head, free from its cradle, lolled to one side. Blood from the cut on his forehead had oozed down to his throat, pooling just beneath his Adam's apple. It reminded me of how he had looked the first time I bit him.

*Vampire's blood,* I thought. During the ritual, it had attracted me powerfully. As powerfully as if the blood were life itself.

Then everything came to me at once:

How drinking Lucas's blood had been part of what maintained my life as a vampire, how I had felt more alive then than at any other time.

How wraiths joined with vampires to create vampire

children like me, because wraiths and vampires were the two halves of life, able together to kindle a flame.

How Mrs. Bethany's ritual of resurrection had been designed to break me down and bring me into a vampire, to merge us into one.

How wraith blood was poisonous to vampires, but their blood was life to us.

How Lucas and I had become a part of each other from the very first time I gave in to my desire and bit into his throat. I was Lucas, and he was me.

And I knew what to do.

"Move back," I said. Everyone sort of stared, but they did what I asked, shuffling backward from Lucas's sprawled body. Dana laid his head down gently before rising to her feet, where Raquel hugged her tightly from behind. Ranulf had bowed his head, and Vic, holding Maxie's hand, sniffled like he was on the verge of tears. My parents stood slightly apart from the rest, but I could see that the concern in their faces for Lucas was real. A few others had gathered, too—just a handful of students, both vampire and human, unsure what to think. Skye stumbled toward us, dazed and weak from her ordeal but unwilling to leave Lucas if he was in trouble. When she swayed on her feet, Balthazar quickly rose to steady her against his shoulder.

The snow around Lucas was stained crimson with his blood. New flakes had begun to fall. A sharp, cold wind gusted past us, ruffling his hair. I held my hand out to Maxie; after a moment's confusion, she understood and handed me my jet brooch, so that

I could be wholly solid once more. I needed that now. The sharp edges of the flower's carved petals cut into my palm.

I thought of how much I loved him, how badly I wanted him to be a part of me. I dreamed of the richness of his blood, and how it had made me feel alive. I remembered being a vampire—and felt my fangs emerge once more, sharp against my lips and tongue. My vampire self remained a part of me, despite my death.

Then I bent low and bit into Lucas's throat.

Blood. Cold, but still his blood, still him. Vampire's blood carried knowledge, and so I felt everything that he had felt, knew everything that he had known. I felt his love for me, and his fear, as he had stood in the tower trying to rescue me. I saw the fight through his eyes, a whirl of blades, blows, and driving snow. I swallowed more deeply, drinking as much of his blood as I possibly could, more than I ever had as a vampire before. Around me, I could dimly hear some of the others protesting, but they were too distant to heed. And then I knew him—Lucas, his spirit, his soul, here at the center of his being.

*Bianca. Where are we?*

*Together.*

*What's happening?*

*I'm drinking your blood. Making it mine. Lucas—drink from me.*

I pushed my hand against his mouth, so that the tender flesh between thumb and forefinger followed the curve of his lips.

*Trust me. Drink.*

He was paralyzed beyond the ability to bite down, so I pressed the soft skin against the sharpness of his teeth until they broke the skin. I felt the pain as sharply as I ever had any mortal injury, but I never flinched.

Blood flowed down his throat. What would have burned him before didn't now, because I had mingled his blood and my own. Now the corrosive power of wraith's blood couldn't touch him any longer. He was free to drink it in. Free to take in life.

I felt myself growing dizzy as the link between us deepened. We were one system now, one being, each of us flowing into the other. As I gave in to it, I felt the outlines of his body as much as I did my own; the cuts on the forehead and chest burned, and the snow was cold underneath. And I knew his dawning wonder as he felt what it was like to be me—the angle of my limbs, the taste of his blood, the nearness of my spirit.

The blood I drank began to warm.

*Is this what it means to die?* Lucas thought. *Because I'm not scared of it anymore. Not if it means I finally get this close to you.*

I concentrated all my energy on him, directing myself into the very core of him, into the redness of his heart. *This isn't death. This is life.*

Lucas gasped in a breath, and I sat up. His blood was sticky on my mouth, and he looked gorier than before, but his eyes were wide open. He took another breath, and another.

"What did you do?" Balthazar said.

Raquel, leaning around Dana, said, "Yeah, was that vampire CPR or something?"

I never looked away from Lucas. The cuts on his face were knitting together, faster than vampire healing, part of his ultimate restoration. He stared up at me, obviously weak from his injuries, but with an incredulous smile spreading across his face. "It's impossible."

"It isn't." I started to laugh from pure joy. "It's real."

"You're healing up, like, crazy fast, but you're still bleeding, man." Vic held out a scrap of cloth.

"Bleeding," Balthazar said, his voice sharp and urgent. He'd seen it now, even if nobody else had. "Bianca, you did it."

"Did what?" Dana said.

I hugged Lucas tightly. This time, when he embraced me in return, he was warm.

"I'm alive," Lucas whispered. "Bianca brought me back to life."

Everyone around us started talking at once—in wonder or confusion or glee. Dana actually jumped into the air with her hands above her head, a victory leap.

I didn't pay any attention. Time for explanations and celebrations later. All I wanted to do at that moment was lie there in Lucas's arms, my head against his chest, listening to the beating of his heart.

Within an hour, the emergency vehicles began showing up—police cars, ambulances, and a couple of fire trucks, although there was nothing left of Mrs. Bethany's carriage house but glowing cinders. My parents had found a landline inside that remained operational after the big freeze-and-thaw, and they made the 911 call.

"The school is dead now," my mother had explained earlier, as Ranulf dragged a couple of vampire corpses into the fire to minimize the awkwardness when the law arrived. "Without Mrs. Bethany, there is no Evernight Academy. These students need to go home to their families."

"What will this place become?" I said, looking at the massive stone towers silhouetted against the snow-cloud sky.

"Some millionaire's mansion, maybe. Or the state might turn it into something—a home for people in trouble. Another school." Mom smiled gently at Dad. "Good thing we never sold the Arrowwood place, huh?"

"We can't go back there," he corrected. "The people who remember us will know we look too young."

"I know, dear. I've been doing this a while, too, remember?" She nudged him, fondly teasing. "But we can sell the house now, and use the money to go somewhere else."

He put an arm around her shoulders. "Homesick for England?"

Mom brightened, and I suspected their new home would be somewhere near her beloved London. But she remained focused on me. "What about you, Bianca?"

"I'm staying with Lucas," I said, "but it doesn't matter now where I stay. I can be with you as quickly as blinking an eye. So we'll visit as much as we want. There's no such thing as being far away from you, not anymore."

She drooped a little. "It's so unfair. That you can give life to someone else, but you're a wraith forever."

"Mom, it's okay." I'd been turning this over in my mind for several days now, and after tonight's astonishing events, I finally knew what I wanted to tell her. "Stop thinking that something terrible happened to me, okay? You guys, of all people, should realize that death's not the end. Besides—I was meant to be a wraith. I feel that now. These powers, these abilities—already I can't imagine not having them. This is my destiny. This is what I'm supposed to be." After a moment's pause, I added, "And it's *fun*."

My parents both started to laugh, and gathered me into their arms for a long hug.

As the cops kept taking extremely confused statements from various students, and a very careful statement from Lucas, the red and blue lights from their vehicles beat raggedly, turning the snow crust on the ground different colors. Vic and Ranulf helped Skye down the front steps of Evernight; I could see that she continued to shake, and was clumsy as she tried to handle a duffle bag half as big as she was. When they walked past us, I heard her say, "Vampires and vampire hunters and ghosts—and they're all at war?"

"Present company excepted," Vic said, with a grin over his shoulder. I could sense that Maxie hovered there, close by his side. "You know, if you ask me, those shouldn't be the sides. Instead, it should be the normal, awesome people versus the bugnut crazy people. Plenty of people and vampires and ghosts on both sides of that equation, you know?"

"We are among the awesome," Ranulf said gravely.

"Whatever you say." Skye looked mostly like she wanted to get the hell away from anything supernatural and take a long nap. I couldn't blame her, but I didn't want to let her go without saying thanks.

"Skye," I called as I walked up. She looked at me tiredly. "What you did up there—I'll always be grateful. Me and Lucas both."

"Lucas saved my life," Skye said. "I wanted to help him, which meant helping you. And, like I said, I'd want somebody to do it for me."

Her voice was so weary, and her eyes remained haunted. Choosing my words with care, I said, "I possessed you for a pretty long time, and some intense supernatural things were happening. Are you sure you're okay?"

Skye's expression hardened. "I'll be okay the sooner I get away from here." She took a deep breath. "Tell Lucas I'm happy for you guys. And . . . tell him good-bye." Then she marched through the snow to the police car without looking back.

In the distance, I saw Balthazar standing apart from everyone else. I walked through the snow to his side. My father's coat hung so large on my shoulders that I felt as though I were wearing a cape. Balthazar didn't turn as I approached, but when I reached him, he said, "Someone will have to take care of the stables."

I followed his gaze to the school stables, where a few students had kept their prize horses for riding. "I hadn't thought of that."

"I'll go down there tonight, make sure the horses are fed and warm," he said quietly. "Their owners will come for them soon enough, probably, but I'll keep checking. Oh, by the way, while we were looking for you today—I grabbed this." From his pocket, Balthazar withdrew my silver and coral bracelet and dropped it into my hand. "It was under the beanbag chair. I guess Mrs. Bethany stashed it there when she replaced it with the trap."

"Thank you," I said, but it wasn't enough. Unspoken words hung between us, and I knew we had to deal with this immediately. "I've drunk your blood, too," I said. "What I did for Lucas—the return to life—it might work for you. If you want."

Drinking somebody's blood was a deeply intimate act, and for any other cause, I would never have offered; it would have been like cheating on Lucas. Yet I knew that Lucas would never begrudge Balthazar the chance to live again.

To my surprise, Balthazar shook his head. "No. There's no guarantee it would work, and if it didn't, I'd be poisoned."

"It's worth a shot."

"It wouldn't work." His eyes narrowed as he stared at the horizon, as if he were blinded by the moonlight on the snow. "What happened tonight—that wasn't about blood. It was about the bond between you. The two of you are parts of one whole. That's something you and I have never been."

I laid my hand on his shoulder. "Balthazar, I'm sorry."

He shrugged. "I'm no worse off than I was before. And—I'm

happy for Lucas. I mean it."

Quickly I stood on tiptoe to kiss him on the cheek. Baltha-zar smiled at me, but I could tell he mostly wanted to be alone. So I went back to help with the cleanup, and hoped that the police believed our version of events.

They would, of course. It was going to be a lot easier for them to decide that a water main had flooded the school, creat-ing some ice on a cold night and shorting out electricity in the carriage house to start the fire. Why would they ever believe some panicked teenagers babbling about ghosts?

There was no telling precisely how the final official reports would read, but I knew how they would end: with the confirma-tion that Evernight Academy existed no more.

Around dawn, Raquel and Dana drove all of us to the town where they lived. Although their motel was anything but ele-gant, it was clean and safe, and there were tons of vacancies. If the tired couple running the motel was confused to suddenly check in seven guests at two A.M., they said nothing.

My parents also said nothing when I went to Lucas's room with him. My mom even checked Lucas's bandage before we walked away and she told him she'd put some Neosporin on it in the morning. He swallowed hard as he nodded, and I could tell he was missing his mother, and the way she had cared for him.

Mom and Dad probably thought we were just going to fall into each other's arms. I liked the idea, but I knew that Lucas and I had to make a lot of decisions tonight—decisions that would shape our whole futures.

When we were alone in the room together, I helped him ease out of his jacket and shirt. Every move made him wince. I said, "You know . . . now that you're human again . . . if you wanted to call Kate—"

"I don't." He looked up at me, and although his eyes were sad, I knew he truly meant what he said. "I still love Mom. I always will. But I know now, she has . . . limitations. She can't see past her own fear. There's no way for her to be a part of our lives. Maybe someday, I might—I don't know, let her know what happened. It would be a load off her mind, knowing I've been changed back. But I'll never see her again."

I sat on the hotel bed next to him. "Are you sad?"

"No. I've known we'd never be together again for a while now." He brought his hand up to the curve of my jaw and smiled. "And how could I be sad today? God, Bianca, you're a—miracle."

I caught his hands in mine. "You're alive again," I said, my voice shaking. "You can have any kind of life you want. So I just want you to know that you're free, okay? You're free to make your own decisions. Even if—even if that means leaving me."

"What?" Lucas stared at me like he couldn't believe a word I'd said. "Why would I ever want to leave you?"

"You don't have to fight vampires or wraiths anymore. You told me how much you always wanted a normal life, and now you can have one. Lucas, you could go to college, like you used to dream about. Meet some girl who's alive and well and never—never had to attack anyone, or to learn how to kill." I couldn't quite meet his eyes anymore. "Someday you could get married. Have children. That's something I can never give you."

Lucas stared at me, shocked into silence. He had to be weighing what I'd just said. I didn't expect him to agree right away, but he had to see the truth of it on some level. Given time, he would choose to fulfill his oldest dream: to live like other people lived. To have a house, a job, a family. To set aside the old battles forever.

Then he said, "How do you know?"

"How do I know what?"

"That we can't have children."

It caught me up short. Honestly, I'd never thought I'd be able to have children; most vampires never did, with my mom and dad as a rare exception. Becoming a ghost had only confirmed its impossibility. "Lucas, I'm *dead*."

"So were your parents."

"I don't have a body."

He cupped my face in his hands, so tenderly it made me shiver. "Feels like it to me."

I could have a body if I wanted one, couldn't I? There didn't seem to be any limit on how long I could keep it. "We don't know that it's possible," I protested. "We can't be sure."

"That means we can't be sure what's impossible, either." Lucas smiled at me, his dark green eyes shining. "Bianca, before tonight, nobody ever dreamed that you would be able to bring me back to life like that. You made that happen. And now we'll find a way. I'm not talking about kids, or at least not just about kids. I mean, no matter what's ahead of us. We'll make it work. Because I love you too much to ever let you go."

Joy rippled through me. "Are you sure?"

"Are you?" For a moment, hesitation flickered across his features. "You're the most amazing supernatural creature in the world, and I'm just some guy who's going to get old eventually."

"I'll make my hair gray to match yours," I promised. "I'll add wrinkles when you do." I hadn't known that I could feel like crying and laughing at the exact same moment. "But, Lucas— what about having a normal life?"

"Forget normal." He grinned. "We're going to be extraordinary."

We kissed, and for the first time since he'd been changed, there was no barrier between us, no hesitation.

It turned out, with a little bit of concentration, I no longer had to take my clothes off. If I wanted them to be gone, they were, so that only my silver and coral bracelet shone on my wrist.

It felt different, being with him now that he was alive and I was not. Somehow, it felt even better. When we were together, I could sense everything he sensed, be aware of his pleasure along with my own. And his touch was no longer a simple connection of nerves and neurons, no longer creating a merely physical response. Instead, I felt his touch as what it was—an expression of the love between us—and that excited me as nothing else ever had or could.

"Bianca," Lucas whispered against my throat, his breath

once again warm, the scent of his skin again all around me. "You're my life."

"And you're mine." It was true. His heartbeat, his muscles, everything that made him human resonated within me as strongly as my own life ever had. Within myself I held everything that was wonderful about being supernatural, and everything that had been wonderful about being alive. This was what it meant to be anchored—to be loved.

Afterward, as we lay tangled up in each other, Lucas combed through my hair with his fingers. As he stared up at the ceiling, he said, "Only one thing bothers me."

"What's that?"

"The only thing I don't like about being mortal means—I have to leave you. Not until the end of my life, and trust me, I intend to live a good long time, but just the same. That's where we're headed, someday."

A sharp pang made me hug him tighter. "I'll face that when the time comes. If I'm able to have the next fifty or sixty years with you—if we can be together and happy for your whole life—then that's what I want. I'd rather mourn when I lose you than not be with you at all."

Lucas kissed me deeply, then folded me back into his arms. "So that's what we'll do."

"What about you?" I whispered. "I know how happy you are to be alive, but . . . you were going to live forever, and now you won't. You lost your immortality. Does that feel weird?"

"I'll never die," he said. Before I could protest, Lucas put two fingers on my lips. His gentle smile seemed to fill the room with light, and I realized he was telling a deeper kind of truth than I'd ever known before. "You'll live forever, and being remembered by you is the only immortality I'll ever need. If I only live on as a part of you—Bianca, that's my idea of heaven."

# FIND OUT HOW IT ALL BEGAN AT EVERNIGHT ACADEMY

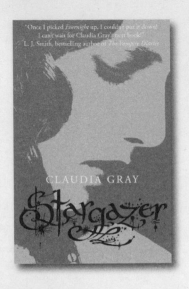

**OUT NOW**